THE BEST STORIES OF Guy De Maupassant

Selected, and with an Introduction by

SAXE COMMINS

THE MODERN LIBRARY · NEW YORK

Random House IS THE PUBLISHER OF

THE MODERN LIBRARY

BENNETT A. CERF · DONALD S. KLOPFER · ROBERT K. HAAS

Manufactured in the United States of America

By H. Wolff

Contents

Contents

Introduction

MORE than a half century has passed since the death of Guy de Maupassant. In that time his writings, and chiefly the short stories, have manifested one of the rarest of all phenomena in letters: they have been self-renewing in vitality and have assumed fresh force and meaning for succeeding generations of readers with changing standards. This is no miraculous regeneration; their vitality resides permanently in the stories themselves and they project the fertility and life-avidity of Maupassant himself during the ten years of his greatest fecundity.

The over-virile and assertively athletic Maupassant imbued his stories with his own surcharged potency and gave them a birthright of independence and a fate of their own. To many good doctors of letters this creates a double misconception: they can find neither biological nor literary precedent for such continuing vigor. Historians who rely upon the conveniences of categories, they have merely overlooked the lustiness of the man himself in order to classify the body of his works. They have tried to file the total of his writings neatly under the heading of "Naturalist" and are confounded because almost all his stories persist in eluding the restrictions of a school and burst forth into the unrestrained world of their own existence. These variegated tales, with the throng of human beings who live in them, belong to no classifiable school. They are the progeny of the man who gave them life and their own irrevocable character. Maupassant himself declared in an early manifesto: "We

vii

Introduction

have but one objective: Man and Life, which must be interpreted artistically."

How well he fulfilled this youthful intention is attested by the prodigious total of his definitive works: six novels, more than three hundred short stories and sketches, three books of travel, a volume of poetry, all achieved within one decade of frenzied application.

At the time of the Franco-Prussian War, in 1870, Maupassant was twenty years old. His childhood and early youth were dominated by his mother, a determined woman who had divorced her gay-blade of a husband and devoted herself and the considerable settlement she received to the upbringing of her two sons, Henri René Albert Guy and the younger Hervé.

Until he was thirteen, Guy attended school at Étretat, and then was transferred to Yvetot, where he incurred the wrath of his teachers for his anti-religious and amorous pronouncements in verse. These peccadilloes brought only a succession of rebukes, but for appropriating, and drinking, the choice wines reserved for the faculty, he was summarily expelled. The Rouen Lycée offered refuge for the erring young Norman and shared the responsibility for his education with the kind of correspondence-school instruction provided in the letters of Gustave Flaubert to his old friend, Laure Lepoitevin de Maupassant, mother of the problem child.

Thanks to the persuasion of Flaubert, Louis Bouilhet, Rouen's own poet-laureate, became interested in the youth who took the trouble to learn all his exalted poetry by heart in order to make a favorable impression. Almost every lesson given in rounded periods by the sage of Rouen emphasized the importance of form and that poetry alone was the medium of expression for an aspirant to literary fame.

Introduction

When the Germans swept through Rouen, the French Army, with Maupassant in the ranks, was in full retreat. The memory of that flight is preserved in some of the scenes of the first story of his to appear in print—"Ball-of-Fat." Eight months after the Armistice was signed, Maupassant was returned to civilian life.

In Paris, while trying to decide whether to study for the law, he frequently visited Flaubert's home, where he met and listened to Turgenev, Zola, Goncourt and Daudet. There he was exposed to endless literary discussions, verbal floggings of the bourgeoisie and scornful allusions to the last champions of Romanticism. Nothing could help him more quickly to a decision; his mind was made up; he would risk everything on a literary career, and to him, as to Flaubert his adviser, that meant only the precarious existence of a poet.

Flaubert was eloquent in bringing him to his resolution and forthwith took him under his protection. In the meantime the question of how to live had to be faced, and, on the suggestion of his father, the literary tyro applied for a job in the Ministry of Marine. First as a temporary clerk and then as a permanent employee in charge of distributing printing and stationery supplies, he served the Third Republic inconspicuously, and unsatisfactorily, for seven years.

Those were the seven years of his apprenticeship to Flaubert, the years of rigid discipline, when, on threat of excommunication from the Master's circle, nothing could be published, when the writer must sacrifice everything to the perfection, first of his craft and then of his art. Nonetheless, Maupassant managed to break into print with occasional, surreptitious pieces of verse and poetic plays, mostly erotic, under the pseudonym of Guy de Valmont, and in 1879, he contrived production of his

Introduction

first play, *Histoire du Vieux Temps,* with one of its acts entirely in verse. Flaubert, laboring on his last great work, *Bouvard et Pécuchet,* was both annoyed and mildly impressed. He could approve of this play and of Maupassant's first volume of poetry, *Des Vers,* especially since the latter gave him the chance to fight the guardians of public morality who had instituted legal proceedings. He, too, had been victimized, and now it was his pupil's turn. Thanks partly to the intervention of Flaubert, the case was dropped.

When Emile Zola prepared an anthology of stories, representative of the work of the group identified with him, under the title of *Les Soirées de Médan,* Maupassant offered his first effort in this genre. It was "Ball-of-Fat." Flaubert, although disappointed because his disciple had not written in verse, without hesitation proclaimed it "a jewel."

The author of *Madame Bovary* did not live to see how far his protégé would go as a story-teller. With the death of the Master, in 1880, the pupil was released from the discipline which could only succeed in making of him an indifferent poet. The dam broken, a deluge of stories flowed from his pen. The influence of Flaubert and his group—Daudet, Goncourt and Turgenev—dwindled, and for a while Maupassant became associated with Zola and his followers, but not for long. Maupassant could no more identify himself with the Naturalists than with the Romanticists; his apprenticeship was over and thenceforward he needed space and freedom for the release of his ungovernable energy.

With the publication, in 1881, of "Madame Tellier's Excursion," demand for his stories increased appreciably, and now Maupassant was entirely on his own and occupied, as he said in reply to a criticism of Francisque Sarcey's, in "catching humanity in the act."

Fame and wealth came quickly, and with them an outpouring of novels, more and more stories and books of travel. Feverish work was never allowed to interfere with amorous adventures. Time was always to be found for dalliance, and a legend grew, formidable even to this day, of Maupassant's centaur-like puissance.

The first of his full-length works of fiction, *Une Vie*, probed with a characteristically fierce intensity into the heart of a woman. Disillusionment was its theme, reality its atmosphere, and the humble truth, as the sub-title insists, its purpose. *Bel Ami*, that bitter biography of a rascal who flourishes in the shady underworld of Parisian journalism, appearing two years later, was denounced violently by the critics as "loathsome," "morbid" and "infamous," and read avidly by the public as if these angry adjectives were commendations.

It is no anomaly, and certainly no discovery, that even in the most robust of men there may be deeply hidden flaws of body and mind. Maupassant, the athlete glorying in his prowess as oarsman and swimmer, the satyriasist and tireless worker, was frequently frightened and distracted by illness. The condition of his eyes especially was a source of pain and anxiety. In many efforts to overcome his terror of blindness and other disabilities, he traveled to Africa, Italy, Sicily, Corsica, and, more frequently, to Southern France. Out of these flights from fear came those travel books and many stories whose pages give back the glaring heat of the desert and make visual the mountain landscapes of the southern islands.

On his return, he sought seclusion, time and again,

in his villa in Étretat, and then, again in search of health, the outwardly sturdy Maupassant was driven elsewhere. In 1885, he went on the same quest to Auvergne, and there began to write *Mont-Oriol*, the third of his six novels, which was finished at Antibes.

One flight followed another, until there grew in him, finally, the tragic need to flee even from himself. Hallucinations tormented him and began to insinuate themselves into his writings. "The Horla" is a foreshadowing of disaster, and "The Diary of a Madman" a portent of disintegration.

Again escape was tried in a cruise at sea, and *Sur l'Eau* was its only reward. Premonitions of complete derangement haunted him and lashed him, together with the stimulus of drugs, to his labor of writing against time. Between 1888 and 1890, he wrote three novels, *Pierre et Jean, Fort comme la Mort* and *Notre Coeur,* in addition to many more stories and one book of travel, *La Vie Errante,* his last.

Then the blow fell. Delusions of persecution and a profound melancholia presaged the final degeneration. In a last effort to escape from himself, he went to Cannes with his faithful valet. The phantoms followed him there, and now only death could exorcise them. He attempted to shoot himself, but by a stroke of good or ill fortune the bullets had been removed from his revolver. In desperation he cut his throat with a paper knife, but the flow of blood was staunched in time. The last vestiges of reason were gone. He became so violent that he had to be bound in a straitjacket. An orderly was summoned from Paris to bring him from Cannes to an asylum in Passy. There, under the constant vigilance of his keepers, he died on July 6, 1893.

The world which Maupassant animated with his

own electric vigor lives on its own abundance. His stories of the Norman peasantry, the demi-monde and the middle-class clerks and shopkeepers of nineteenth-century France are never narrowly national; they have their origin and imperishable life and meaning in themselves. They are transcripts of experience directly observed and set down with such simplicity and fidelity that they become in themselves unforgettable experiences. Far from being strictly naturalistic in treatment, the stories are in almost every instance an inevitable departure from the rigid tenets of style to which Flaubert, Zola and their followers clung so tenaciously. In fact, from the time he wrote *Une Vie* in 1883 until his death, Maupassant showed little evidence of the painful lessons he had learned during his apprenticeship. The stories of the golden decade of his writing gained in dramatic impact as the selectiveness of observation became more and more conscious and deliberate. From then on the focus was sharpened and the characterization became more definite and substantial. The intensity never diminished. But this is not to say that there was a constant evenness of quality during this prolific outpouring of tales. Many were written casually and in sheer exuberance; several should never have been written at all, as is inevitable with a man so lavish.

The forty-five tales of this volume have been chosen as representative of the spirit and substance of Maupassant's work. The order in which they are arranged follows no system, chronological or by type. For example, "Ball-of-Fat," which was written first, appears last, and "The Horla," one of the tales of the twilight period, is offered early in this collection. The reason for the apparently arbitrary sequence is that an attempt was made to give the entire book variety, balance and sustained

Introduction

interest. The cunning practice of heaping the best fruit on the top of the basket has been sedulously avoided.

Every anthologist faces the prospect of reproach, more for his exclusions than his inclusions. In a volume limited to 550 pages, and with the embarrassment of riches of almost 300 stories from which to make a choice, it is manifestly impossible to do more than embody those elements of variety, balance and sustained interest and to be guided by personal preference. By any standard of sampling, these stories provide more than enough evidence of Maupassant's mastery as a story-teller.

SAXE COMMINS

THE BEST STORIES OF
GUY DE MAUPASSANT

Mademoiselle Fifi

T HE Major Graf von Farlsberg, the Prussian commandant, was reading his newspaper, lying back in a great armchair, with his booted feet on the beautiful marble fireplace, where his spurs had made two holes, which grew deeper every day, during the three months that he had been in the château of Urville.

A cup of coffee was steaming on a small, inlaid table, which was stained with liquors, burnt by cigars, notched by the penknife of the victorious officer, who occasionally would stop while sharpening a pencil, to jot down figures, or to make a drawing on it, just as it took his fancy.

When he had read his letters and the German newspapers, which his baggage-master had brought him, he got up, and after throwing three or four enormous pieces of green wood onto the fire—for these gentlemen were gradually cutting down the park in order to keep themselves warm—he went to the window. The rain was descending in torrents, a regular Normandy rain, which looked as if it were being poured out by some furious hand, a slanting rain, which was as thick as a curtain, and which formed a kind of wall with oblique stripes, and which deluged everything, a regular rain, such as one frequently experiences in the neighborhood of Rouen, which is the watering-pot of France.

For a long time the officer looked at the sodden turf and at the swollen Andelle beyond it, which was overflowing its banks, and he was drumming a waltz from the Rhine on the window-panes, with his fingers, when a noise made him turn round; it was his second in command, Captain Baron von Kelweinstein.

The major was a giant, with broad shoulders, and a long, fair beard, which hung like a cloth onto his chest. His whole, solemn person suggested the idea of a military peacock, a peacock who was carrying his tail spread out onto his breast. He had cold, gentle, blue eyes, and the scar from a sword-cut, which he had received in the war with Austria; he was said to be an honorable man, as well as a brave officer.

The captain, a short, red-faced man, who was tightly girthed in at the waist, had his red hair cropped quite close to his head, and in certain lights almost looked as if he had been rubbed over with phosphorus. He had lost two front teeth one night, though he could not quite remember how. This defect made him speak so that he could not always be understood, and he had a bald patch on the top of his head, which made him look rather like a monk, with a fringe of curly, bright, golden hair round the circle of bare skin.

The commandant shook hands with him, and drank his cup of coffee (the sixth that morning) at a draught, while he listened to his subordinate's report of what had occurred; and then they both went to the window, and declared that it was a very unpleasant outlook. The major, who was a quiet man, with a wife at home, could accommodate himself to everything; but the captain, who was rather fast, being in the habit of frequenting low resorts, and much given to women, was mad at having been shut up for three months in the compulsory chastity of that wretched hole.

There was a knock at the door, and when the commandant said, "Come in," one of their automatic soldiers appeared, and by his mere presence announced that

4

breakfast was ready. In the dining-room, they met three
other officers of lower rank: a lieutenant, Otto von Grossling, and two sub-lieutenants, Fritz Scheunebarg, and
Count von Eyrick, a very short, fair-haired man, who
was proud and brutal toward men, harsh toward prisoners, and very violent.

Since he had been in France, his comrades had called
him nothing but "Mademoiselle Fifi." They had given
him that nickname on account of his dandified style and
small waist, which looked as if he wore stays, from his
pale face, on which his budding mustache scarcely
showed, and on account of the habit he had acquired of
employing the French expression, *fi, fi donc,* which he
pronounced with a slight whistle, when he wished to
express his sovereign contempt for persons or things.

The dining-room of the château was a magnificent
long room, whose fine old mirrors, now cracked by pistol
bullets, and Flemish tapestry, now cut to ribbons and
hanging in rags in places, from sword-cuts, told too well
what Mademoiselle Fifi's occupation was during his spare
time.

There were three family portraits on the walls; a
steel-clad knight, a cardinal, and a judge, who were all
smoking long porcelain pipes, which had been inserted
into holes in the canvas, while a lady in a long, pointed
waist proudly exhibited an enormous pair of mustaches,
drawn with a piece of charcoal.

The officers ate their breakfast almost in silence in
that mutilated room, which looked dull in the rain, and
melancholy under its vanquished appearance, although
its old, oak floor had become as solid as the stone floor of
a public-house.

When they had finished eating, and were smoking
and drinking, they began, as usual, to talk about the dull

life they were leading. The bottles of brandy and of liquors passed from hand to hand, and all sat back in their chairs, taking repeated sips from their glasses, and scarcely removing the long, bent stems, which terminated in china bowls painted in a manner to delight a Hottentot, from their mouths.

As soon as their glasses were empty, they filled them again, with a gesture of resigned weariness, but Mademoiselle Fifi emptied his every minute, and a soldier immediately gave him another. They were enveloped in a cloud of strong tobacco smoke; they seemed to be sunk in a state of drowsy, stupid intoxication, in that dull state of drunkenness of men who have nothing to do, when suddenly, the baron sat up, and said: "By heavens! This cannot go on; we must think of something to do." And on hearing this, Lieutenant Otto and Sub-lieutenant Fritz, who pre-eminently possessed the grave, heavy German countenance, said: "What, captain?"

He thought for a few moments, and then replied: "What? Well, we must get up some entertainment, if the commandant will allow us."

"What sort of an entertainment, captain?" the major asked, taking his pipe out of his mouth.

"I will arrange all that, commandant," the baron said. "I will send *Le Devoir* to Rouen, who will bring us some ladies. I know where they can be found. We will have supper here, as all the materials are at hand, and, at least, we shall have a jolly evening."

Graf von Farlsberg shrugged his shoulders with a smile: "You must surely be mad, my friend."

But all the other officers got up, surrounded their chief, and said: "Let the captain have his own way, commandant; it is terribly dull here."

6

And the major ended by yielding. "Very well," he replied, and the baron immediately sent for *Le Devoir*.

The latter was an old corporal who had never been seen to smile, but who carried out all the orders of his superiors to the letter, no matter what they might be. He stood there, with an impassive face, while he received the baron's instructions, and then went out; five minutes later a large wagon belonging to the military train, covered with a miller's tilt, galloped off as fast as four horses could take it, under the pouring rain, and the officers all seemed to awaken from their lethargy, their looks brightened, and they began to talk.

Although it was raining as hard as ever, the major declared that it was not so dull, and Lieutenant von Grossling said with conviction, that the sky was clearing up, while Mademoiselle Fifi did not seem to be able to keep in his place. He got up, and sat down again, and his bright eyes seemed to be looking for something to destroy. Suddenly, looking at the lady with the mustaches, the young fellow pulled out his revolver, and said: "You shall not see it." And without leaving his seat he aimed, and with two successive bullets cut out both the eyes of the portrait.

"Let us make a mine!" he then exclaimed, and the conversation was suddenly interrupted, as if they had found some fresh and powerful subject of interest. The mine was his invention, his method of destruction, and his favorite amusement.

When he left the château, the lawful owner, Count Fernand d'Amoys d'Urville, had not had time to carry away or to hide anything, except the plate, which had been stowed away in a hole made in one of the walls, so that, as he was very rich and had good taste, the large

7

drawing-room, which opened into the dining-room, had looked like the gallery in a museum, before his precipitate flight.

Expensive oil-paintings, water-colors, and drawings hung upon the walls, while on the tables, on the hanging shelves, and in elegant glass cupboards, there were a thousand knickknacks: small vases, statuettes, groups in Dresden china, grotesque Chinese figures, old ivory, and Venetian glass, which filled the large room with their precious and fantastic array.

Scarcely anything was left now; not that the things had been stolen, for the major would not have allowed that, but Mademoiselle Fifi *would have a mine,* and on that occasion all the officers thoroughly enjoyed themselves for five minutes. The little marquis went into the drawing-room to get what he wanted, and he brought back a small, delicate china teapot, which he filled with gunpowder, and carefully introduced a piece of German tinder into it, through the spout. Then he lighted it, and took this infernal machine into the next room; but he came back immediately, and shut the door. The Germans all stood expectantly, their faces full of childish, smiling curiosity, and as soon as the explosion had shaken the château, they all rushed in at once.

Mademoiselle Fifi, who got in first, clapped his hands in delight at the sight of a terra-cotta Venus, whose head had been blown off, and each picked up pieces of porcelain, and wondered at the strange shape of the fragments, while the major was looking with a paternal eye at the large drawing-room which had been wrecked in such a Neronic fashion, and which was strewn with the fragments of works of art. He went out first, and said, with a smile: "He managed that very well!"

But there was such a cloud of smoke in the dining-room, mingled with the tobacco smoke, that they could not breathe, so the commandant opened the window, and all the officers, who had gone into the room for a glass of cognac, went up to it.

The moist air blew into the room, and brought a sort of spray with it, which powdered their beards. They looked at the tall trees which were dripping with the rain, at the broad valley which was covered with mist, and at the church spire in the distance, which rose up like a gray point in the beating rain.

The bells had not rung since their arrival. That was the only resistance which the invaders had met with in the neighborhood. The parish priest had not refused to take in and to feed the Prussian soldiers; he had several times even drunk a bottle of beer or claret with the hostile commandant, who often employed him as a benevolent intermediary; but it was no use to ask him for a single stroke of the bells; he would sooner have allowed himself to be shot. That was his way of protesting against the invasion, a peaceful and silent protest, the only one, he said, which was suitable to a priest, who was a man of mildness, and not of blood; and everyone, for twenty-five miles round, praised Abbé Chantavoine's firmness and heroism, in venturing to proclaim the public mourning by the obstinate silence of his church bells.

The whole village grew enthusiastic over his resistance, and was ready to back up their pastor and to risk anything, as they looked upon that silent protest as the safeguard of the national honor. It seemed to the peasants that thus they had deserved better of their country than Belfort and Strassbourg, that they had set an equally valuable example, and that the name of their little village would become immortalized by that; but with that exception, they refused their Prussian conquerors nothing.

The commandant and his officers laughed among themselves at that inoffensive courage, and as the people in the whole country round showed themselves obliging and compliant toward them, they willingly tolerated their silent patriotism. Only little Count Wilhelm would have liked to have forced them to ring the bells. He was very angry at his superior's politic compliance with the priest's scruples, and every day he begged the commandant to allow him to sound "ding-dong, ding-dong," just once, only just once, just by way of a joke. And he asked it like a wheedling woman, in the tender voice of some mistress who wishes to obtain something, but the commandant would not yield, and to console *herself*, Mademoiselle Fifi made *a mine* in the château.

The five men stood there together for some minutes, inhaling the moist air, and at last, Lieutenant Fritz said, with a laugh: "The ladies will certainly not have fine weather for their drive." Then they separated, each to his own duties, while the captain had plenty to do in seeing about the dinner.

When they met again, as it was growing dark, they began to laugh at seeing each other as dandified and smart as on the day of a grand review. The commandant's hair did not look as gray as it did in the morning, and the captain had shaved—had only kept his mustache on, which made him look as if he had a streak of fire under his nose.

In spite of the rain, they left the window open, and one of them went to listen from time to time. At a quarter past six the baron said he heard a rumbling in the distance. They all rushed down, and soon the wagon drove up at a gallop with its four horses, splashed up to their backs, steaming and panting. Five women got out at the bottom of the steps, five handsome girls whom a comrade of the captain, to whom *Le Devoir* had taken his card, had selected with care.

They had not required much pressing, as they were sure of being well treated, for they had got to know the Prussians in the three months during which they had had to do with them. So they resigned themselves to the men as they did to the state of affairs. "It is part of our business, so it must be done," they said as they drove along; no doubt to allay some slight, secret scruples of conscience.

They went into the dining-room immediately, which looked still more dismal in its dilapidated state, when it was lighted up; while the table covered with choice dishes, the beautiful china and glass, and the plate, which had been found in the hole in the wall where its owner had hidden it, gave to the place the look of a bandits' resort, where they were supping after committing a robbery. The captain was radiant; he took hold of the women as if he were familiar with them; appraising them, kissing them, valuing them for what they were worth as *ladies of pleasure;* and when the three young men wanted to appropriate one each, he opposed them authoritatively, reserving to himself the right to apportion them justly, according to their several ranks, so as not to wound the hierarchy. Therefore, so as to avoid all discussion, jarring, and suspicion of partiality, he placed them all in a line according to height, and addressing the tallest, he said in a voice of command:

"What is your name?"

"Pamela," she replied, raising her voice.

Then he said: "Number One, called Pamela, is adjudged to the commandant."

Then, having kissed Blondina, the second, as a sign of proprietorship, he proffered stout Amanda to Lieutenant

11

Otto, Eva, "the Tomato," to Sub-lieutenant Fritz, and Rachel, the shortest of them all, a very young, dark girl, with eyes as black as ink, a Jewess, whose snub nose confirmed by exception the rule which allots hooked noses to all her race, to the youngest officer, frail Count Wilhelm von Eyrick.

They were all pretty and plump, without any distinctive features, and all were very much alike in look and person, from their daily dissipation, and the life common to houses of public accommodation.

The three younger men wished to carry off their women immediately, under the pretext of finding them brushes and soap; but the captain wisely opposed this, for he said they were quite fit to sit down to dinner, and that those who went up would wish for a change when they came down, and so would disturb the other couples, and his experience in such matters carried the day. There were only many kisses; expectant kisses.

Suddenly Rachel choked, and began to cough until the tears came into her eyes, while smoke came through her nostrils. Under pretense of kissing her, the count had blown a whiff of tobacco into her mouth. She did not fly into a rage, and did not say a word, but she looked at her possessor with latent hatred in her dark eyes.

They sat down to dinner. The commandant seemed delighted; he made Pamela sit on his right, and Blondina on his left, and said, as he unfolded his table napkin: "That was a delightful idea of yours, captain."

Lieutenants Otto and Fritz, who were as polite as if they had been with fashionable ladies, rather intimidated their neighbors, but Baron von Kelweinstein gave the reins to all his vicious propensities, beamed, made doubtful remarks, and seemed on fire with his crown of red hair. He paid them compliments in French from the

other side of the Rhine, and sputtered out gallant remarks, only fit for a low pothouse, from between his two
broken teeth.

They did not understand him, however, and their
intelligence did not seem to be awakened until he uttered
nasty words and broad expressions, which were mangled
by his accent. Then all began to laugh at once, like mad
women, and fell against each other, repeating the words,
which the baron then began to say all wrong, in order
that he might have the pleasure of hearing them say
doubtful things. They gave him as much of that stuff as
he wanted, for they were drunk after the first bottle of
wine, and, becoming themselves once more, and opening
the door to their usual habits, they kissed the mustaches
on the right and left of them, pinched their arms, uttered
furious cries, drank out of every glass, and sang French
couplets, and bits of German songs, which they had
picked up in their daily intercourse with the enemy.

Soon the men themselves, intoxicated by that which
was displayed to their sight and touch, grew very amorous, shouted and broke the plates and dishes, while the
soldiers behind them waited on them stolidly. The commandant was the only one who put any restraint upon
himself.

Mademoiselle Fifi had taken Rachel onto his knees,
and, getting excited, at one moment kissed the little black
curls on her neck, inhaling the pleasant warmth of her
body, and all the savor of her person, through the slight
space there was between her dress and her skin, and at
another pinched her furiously through the material, and
made her scream, for he was seized with a species of fe-
rocity, and tormented by his desire to hurt her. He often
held her close to him, as if to make her part of himself,
and put his lips in a long kiss on the Jewess's rosy mouth,

until she lost her breath; and at last he bit her until a stream of blood ran down her chin and on to her bodice.

For the second time, she looked him full in the face, and as she bathed the wound, she said: "You will have to pay for that!"

But he merely laughed a hard laugh, and said: "I will pay."

At dessert, champagne was served, and the commandant rose, and in the same voice in which he would have drunk to the health of the Empress Augusta, he drank: "To our ladies!" Then a series of toasts began, toasts worthy of the lowest soldiers and of drunkards, mingled with filthy jokes, which were made still more brutal by their ignorance of the language. They got up, one after the other, trying to say something witty, forcing themselves to be funny, and the women, who were so drunk that they almost fell off their chairs, with vacant looks and clammy tongues, applauded madly each time.

The captain, who no doubt wished to impart an appearance of gallantry to the orgy, raised his glass again, and said: "To our victories over hearts!" Thereupon Lieutenant Otto, who was a species of bear from the Black Forest, jumped up, inflamed and saturated with drink, and seized by an access of alcoholic patriotism, cried: "To our victories over France!"

Drunk as they were, the women were silent, and Rachel turned round with a shudder, and said: "Look here, I know some Frenchmen, in whose presence you would not dare to say that." But the little count, still holding her on his knees, began to laugh, for the wine had made him very merry, and said: "Ha! ha! ha! I have never met any of them, myself. As soon as we show ourselves, they run away!"

The girl, who was in a terrible rage, shouted into his face: "You are lying, you dirty scoundrel!"

For a moment, he looked at her steadily, with his bright eyes upon her, as he had looked at the portrait before he destroyed it with revolver bullets, and then he began to laugh: "Ah! yes, talk about them, my dear! Should we be here now, if they were brave?" Then getting excited, he exclaimed: "We are the masters! France belongs to us!" She jumped off his knees with a bound, and threw herself into her chair, while he rose, held out his glass over the table, and repeated: "France and the French, the woods, the fields, and the houses of France belong to us!"

The others, who were quite drunk, and who were suddenly seized by military enthusiasm, the enthusiasm of brutes, seized their glasses, and shouting, "Long live Prussia!" emptied them at a draught.

The girls did not protest, for they were reduced to silence, and were afraid. Even Rachel did not say a word, as she had no reply to make, and then the little count put his champagne glass, which had just been refilled, onto the head of the Jewess, and exclaimed: "All the women in France belong to us, also!"

At that she got up so quickly that the glass upset, spilling the amber colored wine on to her black hair as if to baptize her, and broke into a hundred fragments as it fell on to the floor. With trembling lips, she defied the looks of the officer, who was still laughing, and she stammered out, in a voice choked with rage: "That—that—that—is not true—for you shall certainly not have any French women."

He sat down again, so as to laugh at his ease, and trying ineffectually to speak in the Parisian accent, he

15

said: "That is good, very good! Then what did you come here for, my dear?"

She was thunderstruck, and made no reply for a moment, for in her agitation she did not understand him at first; but as soon as she grasped his meaning, she said to him indignantly and vehemently: "I! I! I am not a woman; I am only a strumpet, and that is all that Prussians want."

Almost before she had finished, he slapped her full in her face; but as he was raising his hand again, as if he would strike her, she, almost mad with passion, took up a small dessert knife from the table, and stabbed him right in the neck, just above the breastbone. Something that he was going to say, was cut short in his throat, and he sat there, with his mouth half open, and a terrible look in his eyes.

All the officers shouted in horror, and leaped up tumultuously; but throwing her chair between Lieutenant Otto's legs, who fell down at full length, she ran to the window, opened it before they could seize her, and jumped out into the night and pouring rain.

In two minutes, Mademoiselle Fifi was dead. Fritz and Otto drew their swords and wanted to kill the women, who threw themselves at their feet and clung to their knees. With some difficulty the major had the four terrified girls locked up in a room under the care of two soldiers. Then he organized the pursuit of the fugitive, as carefully as if he were about to engage in a skirmish, feeling quite sure that she would be caught.

The table, which had been cleared immediately, now served as a bed on which to lay Fifi out, and the four officers made for the window, rigid and sobered, with the stern faces of soldiers on duty, and tried to pierce through the darkness of the night, amid the steady torrent of rain.

Suddenly, a shot was heard, and then another, a long way off; and for four hours they heard from time to time near or distant reports and rallying cries, strange words uttered as a call, in guttural voices.

In the morning they all returned. Two soldiers had been killed and three others wounded by their comrades in the ardor of that chase, and in the confusion of such a nocturnal pursuit, but they had not caught Rachel.

Then the inhabitants of the district were terrorized, the houses were turned topsy-turvy, the country was scoured and beaten up, over and over again, but the Jewess did not seem to have left a single trace of her passage behind her.

When the general was told of it, he gave orders to hush up the affair, so as not to set a bad example to the army, but he severely censured the commandant, who in turn punished his inferiors. The general had said: "One does not go to war in order to amuse oneself, and to caress prostitutes." And Graf von Farlsberg, in his exasperation, made up his mind to have his revenge on the district, but as he required a pretext for showing severity, he sent for the priest, and ordered him to have the bell tolled at the funeral of Count von Eyrick.

Contrary to all expectation, the priest showed himself humble and most respectful, and when Mademoiselle Fifi's body left the Château d'Urville on its way to the cemetery, carried by soldiers, preceded, surrounded, and followed by soldiers, who marched with loaded rifles, for the first time the bell sounded its funereal knell in a lively manner, as if a friendly hand were caressing it. At night it sounded again, and the next day, and every day; it rang as much as anyone could desire. Sometimes even, it would start at night, and sound gently through the darkness, seized by strange joy, awakened, one could not tell why. All the peasants in the neighborhood declared that it was bewitched, and nobody, except the priest and the sacristan would now go near the church tower, and they went because a poor girl was living there in grief and solitude, secretly nourished by those two men.

She remained there until the German troops departed, and then one evening the priest borrowed the baker's cart, and himself drove his prisoner to Rouen. When they got there, he embraced her, and she quickly went back on foot to the establishment from which she had come, where the proprietress, who thought that she was dead, was very glad to see her.

A short time afterward, a patriot who had no prejudices, who liked her because of her bold deed, and who afterward loved her for herself, married her, and made a lady of her.

Vain Beauty

A VERY elegant victoria, with two beautiful black horses, was drawn up in front of the mansion. It was a day in the latter end of June, about half past five in the afternoon, and the sun shone warm and bright into the large courtyard.

The Countess de Mascaret came down just as her husband, who was coming home, appeared in the carriage entrance. He stopped for a few moments to look at his wife and grew rather pale.

She was very beautiful, graceful, and distinguished looking, with her long oval face, her complexion like gilt ivory, her large gray eyes, and her black hair; and she got into her carriage without looking at him, without even seeming to have noticed him, with such a particularly high-bred air, that the furious jealousy by which he had been devoured for so long again gnawed at his heart. He went up to her and said: "You are going for a drive?"

She merely replied disdainfully: "You see I am!"

"In the Bois de Boulogne?"

"Most probably."

"May I come with you?"

"The carriage belongs to you."

Without being surprised at the tone of voice in which she answered him, he got in and sat down by his wife's side, and said: "Bois de Boulogne." The footman jumped up by the coachman's side, and the horses as usual pawed the ground and shook their heads until they were in the street. Husband and wife sat side by side, without speaking. He was thinking how to begin a conversation, but she maintained such an obstinately hard look, that he did not venture to make the attempt. At last, however, he cunningly, accidentally as it were, touched the Countess's gloved hand with his own, but she drew her arm away, with a movement which was so expressive of disgust, that he remained thoughtful, in spite of his usual authoritative and despotic character. "Gabrielle!" said he at last.

"What do you want?"

"I think you are looking adorable."

She did not reply, but remained lying back in the carriage, looking like an irritated queen. By that time they were driving up the Champs-Elysées, toward the Arc de Triomphe. That immense monument, at the end of the long avenue, raised its colossal arch against the red sky, and the sun seemed to be sinking onto it, showering fiery dust on it from the sky.

The streams of carriages, with the sun reflecting from the bright, plated harness and the shining lamps, were like a double current flowing, one toward the town and one toward the wood, and the Count de Mascaret continued: "My dear Gabrielle!"

Then, unable to bear it any longer, she replied in an exasperated voice: "Oh! do leave me in peace, pray; I am not even at liberty to have my carriage to myself, now." He, however, pretended not to hear her, and continued: "You have never looked so pretty as you do today."

Her patience was decidedly at an end, and she replied with irrepressible anger: "You are wrong to notice it, for I swear to you that I will never have anything to do with you in that way again." He was stupefied and agitated, and his violent nature gaining the upper hand, he exclaimed: "What do you mean by that?" in such a manner as revealed rather the brutal master than the amorous man. But she replied in a low voice, so that the servants might not hear, amid the deafening noise of the wheels:

"Ah! What do I mean by that? What do I mean by that? Now I recognize you again! Do you want me to tell everything?"

"Yes."

"Everything that has been in my heart, since I have been the victim of your terrible selfishness?"

He had grown red with surprise and anger, and he growled between his closed teeth: "Yes, tell me everything."

He was a tall, broad-shouldered man, with a big, red beard, a handsome man, a nobleman, a man of the world, who passed as a perfect husband and an excellent father, and now for the first time since they had started she turned toward him, and looked him full in the face: "Ah! You will hear some disagreeable things, but you must know that I am prepared for everything, that I fear nothing, and you less than anyone, today."

He also was looking into her eyes, and already was shaking with passion; then he said in a low voice: "You are mad."

"No, but I will no longer be the victim of the hateful penalty of maternity, which you have inflicted on me for eleven years! I wish to live like a woman of the world, as I have the right to do, as all women have the right to do."

He suddenly grew pale again, and stammered: "I do not understand you."

"Oh! yes; you understand me well enough. It is now three months since I had my last child, and as I am still very beautiful, and as, in spite of all your efforts you cannot spoil my figure, as you just now perceived, when you saw me on the outside flight of steps, you think it is time that I should become *enceinte* again."

"But you are talking nonsense!"

"No, I am not; I am thirty, and I have had seven children, and we have been married eleven years, and you hope that this will go on for ten years longer, after which you will leave off being jealous."

He seized her arm and squeezed it, saying: "I will not allow you to talk to me like that, for long."

"And I shall talk to you till the end, until I have finished all I have to say to you, and if you try to prevent me, I shall raise my voice so that the two servants, who are on the box, may hear. I only allowed you to come with me for that object, for I have these witnesses, who will oblige you to listen to me, and to contain yourself; so now, pay attention to what I say. I have always felt an antipathy for you, and I have always let you see it, for I have never lied, Monsieur. You married me in spite of myself; you forced my parents, who were in embarrassed circumstances, to give me to you, because you were rich, and they obliged me to marry you, in spite of my tears.

"So you bought me, and as soon as I was in your power, as soon as I had become your companion, ready to attach myself to you, to forget your coercive and threatening proceedings, in order that I might only remember that I ought to be a devoted wife and to love you as much as it might be possible for me to love you, you became jealous—you—as no man has ever been before, with the base, ignoble jealousy of a spy, which was as degrading for you as it was for me. I had not been married eight months, when you suspected me of every perfidiousness, and you even told me so. What a disgrace! And as you could not prevent me from being beautiful, and from pleasing people, from being called in drawing-rooms, and also in the newspapers, one of the most beautiful women in Paris, you tried everything you could think of to keep admirers from me, and you hit upon the abominable idea of making me spend my life in a constant state of mother-hood, until the time when I should disgust every man. Oh! do not deny it! I did not understand it for some time, but then I guessed it. You even boasted about it to your sister, who told me of it, for she is fond of me and was disgusted at your boorish coarseness.

"Ah! Remember our struggles, doors smashed in, and locks forced! For eleven years you have condemned me to the existence of a brood mare. Then as soon as I was pregnant, you grew disgusted with me, and I saw nothing of you for months, and I was sent into the country, to the family mansion, among fields and meadows, to bring forth my child. And when I reappeared, fresh, pretty, and indestructible, still seductive and constantly surrounded by admirers, hoping that at last I should live a little like a young rich woman who belongs to society, you were seized by jealousy again, and you recommenced to perse-cute me with that infamous and hateful desire from which you are suffering at this moment, by my side. And it is not the desire of possessing me—for I should never have refused myself to you—but it is the wish to make me unsightly.

"Besides this, that abominable and mysterious cir-cumstance took place, which I was a long time in pene-trating (but I grew acute by dint of watching your thoughts and actions). You attached yourself to your chil-dren with all the security which they gave you while I bore them in my womb. You felt affection for them, with

23

all your aversion for me, and in spite of your ignoble fears, which were momentarily allayed by your pleasure in seeing me a mother.

"Oh! how often have I noticed that joy in you! I have seen it in your eyes and guessed it. You loved your children as victories, and not because they were of your own blood. They were victories over me, over my youth, over my beauty, over my charms, over the compliments which were paid me, and over those who whispered round me, without paying them to me. And you are proud of them, you make a parade of them, you take them out for drives in your coach in the Bois de Boulogne, and you give them donkey rides at Montmorency. You take them to theatrical matinées so that you may be seen in the midst of them, and that people may say: 'What a kind father!' and that it may be repeated."

He had seized her wrist with savage brutality, and squeezed it so violently that she was quiet, though she nearly cried out with the pain. Then he said to her in a whisper:

"I love my children, do you hear? What you have just told me is disgraceful in a mother. But you belong to me; I am master—your master. I can exact from you what I like and when I like—and I have the law on my side."

He was trying to crush her fingers in the strong grip of his large, muscular hand, and she, livid with pain, tried in vain to free them from that vise which was crushing them; the agony made her pant, and the tears came into her eyes. "You see that I am the master, and the stronger," he said. And when he somewhat loosened his grip, she asked him: "Do you think that I am a religious woman?"

He was surprised and stammered: "Yes."

"Do you think that I could lie, if I swore to the truth

24

of anything to you, before an altar on which Christ's body is?"

"No."

"Will you go with me to some church?"

"What for?"

"You shall see. Will you?"

"If you absolutely wish it, yes."

She raised her voice and said: "Philip!" And the coachman, bending down a little, without taking his eyes from his horses, seemed to turn his ear alone toward his mistress, who said: "Drive to St. Philip-du-Roule's." And the victoria, which had reached the entrance of the Bois de Boulogne, returned to Paris.

Husband and wife did not exchange a word during the drive. When the carriage stopped before the church, Madame de Mascaret jumped out, and entered it, followed by the Count, a few yards behind her. She went, without stopping, as far as the choir-screen, and falling on her knees at a chair, she buried her face in her hands. She prayed for a long time, and he, standing behind her, could see that she was crying. She wept noiselessly, like women do weep when they are in great and poignant grief. There was a kind of undulation in her body, which ended in a little sob, hidden and stifled by her fingers.

But Count de Mascaret thought that the situation was long drawn out, and he touched her on the shoulder. That contact recalled her to herself, as if she had been burned, and getting up, she looked straight into his eyes.

"This is what I have to say to you. I am afraid of nothing, whatever you may do to me. You may kill me if you like. One of your children is not yours, and one only; that I swear to you before God, who hears me here. That is the only revenge which was possible for me, in return

25

for all your abominable male tyrannies, in return for the penal servitude of childbearing to which you have condemned me. Who was my lover? That you will never know! You may suspect everyone, but you will never find out. I gave myself up to him, without love and without pleasure, only for the sake of betraying you, and he made me a mother. Which is his child? That also you will never know. I have seven; try and find out! I intended to tell you this later, for one cannot completely avenge oneself on a man by deceiving him, unless he knows it. You have driven me to confess it today; now I have finished."

She hurried through the church, toward the open door, expecting to hear behind her the quick steps of her husband whom she had defied, and to be knocked to the ground by a blow of his fist, but she heard nothing, and reached her carriage. She jumped into it at a bound, overwhelmed with anguish, and breathless with fear; she called out to the coachman, "Home!" and the horses set off at a quick trot.

II

The Countess de Mascaret was waiting in her room for dinner time, like a criminal sentenced to death awaits the hour of his execution. What was he going to do? Had he come home? Despotic, passionate, ready for any violence as he was, what was he meditating, what had he made up his mind to do? There was no sound in the house, and every moment she looked at the clock. Her maid had come and dressed her for the evening, and had then left the room again. Eight o'clock struck; almost at the same moment there were two knocks at the door, and the butler came in and told her that dinner was ready.

"Has the Count come in?"

"Yes, Madame la Comtesse; he is in the dining-room."

For a moment she felt inclined to arm herself with a small revolver, which she had bought some weeks before, foreseeing the tragedy which was being rehearsed in her heart. But she remembered that all the children would be there, and she took nothing except a smelling-bottle. He rose somewhat ceremoniously from his chair. They exchanged a slight bow, and sat down. The three boys, with their tutor, Abbé Martin, were on her right, and the three girls, with Miss Smith, their English governess, were on her left. The youngest child, who was only three months old, remained upstairs with his nurse.

The Abbé said grace, as was usual when there was no company, for the children did not come down to dinner when there were guests present; then they began dinner. The Countess, suffering from emotion which she had not at all calculated upon, remained with her eyes cast down, while the Count scrutinized, now the three boys, and now the three girls with uncertain, unhappy looks, which traveled from one to the other. Suddenly, pushing his wineglass from him, it broke, and the wine was spilt on the tablecloth, and at the slight noise caused by this little accident, the Countess started up from her chair, and for the first time they looked at each other. Then, almost every moment, in spite of themselves, in spite of the irritation of their nerves caused by every glance, they did not cease to exchange looks, rapid as pistol shots.

The Abbé, who felt that there was some cause for embarrassment which he could not divine, tried to get up a conversation, and started various subjects, but his useless efforts gave rise to no ideas and did not bring out a word. The Countess, with feminine tact and obeying the instincts of a woman of the world, tried to answer him two or three times, but in vain. She could not find words, in the perplexity of her mind, and her own voice almost frightened her in the silence of the large room, where nothing else was heard except the slight sound of plates and knives and forks.

Suddenly, her husband said to her, bending forward: "Here, amid your children, will you swear to me that what you told me just now is true?"

The hatred which was fermenting in her veins suddenly roused her, and replying to that question with the same firmness with which she had replied to his looks, she raised both her hands, the right pointing toward the boys and the left toward the girls, and said in a firm, resolute voice, and without any hesitation: "On the heads of my children, I swear that I have told you the truth."

He got up, and throwing his table napkin onto the table with an exasperated movement, turned round and flung his chair against the wall. Then he went out without another word, while she, uttering a deep sigh, as if after a first victory, went on in a calm voice: "You must not pay any attention to what your father has just said, my darlings; he was very much upset a short time ago, but he will be all right again, in a few days."

Then she talked with the Abbé and with Miss Smith, and had tender, pretty words for all her children; those sweet spoiling mother's ways which unlock little hearts.

When dinner was over, she went into the drawing-room with all her little following. She made the elder ones chatter, and when their bedtime came she kissed them for a long time, and then went alone into her room.

She waited, for she had no doubt that he would come, and she made up her mind then, as her children were not with her, to defend her human flesh, as she defended her life as a woman of the world; and in the pocket of her dress she put the little loaded revolver which she had bought a few weeks before. The hours went by, the hours struck, and every sound was hushed in the house. Only the cabs continued to rumble through the streets, but their noise was heard only vaguely through the shuttered and curtained windows.

She waited, energetic and nervous, without any fear of him now, ready for anything, and almost triumphant, for she had found means of torturing him continually, during every moment of his life.

But the first gleams of dawn came in through the fringe at the bottom of her curtains, without his having come into her room, and then she awoke to the fact, much to her surprise that he was not coming. Having locked and bolted her door, for greater security, she went to bed at last, and remained there, with her eyes open, thinking, and barely understanding it all, without being able to guess what he was going to do.

When her maid brought her tea, she at the same time gave her a letter from her husband. He told her that he was going to undertake a longish journey, and in a post-script he added that his lawyer would provide her with such money as she might require for her expenses.

III

It was at the opera, between two of the acts in "Robert the Devil." In the stalls, the men were standing up, with their hats on, their waistcoats cut very low so as to show a large amount of white shirt front, in which the gold and precious stones of their studs glistened. They were looking at the boxes crowded with ladies in low dresses, covered with diamonds and pearls, women who seemed to expand like flowers in that illuminated hot-house, where the beauty of their faces and the whiteness of their shoulders seemed to bloom for inspection, in the midst of the music and of human voices.

Vain Beauty

Two friends, with their backs to the orchestra, were scanning those parterres of elegance, that exhibition of real or false charms, of jewels, of luxury, and of pretension which showed itself off all round the Grand Theater. One of them, Roger de Salnis, said to his companion, Bernard Grandin: "Just look how beautiful Countess de Mascaret still is."

Then the elder, in turn, looked through his opera glasses at a tall lady in a box opposite, who appeared to be still very young, and whose striking beauty seemed to appeal to men's eyes in every corner of the house. Her pale complexion, of an ivory tint, gave her the appearance of a statue, while a small, diamond coronet glistened in her black hair like a cluster of stars.

When he had looked at her for some time, Bernard Grandin replied with a jocular accent of sincere conviction: "You may well call her beautiful!"

"How old do you think she is?"

"Wait a moment. I can tell you exactly, for I have known her since she was a child, and I saw her make her *début* into society when she was quite a girl. She is—she is—thirty—thirty-six."

"Impossible!"

"I am sure of it."

"She looks twenty-five."

"She has had seven children."

"It is incredible."

"And what is more, they are all seven alive, as she is a very good mother. I go to the house, which is a very quiet and pleasant one, occasionally, and she presents the phenomenon of the family in the midst of the world."

"How very strange! And have there never been any reports about her?"

"Never."

"But what about her husband? He is peculiar, is he not?"

"Yes and no. Very likely there has been a little drama between them, one of those little domestic dramas which one suspects, which one never finds out exactly, but which one guesses pretty nearly."

"What is it?"

"I do not know anything about it. Mascaret leads a very fast life now, after having been a model husband. As long as he remained a good spouse, he had a shocking temper and was crabbed and easily took offense, but since he has been leading his present, rackety life, he has become quite indifferent; but one would guess that he has some trouble, a worm gnawing somewhere, for he has aged very much."

Thereupon the two friends talked philosophically for some minutes about the secret, unknowable troubles, which differences of character or perhaps physical antipathies, which were not perceived at first, give rise to in families. Then Roger de Salnis, who was still looking at Madame de Mascaret through his opera-glasses, said:

"It is almost incredible that that woman has had seven children!"

"Yes, in eleven years; after which, when she was thirty, she put a stop to her period of production in order to enter into the brilliant period of entertaining, which does not seem near coming to an end."

"Poor women!"

"Why do you pity them?"

"Why? Ah! my dear fellow, just consider! Eleven years of maternity, for such a woman! What a hell! All her youth, all her beauty, every hope of success, every poetical ideal of a bright life, sacrificed to that abominable law of reproduction which turns the normal woman into a mere machine for maternity."

"What would you have? It is only Nature!"

"Yes, but I say that Nature is our enemy, that we must always fight against Nature, for she is continually bringing us back to an animal state. You may be sure that God has not put anything on this earth that is clean, pretty, elegant, or accessory to our ideal, but the human brain has done it. It is we who have introduced a little grace, beauty, unknown charm, and mystery into creation by singing about it, interpreting it, by admiring it as poets, idealizing it as artists, and by explaining it as learned men who make mistakes, but who find ingenious reasons, some grace and beauty, some unknown charm and mystery in the various phenomena of nature.

"God only created coarse beings, full of the germs of disease, and who, after a few years of bestial enjoyment, grow old and infirm, with all the ugliness and all the want of power of human decrepitude. He only seems to have made them in order that they may reproduce their species in a repulsive manner, and then die like ephemeral insects. I said, *reproduce their species in a repulsive manner*, and I adhere to that expression. What is there as a matter of fact, more ignoble and more repugnant than that ridiculous act of the reproduction of living beings, against which all delicate minds always have revolted, and always will revolt? Since all the organs which have been invented by this economical and malicious Creator serve two purposes, why did he not choose those that were unsullied, in order to intrust them with that sacred mission, which is the noblest and the most exalted of all human functions? The mouth which nourishes the body by means of material food, also diffuses abroad speech and thought. Our flesh revives itself by means of itself, and at the same time, ideas are communicated by it. The sense of smell, which gives the vital air to the lungs, imparts all the perfumes of the world to the brain: the smell of flowers, of woods, of trees, of the sea. The ear, which enables us to communicate with our fellow-men, has also allowed us to invent music, to create dreams, happiness, the infinite, and even physical pleasure, by means of sounds!

"But one might say that the Creator wished to prohibit men from ever ennobling and idealizing his commerce with women. Nevertheless, man has found love, which is not a bad reply to that sly Deity, and he has ornamented it so much with literary poetry, that woman often forgets the contact she is obliged to submit to. Those among us who are powerless to deceive themselves have invented vice and refined debauchery, which is another way of laughing at God, and of paying homage, immodest homage, to beauty.

"But the normal man makes children; just a beast that is coupled with another by law.

"Look at that woman! Is it not abominable to think that such a jewel, such a pearl, born to be beautiful, admired, fêted, and adored, has spent eleven years of her life in providing heirs for the Count de Mascaret?"

Bernard Grandin replied with a laugh: "There is a great deal of truth in all that, but very few people would understand you."

Salnis got more and more animated. "Do you know how I picture God myself?" he said. "As an enormous, creative organ unknown to us, who scatters millions of worlds into space, just as one single fish would deposit its spawn in the sea. He creates, because it is His function as God to do so, but He does not know what He is doing, and is stupidly prolific in His work, and is ignorant of the combinations of all kinds which are produced by His scattered germs. Human thought is a lucky little local, passing accident, which was totally unforeseen, and is condemned to disappear with this earth, and to recommence perhaps here or elsewhere, the same or different, with fresh combinations of eternally new beginnings. We owe it to this slight accident which has happened to His intellect, that we are very uncomfortable in this world which was not made for us, which had not been prepared to receive us, to lodge and feed us, or to satisfy reflecting beings, and we owe it to Him also that we have to struggle without ceasing against what are still called the designs of Providence, when we are really refined and civilized beings."

Grandin, who was listening to him attentively, as he had long known the surprising outbursts of his fancy, asked him: "Then you believe that human thought is the spontaneous product of blind, divine parturition?"

"Naturally? A fortuitous function of the nerve-centers of our brain, like some unforeseen chemical action which is due to new mixtures, and which also resembles a product of electricity, caused by friction or the unexpected proximity of some substance, and which, lastly, resembles the phenomena caused by the infinite and fruitful fermentations of living matter.

"But, my dear fellow, the truth of this must be evident to anyone who looks about him. If human thought, ordained by an omniscient Creator, had been intended to be what it has become, altogether different from mechanical thoughts and resignation, so exacting, inquiring, agitated, tormented, would the world which was created to receive the beings which we now are have been this unpleasant little dwelling place for poor fools, this salad plot, this rocky, wooded, and spherical kitchen garden where your improvident Providence has destined us to live naked, in caves or under trees, nourished on the flesh of slaughtered animals, our brethren, or on raw vegetables nourished by the sun and the rain?

"But it is sufficient to reflect for a moment, in order to understand that this world was not made for such creatures as we are. Thought, which is developed by a miracle in the nerves of the cells in our brain, powerless, ignorant, and confused as it is, and as it will always remain, makes all of us who are intellectual beings eternal and wretched exiles on earth.

"Look at this earth, as God has given it to those who inhabit it. Is it not visibly and solely made, planted and covered with forests, for the sake of animals? What is there for us? Nothing. And for them? Everything. They have nothing to do but to eat, or go hunting and eat each other, according to their instincts, for God never foresaw gentleness and peaceable manners; He only foresaw the death of creatures which were bent on destroying and devouring each other. Are not the quail, the pigeon, and the partridge the natural prey of the hawk? the sheep, the stag, and the ox that of the great flesh-eating animals, rather than meat that has been fattened to be served up to us with truffles, which have been unearthed by pigs, for our special benefit?

"As to ourselves, the more civilized, intellectual, and refined we are, the more we ought to conquer and subdue that animal instinct, which represents the will of God in us. And so, in order to mitigate our lot as brutes, we have discovered and made everything, beginning with houses, then exquisite food, sauces, sweetmeats, pastry, drink, stuffs, clothes, ornaments, beds, mattresses, carriages, railways, and innumerable machines, besides arts and sciences, writing and poetry. Every ideal comes from us as well as the amenities of life, in order to make our existence as simple reproducers, for which divine Providence solely intended us, less monotonous and less hard.

"Look at this theater. Is there not here a human world created by us, unforeseen and unknown by Eternal destinies, comprehensible by our minds alone, a sensual and intellectual distraction, which has been invented solely by and for that discontented and restless little animal that we are.

"Look at that woman, Madame de Mascaret. God intended her to live in a cave naked, or wrapped up in the skins of wild animals, but is she not better as she is? But, speaking of her, does anyone know why and how her brute of a husband, having such a companion by his side, and especially after having been boorish enough to make her a mother seven times, has suddenly left her, to run after bad women?"

Grandin replied: "Oh! my dear fellow, this is probably the only reason. He found that always living with her was becoming too expensive in the end, and from reasons of domestic economy, he has arrived at the same principles which you lay down as a philosopher."

Just then the curtain rose for the third act, and they turned round, took off their hats, and sat down.

IV

The Count and Countess Mascaret were sitting side by side in the carriage which was taking them home from the opera, without speaking. But suddenly the husband said to his wife: "Gabrielle!"

"What do you want?"

"Don't you think that this has lasted long enough?"

"What?"

"The horrible punishment to which you have con
demned me for the last six years."

"What do you want? I cannot help it."

"Then tell me which of them it is?"

"Never."

"Think that I can no longer see my children or feel
them round me, without having my heart burdened with
this doubt. Tell me which of them it is, and I swear that
I will forgive you, and treat it like the others."

"I have not the right to."

"You do not see that I can no longer endure this life,
this thought which is wearing me out, or this question
which I am constantly asking myself, this question which
tortures me each time I look at them. It is driving
me mad."

"Then you have suffered a great deal?" she said.

"Terribly. Should I, without that, have accepted the
horror of living by your side, and the still greater horror
of feeling and knowing that there is one among them
whom I cannot recognize, and who prevents me from
loving the others?"

She repeated: "Then you have really suffered very
much?" And he replied in a constrained and sorrowful
voice:

"Yes, for do I not tell you every day that it is intolerable torture to me? Should I have remained in that
house, near you and them, if I did not love them? Oh!
You have behaved abominably toward me. All the affection of my heart I have bestowed upon my children, and
that you know. I am for them a father of the olden time,
as I was for you a husband of one of the families of old,
for by instinct I have remained a natural man, a man of
former days. Yes, I will confess it, you have made me
terribly jealous, because you are a woman of another

race, of another soul, with other requirements. Oh! I shall never forget the things that you told me, but from that day, I troubled myself no more about you. I did not kill you, because then I should have had no means on earth of ever discovering which of our—of your children is not mine. I have waited, but I have suffered more than you would believe, for I can no longer venture to love them, except, perhaps, the two eldest; I no longer venture to look at them, to call them to me, to kiss them; I cannot take them on to my knee without asking myself: 'Can it be this one?' I have been correct in my behavior toward you for six years, and even kind and complaisant; tell me the truth, and I swear that I will do nothing unkind."

He thought, in spite of the darkness of the carriage, that he could perceive that she was moved, and feeling certain that she was going to speak at last, he said: "I beg you, I beseech you to tell me."

"I have been more guilty than you think perhaps," she replied; "but I could no longer endure that life of continual pregnancy, and I had only one means of driving you from my bed. I lied before God, and I lied, with my hand raised to my children's heads, for I have never wronged you."

He seized her arm in the darkness, and squeezing it as he had done on that terrible day of their drive in the Bois de Boulogne, he stammered: "Is that true?"

"It is true."

But he in terrible grief said with a groan: "I shall have fresh doubts that will never end! When did you lie, the last time or now? How am I to believe you at present? How can one believe a woman after that? I shall never again know what I am to think. I would rather you had said to me: 'It is Jacques, or, it is Jeanne.' "

Vain Beauty

The carriage drove them into the courtyard of their mansion, and when it had drawn up in front of the steps, the Count got down first as usual, and offered his wife his arm, to help her up. And then, as soon as they had reached the first floor he said: "May I speak to you for a few moments longer?"

And she replied: "I am quite willing."

They went into a small drawing-room, while a footman in some surprise, lit the wax candles. As soon as he had left the room and they were alone, he continued: "How am I to know the truth? I have begged you a thousand times to speak, but you have remained dumb, impenetrable, inflexible, inexorable, and now today, you tell me that you have been lying. For six years you have actually allowed me to believe such a thing! No, you are lying now, I do not know why, but out of pity for me, perhaps?"

She replied in a sincere and convincing manner: "If I had not done so, I should have had four more children in the last six years!"

And he exclaimed: "Can a mother speak like that?"

"Oh!" she replied, "I do not at all feel that I am the mother of children who have never been born, it is enough for me to be the mother of those that I have, and to love them with all my heart. I am—we are—women who belong to the civilized world, Monsieur, and we are no longer, and we refuse to be, mere females who restock the earth."

She got up, but he seized her hands. "Only one word, Gabrielle. Tell me the truth!"

"I have just told you. I have never dishonored you."

He looked her full in the face, and how beautiful she was, with her gray eyes, like the cold sky. In her dark hairdress, on that opaque night of black hair, there shone the diamond coronet, like a cluster of stars. Then he suddenly felt, felt by a kind of intuition, that this grand creature was not merely a being destined to perpetuate his race, but the strange and mysterious product of all the complicated desires which have been accumulating in us for centuries but which have been turned aside from their primitive and divine object, and which have wandered after a mystic, imperfectly seen, and intangible beauty. There are some women like that, women who blossom only for our dreams, adorned with every poetical attribute of civilization, with that ideal luxury, coquetry, and æsthetic charm which should surround the living statue who brightens our life.

Her husband remained standing before her, stupefied at the tardy and obscure discovery, confusedly hitting on the cause of his former jealousy, and understanding it all very imperfectly. At last he said: "I believe you, for I feel at this moment that you are not lying, and formerly, I really thought that you were."

She put out her hand to him: "We are friends then?"

He took her hand and kissed it, and replied: "We are friends. Thank you, Gabrielle."

Then he went out, still looking at her, and surprised that she was still so beautiful, and feeling a strange emotion arising in him, which was, perhaps, more formidable than antique and simple love.

The Horla

MAR. 8. What a lovely day! I have spent all the morning lying on the grass in front of my house, under the enormous plantain tree which covers and shades and shelters the whole of it. I like this part of the country; I am fond of living here because I am attached to it by deep roots, the profound and delicate roots which attach a man to the soil on which his ancestors were born and died, to their traditions, their usages, their food, the local expressions, the peculiar language of the peasants, the smell of the soil, the hamlets, and to the atmosphere itself.

I love the house in which I grew up. From my windows I can see the Seine, which flows by the side of my garden, on the other side of the road, almost through my grounds, the great and wide Seine, which goes to Rouen and Havre, and which is covered with boats passing to and fro.

On the left, down yonder, lies Rouen, populous Rouen with its blue roofs massing under pointed Gothic towers. Innumerable are they, delicate or broad, dominated by the spire of the cathedral, full of bells which sound through the blue air on fine mornings, sending their sweet and distant iron clang to me, their metallic sounds, now stronger and now weaker, according as the wind is strong or light.

What a delicious morning it was! About eleven o'clock, a long line of boats drawn by a steam-tug, as big as a fly, and which scarcely puffed while emitting its thick smoke, passed my gate.

After two English schooners, whose red flags fluttered toward the sky, there came a magnificent Brazilian three-master; it was perfectly white and wonderfully clean and shining. I saluted it, I hardly know why, except that the sight of the vessel gave me great pleasure.

May 12. I have had a slight feverish attack for the last few days, and I feel ill, or rather I feel low-spirited.

Whence come those mysterious influences which change our happiness into discouragement, and our self-confidence into diffidence? One might almost say that the air, the invisible air, is full of unknowable Forces, whose mysterious presence we have to endure. I wake up in the best of spirits, with an inclination to sing in my heart. Why? I go down by the side of the water, and suddenly, after walking a short distance, I return home wretched, as if some misfortune were awaiting me there. Why? Is it a cold shiver which, passing over my skin, has upset my nerves and given me a fit of low spirits? Is it the form of the clouds, or the tints of the sky, or the colors of the surrounding objects which are so changeable, which have troubled my thoughts as they passed before my eyes? Who can tell? Everything that surrounds us, everything that we see without looking at it, everything that we touch without knowing it, everything that we handle without feeling it, everything that we meet without clearly distinguishing it, has a rapid, surprising, and inexplicable effect upon us and upon our organs, and through them on our ideas and on our being itself.

How profound that mystery of the Invisible is! We cannot fathom it with our miserable senses: our eyes are unable to perceive what is either too small or too great, too near to or too far from us; we can see neither the inhabitants of a star nor of a drop of water; our ears deceive us, for they transmit to us the vibrations of the air in sonorous notes. Our senses are fairies who work the miracle of changing that movement into noise, and by that metamorphosis give birth to music, which makes the mute agitation of nature a harmony. So with our sense of smell, which is weaker than that of a dog, and so with our sense of taste, which can scarcely distinguish the age of a wine!

Oh! If we only had other organs which could work other miracles in our favor, what a number of fresh things we might discover around us!

May 16. I am ill, decidedly! I was so well last month! I am feverish, horribly feverish, or rather I am in a state of feverish enervation, which makes my mind suffer as much as my body. I have without ceasing the horrible sensation of some danger threatening me, the apprehension of some coming misfortune or of approaching death, a presentiment which is, no doubt, an attack of some illness still unnamed, which germinates in the flesh and in the blood.

May 18. I have just come from consulting my medical man, for I can no longer get my sleep. He found that my pulse was high, my eyes dilated, my nerves highly strung, but no alarming symptoms. I must have a course of shower baths and of bromide of potassium.

May 25. No change! My state is really very peculiar. As the evening comes on, an incomprehensible feeling of disquietude seizes me, just as if night concealed some terrible menace toward me. I dine quickly, and then try to read, but I do not understand the words, and can scarcely distinguish the letters. Then I walk up and down my drawing-room, oppressed by a feeling of confused and irresistible fear, a fear of sleep and a fear of my bed.

About ten o'clock I go up to my room. As soon as I have entered I lock and bolt the door. I am frightened—

of what? Up till the present time I have been frightened of nothing. I open my cupboards, and look under my bed; I listen—I listen—to what? How strange it is that a simple feeling of discomfort, of impeded or heightened circulation, perhaps the irritation of a nervous center, a slight congestion, a small disturbance in the imperfect and delicate functions of our living machinery, can turn the most light-hearted of men into a melancholy one, and make a coward of the bravest? Then, I go to bed, and I wait for sleep as a man might wait for the executioner. I wait for its coming with dread, and my heart beats and my legs tremble, while my whole body shivers beneath the warmth of the bedclothes, until the moment when I suddenly fall asleep, as a man throws himself into a pool of stagnant water in order to drown. I do not feel this perfidious sleep coming over me as I used to, but a sleep which is close to me and watching me, which is going to seize me by the head, to close my eyes and annihilate me.

I sleep—a long time—two or three hours perhaps—then a dream—no—a nightmare lays hold of me. I feel that I am in bed and asleep—I feel it and I know it—and I feel also that somebody is coming close to me, is looking at me, touching me, is getting onto my bed, is kneeling on my chest, is taking my neck between his hands and squeezing it—squeezing it with all his might in order to strangle me.

I struggle, bound by that terrible powerlessness which paralyzes us in our dreams; I try to cry out—but I cannot; I want to move—I cannot; I try, with the most violent efforts and out of breath, to turn over and throw off this being which is crushing and suffocating me—I cannot!

And then suddenly I wake up, shaken and bathed in

perspiration; I light a candle and find that I am alone, and after that crisis, which occurs every night, I at length fall asleep and slumber tranquilly till morning.

June 2. My state has grown worse. What is the matter with me? The bromide does me no good, and the shower-baths have no effect whatever. Sometimes, in order to tire myself out, though I am fatigued enough already, I go for a walk in the forest of Roumare. I used to think at first that the fresh light and soft air, impregnated with the odor of herbs and leaves, would instill new life into my veins and impart fresh energy to my heart. One day I turned into a broad ride in the wood, and then I diverged toward La Bouille, through a narrow path, between two rows of exceedingly tall trees, which placed a thick, green, almost black roof between the sky and me.

A sudden shiver ran through me, not a cold shiver, but a shiver of agony, and so I hastened my steps, uneasy at being alone in the wood, frightened stupidly and without reason, at the profound solitude. Suddenly it seemed as if I were being followed, that somebody was walking at my heels, close, quite close to me, near enough to touch me.

I turned round suddenly, but I was alone. I saw nothing behind me except the straight, broad ride, empty and bordered by high trees, horribly empty; on the other side also it extended until it was lost in the distance, and looked just the same—terrible.

I closed my eyes. Why? And then I began to turn round on one heel very quickly, just like a top. I nearly fell down, and opened my eyes; the trees were dancing round me and the earth heaved; I was obliged to sit down. Then, ah! I no longer remembered how I had come! What a strange idea! What a strange, strange idea!

I did not the least know. I started off to the right, and got back into the avenue which had led me into the middle of the forest.

June 3. I have had a terrible night. I shall go away for a few weeks, for no doubt a journey will set me up again.

July 2. I have come back, quite cured, and have had a most delightful trip into the bargain. I have been to Mont Saint-Michel, which I had not seen before.

What a sight, when one arrives as I did, at Avranches toward the end of the day! The town stands on a hill, and I was taken into the public garden at the extremity of the town. I uttered a cry of astonishment. An extraordinarily large bay lay extended before me, as far as my eyes could reach, between two hills which were lost to sight in the mist; and in the middle of this immense yellow bay, under a clear, golden sky, a peculiar hill rose up, somber and pointed in the midst of the sand. The sun had just disappeared, and under the still flaming sky stood out the outline of that fantastic rock, which bears on its summit a picturesque monument.

At daybreak I went to it. The tide was low, as it had been the night before, and I saw that wonderful abbey rise up before me as I approached it. After several hours' walking, I reached the enormous mass of rock which supports the little town, dominated by the great church. Having climbed the steep and narrow street, I entered the most wonderful Gothic building that has ever been erected to God on earth, large as a town, and full of low rooms which seem buried beneath vaulted roofs, and of lofty galleries supported by delicate columns.

I entered this gigantic granite jewel, which is as light in its effect as a bit of lace and is covered with towers, with slender belfries to which spiral staircases ascend.

The flying buttresses raise strange heads that bristle with chimeras, with devils, with fantastic animals, with monstrous flowers, are joined together by finely carved arches, to the blue sky by day, and to the black sky by night.

When I had reached the summit, I said to the monk who accompanied me: "Father, how happy you must be here!" And he replied: "It is very windy, Monsieur"; and so we began to talk while watching the rising tide, which ran over the sand and covered it with a steel cuirass.

And then the monk told me stories, all the old stories belonging to the place—legends, nothing but legends.

One of them struck me forcibly. The country people, those belonging to the Mornet, declare that at night one can hear talking going on in the sand, and also that two goats bleat, one with a strong, the other with a weak voice. Incredulous people declare that it is nothing but the screaming of the sea birds, which occasionally resembles bleatings, and occasionally human lamentations; but belated fishermen swear that they have met an old shepherd, whose cloak-covered head they can never see, wandering on the sand, between two tides, round the little town placed so far out of the world. They declare he is guiding and walking before a he-goat with a man's face and a she-goat with a woman's face, both with white hair, who talk incessantly, quarreling in a strange language, and then suddenly cease talking in order to bleat with all their might.

"Do you believe it?" I asked the monk. "I scarcely know," he replied; and I continued: "If there are other beings besides ourselves on this earth, how comes it that we have not known it for so long a time, or why have you not seen them? How is it that I have not seen them?"

He replied: "Do we see the hundred-thousandth part of what exists? Look here; there is the wind, which is the strongest force in nature. It knocks down men, and blows down buildings, uproots trees, raises the sea into mountains of water, destroys cliffs and casts great ships onto the breakers; it kills, it whistles, it sighs, it roars. But have you ever seen it, and can you see it? Yet it exists for all that."

I was silent before this simple reasoning. That man was a philosopher, or perhaps a fool; I could not say which exactly, so I held my tongue. What he had said had often been in my own thoughts.

July 3. I have slept badly; certainly there is some feverish influence here, for my coachman is suffering in the same way as I am. When I went back home yesterday, I noticed his singular paleness, and I asked him: "What it the matter with you, Jean?"

"The matter is that I never get any rest, and my nights devour my days. Since your departure, Monsieur, there has been a spell over me."

However, the other servants are all well, but I am very frightened of having another attack, myself.

July 4. I am decidedly taken again; for my old nightmares have returned. Last night I felt somebody leaning on me who was sucking my life from between my lips with his mouth. Yes, he was sucking it out of my neck as a leech would have done. Then he got up, satiated, and I woke up, so beaten, crushed, and annihilated that I could not move. If this continues for a few days, I shall certainly go away again.

July 5. Have I lost my reason? What has happened? What I saw last night is so strange that my head wanders when I think of it!

As I do now every evening, I had locked my door; then, being thirsty, I drank half a glass of water, and I accidentally noticed that the water-bottle was full up to the cut-glass stopper.

Then I went to bed and fell into one of my terrible sleeps, from which I was aroused in about two hours by a still more terrible shock.

Picture to yourself a sleeping man who is being murdered, who wakes up with a knife in his chest, a gurgling in his throat, is covered with blood, can no longer breathe, is going to die and does not understand anything at all about it—there you have it.

Having recovered my senses, I was thirsty again, so I lighted a candle and went to the table on which my water-bottle was. I lifted it up and tilted it over my glass, but nothing came out. It was empty! It was completely empty! At first I could not understand it at all; then suddenly I was seized by such a terrible feeling that I had to sit down, or rather fall into a chair! Then I sprang up with a bound to look about me; then I sat down again, overcome by astonishment and fear, in front of the transparent crystal bottle! I looked at it with fixed eyes, trying to solve the puzzle, and my hands trembled! Somebody had drunk the water, but who? I? I without any doubt. It could surely only be I? In that case I was a somnambulist—was living, without knowing it, that double, mysterious life which makes us doubt whether there are not two beings in us—whether a strange, unknowable, and invisible being does not, during our moments of mental and physical torpor, animate the inert body, forcing it to a more willing obedience than it yields to ourselves.

Oh! Who will understand my horrible agony? Who will understand the emotion of a man sound in mind, wide-awake, full of sense, who looks in horror at the disappearance of a little water while he was asleep, through the glass of a water-bottle! And I remained sitting until it was daylight, without venturing to go to bed again.

July 6. I am going mad. Again all the contents of my water-bottle have been drunk during the night; or rather I have drunk it!

But is it I? Is it I? Who could it be? Who? Oh! God! Am I going mad? Who will save me?

July 10. I have just been through some surprising ordeals. Undoubtedly I must be mad! And yet!

On July 6, before going to bed, I put some wine, milk, water, bread, and strawberries on my table. Somebody drank—I drank—all the water and a little of the milk, but neither the wine, nor the bread, nor the strawberries were touched.

On the seventh of July I renewed the same experiment, with the same results, and on July 8 I left out the water and the milk and nothing was touched.

Lastly, on July 9 I put only water and milk on my table, taking care to wrap up the bottles in white muslin and to tie down the stoppers. Then I rubbed my lips, my beard, and my hands with pencil lead, and went to bed.

Deep slumber seized me, soon followed by a terrible awakening. I had not moved, and my sheets were not marked. I rushed to the table. The muslin round the bottles remained intact; I undid the string, trembling with fear. All the water had been drunk, and so had the milk! Ah! Great God! I must start for Paris immediately.

July 12. Paris. I must have lost my head during the last few days! I must be the plaything of my enervated imagination, unless I am really a somnambulist, or I have been brought under the power of one of those influences—hypnotic suggestion, for example—which are known to exist, but have hitherto been inexplicable. In any case, my mental state bordered on madness, and twenty-four hours of Paris sufficed to restore me to my equilibrium.

Yesterday after doing some business and paying some visits, which instilled fresh and invigorating mental air into me, I wound up my evening at the Théâtre Français. A drama by Alexander Dumas the Younger was being acted, and his brilliant and powerful play completed my cure. Certainly solitude is dangerous for active minds. We need men around us who can think and can talk. When we are alone for a long time, we people space with phantoms.

I returned along the boulevards to my hotel in excellent spirits. Amid the jostling of the crowd I thought, not without irony, of my terrors and surmises of the previous week, because I believed, yes, I believed, that an invisible being lived beneath my roof. How weak our mind is; how quickly it is terrified and unbalanced as soon as we are confronted with a small, incomprehensible fact. Instead of dismissing the problem with: "We do not understand because we cannot find the cause," we immediately imagine terrible mysteries and supernatural powers.

July 14. Fête of the Republic. I walked through the streets, and the crackers and flags amused me like a child. Still, it is very foolish to make merry on a set date, by Government decree. People are like a flock of sheep, now steadily patient, now in ferocious revolt. Say to it: "Amuse yourself," and it amuses itself. Say to it: "Go and fight with your neighbor," and it goes and fights. Say to it: "Vote for the Emperor," and it votes for the Emperor; then say to it: "Vote for the Republic," and it votes for the Republic.

Those who direct it are stupid, too; but instead of obeying men they obey principles, a course which can only be foolish, ineffective, and false, for the very reason that principles are ideas which are considered as certain and unchangeable, whereas in this world one is certain of nothing, since light is an illusion and noise is deception.

July 16. I saw some things yesterday that troubled me very much.

I was dining at my cousin's, Madame Sablé, whose husband is colonel of the Seventy-sixth Chasseurs at Limoges. There were two young women there, one of whom had married a medical man, Dr. Parent, who devotes himself a great deal to nervous diseases and to the extraordinary manifestations which just now experiments in hypnotism and suggestion are producing.

He related to us at some length the enormous results obtained by English scientists and the doctors of the medical school at Nancy, and the facts which he adduced appeared to me so strange that I declared that I was altogether incredulous.

"We are," he declared, "on the point of discovering one of the most important secrets of nature, I mean to say, one of its most important secrets on this earth, for assuredly there are some up in the stars, yonder, of a different kind of importance. Ever since man has thought, since he has been able to express and write down his thoughts, he has felt himself close to a mystery which is impenetrable to his coarse and imperfect senses, and he endeavors to supplement the feeble penetration of his organs by the efforts of his intellect. As long as that intellect remained in its elementary stage, this intercourse with invisible spirits assumed forms which were commonplace though terrifying. Thence sprang the popular belief in the supernatural, the legends of wandering spirits, of fairies, of gnomes, of ghosts, I might even say the conception of God, for our ideas of the Workman-Creator, from whatever religion they may have come down to us, are certainly the most mediocre, the stupidest, and the most unacceptable inventions that ever sprang from the frightened brain of any human creature. Nothing is truer than what Voltaire says: 'If God made man in His own image, man has certainly paid Him back again.'

"But for rather more than a century, men seem to have had a presentiment of something new. Mesmer and some others have put us on an unexpected track, and within the last two or three years especially, we have arrived at results really surprising."

My cousin, who is also very incredulous, smiled, and Dr. Parent said to her: "Would you like me to try and send you to sleep, Madame?"

"Yes, certainly."

She sat down in an easy-chair, and he began to look at her fixedly, as if to fascinate her. I suddenly felt myself somewhat discomposed; my heart beat rapidly and I had a choking feeling in my throat. I saw that Madame Sablé's eyes were growing heavy, her mouth twitched, and her bosom heaved, and at the end of ten minutes she was asleep.

"Go behind her," the doctor said to me; so I took a seat behind her. He put a visiting-card into her hands, and said to her: "This is a looking-glass; what do you see in it?"

She replied: "I see my cousin."

"What is he doing?"

"He is twisting his mustache."

"And now?"

"He is taking a photograph out of his pocket."

"Whose photograph is it?"

"His own."

That was true, for the photograph had been given me that same evening at the hotel.

"What is his attitude in this portrait?"

"He is standing up with his hat in his hand."

She saw these things in that card, in that piece of white pasteboard, as if she had seen them in a looking-glass.

The young women were frightened, and exclaimed: "That is quite enough! Quite, quite enough!"

But the doctor said to her authoritatively: "You will get up at eight o'clock tomorrow morning; then you will go and call on your cousin at his hotel and ask him to lend you the five thousand francs which your husband asks of you, and which he will ask for when he sets out on his coming journey."

Then he woke her up.

On returning to my hotel, I thought over this curious *séance* and I was assailed by doubts, not as to my cousin's absolute and undoubted good faith, for I had known her as well as if she had been my own sister ever since she was a child, but as to a possible trick on the doctor's part. Had not he, perhaps, kept a glass hidden in his hand, which he showed to the young woman in her sleep at the same time as he did the card? Professional conjurers do things which are just as singular.

However, I went to bed, and this morning, at about half past eight, I was awakened by my footman, who said to me: "Madame Sablé has asked to see you immediately, Monsieur." I dressed hastily and went to her.

She sat down in some agitation, with her eyes on the floor, and without raising her veil said to me: "My dear cousin, I am going to ask a great favor of you."

"What is it, cousin?"

"I do not like to tell you, and yet I must. I am in absolute want of five thousand francs."

"What, you?"

"Yes, I, or rather my husband, who has asked me to procure them for him."

I was so stupefied that I hesitated to answer. I asked myself whether she had not really been making fun of me with Dr. Parent, if it were not merely a very well-acted farce which had been got up beforehand. On looking at her attentively, however, my doubts disappeared. She was trembling with grief, so painful was this step to her, and I was sure that her throat was full of sobs.

I knew that she was very rich and so I continued: "What! Has not your husband five thousand francs at his disposal? Come, think. Are you sure that he commissioned you to ask me for them? Are you absolutely sure?"

She hesitated for a few seconds, as if she were making a great effort to search her memory, and then she replied: "Yes—yes, I am quite sure of it."

"He has written to you?"

She hesitated again and reflected, and I guessed the torture of her thoughts. She did not know. She only knew that she was to borrow five thousand francs of me for her husband. So she told a lie.

"Yes, he has written to me."

"When, pray? You did not mention it to me yesterday."

"I received his letter this morning."

"Can you show it to me?"

"No; no—no—it contained private matters, things too personal to ourselves. I burned it."

"So your husband runs into debt?"

She hesitated again, and then murmured: "I do not know."

Thereupon I said bluntly: "I have not five thousand francs at my disposal at this moment, my dear cousin."

She uttered a cry, as if she were in pain and said: "Oh! oh! I beseech you, I beseech you to get them for me."

She got excited and clasped her hands as if she were praying to me! I heard her voice change its tone; she wept and sobbed, harassed and dominated by the irresistible order that she had received.

"Oh! oh! I beg you to—if you knew what I am suffering—I want them today."

I had pity on her: "You shall have them by and by, I swear to you."

"Oh! thank you! thank you! How kind you are."

I continued: "Do you remember what took place at your house last night?"

"Yes."

"Do you remember that Dr. Parent sent you to sleep?"

"Yes."

"Oh! Very well then; he ordered you to come to me this morning to borrow five thousand francs, and at this moment you are obeying that suggestion."

She considered for a few moments, and then replied: "But as it is my husband who wants them—"

For a whole hour I tried to convince her, but could not succeed, and when she had gone I went to the doctor. He was just going out, and he listened to me with a smile, and said: "Do you believe now?"

"Yes, I cannot help it."

"Let us go to your cousin's."

She was already resting on a couch, overcome with fatigue. The doctor felt her pulse, looked at her for some tıme with one hand raised toward her eyes, which she closed by degrees under the irresistible power of this magnetic influence. When she was asleep, he said:

"Your husband does not require the five thousand francs any longer! You must, therefore, forget that you asked your cousin to lend them to you, and, if he speaks to you about it, you will not understand him."

Then he woke her up, and I took out a pocketbook and said: "Here is what you asked me for this morning, my dear cousin." But she was so surprised, that I did not venture to persist; nevertheless, I tried to recall the cir, cumstance to her, but she denied it vigorously, thought that I was making fun of her, and in the end, very nearly lost her temper.

There! I have just come back, and I have not been able to eat any lunch, for this experiment has altogether upset me.

July 19. Many people to whom I have told the adventure have laughed at me. I no longer know what to think. The wise man says: Perhaps?

July 21. I dined at Bougival, and then I spent the evening at a boatmen's ball. Decidedly everything depends on place and surroundings. It would be the height of folly to believe in the supernatural on the *Ile de la Grenouillière*.* But on the top of Mont Saint-Michel or in India, we are terribly under the influence of our surroundings. I shall return home next week.

July 30. I came back to my own house yesterday. Everything is going on well.

August 2. Nothing fresh; it is splendid weather, and I spend my days in watching the Seine flow past.

August 4. Quarrels among my servants. They declare

* Frog-island.

that the glasses are broken in the cupboards at night. The footman accuses the cook, she accuses the needle-woman, and the latter accuses the other two. Who is the culprit? It would take a clever person to tell.

August 6. This time, I am not mad. I have seen—I have seen—I have seen!—I can doubt no longer—*I have seen it!*

I was walking at two o'clock among my rose-trees, in the full sunlight—in the walk bordered by autumn roses which are beginning to fall. As I stopped to look at a Géant de Bataille, which had three splendid blooms, I distinctly saw the stalk of one of the roses bend close to me, as if an invisible hand had bent it, and then break, as if that hand had picked it! Then the flower raised it-self, following the curve which a hand would have de-scribed in carrying it toward a mouth, and remained sus-pended in the transparent air, alone and motionless, a terrible red spot, three yards from my eyes. In despera-tion I rushed at it to take it! I found nothing; it had dis-appeared. Then I was seized with furious rage against myself, for it is not wholesome for a reasonable and seri-ous man to have such hallucinations.

But was it a hallucination? I turned to look for the stalk, and I found it immediately under the bush, freshly broken, between the two other roses which remained on the branch. I returned home, then, with a much dis-turbed mind; for I am certain now, certain as I am of the alternation of day and night, that there exists close to me an invisible being who lives on milk and on water, who can touch objects, take them and change their places; who is, consequently, endowed with a material nature, al-though imperceptible to sense, and who lives as I do, un-der my roof—

August 7. I slept tranquilly. He drank the water out of my decanter, but did not disturb my sleep.

I ask myself whether I am mad. As I was walking just now in the sun by the riverside, doubts as to my own sanity arose in me; not vague doubts such as I have had hitherto, but precise and absolute doubts. I have seen mad people, and I have known some who were quite intelligent, lucid, even clear-sighted in every concern of life, except on one point. They could speak clearly, readily, profoundly on everything; till their thoughts were caught in the breakers of their delusions and went to pieces there, were dispersed and swamped in that furious and terrible sea of fogs and squalls which is called *madness.*

I certainly should think that I was mad, absolutely mad, if I were not conscious that I knew my state, if I could not fathom it and analyze it with the most complete lucidity. I should, in fact, be a reasonable man laboring under a hallucination. Some unknown disturbance must have been excited in my brain, one of those disturbances which physiologists of the present day try to note and to fix precisely, and that disturbance must have caused a profound gulf in my mind and in the order and logic of my ideas. Similar phenomena occur in dreams, and lead us through the most unlikely phantasmagoria, without causing us any surprise, because our verifying apparatus and our sense of control have gone to sleep, while our imaginative faculty wakes and works. Was it not possible that one of the imperceptible keys of the cerebral finger-board had been paralyzed in me? Some men lose the recollection of proper names, or of verbs, or of numbers, or merely of dates, in consequence of an accident. The localization of all the avenues of thought has been accomplished nowadays; what, then, would there be surprising in the fact that my faculty of controlling the unreality of certain hallucinations should be destroyed for the time being?

I thought of all this as I walked by the side of the water. The sun was shining brightly on the river and made earth delightful, while it filled me with love for life, for the swallows, whose swift agility is always delightful in my eyes, for the plants by the riverside, whose rustling is a pleasure to my ears.

By degrees, however, an inexplicable feeling of discomfort seized me. It seemed to me as if some unknown force were numbing and stopping me, were preventing me from going further and were calling me back. I felt that painful wish to return which comes on you when you have left a beloved invalid at home, and are seized by a presentiment that he is worse.

I, therefore, returned despite myself, feeling certain that I should find some bad news awaiting me, a letter or a telegram. There was nothing, however, and I was surprised and uneasy, more so than if I had had another fantastic vision.

August 8. I spent a terrible evening, yesterday. He does not show himself any more, but I feel that He is near me, watching me, looking at me, penetrating me, dominating me, and more terrible to me when He hides himself thus than if He were to manifest his constant and invisible presence by supernatural phenomena. However, I slept.

August 9. Nothing, but I am afraid.

August 10. Nothing; but what will happen tomorrow?

August 11. Still nothing. I cannot stop at home with

this fear hanging over me and these thoughts in my mind; I shall go away.

August 12. Ten o'clock at night. All day long I have been trying to get away, and have not been able. I contemplated a simple and easy act of liberty, a carriage ride to Rouen—and I have not been able to do it. What is the reason?

August 13. When one is attacked by certain maladies, the springs of our physical being seem broken, our energies destroyed, our muscles relaxed, our bones to be as soft as our flesh, and our blood as liquid as water. I am experiencing the same in my moral being, in a strange and distressing manner. I have no longer any strength, any courage, any self-control, nor even any power to set my own will in motion. I have no power left to *will* anything, but some one does it for me and I obey.

August 14. I am lost! Somebody possesses my soul and governs it! Somebody orders all my acts, all my movements, all my thoughts. I am no longer master of myself, nothing except an enslaved and terrified spectator of the things which I do. I wish to go out; I cannot. *He* does not wish to; and so I remain, trembling and distracted in the armchair in which he keeps me sitting. I merely wish to get up and to rouse myself, so as to think that I am still master of myself: I cannot! I am riveted to my chair, and my chair adheres to the floor in such a manner that no force of mine can move us.

Then suddenly, I must, I *must* go to the foot of my garden to pick some strawberries and eat them—and I go there. I pick the strawberries and I eat them! Oh! my God! my God! Is there a God? If there be one, deliver me! save me! succor me! Pardon! Pity! Mercy! Save me! Oh! what sufferings! what torture! what horror!

The Horla

August 15. Certainly this is the way in which my poor cousin was possessed and swayed, when she came to borrow five thousand francs of me. She was under the power of a strange will which had entered into her, like another soul, a parasitic and ruling soul. Is the world coming to an end?

But who is He, this invisible being that rules me, this unknowable being, this rover of a supernatural race?

Invisible beings exist, then! How is it, then, that since the beginning of the world they have never manifested themselves in such a manner as they do to me? I have never read anything that resembles what goes on in my house. Oh! If I could only leave it, if I could only go away and flee, and never return, I should be saved; but I cannot.

August 16. I managed to escape today for two hours, like a prisoner who finds the door of his dungeon accidentally open. I suddenly felt that I was free and that He was far away, and so I gave orders to put the horses in as quickly as possible, and I drove to Rouen. Oh! how delightful to be able to say to my coachman: "Go to Rouen!"

I made him pull up before the library, and I begged them to lend me Dr. Herrmann Herestauss's treatise on the unknown inhabitants of the ancient and modern world.

Then, as I was getting into my carriage, I intended to say: "To the railway station!" but instead of this I shouted—I did not speak, but I shouted—in such a loud voice that all the passers-by turned round: "Home!" and I fell back onto the cushion of my carriage, overcome by mental agony. He had found me out and regained possession of me.

August 17. Oh! What a night! what a night! And yet

62

it seems to me that I ought to rejoice. I read until one o'clock in the morning! Herestauss, Doctor of Philosophy and Theogony, wrote the history and the manifestation of all those invisible beings which hover around man, or of whom he dreams. He describes their origin, their domains, their power; but none of them resembles the one which haunts me. One might say that man, ever since he has thought, has had a foreboding and a fear of a new being, stronger than himself, his successor in this world, and that, feeling him near, and not being able to foretell the nature of the unseen one, he has, in his terror, created the whole race of hidden beings, vague phantoms born of fear.

Having, therefore, read until one o'clock in the morning, I went and sat down at the open window, in order to cool my forehead and my thoughts in the calm night air. It was very pleasant and warm! How I should have enjoyed such a night formerly!

There was no moon, but the stars darted out their rays in the dark heavens. Who inhabits those worlds? What forms, what living beings, what animals are there yonder? Do those who are thinkers in those distant worlds know more than we do? What can they do more than we? What do they see which we do not? Will not one of them, some day or other, traversing space, appear on our earth to conquer it, just as formerly the Norsemen crossed the sea in order to subjugate nations feebler than themselves?

We are so weak, so powerless, so ignorant, so small— we who live on this particle of mud which revolves in liquid air.

I fell asleep, dreaming thus in the cool night air, and then, having slept for about three quarters of an hour, I opened my eyes without moving, awakened by an indescribably confused and strange sensation. At first I

saw nothing, and then suddenly it appeared to me as if
a page of the book, which had remained open on my
table, turned over of its own accord. Not a breath of air
had come in at my window, and I was surprised and
waited. In about four minutes, I saw, I saw—yes I saw
with my own eyes—another page lift itself up and fall
down on the others, as if a finger had turned it over. My
armchair was empty, appeared empty, but I knew that
He was there, He, and sitting in my place, and that He
was reading. With a furious bound, the bound of an enraged wild beast that wishes to disembowel its tamer, I
crossed my room to seize Him, to strangle Him, to kill
Him! But before I could reach it, my chair fell over as if
somebody had run away from me. My table rocked, my
lamp fell and went out, and my window closed as if some
thief had been surprised and had fled out into the night,
shutting it behind him.

So He had run away; He had been afraid; He, afraid
of me!

So tomorrow, or later—some day or other, I should
be able to hold him in my clutches and crush him against
the ground! Do not dogs occasionally bite and strangle
their masters?

August 18. I have been thinking the whole day long.
Oh! yes, I will obey Him, follow His impulses, fulfill all
His wishes, show myself humble, submissive, a coward.
He is the stronger; but an hour will come.

August 19. I know, I know, I know all! I have just
read the following in the *Revue du Monde Scientif-
ique*: "A curious piece of news comes to us from Rio
de Janeiro. Madness, an epidemic of madness, which may
be compared to that contagious madness which attacked
the people of Europe in the Middle Ages, is at this moment raging in the Province of San-Paulo. The frightened

inhabitants are leaving their houses, deserting their villages, abandoning their land, saying that they are pursued, possessed, governed like human cattle by invisible, though tangible beings, by a species of vampire, which feeds on their life while they are asleep, and which, besides, drinks water and milk without appearing to touch any other nourishment.

"Professor Don Pedro Henriques, accompanied by several medical savants, has gone to the Province of San-Paulo, in order to study the origin and the manifestations of this surprising madness on the spot, and to propose such measures to the Emperor as may appear to him to be most fitted to restore the mad population to reason."

Ah! Ah! I remember now that fine Brazilian three-master which passed in front of my windows as it was going up the Seine, on the eighth of last May! I thought it looked so pretty, so white and bright! That Being was on board of her, coming from there, where its race sprang from. And it saw me! It saw my house, which was also white, and He sprang from the ship on to the land. Oh! Good heavens!

Now I know, I can divine. The reign of man is over, and He has come. He whom disquieted priests exorcised, whom sorcerers evoked on dark nights, without seeing him appear, He to whom the imaginations of the transient masters of the world lent all the monstrous or graceful forms of gnomes, spirits, genii, fairies, and familiar spirits. After the coarse conceptions of primitive fear, men more enlightened gave him a truer form. Mesmer divined him, and ten years ago physicians accurately discovered the nature of his power, even before He exercised it himself. They played with that weapon of their new Lord, the sway of a mysterious will over the human soul, which had become enslaved. They called it mesmerism, hypnotism, suggestion, I know not what. I have seen them diverting themselves like rash children with this horrible power! Woe to us! Woe to man! He has come, the—the—what does He call Himself—the—I fancy that He is shouting out His name to me and I do not hear Him—the—yes—He is shouting it out—I am listening—I cannot—repeat—it—Horla—I have heard—the Horla —it is He—the Horla—He has come!—

Ah! the vulture has eaten the pigeon, the wolf has eaten the lamb; the lion has devoured the sharp-horned buffalo; man has killed the lion with an arrow, with a spear, with gunpowder; but the Horla will make of man what man has made of the horse and of the ox: His chattel, His slave, and His food, by the mere power of His will. Woe to us!

But, nevertheless, sometimes the animal rebels and kills the man who has subjugated it. I should also like—I shall be able to—but I must know Him, touch Him, see Him! Learned men say that eyes of animals, as they differ from ours, do not distinguish as ours do. And my eye cannot distinguish this newcomer who is oppressing me.

Why? Oh! Now I remember the words of the monk at Mont Saint-Michel: "Can we see the hundred-thousandth part of what exists? Listen; there is the wind which is the strongest force in nature; it knocks men down, blows down buildings, uproots trees, raises the sea into mountains of water, destroys cliffs, and casts great ships onto the breakers; it kills, it whistles, it sighs, it roars—have you ever seen it, and can you see it? It exists for all that, however!"

And I went on thinking: my eyes are so weak, so imperfect, that they do not even distinguish hard bodies, if they are as transparent as glass! If a glass without quicksilver behind it were to bar my way, I should run into it, just like a bird which has flown into a room breaks its head against the windowpanes. A thousand things, moreover, deceive a man and lead him astray. How then is it surprising that he cannot perceive a new body which is penetrated and pervaded by the light?

A new being! Why not? It was assuredly bound to come! Why should we be the last? We do not distinguish it, like all the others created before us? The reason is, that its nature is more delicate, its body finer and more finished than ours. Our make-up is so weak, so awkwardly conceived; our body is encumbered with organs that are always tired, always being strained like locks that are too complicated; it lives like a plant and like an animal nourishing itself with difficulty on air, herbs, and flesh; it is a brute machine which is a prey to maladies, to malformations, to decay; it is broken-winded, badly regulated, simple and eccentric, ingeniously yet badly made, a coarse and yet a delicate mechanism, in brief, the outline of a being which might become intelligent and great.

There are only a few—so few—stages of development in this world, from the oyster up to man. Why should there not be one more, when once that period is accomplished which separates the successive products one from the other?

Why not one more? Why not, also, other trees with immense, splendid flowers, perfuming whole regions? Why not other elements besides fire, air, earth, and water? There are four, only four, nursing fathers of various beings! What a pity! Why should not there be forty, four hundred, four thousand! How poor everything is, how mean and wretched—grudgingly given, poorly invented, clumsily made! Ah! the elephant and the hippopotamus, what power! And the camel, what suppleness!

But the butterfly, you will say, a flying flower! I

dream of one that should be as large as a hundred worlds, with wings whose shape, beauty, colors, and motion I cannot even express. But I see it—it flutters from star to star, refreshing them and perfuming them with the light and harmonious breath of its flight! And the people up there gaze at it as it passes in an ecstasy of delight!

What is the matter with me? It is He, the Horla who haunts me, and who makes me think of these foolish things! He is within me, He is becoming my soul; I shall kill Him!

August 20. I shall kill Him. I have seen Him! Yesterday I sat down at my table and pretended to write very assiduously. I knew quite well that He would come prowling round me, quite close to me, so close that I might perhaps be able to touch Him, to seize Him. And then— then I should have the strength of desperation; I should have my hands, my knees, my chest, my forehead, my teeth to strangle Him, to crush Him, to bite Him, to tear Him to pieces. And I watched for Him with all my overexcited nerves.

I had lighted my two lamps and the eight wax candles on my mantelpiece, as if, by this light I should discover Him.

My bed, my old oak bed with its columns, was opposite to me; on my right was the fireplace; on my left the door, which was carefully closed, after I had left it open for some time, in order to attract Him; behind me was a very high wardrobe with a looking-glass in it, which served me to dress by every day, and in which I was in the habit of inspecting myself from head to foot every time I passed it.

So I pretended to be writing in order to deceive Him, for He also was watching me, and suddenly I felt,

The Horla

I was certain, that He was reading over my shoulder, that He was there, almost touching my ear.

I got up so quickly, with my hands extended, that I almost fell. Horror! It was as bright as at midday, but I did not see myself in the glass! It was empty, clear, profound, full of light! But my figure was not reflected in it —and I, I was opposite to it! I saw the large, clear glass from top to bottom, and I looked at it with unsteady eyes. I did not dare advance; I did not venture to make a movement; feeling certain, nevertheless, that He was there, but that He would escape me again, He whose imperceptible body had absorbed my reflection.

How frightened I was! And then suddenly I began to see myself through a mist in the depths of the looking-glass, in a mist as it were, or through a veil of water; and it seemed to me as if this water were flowing slowly from left to right, and making my figure clearer every moment. It was like the end of an eclipse. Whatever hid me did not appear to possess any clearly defined outlines, but was a sort of opaque transparency, which gradually grew clearer.

At last I was able to distinguish myself completely, as I do every day when I look at myself.

I had seen Him! And the horror of it remained with me, and makes me shudder even now.

August 21. How could I kill Him, since I could not get hold of Him? Poison? But He would see me mix it with the water; and then, would our poisons have any effect on His impalpable body? No—no—no doubt about the matter. Then?—then?

August 22. I sent for a blacksmith from Rouen and ordered iron shutters of him for my room, such as some private hotels in Paris have on the ground floor, for fear of thieves, and he is going to make me a similar door as

69

well. I have made myself out a coward, but I do not care about that!

September 10. Rouen, Hotel Continental. It is done; it is done—but is He dead? My mind is thoroughly upset by what I have seen.

Well then, yesterday, the locksmith having put on the iron shutters and door, I left everything open until midnight, although it was getting cold.

Suddenly I felt that He was there, and joy, mad joy took possession of me. I got up softly, and I walked to the right and left for some time, so that He might not guess anything; then I took off my boots and put on my slippers carelessly; then I fastened the iron shutters and going back to the door quickly I double-locked it with a padlock, putting the key into my pocket.

Suddenly I noticed that He was moving restlessly round me, that in His turn He was frightened and was ordering me to let Him out. I nearly yielded, though I did not quite, but putting my back to the door, I half opened it, just enough to allow me to go out backward, and as I am very tall, my head touched the lintel. I was sure that He had not been able to escape, and I shut Him up quite alone, quite alone. What happiness! I had Him fast. Then I ran downstairs into the drawing-room which was under my bedroom. I took the two lamps and poured all the oil onto the carpet, the furniture, everywhere; then I set fire to it and made my escape, after having carefully double-locked the door.

I went and hid myself at the bottom of the garden, in a clump of laurel bushes. How long it was! how long it was! Everything was dark, silent, motionless, not a breath of air and not a star, but heavy banks of clouds which one could not see, but which weighed, oh! so heavily on my soul.

I looked at my house and waited. How long it was! I already began to think that the fire had gone out of its own accord, or that He had extinguished it, when one of the lower windows gave way under the violence of the flames, and a long, soft, caressing sheet of red flame mounted up the white wall, and kissed it as high as the roof. The light fell on to the trees, the branches, and the leaves, and a shiver of fear pervaded them also! The birds awoke; a dog began to howl, and it seemed to me as if the day were breaking! Almost immediately two other windows flew into fragments, and I saw that the whole of the lower part of my house was nothing but a terrible furnace. But a cry, a horrible, shrill, heart-rending cry, a woman's cry, sounded through the night, and two garret windows were opened! I had forgotten the servants! I saw the terror-struck faces, and the frantic waving of their arms!

Then, overwhelmed with horror, I ran off to the village, shouting: "Help! help! fire! fire!" Meeting some people who were already coming on to the scene, I went back with them to see!

By this time the house was nothing but a horrible and magnificent funeral pile, a monstrous pyre which lit up the whole country, a pyre where men were burning, and where He was burning also, He, He, my prisoner, that new Being, the new Master, the Horla!

Suddenly the whole roof fell in between the walls, and a volcano of flames darted up to the sky. Through all the windows which opened on to that furnace, I saw the flames darting, and I reflected that He was there, in that kiln, dead.

Dead? Perhaps? His body? Was not his body, which was transparent, indestructible by such means as would kill ours?

If He were not dead? Perhaps time alone has power over that Invisible and Redoubtable Being. Why this transparent, unrecognizable body, this body belonging to a spirit, if it also had to fear ills, infirmities, and premature destruction?

Premature destruction? All human terror springs from that! After man the Horla. After him who can die every day, at any hour, at any moment, by any accident, He came, He who was only to die at his own proper hour and minute, because He had touched the limits of his existence!

No—no—there is no doubt about it—He is not dead. Then—then—I suppose I must kill *myself!*

Madame Tellier's Excursion

MEN went there every evening at about eleven o'clock, just as they went to the *café*. Six or eight of them used to meet there; always the same set, not fast men, but respectable tradesmen, and young men in government or some other employ; and they used to drink their Chartreuse, and tease the girls, or else they would talk seriously with Madame, whom everybody respected, and then would go home at twelve o'clock! The younger men would sometimes stay the night.

It was a small, comfortable house, at the corner of a street behind Saint Etienne's church. From the windows one could see the docks, full of ships which were being unloaded, and on the hill the old, gray chapel, dedicated to the Virgin.

Madame, who came of a respectable family of peasant proprietors in the department of the Eure, had taken up her profession, just as she would have become a milliner or dressmaker. The prejudice against prostitution, which is so violent and deeply rooted in large towns, does not exist in the country places in Normandy. The peasant simply says: "It is a paying business," and sends his daughter to keep a harem of fast girls, just as he would send her to keep a girls' school.

She had inherited the house from an old uncle, to whom it had belonged. Monsieur and Madame, who had formerly been innkeepers near Yvetot, had immediately sold their house, as they thought that the business at Fécamp was more profitable. They arrived one fine morning to assume the direction of the enterprise, which was declining on account of the absence of a head. They were good people enough in their way, and soon made themselves liked by their staff and their neighbors.

Monsieur died of apoplexy two years later, for as his new profession kept him in idleness and without exercise, he had grown excessively stout, and his health had suffered. Since Madame had been a widow, all the frequenters of the establishment had wanted her; but people said that personally she was quite virtuous, and even the girls in the house could not discover anything against her. She was tall, stout, and affable, and her complexion, which had become pale in the dimness of her house, the shutters of which were scarcely ever opened, shone as if it had been varnished. She had a fringe of curly, false hair, which gave her a juvenile look, which in turn contrasted strongly with her matronly figure. She was always smiling and cheerful, and was fond of a joke, but there was a shade of reserve about her which her new occupation had not quite made her lose. Coarse words always shocked her, and when any young fellow who had been badly brought up called her establishment by its right name, she was angry and disgusted.

In a word, she had a refined mind, and although she treated her women as friends, yet she very frequently used to say that she and they were not made of the same stuff.

Sometimes during the week she would hire a carriage and take some of her girls into the country, where they used to enjoy themselves on the grass by the side of the little river. They behaved like a lot of girls let out from a school, and used to run races, and play childish games. They would have a cold dinner on the grass, and drink cider, and go home at night with a delicious feeling of fatigue, and in the carriage kiss Madame as a kind mother who was full of goodness and complaisance.

The house had two entrances. At the corner there was a sort of low *café*, which sailors and the lower orders frequented at night, and she had two girls whose special duty it was to attend to that part of the business. With the assistance of the waiter, whose name was Frederic, and who was a short, light-haired, beardless fellow, as strong as a horse, they set the half bottles of wine and the jugs of beer on the shaky marble tables and then, sitting astride on the customers' knees, would urge them to drink.

The three other girls (there were only five in all), formed a kind of aristocracy, and were reserved for the company on the first floor, unless they were wanted downstairs, and there was nobody on the first floor. The salon of Jupiter, where the tradesmen used to meet, was papered in blue, and embellished with a large drawing representing Leda stretched out under the swan. That room was reached by a winding staircase, which ended at a narrow door opening onto the street, and above it, all night long a little lamp burned, behind wire bars, such as one still sees in some towns, at the foot of the shrine of some saint.

The house, which was old and damp, rather smelled of mildew. At times there was an odor of eau de Cologne in the passages, or a half open door downstairs allowed the noise of the common men sitting and drinking downstairs to reach the first floor, much to the disgust of the gentlemen who were there. Madame, who was quite familiar with those of her customers with whom she was on friendly terms, did not leave the salon. She took much interest in what was going on in the town, and they regularly told her all the news. Her serious conversation was a change from the ceaseless chatter of the three women; it was a rest from the doubtful jokes of those stout individuals who every evening indulged in the common-place amusement of drinking a glass of liquor in company with girls of easy virtue.

The names of the girls on the first floor were Fernande, Raphaelle, and Rosa "the Jade." As the staff was limited, Madame had endeavored that each member of it should be a pattern, an epitome of each feminine type so that every customer might find as nearly as possible, the realization of his ideal. Fernande represented the handsome blonde; she was very tall, rather fat, and lazy; a country girl, who could not get rid of her freckles, and whose short, light, almost colorless, tow-like hair, which was like combed-out flax, barely covered her head.

Raphaelle, who came from Marseilles, played the indispensable part of the handsome Jewess. She was thin, with high cheek-bones covered with rouge, and her black hair, which was always covered with pomatum, curled on to her forehead. Her eyes would have been handsome, if the right one had not had a speck in it. Her Roman nose came down over a square jaw, where two false upper teeth contrasted strangely with the bad color of the rest.

Rosa the Jade was a little roll of fat, nearly all stomach, with very short legs. From morning till night she sang songs, which were alternately indecent or sentimental, in a harsh voice, told silly, interminable tales, and only stopped talking in order to eat, or left off eating in order to talk. She was never still, was as active as a squirrel, in spite of her fat and her short legs; and her laugh, which was a torrent of shrill cries, resounded here and there, ceaselessly, in a bedroom, in the loft, in the *café*, everywhere, and always about nothing.

The two women on the ground floor were Louise, who was nicknamed "la Cocotte," and Flora, whom they called "Balançière," † because she limped a little. The former always dressed as Liberty, with a tri-colored sash, and the other as a Spanish woman, in whose carroty hair was a string of copper coins which jingled at every step she took. Both looked like cooks dressed up for the carnival, and were like all other women of the lower orders, neither uglier nor better looking than they usually are. In fact they looked just like servants at an inn, and were generally called "the Two Pumps."

A jealous peace, very rarely disturbed, reigned among these five women, thanks to Madame's conciliatory wisdom and to her constant good humor; and the establishment, which was the only one of the kind in the little town, was very much frequented. Madame had succeeded in giving it such a respectable appearance; she was so amiable and obliging to everybody, her good heart was so well known, that she was treated with a certain amount of consideration. The regular customers spent money on her, and were delighted when she was especially friendly toward them. When they met during the day, they would say: "This evening, you know where," just as men say: "At the *café*, after dinner." In a word Madame Tellier's house was somewhere to go to, and her customers very rarely missed their daily meetings there.

One evening, toward the end of May, the first arrival, Monsieur Poulin, who was a timber merchant, and had been mayor, found the door shut. The little lantern behind the grating was not alight; there was not a sound in the house; everything seemed dead. He knocked, gently at first, and then more loudly, but nobody answered the door. Then he went slowly up the street, and when he got to the market place, he met Monsieur Duvert, the

† Swing, or seesaw.

gun-maker, who was going to the same place, so they went back together, but did not meet with any better success. But suddenly they heard a loud noise close to them, and on going round the corner of the house, they saw a number of English and French sailors, who were hammering at the closed shutters of the *café* with their fists.

The two tradesmen immediately made their escape, for fear of being compromised, but a low *Pst* stopped them; it was Monsieur Tournevau, the fish-curer, who had recognized them, and was trying to attract their attention. They told him what had happened, and he was all the more vexed at it, as he, a married man, and father of a family, only went there on Saturdays—*securitatis causa,* as he said, alluding to a measure of sanitary policy, which his friend Doctor Borde had advised him to observe. That was his regular evening, and now he would be deprived of it for the whole week.

The three men went as far as the quay together, and on the way they met young Monsieur Philippe, the banker's son, who frequented the place regularly, and Monsieur Pinipesse, the collector. They all returned to the Rue aux Juifs together, to make a last attempt. But the exasperated sailors were besieging the house, throwing stones at the shutters, and shouting, and the five first-floor customers went away as quickly as possible, and walked aimlessly about the streets.

Presently they met Monsieur Dupuis, the insurance agent, and then Monsieur Vassi, the Judge of the Tribunal of Commerce, and they all took a long walk, going to the pier first of all. There they sat down in a row on the granite parapet, and watched the rising tide, and when the promenaders had sat there for some time, Monsieur Tournevau said: "This is not very amusing!"

"Decidedly not," Monsieur Pinipesse replied, and they started off to walk again.

After going through the street on the top of the hill, they returned over the wooden bridge which crosses the Retenue, passed close to the railway, and came out again in the market place, when suddenly a quarrel arose between Monsieur Pinipesse and Monsieur Tournevau, about an edible fungus which one of them declared he had found in the neighborhood.

As they were out of temper already from annoyance, they would very probably have come to blows, if the others had not interfered. Monsieur Pinipesse went off furious, and soon another altercation arose between the ex-mayor, Monsieur Poulin, and Monsieur Dupuis, the insurance agent, on the subject of the tax-collector's salary, and the profits which he might make. Insulting remarks were freely passing between them, when a torrent of formidable cries were heard, and the body of sailors, who were tired of waiting so long outside a closed house, came into the square. They were walking arm-in-arm, two and two, and formed a long procession, and were shouting furiously. The landsmen went and hid themselves under a gateway, and the yelling crew disappeared in the direction of the abbey. For a long time they still heard the noise, which diminished like a storm in the distance, and then silence was restored. Monsieur Poulin and Monsieur Dupuis, who were enraged with each other, went in different directions, without wishing each other good-bye.

The other four set off again, and instinctively went in the direction of Madame Tellier's establishment, which was still closed, silent, impenetrable. A quiet, but obstinate, drunken man was knocking at the door of the *café;* then he stopped and called Frederic, the waiter, in a low voice, but finding that he got no answer, he sat down on the doorstep, and awaited the course of events.

The others were just going to retire, when the noisy band of sailors reappeared at the end of the street. The French sailors were shouting the "Marseillaise," and the Englishmen, "Rule Britannia." There was a general lurching against the wall, and then the drunken brutes went on their way toward the quay, where a fight broke out between the two nations, in the course of which an Englishman had his arm broken, and a Frenchman his nose split.

The drunken man, who had stopped outside the door, was crying by this time, as drunken men and children cry when they are vexed, and the others went away. By degrees, calm was restored in the noisy town; here and there, at moments, the distant sound of voices could be heard, only to die away in the distance.

One man was still wandering about, Monsieur Tournevau, the fish-curer, who was vexed at having to wait until the next Saturday. He hoped for something to turn up, he did not know what; but he was exasperated at the police for thus allowing an establishment of such public utility, which they had under their control, to be thus closed.

He went back to it, examined the walls, and tried to find out the reason. On the shutter he saw a notice stuck up, so he struck a wax vesta, and read the following, in a large, uneven hand: "Closed on account of the Confirmation."

Then he went away, as he saw it was useless to remain, and left the drunken man lying on the pavement fast asleep, outside the inhospitable door.

The next day, all the regular customers, one after the

other, found some reason for going through the Rue aux Juifs with a bundle of papers under their arm, to keep them in countenance, and with a furtive glance they all read that mysterious notice:

"CLOSED ON ACCOUNT OF THE CONFIRMATION."

II

Madame had a brother, who was a carpenter in their native place, Virville, in the department of Eure. When Madame had still kept the inn at Yvetot, she had stood godmother to that brother's daughter, who had received the name of Constance, Constance Rivet; she herself being a Rivet on her father's side. The carpenter, who knew that his sister was in a good position, did not lose sight of her, although they did not meet often, as they were both kept at home by their occupations, and lived a long way from each other. But when the girl was twelve years old, and about to be confirmed, he seized the opportunity to write to his sister, and ask her to come and be present at the ceremony. Their old parents were dead, and as Madame could not well refuse, she accepted the invitation. Her brother, whose name was Joseph, hoped that by dint of showing his sister attentions, she might be induced to make her will in the girl's favor, as she had no children of her own.

His sister's occupation did not trouble his scruples in the least, and, besides, nobody knew anything about it at Virville. When they spoke of her, they only said: "Madame Tellier is living at Fécamp," which might mean that she was living on her own private income. It was quite twenty leagues from Fécamp to Virville, and for a peasant, twenty leagues on land are more than is crossing the ocean to an educated person. The people at Virville had never been further than Rouen, and nothing attracted the people from Fécamp to a village of five hundred houses, in the middle of a plain, and situated in another department. At any rate, nothing was known about her business.

But the Confirmation was coming on, and Madame was in great embarrassment. She had no under-mistress, and did not at all care to leave her house, even for a day. She feared the rivalries between the girls upstairs and those downstairs would certainly break out; that Frederic would get drunk, for when he was in that state, he would knock anybody down for a mere word. At last, however, she made up her mind to take them all with her, with the exception of the man, to whom she gave a holiday, until the next day but one.

When she asked her brother, he made no objection, but undertook to put them all up for a night. So on Saturday morning the eight o'clock express carried off Madame and her companions in a second-class carriage. As far as Beuzeille they were alone, and chattered like magpies, but at that station a couple got in. The man, an aged peasant dressed in a blue blouse with a folding collar, wide sleeves tight at the wrist, and ornamented with white embroidery, wore an old high hat with long nap. He held an enormous green umbrella in one hand, and a large basket in the other, from which the heads of three frightened ducks protruded. The woman, who sat stiffly in her rustic finery, had a face like a fowl, and a nose that was as pointed as a bill. She sat down opposite her husband and did not stir, as she was startled at finding herself in such smart company.

There was certainly an array of striking colors in the carriage. Madame was dressed in blue silk from head to foot, and had over her dress a dazzling red shawl of imitation French cashmere. Fernande was panting in a Scottish plaid dress, whose bodice, which her companions had laced as tight as they could, had forced up her falling bosom into a double dome, that was continually heaving up and down, and which seemed liquid beneath the material. Raphaelle, with a bonnet covered with feathers, so that it looked like a nest full of birds, had on a lilac dress with gold spots on it; there was something Oriental about it that suited her Jewish face. Rosa the Jade had on a pink petticoat with large flounces, and looked like a very fat child, an obese dwarf; while the Two Pumps looked as if they had cut their dresses out of old, flowered curtains, dating from the Restoration.

Perceiving that they were no longer alone in the compartment, the ladies put on staid looks, and began to talk of subjects which might give the others a high opinion of them. But at Bolbec a gentleman with light whiskers, with a gold chain, and wearing two or three rings, got in, and put several parcels wrapped in oilcloth into the net over his head. He looked inclined for a joke, and a good-natured fellow.

"Are you ladies changing your quarters?" he asked. The question embarrassed them all considerably. Madame, however, quickly recovered her composure, and said sharply, to avenge the honor of her corps:

"I think you might try and be polite!"

He excused himself, and said: "I beg your pardon, I ought to have said your nunnery."

As Madame could not think of a retort, or perhaps as she thought herself justified sufficiently, she gave him a dignified bow, and pinched in her lips.

Then the gentleman, who was sitting between Rosa the Jade and the old peasant, began to wink knowingly at the ducks, whose heads were sticking out of the basket.

When he felt that he had fixed the attention of his public, he began to tickle them under their bills, and spoke funnily to them, to make the company smile.

"We have left our little pond, qu-ack! qu-ack! to make the acquaintance of the little spit, qu-ack! qu-ack!"

The unfortunate creatures turned their necks away to avoid his caresses, and made desperate efforts to get out of their wicker prison, and then, suddenly, all at once, uttered the most lamentable quacks of distress. The women exploded with laughter. They leaned forward and pushed each other, so as to see better; they were very much interested in the ducks, and the gentleman redoubled his airs, his wit, and his teasing.

Rosa joined in, and leaning over her neighbor's legs, she kissed the three animals on the head. Immediately all the girls wanted to kiss them in turn, and the gentleman took them on to his knees, made them jump up and down and pinched them. The two peasants, who were even in greater consternation than their poultry, rolled their eyes as if they were possessed, without venturing to move, and their old wrinkled faces had not a smile nor a movement.

Then the gentleman, who was a commercial traveler, offered the ladies braces by way of a joke, and taking up one of his packages, he opened it. It was a trick, for the parcel contained garters. There were blue silk, pink silk, red silk, violet silk, mauve silk garters, and the buckles were made of two gilt metal Cupids, embracing each other. The girls uttered exclamations of delight, and looked at them with that gravity which is natural to a woman when she is hankering after a bargain. They consulted one another by their looks or in a whisper, and replied in the same manner, and Madame was longingly handling a pair of orange garters that were broader and more imposing than the rest; really fit for the mistress of such an establishment.

The gentleman waited, for he was nourishing an idea.

"Come, my kittens," he said, "you must try them on."

There was a torrent of exclamations, and they squeezed their petticoats between their legs, as if they thought he was going to ravish them, but he quietly waited his time, and said: "Well, if you will not, I shall pack them up again."

And he added cunningly: "I offer any pair they like, to those who will try them on."

But they would not, and sat up very straight, and looked dignified.

But the Two Pumps looked so distressed that he renewed the offer to them. Flora especially hesitated, and he pressed her:

"Come, my dear, a little courage! Just look at that lilac pair; it will suit your dress admirably."

That decided her, and pulling up her dress she showed a thick leg fit for a milk-maid, in a badly-fitting, coarse stocking. The commercial traveler stooped down and fastened the garter below the knee first of all and then above it; and he tickled the girl gently, which made her scream and jump. When he had done, he gave her the lilac pair, and asked: "Who next?"

"I! I!" they all shouted at once, and he began on Rosa the Jade, who uncovered a shapeless, round thing without any ankle, a regular "sausage of a leg," as Raphaelle used to say.

The commercial traveler complimented Fernande, and grew quite enthusiastic over her powerful columns.

The thin tibias of the handsome Jewess met with less flattery, and Louise Cocotte, by way of a joke, put her petticoats over the man's head, so that Madame was obliged to interfere to check such unseemly behavior.

Lastly, Madame herself put out her leg, a handsome, muscular, Norman leg, and in his surprise and pleasure the commercial traveler gallantly took off his hat to salute that master calf, like a true French cavalier.

The two peasants, who were speechless from surprise, looked askance, out of the corners of their eyes. They looked so exactly like fowls, that the man with the light whiskers, when he sat up, said "Co—co—ri—co," under their very noses, and that gave rise to another storm of amusement.

The old people got out at Motteville, with their basket, their ducks, and their umbrella, and they heard the woman say to her husband, as they went away:

"They are sluts, who are off to that cursed place, Paris."

The funny commercial traveler himself got out at Rouen, after behaving so coarsely that Madame was obliged sharply to put him into his right place. She added, as a moral: "This will teach us not to talk to the first comer."

At Oissel they changed trains, and at a little station further on Monsieur Joseph Rivet was waiting for them with a large cart and a number of chairs in it, which was drawn by a white horse.

The carpenter politely kissed all the ladies, and then helped them into his conveyance.

Three of them sat on three chairs at the back, Raphaelle, Madame, and her brother on the three chairs in front, and Rosa, who had no seat, settled herself as comfortably as she could on tall Fernande's knees, and then they set off.

But the horse's jerky trot shook the cart so terribly,

that the chairs began to dance, throwing the travelers into the air, to the right and to the left, as if they had been dancing puppets. This made them make horrible grimaces and screams, which, however, were cut short by another jolt of the cart.

They clung to the sides of the vehicle, their bonnets fell onto their backs, their noses on their shoulders, and the white horse trotted on, stretching out his head and holding out his tail quite straight, a little hairless rat's tail, with which he whisked his buttocks from time to time.

Joseph Rivet, with one leg on the shafts and the other bent under him, held the reins with elbows high and kept uttering a kind of chuckling sound, which made the horse prick up its ears and go faster.

The green country extended on either side of the road, and here and there the colza in flower presented a waving expanse of yellow, from which there arose a strong, wholesome, sweet and penetrating smell, which the wind carried to some distance.

The cornflowers showed their little blue heads among the rye, and the women wanted to pick them, but Monsieur Rivet refused to stop.

Then sometimes a whole field appeared to be covered with blood, so thickly were the poppies growing, and the cart, which looked as if it were filled with flowers of more brilliant hue, drove on through the fields colored with wild flowers, to disappear behind the trees of a farm, then to reappear and go on again through the yellow or green standing crops studded with red or blue.

One o'clock struck as they drove up to the carpenter's door. They were tired out, and very hungry, as they had eaten nothing since they left home. Madame Rivet ran out, and made them alight, one after another, kissing them as soon as they were on the ground. She seemed as if she would never tire of kissing her sister-in-law, whom she apparently wanted to monopolize. They had lunch in the workshop, which had been cleared out for the next day's dinner.

A capital omelette, followed by boiled chitterlings, and washed down by good, sharp cider, made them all feel comfortable.

Rivet had taken a glass so that he might hob-nob with them, and his wife cooked, waited on them, brought in the dishes, took them out, and asked all of them in a whisper whether they had everything they wanted. A number of boards standing against the walls, and heaps of shavings that had been swept into the corners, gave out the smell of planed wood, of carpentering, that resinous odor which penetrates the lungs.

They wanted to see the little girl, but she had gone to church, and would not be back until evening, so they all went out for a stroll in the country.

It was a small village, through which the high road passed. Ten or a dozen houses on either side of the single street had for tenants the butcher, the grocer, the carpenter, the innkeeper, the shoemaker, and the baker, and others.

The church was at the end of the street. It was surrounded by a small churchyard, and four enormous lime-trees, which stood just outside the porch, shaded it completely. It was built of flint, in no particular style, and had a slated steeple. When you got past it, you were in the open country again, which was broken here and there by clumps of trees which hid some homestead.

Rivet had given his arm to his sister, out of politeness, although he was in his working clothes, and was

walking with her majestically. His wife, who was overwhelmed by Raphaelle's gold-striped dress, was walking
between her and Fernande, and rotund Rosa was trotting
behind with Louise Cocotte and Flora, the see-saw, who
was limping along, quite tired out.

The inhabitants came to their doors, the children
left off playing, and a window curtain would be raised,
so as to show a muslin cap, while an old woman with a
crutch, who was almost blind, crossed herself as if it were
a religious procession. They all looked for a long time
after those handsome ladies from the town, who had
come so far to be present at the confirmation of Joseph
Rivet's little girl, and the carpenter rose very much in the
public estimation.

As they passed the church, they heard some children
singing; little shrill voices were singing a hymn, but Madame would not let them go in, for fear of disturbing the
little cherubs.

After a walk, during which Joseph Rivet enumerated
the principal landed proprietors, spoke about the yield
of the land, and the productiveness of the cows and sheep,
he took his flock of women home and installed them in
his house, and as it was very small, he had put them into
the rooms, two and two.

Just for once, Rivet would sleep in the workshop on
the shavings; his wife was going to share her bed with her
sister-in-law, and Fernande and Raphaelle were to sleep
together in the next room. Louise and Flora were put
into the kitchen, where they had a mattress on the floor,
and Rosa had a little dark cupboard at the top of the
stairs to herself, close to the loft, where the candidate for
confirmation was to sleep.

When the girl came in, she was overwhelmed with

kisses; all the women wished to caress her, with that need of tender expansion, that habit of professional wheedling, which had made them kiss the ducks in the railway carriage.

They took her onto their laps, stroked her soft, light hair, and pressed her in their arms with vehement and spontaneous outbursts of affection, and the child, who was very good-natured and docile, bore it all patiently.

As the day had been a fatiguing one for everybody, they all went to bed soon after dinner. The whole village was wrapped in that perfect stillness of the country, which is almost like a religious silence, and the girls, who were accustomed to the noisy evenings of their establishment, felt rather impressed by the perfect repose of the sleeping village. They shivered, not with cold, but with those little shivers of solitude which come over uneasy and troubled hearts.

As soon as they were in bed, two and two together, they clasped each other in their arms, as if to protect themselves against this feeling of the calm and profound slumber of the earth. But Rosa the Jade, who was alone in her little dark cupboard, felt a vague and painful emotion come over her.

She was tossing about in bed, unable to get to sleep, when she heard the faint sobs of a crying child close to her head, through the partition. She was frightened, and called out, and was answered by a weak voice, broken by sobs. It was the little girl who, being used to sleeping in her mother's room, was frightened in her small attic.

Rosa was delighted, got up softly so as not to awaken anyone, and went and fetched the child. She took her into her warm bed, kissed her and pressed her to her bosom, caressed her, lavished exaggerated manifestations of tenderness on her, and at last grew calmer herself and went to sleep. And till morning, the candidate for confirmation slept with her head on Rosa's naked bosom.

At five o'clock, the little church bell ringing the "Angelus" woke these women up, who as a rule slept the whole morning long.

The peasants were up already, and the women went busily from house to house, carefully bringing short, starched, muslin dresses in bandboxes, or very long wax tapers, with a bow of silk fringed with gold in the middle, and with dents in the wax for the fingers.

The sun was already high in the blue sky, which still had a rosy tint toward the horizon, like a faint trace of dawn, remaining. Families of fowls were walking about the henhouses, and here and there a black cock, with a glistening breast, raised his head, crowned by his red comb, flapped his wings, and uttered his shrill crow, which the other cocks repeated.

Vehicles of all sorts came from neighboring parishes, and discharged tall, Norman women, in dark dresses, with neck-handkerchiefs crossed over the bosom, and fastened with silver brooches, a hundred years old.

The men had put on blouses over their new frock coats, or over their old dress coats of green cloth, the tails of which hung down below their blouses. When the horses were in the stable, there was a double line of rustic conveyances along the road; carts, cabriolets, tilburies, char-à-bancs, traps of every shape and age, resting on their shafts, or pointing them in the air.

The carpenter's house was as busy as a beehive. The ladies, in dressing jackets and petticoats, with their long, thin, light hair, which looked as if it were faded and worn by dyeing, were busy dressing the child, who was standing motionless on a table, while Madame Tellier was directing the movements of her battalion. They washed her, did her hair, dressed her, and with the help of a number of pins, they arranged the folds of her dress, and took in the waist, which was too large.

Then, when she was ready, she was told to sit down and not to move, and the women hurried off to get ready themselves.

The church bell began to ring again, and its tinkle was lost in the air, like a feeble voice which is soon drowned in space. The candidates came out of the houses, and went toward the parochial building which contained the school and the mansion house. This stood quite at one end of the village, while the church was situated at the other.

The parents, in their very best clothes, followed their children with awkward looks, and with the clumsy movements of bodies that are always bent at work.

The little girls disappeared in a cloud of muslin, which looked like whipped cream, while the lads, who looked like embryo waiters in a *café*, and whose heads shone with pomatum, walked with their legs apart, so as not to get any dust or dirt onto their black trousers.

It was something for the family to be proud of; a large number of relatives from distant parts surrounded the child, and, consequently, the carpenter's triumph was complete.

Madame Tellier's regiment, with its mistress at its head, followed Constance; her father gave his arm to his sister, her mother walked by the side of Raphaelle, Fernande with Rosa, and the Two Pumps together. Thus they walked majestically through the village, like a general's staff in full uniform, while the effect on the village was startling.

At the school, the girls arranged themselves under

the Sister of Mercy, and the boys under the schoolmaster, and they started off, singing a hymn as they went. The boys led the way, in two files, between the two rows of vehicles, from which the horses had been taken out, and the girls followed in the same order. As all the people in the village had given the town ladies the precedence out of politeness, they came immediately behind the girls, and lengthened the double line of the procession still more, three on the right and three on the left, while their dresses were as striking as a bouquet of fireworks.

When they went into the church, the congregation grew quite excited. They pressed against each other, they turned round, they jostled one another in order to see. Some of the devout ones almost spoke aloud, so astonished were they at the sight of these ladies, whose dresses were trimmed more elaborately than the priest's chasuble.

The Mayor offered them his pew, the first one on the right, close to the choir, and Madame Tellier sat there with her sister-in-law; Fernande and Raphaelle, Rosa the Jade, and the Two Pumps occupied the second seat, in company with the carpenter.

The choir was full of kneeling children, the girls on one side, and the boys on the other, and the long wax tapers which they held, looked like lances, pointing in all directions. Three men were standing in front of the lectern, singing as loud as they could.

They prolonged the syllables of the sonorous Latin indefinitely, holding on to the Amens with interminable *a—a's*, which the serpent of the organ kept up in the monotonous, long-drawn-out notes, emitted by the deep-throated pipes.

A child's shrill voice took up the reply, and from time to time a priest sitting in a stall and wearing a biretta, got up, muttered something, and sat down again. The three singers continued, with their eyes fixed on the big book of plain-song lying open before them on the outstretched wings of an eagle, mounted on a pivot.

Then silence ensued. The service went on, and toward the end of it, Rosa, with her head in both her hands, suddenly thought of her mother, and her village church on a similar occasion. She almost fancied that that day had returned, when she was so small, and almost hidden in her white dress, and she began to cry.

First of all she wept silently, the tears dropped slowly from her eyes, but her emotion increased with her recollections, and she began to sob. She took out her pocket-handkerchief, wiped her eyes, and held it to her mouth, so as not to scream, but it was useless.

A sort of rattle escaped her throat, and she was answered by two other profound, heart-breaking sobs; for her two neighbors, Louise and Flora, who were kneeling near her, overcome by similar recollections, were sobbing by her side. There was a flood of tears, and as weeping is contagious, Madame soon found that her eyes were wet, and on turning to her sister-in-law, she saw that all the occupants of the pew were crying.

Soon, throughout the church, here and there, a wife, a mother, a sister, seized by the strange sympathy of poignant emotion, and agitated by the grief of those handsome ladies on their knees, who were shaken by their sobs, was moistening her cambric pocket-handkerchief, and pressing her beating heart with her left hand.

Just as the sparks from an engine will set fire to dry grass, so the tears of Rosa and of her companions infected the whole congregation in a moment. Men, women, old men, and lads in new blouses were soon sobbing; something superhuman seemed to be hovering over their heads

—a spirit, the powerful breath of an invisible and all-powerful being.

Suddenly a species of madness seemed to pervade the church, the noise of a crowd in a state of frenzy, a tempest of sobs and of stifled cries. It passed over the people like gusts of wind which bow the trees in a forest, and the priest, overcome by emotion, stammered out incoherent prayers, those inarticulate prayers of the soul, when it soars toward heaven.

The people behind him gradually grew calmer. The cantors, in all the dignity of their white surplices, went on in somewhat uncertain voices, and the organ itself seemed hoarse, as if the instrument had been weeping. The priest, however, raised his hand, as a sign for them to be still, and went to the chancel steps. All were silent, immediately.

After a few remarks on what had just taken place, which he attributed to a miracle, he continued, turning to the seats where the carpenter's guests were sitting:

"I especially thank you, my dear sisters, who have come from such a distance, and whose presence among us, whose evident faith and ardent piety have set such a salutary example to all. You have edified my parish; your emotion has warmed all hearts; without you, this day would not, perhaps, have had this really divine character. It is sufficient, at times, that there should be one chosen to keep in the flock, to make the whole flock blessed."

His voice failed him again, from emotion, and he said no more, but concluded the service.

They all left the church as quickly as possible; the children themselves were restless, tired with such a prolonged tension of the mind. Besides, the elders were hungry, and one after another left the churchyard, to see about dinner.

There was a crowd outside, a noisy crowd, a babel of loud voices, in which the shrill Norman accent was discernible. The villagers formed two ranks, and when the children appeared, each family seized their own.

The whole houseful of women caught hold of Constance, surrounded her and kissed her, and Rosa was especially demonstrative. At last she took hold of one hand, while Madame Tellier held the other, and Raphaelle and Fernande held up her long muslin petticoat, so that it might not drag in the dust. Louise and Flora brought up the rear with Madame Rivet, and the child, who was very silent and thoughtful, set off home, in the midst of this guard of honor.

The dinner was served in the workshop, on long boards supported by trestles, and through the open door they could see all the enjoyment that was going on. Everywhere people were feasting; through every window could be seen tables surrounded by people in their Sunday clothes. There was merriment in every house—men sitting in their shirt sleeves, drinking cider, glass after glass.

In the carpenter's house the gaiety took on somewhat of an air of reserve, the consequence of the emotion of the girls in the morning. Rivet was the only one who was in good cue, and he was drinking to excess. Madame Tellier was looking at the clock every moment, for, in order not to lose two days following, they ought to take the 3.55 train, which would bring them to Fécamp by dark.

The carpenter tried very hard to distract her attention, so as to keep his guests until the next day. But he did not succeed, for she never joked when there was business to be done, and as soon as they had had their coffee she ordered her girls to make haste and get ready. Then, turning to her brother, she said:

"You must have the horse put in immediately," and she herself went to complete her preparations.

When she came down again, her sister-in-law was waiting to speak to her about the child, and a long conversation took place, in which, however, nothing was settled. The carpenter's wife finessed, and pretended to be very much moved, and Madame Tellier, who was holding the girl on her knees, would not pledge herself to anything definite, but merely gave vague promises: she would not forget her, there was plenty of time, and then, they were sure to meet again.

But the conveyance did not come to the door, and the women did not come downstairs. Upstairs, they even heard loud laughter, falls, little screams, and much clapping of hands, and so, while the carpenter's wife went to the stable to see whether the cart was ready, Madame went upstairs.

Rivet, who was very drunk and half undressed, was vainly trying to kiss Rosa, who was choking with laughter. The Two Pumps were holding him by the arms and trying to calm him, as they were shocked at such a scene after that morning's ceremony; but Raphaelle and Fernande were urging him on, writhing and holding their sides with laughter, and they uttered shrill cries at every useless attempt that the drunken fellow made.

The man was furious, his face was red, his dress disordered, and he was trying to shake off the two women who were clinging to him, while he was pulling Rosa's bodice, with all his might, and ejaculating: "Won't you, you slut?"

But Madame, who was very indignant, went up to her brother, seized him by the shoulders, and threw him out of the room with such violence that he fell against a wall in the passage, and a minute afterward, they heard him pumping water on to his head in the yard. When he came back with the cart, he was already quite calmed down.

They seated themselves in the same way as they had done the day before, and the little white horse started off with his quick, dancing trot. Under the hot sun, their fun, which had been checked during dinner, broke out again. The girls now were amused at the jolts which the wagon gave, pushed their neighbors' chairs, and burst out laughing every moment, for they were in the vein for it, after Rivet's vain attempt.

There was a haze over the country, the roads were glaring, and dazzled their eyes. The wheels raised up two trails of dust, which followed the cart for a long time along the highroad, and presently Fernande, who was fond of music, asked Rosa to sing something. She boldly struck up the "Gros Curé de Meudon," but Madame made her stop immediately, as she thought it a song which was very unsuitable for such a day, and added:

"Sing us something of Béranger's."

After a moment's hesitation, Rosa began Béranger's song, "The Grandmother," in her worn-out voice, and all the girls, and even Madame herself, joined in the chorus:

> "How I regret
> My dimpled arms,
> My well-made legs,
> And my vanished charms."

"That is first-rate," Rivet declared, carried away by the rhythm. They shouted the refrain to every verse, while Rivet beat time on the shafts with his foot, and on the horse's back with the reins. The animal, himself, carried away by the rhythm, broke into a wild gallop, and threw all the women in a heap, one on the top of the other, in the bottom of the conveyance.

They got up, laughing as if they were crazy, and the song went on, shouted at the top of their voices, beneath the burning sky and among the ripening grain, to the rapid gallop of the little horse, who set off every time the refrain was sung, and galloped a hundred yards, to their great delight. Occasionally a stone breaker by the road-side sat up, and looked at the wild and shouting female load, through his wire spectacles.

When they got out at the station, the carpenter said:

"I am sorry you are going; we might have had some fun together."

But Madame replied very sensibly: "Everything has its right time, and we cannot always be enjoying ourselves."

And then he had a sudden inspiration: "Look here, I will come and see you at Fécamp next month." And he gave a knowing look, with his bright and roguish eyes.

"Come," Madame said, "you must be sensible; you may come if you like, but you are not to be up to any of your tricks."

He did not reply, and as they heard the whistle of the train he immediately began to kiss them all. When it came to Rosa's turn, he tried to get to her mouth, which she, however, smiling with her lips closed, turned away from him each time by a rapid movement of her head to one side. He held her in his arms, but he could not attain his object, as his large whip, which he was holding in his hand and waving behind the girl's back in desperation, interfered with his efforts.

"Passengers for Rouen, take your seats, please!" a guard cried, and they got in. There was a slight whistle followed by a loud one from the engine, which noisily puffed out its first jet of steam, while the wheels began to turn a little, with visible effort. Rivet left the station and went to the gate by the side of the line to get another look at Rosa, and as the carriage full of human merchandise passed him, he began to crack his whip and to jump, singing at the top of his voice:

> "How I regret
> My dimpled arms,
> My well-made legs,
> And my vanished charms!"

And then he watched a white pocket-handkerchief, which somebody was waving, as it disappeared in the distance.

III

They slept the peaceful sleep of quiet consciences, until they got to Rouen. When they returned to the house, refreshed and rested, Madame could not help saying:

"It was all very well, but I was already longing to get home."

They hurried over their supper, and then, when they had put on their usual light evening costumes, waited for their usual customers. The little colored lamp outside the door told the passers-by that the flock had returned to the fold, and in a moment the news spread, nobody knew how, or by whom.

Monsieur Philippe, the banker's son, even carried his audacity so far as to send a special messenger to Monsieur Tournevau, who was in the bosom of his family.

Every Sunday the fish-curer used to have several cousins to dinner, and they were having coffee, when a

man came in with a letter in his hand. Monsieur Tournevau was much excited; he opened the envelope and grew
pale; it only contained these words in pencil:

"The cargo of fish has been found; the ship has come into
port; good business for you. Come immediately."

He felt in his pockets, gave the messenger two-pence,
and suddenly blushing to his ears, he said: "I must go
out." He handed his wife the laconic and mysterious
note, rang the bell, and when the servant came in, he
asked her to bring him his hat and overcoat immediately.
As soon as he was in the street, he began to run, and the
way seemed to him to be twice as long as usual, in consequence of his impatience.

Madame Tellier's establishment had put on quite
a holiday look. On the ground floor, a number of sailors
were making a deafening noise, and Louise and Flora
drank with one and the other, so as to merit their name
of the Two Pumps more than ever. They were being
called for everywhere at once; already they were not quite
sober enough for their business, and the night bid fair
to be a very jolly one.

The upstairs room was full by nine o'clock. Monsieur Vassi, the Judge of the Tribunal of Commerce,
Madame's usual Platonic wooer, was talking to her in a
corner, in a low voice, and they were both smiling, as if
they were about to come to an understanding.

Monsieur Poulin, the ex-mayor, was holding Rosa on
his knees; and she, with her nose close to his, was running her hands through the old gentleman's white whiskers.

Tall Fernande, who was lying on the sofa, had both
her feet on Monsieur Pinipesse the tax-collector's stomach, and her back on young Monsieur Philippe's waist-

coat; her right arm was round his neck, and she held a cigarette in her left.

Raphaelle appeared to be discussing matters with Monsieur Dupuis, the insurance agent, and she finished by saying: "Yes, my dear, I will."

Just then, the door opened suddenly, and Monsieur Tournevau came in. He was greeted with enthusiastic cries of: "Long live Tournevau!" and Raphaelle, who was twirling round, went and threw herself into his arms. He seized her in a vigorous embrace, and without saying a word, lifting her up as if she had been a feather, he carried her through the room.

Rosa was chatting to the ex-mayor, kissing him every moment, and pulling both his whiskers at the same time in order to keep his head straight.

Fernande and Madame remained with the four men, and Monsieur Philippe exclaimed: "I will pay for some champagne; get three bottles, Madame Tellier." And Fernande gave him a hug, and whispered to him: "Play us a waltz, will you?" So he rose and sat down at the old piano in the corner, and managed to get a hoarse waltz out of the entrails of the instrument.

The tall girl put her arms round the tax-collector, Madame asked Monsieur Vassi to take her in his arms, and the two couples turned round, kissing as they danced. Monsieur Vassi, who had formerly danced in good society, waltzed with such elegance that Madame was quite captivated.

Frederic brought the champagne; the first cork popped, and Monsieur Philippe played the introduction to a quadrille, through which the four dancers walked in society fashion, decorously, with propriety of deportment, with bows, and curtsies, and then they began to drink.

Monsieur Philippe next struck up a lively polka,

and Monsieur Tournevau started off with the handsome Jewess, whom he held up in the air, without letting her feet touch the ground. Monsieur Pinipesse and Monsieur Vassi had started off with renewed vigor and from time to time one or another couple would stop to toss off a long glass of sparkling wine. The dance was threatening to become never-ending, when Rosa opened the door.

"I want to dance," she exclaimed. And she caught hold of Monsieur Dupuis, who was sitting idle on the couch, and the dance began again.

But the bottles were empty. "I will pay for one," Monsieur Tournevau said.

"So will I," Monsieur Vassi declared.

"And I will do the same," Monsieur Dupuis remarked.

They all began to clap their hands, and it soon became a regular ball. From time to time, Louise and Flora ran upstairs quickly, had a few turns while their customers downstairs grew impatient, and then they returned regretfully to the *café*. At midnight they were still dancing.

Madame shut her eyes to what was going on, and she had long private talks in corners with Monsieur Vassi, as if to settle the last details of something that had already been agreed upon.

At last, at one o'clock, the two married men, Monsieur Tournevau and Monsieur Pinipesse, declared that they were going home, and wanted to pay. Nothing was charged for except the champagne, and that only cost six francs a bottle, instead of ten, which was the usual price, and when they expressed their surprise at such generosity, Madame, who was beaming, said to them:

"We don't have a holiday every day."

The Piece of String

ALONG all the roads around Goderville the peasants and their wives were coming toward the town because it was market day. The men were proceeding with slow steps, the whole body bent forward at each movement of their long twisted legs, deformed by their hard work, by the weight on the plow which, at the same time, raised the left shoulder and swerved the figure, by the reaping of the wheat which made the knees spread to make a firm "purchase," by all the slow and painful labors of the country. Their blouses, blue, "stiff-starched," shining as if varnished, ornamented with a little design in white at the neck and wrists, puffed about their bony bodies, seemed like balloons ready to carry them off. From each of them a head, two arms, and two feet protruded.

Some led a cow or a calf by a cord, and their wives, walking behind the animal, whipped its haunches with a leafy branch to hasten its progress. On their arms they carried large baskets from which, in some cases, chickens and, in others, ducks thrust out their heads. And they walked with a quicker, livelier step than their husbands. Their spare straight figures were wrapped in scanty little shawls, pinned over their flat bosoms, and their heads were enveloped in white cloths glued to the hair and surmounted by caps.

Then a wagon passed at the jerky trot of a nag, shaking strangely, two men seated side by side and a woman in the bottom of the vehicle, the latter holding on to the sides to lessen the hard jolts.

The Piece of String

In the public square of Goderville there was a crowd, a throng of human beings and animals mixed together. The horns of the cattle, the tall hats with the long nap of the rich peasant, and the headgear of the peasant women rose above the surface of the assembly. And the clamorous, shrill, screaming voices made a continuous and savage din which sometimes was dominated by the robust lungs of some country-man's laugh, or the long lowing of a cow tied to the wall of a house.

All that smacked of the stable, the dairy and the dirt heap, hay and sweat, giving forth that unpleasant odor, human and animal, peculiar to the people of the field.

Maître Hauchecome, of Breaute, had just arrived at Goderville, and he was directing his steps toward the public square, when he perceived upon the ground a little piece of string. Maître Hauchecome, economical like a true Norman, thought that everything useful ought to be picked up, and he bent painfully, for he suffered from rheumatism. He took the bit of thin cord from the ground and began to roll it carefully when he noticed Maître Malandain, the harness-maker, on the threshold of his door, looking at him. They had heretofore had business together on the subject of a halter, and they were on bad terms, being both good haters. Maître Hauchecome was seized with a sort of shame to be seen thus by his enemy, picking a bit of string out of the dirt. He concealed his "find" quickly under his blouse, then in his trousers' pocket; then he pretended to be still looking on the ground for something which he did not find, and he went toward the market, his head forward, bent double by his pains.

He was soon lost in the noisy and slowly moving crowd, which was busy with interminable bargainings.

The peasants milked, went and came, perplexed, always in fear of being cheated, not daring to decide, watching the vendor's eye, ever trying to find the trick in the man and the flaw in the beast.

The women, having placed their great baskets at their feet, had taken out the poultry which lay upon the ground, tied together by the feet, with terrified eyes and scarlet crests.

They heard offers, stated their prices with a dry air and impassive face, or perhaps, suddenly deciding on some proposed reduction, shouted to the customer who was slowly going away: "All right, Maître Authirne, I'll give it to you for that."

Then little by little the square was deserted, and when the Angelus rang at noon, those who had stayed too long, scattered to their shops.

At Jourdain's the great room was full of people eating, as the big court was full of vehicles of all kinds, carts, gigs, wagons, dump carts, yellow with dirt, mended and patched, raising their shafts to the sky like two arms, or perhaps with their shafts in the ground and their backs in the air.

Just opposite the diners seated at the table, the immense fireplace, filled with bright flames, cast a lively heat on the backs of the row on the right. Three spits were turning on which were chickens, pigeons, and legs of mutton; and an appetizing odor of roast beef and gravy dripping over the nicely browned skin rose from the hearth, increased the jovialness, and made everybody's mouth water.

All the aristocracy of the plow ate there, at Maître Jourdain's, tavern keeper and horse dealer, a rascal who had money.

The dishes were passed and emptied, as were the

jugs of yellow cider. Everyone told his affairs, his purchases, and sales. They discussed the crops. The weather was favorable for the green things but not for the wheat.

Suddenly the drum beat in the court, before the house. Everybody rose except a few indifferent persons, and ran to the door, or to the windows, their mouths still full and napkins in their hands.

After the public crier had ceased his drum-beating, he called out in a jerky voice, speaking his phrases irregularly:

"It is hereby made known to the inhabitants of Goderville, and in general to all persons present at the market, that there was lost this morning, on the road to Benzeville, between nine and ten o'clock, a black leather pocketbook containing five hundred francs and some business papers. The finder is requested to return same with all haste to the mayor's office or to Maître Fortune Houlbreque of Manneville. There will be twenty francs reward."

Then the man went away. The heavy roll of the drum and the crier's voice were again heard at a distance.

Then they began to talk of this event discussing the chances that Maître Houlbreque had of finding or not finding his pocketbook.

And the meal concluded. They were finishing their coffee when a chief of the gendarmes appeared upon the threshold.

He inquired: "Is Maître Hauchecome, of Breaute, here?"

Maître Hauchecome, seated at the other end of the table, replied: "Here I am."

And the officer resumed: "Maître Hauchecome, will you have the goodness to accompany me to the mayor's office? The mayor would like to talk to you."

The Piece of String

The peasant, surprised and disturbed, swallowed at a draught his tiny glass of brandy, rose, and, even more bent than in the morning, for the first steps after each rest were specially difficult, set out, repeating: "Here I am, here I am."

The mayor was awaiting him, seated on an armchair. He was the notary of the vicinity, a stout, serious man, with pompous phrases.

"Maître Hauchecome," said he, "you were seen this morning to pick up, on the road to Benzeville, the pocketbook lost by Maître Houlbreque, of Manneville."

The countryman, astounded, looked at the mayor, already terrified, by this suspicion resting on him without his knowing why.

"Me? Me? Me pick up the pocketbook?"

"Yes, you, yourself."

"Word of honor, I never heard of it."

"But you were seen."

"I was seen, me? Who says he saw me?"

"Monsieur Malandain, the harness-maker."

The old man remembered, understood, and flushed with anger.

"Ah, he saw me, the clodhopper, he saw me pick up this string, here, M'sieu' the Mayor." And rummaging in his pocket he drew out the little piece of string.

But the mayor, incredulous, shook his head.

"You will not make me believe, Maître Hauchecome, that Monsieur Malandain, who is a man worthy of credence, mistook this cord for a pocketbook."

The peasant, furious, lifted his hand, spat at one side to attest his honor, repeating: "It is nevertheless the truth of the good God, the sacred truth, M'sieu' the Mayor. I repeat it on my soul and my salvation."

The mayor resumed: "After picking up the object,

you stood like a stilt, looking a long while in the mud to see if any piece of money had fallen out."

The good, old man choked with indignation and fear.

"How anyone can tell—how anyone can tell—such lies to take away an honest man's reputation! How can anyone—"

There was no use in his protesting; nobody believed him. He was confronted with Monsieur Malandain, who repeated and maintained his affirmation. They abused each other for an hour. At his own request, Maître Hauchecome was searched; nothing was found on him.

Finally the mayor, very much perplexed, discharged him with the warning that he would consult the public prosecutor and ask for further orders.

The news had spread. As he left the mayor's office, the old man was surrounded and questioned with a serious or bantering curiosity, in which there was no indignation. He began to tell the story of the string. No one believed him. They laughed at him.

He went along, stopping his friends, beginning endlessly his statement and his protestations, showing his pockets turned inside out, to prove that he had nothing.

They said: "Old rascal, get out!"

And he grew angry, becoming exasperated, hot, and distressed at not being believed, not knowing what to do and always repeating himself.

Night came. He must depart. He started on his way with three neighbors to whom he pointed out the place where he had picked up the bit of string; and all along the road he spoke of his adventure.

In the evening he took a turn in the village of

Breaute, in order to tell it to everybody. He only met with incredulity.

It made him ill at night.

The next day about one o'clock in the afternoon, Marius Paumelle, a hired man in the employ of Maître Breton, husbandman at Ymanville, returned the pocketbook and its contents to Maître Houlbreque of Manneville.

This man claimed to have found the object in the road; but not knowing how to read, he had carried it to the house and given it to his employer.

The news spread through the neighborhood. Maître Hauchecome was informed of it. He immediately went the circuit and began to recount his story completed by the happy climax. He was in triumph.

"What grieved me so much was not the thing itself, as the lying. There is nothing so shameful as to be placed under a cloud on account of a lie."

He talked of his adventure all day long; he told it on the highway to people who were passing by, in the wine-shop to people who were drinking there, and to persons coming out of church the following Sunday. He stopped strangers to tell them about it. He was calm now, and yet something disturbed him without his knowing exactly what it was. People had the air of joking while they listened. They did not seem convinced. He seemed to feel that remarks were being made behind his back.

On Tuesday of the next week he went to the market at Goderville, urged solely by the necessity he felt of discussing the case.

Malandain, standing at his door, began to laugh on seeing him pass. Why?

He approached a farmer from Crequetot, who did

not let him finish, and giving him a thump in the stomach said to his face: "You big rascal."

Then he turned his back on him.

Maître Hauchecome was confused. Why was he called a big rascal?

When he was seated at the table, in Jourdain's tavern he commenced to explain "the affair."

A horse dealer from Monvilliers called to him: "Come, come, old sharper, that's an old trick; I know all about your piece of string!"

Hauchecome stammered: "But since the pocketbook was found."

But the other man replied: "Shut up, papa, there is one that finds, and there is one that reports. At any rate you are mixed up with it."

The peasant stood choking. He understood. They accused him of having had the pocketbook returned by a confederate, by an accomplice.

He tried to protest. All the table began to laugh.

He could not finish his dinner and went away, in the midst of jeers.

He went home ashamed and indignant, choking with anger and confusion, the more dejected that he was capable with his Norman cunning of doing what they had accused him of, and even boasting of it as of a good turn. His innocence to him, in a confused way, was impossible to prove, as his sharpness was known. And he was stricken to the heart by the injustice of the suspicion.

Then he began to recount the adventures again, prolonging his history every day, adding each time, new reasons, more energetic protestations, more solemn oaths which he imagined and prepared in his hours of solitude, his whole mind given up to the story of the string. He was believed so much the less as his defense was more complicated and his arguing more subtle.

"Those are lying excuses," they said behind his back.

He felt it, consumed his heart over it, and wore himself out with useless efforts. He wasted away before their very eyes.

The wags now made him tell about the string to amuse them, as they make a soldier who has been on a campaign tell about his battles. His mind, touched to the depth, began to weaken.

Toward the end of December he took to his bed.

He died in the first days of January, and in the delirium of his death struggles he kept claiming his innocence, reiterating.

"A piece of string, a piece of string—look—here it is, M'sieu' the Mayor."

The Story of a Farm-Girl

As the weather was very fine, the people on the farm had dined more quickly than usual, and had returned to the fields.

The female servant, Rose, remained alone in the large kitchen, where the fire on the hearth was dying out, under the large boiler of hot water. From time to time she took some water out of it, and slowly washed her plates and dishes, stopping occasionally to look at the two streaks of light which the sun threw onto the long table through the window, and which showed the defects in the glass.

Three venturesome hens were picking up the crumbs under the chairs, while the smell of the poultry yard and the warmth from the cow-stall came in through the half open door, and a cock was heard crowing in the distance.

When she had finished her work, wiped down the table, dusted the mantelpiece, and put the plates on the high dresser, close to the wooden clock, with its enormous pendulum, she drew a long breath, as she felt rather oppressed, without exactly knowing why. She looked at the black clay walls, the rafters that were blackened with smoke, from which spiders' webs were hanging amid pickled herrings and strings of onions, and then she sat down, rather overcome by the stale emanations from the floor, on which so many things had been spilled. With these was mingled the smell of the pans of milk, which were set out to raise the cream in the adjoining dairy.

She wanted to sew, as usual, but she did not feel strong enough for it, and so she went to get a mouthful of fresh air at the door, which seemed to do her good.

The fowls were lying on the smoking dung-hill; some of them were scratching with one claw in search of worms, while the cock stood up proudly among them. Now and then he selected one of them, and walked round her with a slight cluck of amorous invitation. The hen got up in a careless way as she received his attentions, supported herself on her legs and spread out her wings; then she shook her feathers to shake out the dust, and stretched herself out on the dung-hill again, while he crowed, in sign of triumph, and the cocks in all the neighboring farmyards replied to him, as if they were uttering amorous challenges from farm to farm.

The girl looked at them without thinking; then she raised her eyes and was almost dazzled at the sight of the apple-trees in blossom, which looked almost like powdered heads. Just then, a colt, full of life and friskiness, galloped past her. Twice he jumped over the ditches, and then stopped suddenly, as if surprised at being alone.

She also felt inclined to run; she felt inclined to move and to stretch her limbs, and to repose in the warm, breathless air. She took a few undecided steps, and closed her eyes, for she was seized with a feeling of animal comfort; then she went to look for the eggs in the hen loft. There were thirteen of them, which she took in and put into the storeroom; but the smell from the kitchen disgusted her again, and she went out to sit on the grass for a time.

The farmyard, which was surrounded by trees, seemed to be asleep. The tall grass, among which the tall yellow dandelions rose up like streaks of yellow light, was of a vivid green, the fresh spring green. The apple-trees threw their shade all round them, and the thatched houses, on which the blue and yellow iris flowers, with their sword-like leaves, grew, smoked as if the moisture of the stables and barns was coming through the straw.

The girl went to the shed where the carts and traps were kept. Close to it, in a ditch, there was a large patch of violets whose scent was perceptible all round, while beyond it could be seen the open country where the corn was growing, with clumps of trees in the distance, and groups of laborers here and there, who looked as small as dolls, and white horses like toys, who were pulling a child's cart, driven by a man as tall as one's finger.

She took up a bundle of straw, threw it into the ditch and sat down upon it; then, not feeling comfortable, she undid it, spread it out and lay down upon it at full length, on her back, with both arms under her head, and her limbs stretched out.

Gradually her eyes closed, and she was falling into a state of delightful languor. She was, in fact, almost asleep, when she felt two hands on her bosom, and then she sprang up at a bound. It was Jacques, one of the farm laborers, a tall fellow from Picardy, who had been making love to her for a long time. He had been looking after the sheep, and seeing her lying down in the shade, he had come stealthily, and holding his breath, with glistening eyes, and bits of straw in his hair.

He tried to kiss her, but she gave him a smack in the face, for she was as strong as he, and he was shrewd enough to beg her pardon: so they sat down side by side and talked amicably. They spoke about the favorable weather, of their master, who was a good fellow, then of their neighbors, of all the people in the country round, of themselves, of their village, of their youthful days, of their recollections, of their relatives, whom they had not seen for a long time, and might not see again. She grew sad, as she thought of it, while he, with one fixed idea in his head, rubbed against her with a kind of a shiver, overcome by desire.

"I have not seen my mother for a long time," she said. "It is very hard to be separated like that." And she directed her looks into the distance, toward the village in the North, which she had left.

Suddenly, however, he seized her by the neck and kissed her again! but she struck him so violently in the face with her clenched fist, that his nose began to bleed, and he got up and laid his head against the branch of a tree. When she saw that, she was sorry, and going up to him, she said:

"Have I hurt you?"

He, however, only laughed. "No, it was a mere nothing;" though she had hit him right on the middle of the nose. "What a devil!" he said, and he looked at her with admiration, for she had inspired him with a feeling of respect and of a very different kind of admiration, which was the beginning of real love for that tall, strong wench.

When the bleeding had stopped, he proposed a walk, as he was afraid of his neighbor's heavy hand, if they remained side by side like that much longer; but she took his arm of her own accord, in the avenue, as if they had been out for an evening walk, and said: "It is not nice of you to despise me like that, Jacques."

He protested, however. No, he did not despise her. He was in love with her, that was all.

"So you really want to marry me?" she asked.

The Story of a Farm-Girl

He hesitated, and then looked at her aside, while she looked straight ahead of her. She had fat, red cheeks, a full, protuberant bust under her muslin dress, thick, red lips, and her neck, which was almost bare, was covered with small beads of perspiration. He felt a fresh access of desire, and putting his lips to her ear, he murmured: "Yes, of course I do."

Then she threw her arms round his neck, and kissed him for such a long time, that both of them lost their breath. From that moment the eternal story of love began between them. They plagued each other in corners; they met in the moonlight under a haystack, and gave each other bruises on the legs, with their heavy nailed boots. By degrees, however, Jacques seemed to grow tired of her: he avoided her; scarcely spoke to her, and did not try any longer to meet her alone, which made her sad and anxious, especially when she found that she was pregnant.

At first, she was in a state of consternation; then she got angry, and her rage increased every day, because she could not meet him, as he avoided her most carefully. At last, one night when everyone in the farmhouse was asleep, she went out noiselessly in her petticoat, with bare feet, crossed the yard and opened the door of the stable where Jacques was lying in a large box of straw, over his horses. He pretended to snore when he heard her coming, but she knelt down by his side and shook him until he sat up.

"What do you want?" he then asked of her. And she with clenched teeth, and trembling with anger, replied:

"I want—I want you to marry me, as you promised."

But he only laughed, and replied: "Oh! If a man were to marry all the girls with whom he has made a slip, he would have more than enough to do."

Then she seized him by the throat, threw him onto his back, so that he could not disengage himself from her, and half strangling him, she shouted into his face: "I am *enceinte*, do you hear? I am *enceinte!*"

He gasped for breath, as he was nearly choked, and so they remained, both of them, motionless and without speaking, in the dark silence, which was only broken by the noise that a horse made as he pulled the hay out of the manger, and then slowly chewed it.

When Jacques found that she was the stronger, he stammered out: "Very well, I will marry you, as that is the case."

But she did not believe his promises. "It must be at once," she said. "You must have the banns put up."

"At once," he replied.

"Swear solemnly that you will."

He hesitated for a few moments, and then said: "I swear it, by heaven."

Then she released her grasp, and went away without another word.

She had no chance of speaking to him for several days, and as the stable was now always locked at night, she was afraid to make any noise, for fear of creating a scandal. One day, however, she saw another man come in at dinner-time, and so she said: "Has Jacques left?"

"Yes," the man replied; "I have got his place."

This made her tremble so violently, that she could not take the saucepan off the fire; and later when they were all at work, she went up into her room and cried, burying her head in her bolster, so that she might not be heard. During the day, however, she tried to obtain some information without exciting any suspicions, but she was so overwhelmed by the thoughts of her misfortune, that she fancied that all the people whom she asked, laughed maliciously. All she learned, however, was, that he had left the neighborhood altogether.

II

Then a cloud of constant misery began for her. She worked mechanically, without thinking of what she was doing, with one fixed idea in her head: "Suppose people were to know."

This continual feeling made her so incapable of reasoning, that she did not even try to think of any means of avoiding the disgrace that she knew must ensue, which was irreparable, and drawing nearer every day, and which was as sure as death itself. She got up every morning long before the others, and persistently tried to look at her figure in a piece of broken looking-glass at which she did her hair, as she was very anxious to know whether anybody would notice a change in her, and during the day she stopped working every few minutes to look at herself from top to toe, to see whether the size of her abdomen did not make her apron look too short.

The months went on. She scarcely spoke now, and when she was asked a question, she did not appear to understand. She had a frightened look, with haggard eyes and trembling hands, which made her master say to her occasionally: "My poor girl, how stupid you have grown lately."

In church, she hid behind a pillar, and no longer ventured to go to confession. She feared to face the priest, to whom she attributed a superhuman power, which enabled him to read people's consciences; and at meal times, the looks of her fellow-servants almost made her faint with mental agony. She was always fancying that she had been found out by the cowherd, a precocious and cunning little lad, whose bright eyes seemed always to be watching her.

One morning the postman brought her a letter, and as she had never received one in her life before, she was so upset by it, that she was obliged to sit down. Perhaps it was from him? But as she could not read, she sat anxious and trembling with that piece of paper covered with ink in her hand; after a time, however, she put it into her pocket, as she did not venture to confide her secret to anyone. She often stopped in her work to look at the lines, written at regular intervals, and terminating in a signature, imagining vaguely that she would suddenly discover their meaning. At last, as she felt half mad with impatience and anxiety, she went to the schoolmaster, who told her to sit down, and read the letter to her, as follows:

"MY DEAR DAUGHTER: I write to tell you that I am very ill. Our neighbor, Monsieur Dentu, begs you to come, if you can,
"For your affectionate mother.
"CÉSAIRE DENTU,
"*Deputy Mayor.*"

She did not say a word, and went away, but as soon as she was alone, her legs gave way, and she fell down by the roadside, and remained there till night.

When she got back, she told the farmer her trouble. He allowed her to go home for as long as she wanted, promised to have her work done by a charwoman, and to take her back when she returned.

Her mother died soon after she got there, and the next day Rose gave birth to a seven months' child, a miserable little skeleton, thin enough to make anybody shudder. It seemed to be suffering continually, to judge from the painful manner in which it moved its poor little limbs, which were as thin as a crab's legs, but it lived, for all that. She said that she was married, but that she could not saddle herself with the child, so she left it with some neighbors, who promised to take great care of it, and she went back to the farm.

But then, in her heart, which had been wounded so long, there arose something like brightness, an unknown love for that frail little creature which she had left behind her, but there was fresh suffering in that very love, suffering which she felt every hour and every minute, because she was parted from the child. What pained her most, however, was a mad longing to kiss it, to press it in her arms, to feel the warmth of its little body against her skin. She could not sleep at night; she thought of it the whole day long, and in the evening, when her work was done, she used to sit in front of the fire and look at it intently, as people do whose thoughts are far away.

They began to talk about her, and to tease her about her lover. They asked her whether he was tall, handsome, and rich. When was the wedding to be, and the christening? And often she ran away to cry by herself, for these questions seemed to hurt her, like the prick of a pin, and in order to forget their jokes, she began to work still more energetically, and still thinking of her child, she sought for the means of saving up money for it, and determined to work so that her master would be obliged to raise her wages.

Then, by degrees, she almost monopolized the work, and persuaded him to get rid of one servant girl, who had become useless since she had taken to working like two; she economized in the bread, oil, and candles, in the corn which they gave to the fowls too extravagantly, and in the fodder for the horses and cattle, which was rather wasted. She was as miserly about her master's money as if it had been her own, and by dint of making good bargains, of getting high prices for all their produce, and by baffling the peasants' tricks when they offered anything for sale, he at last intrusted her with buying and selling everything, with the direction of all the laborers, and with the quantity of provisions necessary for the household, so that in a short time she became indispensable to him. She kept such a strict eye on everything about her, that under her direction the farm prospered wonderfully, and for five miles round people talked of "Master Vallin's servant," and the farmer himself said everywhere: "That girl is worth more than her weight in gold."

But time passed by, and her wages remained the same. Her hard work was accepted as something that was due from every good servant, and as a mere token of her good-will; and she began to think rather bitterly, that if the farmer could put fifty or a hundred crowns extra into the bank every month, thanks to her, she was still only earning her two hundred francs a year, neither more nor less, and so she made up her mind to ask for an increase of wages. She went to see the schoolmaster three times about it, but when she got there, she spoke about something else. She felt a kind of modesty in asking for money, as if it were something disgraceful; but at last, one day, when the farmer was having breakfast by himself in the kitchen, she said to him, with some embarrassment, that she wished to speak to him particularly. He raised his head in surprise, with both his hands on the table, holding his knife, with its point in the air, in one, and a piece of bread in the other. He looked fixedly at the girl, who felt uncomfortable under his gaze, but asked for a week's holiday, so that she might get away, as she was not very well. He acceded to her request immediately, and then added, in some embarrassment, himself:

"When you come back, I shall have something to say to you, myself."

III

The child was nearly eight months old. It had grown rosy and chubby all over like a little bundle of living fat. She threw herself onto it as if it had been some prey, and kissed it so violently that it began to scream with terror, and then she began to cry herself, because it did not know her, and stretched out its arms to its nurse, as soon as it saw her. But the next day, it began to get used to her, and laughed when it saw her, and she took it into the fields and ran about excitedly with it, and sat down under the shade of the trees, and then, for the first time in her life, she opened her heart to somebody and told the infant her troubles, how hard her work was, her anxieties and her hopes, and she quite tired the child with the violence of her caresses.

She took the greatest pleasure in handling it, in washing and dressing it, for it seemed to her that all this was the confirmation of her maternity, and she would look at it, almost feeling surprised that it was hers, and she used to say to herself in a low voice, as she danced it in her arms: "It is my baby, it is my baby."

She cried all the way home as she returned to the farm, and had scarcely got in, before her master called her into his room. She went in, feeling astonished and nervous, without knowing why.

"Sit down there," he said.

She sat down, and for some moments they remained side by side, in some embarrassment, with their arms hanging at their sides, as if they did not know what to do with them, and looking each other in the face, after the manner of peasants.

The farmer, a stout, jovial, obstinate man of forty-five, who had lost two wives, evidently felt embarrassed, which was very unusual with him. But at last he made up his mind, and began to speak vaguely, hesitating a little, and looking out of the window as he talked.

"How is it, Rose," he said, "that you have never thought of settling in life?"

She grew as pale as death, and seeing that she gave him no answer, he went on:

"You are a good, steady, active, and economical girl, and a wife like you would make a man's fortune."

She did not move, but looked frightened; she did not even try to comprehend his meaning, for her thoughts were in a whirl, as if at the approach of some great danger; so after waiting for a few seconds, he went on:

"You see, a farm without a mistress can never succeed, even with a servant like you are."

Then he stopped, for he did not know what else to say, and Rose looked at him with the air of a person who thinks that he is face to face with a murderer, and ready to flee at the slightest movement he may make; but after waiting for about five minutes, he asked her:

"Well, will it suit you?"

"Will what suit me, master?"

And he said, quickly: "Why, to marry me, by Jove!"

She jumped up, but fell back on to her chair as if she had been struck, and there she remained motionless, like a person who is overwhelmed by some great misfortune. But at last the farmer grew impatient, and said: "Come, what more do you want?"

She looked at him almost in terror; then suddenly the tears came into her eyes, and she said twice, in a choking voice: "I cannot, I cannot!"

"Why not?" he asked. "Come, don't be silly; I will give you until tomorrow to think it over."

And he hurried out of the room, very glad to have finished a matter which had troubled him a good deal. He had no doubt that she would the next morning accept a proposal which she could never have expected, and which would be a capital bargain for him, as he thus bound a woman to himself who would certainly bring him more than if she had the best dowry in the district.

Neither could there be any scruples about an unequal match between them, for in the country everyone is very nearly equal. The farmer works just as his laborers do; the latter frequently become masters in their turn, and the female servants constantly become the mistresses of the establishment, without making any change in their life or habits.

Rose did not go to bed that night. She threw herself, dressed as she was, onto her bed, and she had not even strength to cry left in her, she was so thoroughly astonished. She remained quite inert, scarcely knowing that she had a body, and without being at all able to collect her thoughts, though at moments she remembered a part of what had happened, and then she was frightened at the idea of what might happen. Her terror increased, and every time the great kitchen clock struck the hour, she broke into a perspiration from grief. She lost her head, and had a nightmare; her candle went out, and then she began to imagine that some one had thrown a spell over her, as country people so often fancy, and she felt a mad inclination to run away, to escape and flee before her misfortune, as a ship scuds before the wind.

An owl hooted, and she shivered, sat up, put her hands to her face, into her hair, and all over her body, and then she went downstairs, as if she were walking in her sleep. When she got into the yard, she stooped down, so as not to be seen by any prowling scamp, for the moon, which was setting, shed a bright light over the fields. Instead of opening the gate, she scrambled over the fence, and as soon as she was outside, she started off. She went on straight before her, with a quick, elastic trot, and from time to time, she unconsciously uttered a piercing cry. Her long shadow accompanied her, and now and then some night-bird flew over her head, while the dogs in the farmyards barked, as they heard her pass. One even jumped over the ditch, followed her, and tried to bite her, but she turned round at it, and gave such a terrible yell that the frightened animal ran back, and cowered in silence in its kennel.

The stars grew dim, and the birds began to twitter; day was breaking. The girl was worn out and panting, and when the sun rose in the purple sky, she stopped, for her swollen feet refused to go any further. But she saw a pond in the distance, a large pond whose stagnant water looked like blood under the reflection of this new day, and she limped on with short steps and with her hand on her heart, in order to dip both her feet in it.

She sat down on a tuft of grass, took off her sabots which were full of dust, pulled off her stockings and plunged her legs into the still water, from which bubbles were rising here and there.

A feeling of delicious coolness pervaded her from head to foot, and suddenly, while she was looking fixedly at the deep pool, she was seized with giddiness, and with a mad longing to throw herself into it. All her sufferings would be over in there; over forever. She no longer thought of her child; she only wanted peace, complete rest, and to sleep forever, and she got up with raised arms and took two steps forward. She was in the water up to her thighs, and she was just about to throw herself in, when sharp, pricking pains in her ankles made her jump back. She uttered a cry of despair, for, from her knees to the tips of her feet, long, black leeches were sucking in her life blood, and were swelling, as they adhered to her flesh. She did not dare to touch them, and screamed with horror, so that her cries of despair attracted a peasant, who was driving along at some distance, to the spot. He pulled off the leeches one by one, applied herbs to the wounds, and drove the girl to her master's farm, in his gig.

She was in bed for a fortnight, and as she was sitting outside the door on the first morning that she got up, the farmer suddenly came and planted himself before her.

"Well," he said, "I suppose the affair is settled, isn't it?"

She did not reply at first, and then, as he remained standing and looking at her intently with his piercing eyes, she said with difficulty: "No, master, I cannot."

But he immediately flew into a rage. "You cannot, girl; you cannot? I should just like to know the reason why?"

She began to cry, and repeated: "I cannot."

He looked at her, and then exclaimed, angrily: "Then I suppose you have a lover?"

"Perhaps that is it," she replied, trembling with shame.

The man got as red as a poppy, and stammered out

in a rage: "Ah! So you confess it, you slut! And pray who is the fellow? Some penniless, half-starved ragamuffin, without a roof to his head, I suppose? Who is it, I say?"

And as she gave him no answer, he continued: "Ah! So you will not tell me. Then I will tell you; it is Jean Bauda!"

"No, not he," she exclaimed.

"Then it is Pierre Martin?"

"Oh! no, master."

And he angrily mentioned all the young fellows in the neighborhood, while she denied that he had hit upon the right one, and every moment wiped her eyes with the corner of her blue apron. But he still tried to find it out, with his brutish obstinacy, and, as it were, scratched her heart to discover her secret, as a terrier scratches at a hole to try and get at the animal which he scents in it. Suddenly, however, the man shouted: "By George! It is Jacques, the man who was here last year. They used to say that you were always talking together, and that you thought about getting married."

Rose was choking, and she grew scarlet, while her tears suddenly stopped, and dried up on her cheeks, like drops of water on hot iron, and she exclaimed: "No, it is not he, it is not he!"

"Is that really a fact?" asked the cunning farmer, who partly guessed the truth, and she replied hastily:

"I will swear it; I will swear it to you." She tried to think of something by which to swear, as she did not dare to invoke sacred things.

But he interrupted her: "At any rate, he used to follow you into every corner, and devoured you with his eyes at meal times. Did you ever give him your promise, eh?"

This time she looked her master straight in the face.

"No, never, never; I will solemnly swear to you, that if he were to come today and ask me to marry him, I would have nothing to do with him."

She spoke with such an air of sincerity, that the farmer hesitated, and then he continued, as if speaking to himself: "What, then? You have not had *a misfortune,* as they call it, or it would have been known, and as it has no consequences, no girl would refuse her master on that account. There must be something at the bottom of it, however."

She could say nothing; she had not the strength to speak, and he asked her again: "You will not?"

"I cannot, master," she said, with a sigh, and he turned on his heel.

She thought she had got rid of him altogether, and spent the rest of the day almost tranquilly, but as worn out as if she, instead of the old white horse, had been turning the threshing machine all day. She went to bed as soon as she could, and fell asleep immediately. In the middle of the night, however, two hands touching the bed woke her. She trembled with fear, but she immediately recognized the farmer's voice, when he said to her: "Don't be frightened, Rose; I have come to speak to you."

She was surprised at first, but when he tried to take liberties with her, she understood what he wanted, and began to tremble violently. She felt quite alone in the darkness, still heavy from sleep, and quite unprotected, by the side of the man who stood near her. She certainly did not consent, but resisted carelessly, herself struggling against that instinct which is always strong in simple natures, and very imperfectly protected, by the undecided will of an exhausted body. She turned her head now to the wall, and now toward the room, in order to avoid the attentions which the farmer tried to press on her, and her body writhed under the coverlet, weakened as she was by the fatigue of the struggle, while he became brutal, intoxicated by desire.

They lived together as man and wife, and one morning he said to her: "I have put up our banns, and we will get married next month."

She did not reply, for what could she say? She did not resist, for what could she do?

IV

She married him. She felt as if she were in a pit with inaccessible edges, from which she could never get out, and all kinds of misfortunes remained hanging over her head, like huge rocks, which would fall on the first occasion. Her husband gave her the impression of a man whom she had stolen, and who would find it out some day or other. And then she thought of her child, who was the cause of her misfortunes, but was also the cause of all her happiness on earth. She went to see him twice a year, and she came back more unhappy each time.

But she gradually grew accustomed to her life, her fears were allayed, her heart was at rest, and she lived with an easier mind, though still with some vague fear floating in her mind. So years went on, and the child was six. She was almost happy now, when suddenly the farmer's temper grew very bad.

For two or three years, he seemed to have been nursing some secret anxiety, to be troubled by some care, some mental disturbance, which was gradually increasing. He remained at table a long time after dinner, with his head in his hands, sad and devoured by sorrow. He always spoke hastily, sometimes even brutally, and it even seemed as if he bore a grudge against his wife, for at times he answered her roughly, almost angrily.

One day, when a neighbor's boy came for some eggs, and she spoke rather crossly to him, for she was very busy, her husband suddenly came in, and said to her in his unpleasant voice: "If that were your own child, you would not treat him so."

She was hurt and did not reply, and then she went back into the house with all her grief awakened afresh. At dinner, the farmer neither spoke to her nor looked at her, and seemed to hate her, to despise her, to know something about the affair at last. In consequence, she lost her head and did not venture to remain alone with him after the meal was over, but left the room and hastened to the church.

It was getting dusk; the narrow nave was in total darkness, but she heard footsteps in the choir, for the sacristan was preparing the tabernacle lamp for the night. That spot of trembling light, which was lost in the darkness of the arches, looked to Rose like her last hope, and with her eyes fixed on it, she fell on her knees. The chain rattled as the little lamp swung up into the air, and almost immediately the small bell rang out the "Angelus" through the increasing mist. She went up to him, as he was going out.

"Is Monsieur le Curé at home?" she asked.

"Of course he is; this is his dinner-time."

She trembled as she rang the bell of the parsonage. The priest was just sitting down to dinner, and he made her sit down also. "Yes, yes, I know all about it; your husband has mentioned the matter to me that brings you here."

The poor woman nearly fainted, and the priest continued: "What do you want, my child?" And he hastily swallowed several spoonfuls of soup, some of which dropped on to his greasy cassock. But Rose did not venture to say anything more, but got up to go, while the priest said: "Courage."

So she went out, and returned to the farm, without knowing what she was doing. The farmer was waiting for her, as the laborers had gone away during her absence, and she fell heavily at his feet, and shedding a flood of tears, she said to him: "What have you got against me?"

He began to shout and to swear: "What have I got against you? That I have no children, by God! When a man takes a wife, he does not want to be left alone with her until the end of his days. That is what I have against you. When a cow has no calves, she is not worth anything, and when a woman has no children, she is also not worth anything."

She began to cry, and said: "It is not my fault! It is not my fault!"

He grew rather more gentle when he heard that, and added: "I do not say that it is, but it is very annoying, all the same."

V

From that day forward, she had only one thought— to have a child, another child. She confided her wish to everybody, and in consequence of this, a neighbor told her of an infallible method. This was, to make her husband a glass of water with a pinch of ashes in it, every evening. The farmer consented to try it, but without success; so they said to each other: "Perhaps there are some secret ways?" And they tried to find out. They were told of a shepherd who lived ten leagues off, and so Vallin one day drove off to consult him. The shepherd gave him a loaf on which he had made some marks; it was kneaded up with herbs, and both of them were to eat a piece of it before and after their mutual caresses; but they ate the whole loaf without obtaining any results from it.

Next, a schoolmaster unveiled mysteries and processes of love which were unknown in the country, but infallible, so he declared; but none of them had the desired effect. Then the priest advised them to make a pilgrimage to the shrine at Fécamp. Rose went with the crowd and prostrated herself in the abbey, and mingling her prayers with the coarse wishes of the peasants around her, she prayed that she might be fruitful a second time; but it was in vain, and then she thought that she was being punished for her first fault, and she was seized by terrible grief. She was wasting away with sorrow; her husband was growing old prematurely, and was wearing himself out in useless hopes.

Then war broke out between them; he called her names and beat her. They quarreled all day long, and when they were in bed together at night he flung insults and obscenities at her, panting with rage, until one night, not being able to think of any means of making her suffer more, he ordered her to get up and go and stand out of doors in the rain, until daylight. As she did not obey him, he seized her by the neck, and began to strike her in the face with his fists, but she said nothing, and did not move. In his exasperation he knelt on her, and with clenched teeth and mad with rage began to beat her. Then in her despair she rebelled, and flinging him against the wall with a furious gesture, she sat up, and in an altered voice, she hissed: "I have had a child, I have had one! I had it by Jacques; you know Jacques well. He promised to marry me, but he left this neighborhood without keeping his word."

The man was thunderstruck, and could hardly speak, but at last he stammered out: "What are you saying? What are you saying?"

Then she began to sob, and amid her tears she said: "That was the reason why I did not want to marry you. I could not tell you, for you would have left me without any bread for my child. You have never had any children, so you cannot understand, you cannot understand!"

He said again, mechanically, with increasing surprise: "You have a child? You have a child?"

"You won me by force, as I suppose you know. I did not want to marry you," she said, still sobbing.

Then he got up, lighted the candle, and began to walk up and down, with his arms behind him. She was cowering on the bed and crying, and suddenly he stopped in front of her, and said: "Then it is my fault that you have no children?"

She gave him no answer, and he began to walk up and down again, and then, stopping again, he continued: "How old is your child?"

"Just six," she whispered.

"Why did you not tell me about it?" he asked.

"How could I?" she replied, with a sigh.

He remained standing, motionless. "Come, get up," he said.

She got up, with some difficulty, and then when she was standing on the floor, he suddenly began to laugh, with his hearty laugh of his good days, and seeing how surprised she was, he added: "Very well, we will go and fetch the child, as you and I can have none together."

She was so frightened that if she had the strength she would assuredly have run away, but the farmer rubbed his hands and said: "I wanted to adopt one, and now we have found one. I asked the Curé about an orphan, some time ago."

Then, still laughing, he kissed his weeping and agitated wife on both cheeks, and shouted out, as if she could not hear him: "Come along, mother, we will go and see whether there is any soup left; I should not mind a plateful."

She put on her petticoat, and they went downstairs; and while she was kneeling in front of the fireplace, and lighting the fire under the saucepan, he continued to walk up and down the kitchen with long strides, and said: "Well, I am really glad at this; I am not saying it for form's sake, but I am glad, I am really very glad."

That Pig of a Morin

"THERE, my friend," I said to Labarbe, "you have just repeated those five words, 'That pig of a Morin.' Why on earth do I never hear Morin's name mentioned without his being called *a pig?*"

Labarbe, who is a Deputy, looked at me with eyes like an owl's, and said: "Do you mean to say that you do not know Morin's story, and yet come from La Rochelle?" I was obliged to declare that I did not know Morin's story, and then Labarbe rubbed his hands, and began his recital.

"You knew Morin, did you not, and you remember his large linen-draper's shop on the Quai de la Rochelle?"

"Yes, perfectly."

"All right, then. You must know that in 1862 or '63 Morin went to spend a fortnight in Paris for pleasure, or for his pleasures, but under the pretext of renewing his stock, and you also know what a fortnight in Paris means for a country shopkeeper; it makes his blood grow hot. The theater every evening, women's dresses rustling up against you, and continual excitement; one goes almost mad with it. One sees nothing but dancers in tights, actresses in very low dresses, round legs, fat shoulders, all nearly within reach of one's hands, without daring or being able to touch, and one scarcely ever tastes an inferior dish. And one leaves it, with heart still all in a flutter, and a mind still exhilarated by a sort of longing for kisses which tickle one's lips.

"Morin was in that state when he took his ticket for La Rochelle by the 8.40 night express. And he was walking up and down the waiting-room at the station, when he stopped suddenly in front of a young lady who was kissing an old one. She had her veil up, and Morin murmured with delight: 'By Jove what a pretty woman!'

"When she had said 'Good-bye' to the old lady, she went into the waiting-room, and Morin followed her; then she went onto the platform and Morin still followed her; then she got into an empty carriage, and he again followed her. There were very few travelers by the express, the engine whistled, and the train started. They were alone. Morin devoured her with his eyes. She appeared to be about nineteen or twenty, and was fair, tall, and with demure looks. She wrapped a railway rug round her legs and stretched herself on the seat to sleep.

"Morin asked himself: 'I wonder who she is?' And a thousand conjectures, a thousand projects went through his head. He said to himself: 'So many adventures are told as happening on railway journeys, that this may be one that is going to present itself to me. Who knows? A piece of good luck like that happens very quickly, and perhaps I need only be a little venturesome. Was it not Danton who said: "Audacity, more audacity, and always audacity." If it was not Danton it was Mirabeau, but that does not matter. But then, I have no audacity, and that is the difficulty. Oh! If one only knew, if one could only read people's minds! I will bet that every day one passes by magnificent opportunities without knowing it, though a gesture would be enough to let me know that she did not ask for anything better.'

"Then he imagined to himself combinations which led him to triumph. He pictured some chivalrous deed, or merely some slight service which he rendered her, a lively, gallant conversation which ended in a declaration, which ended in—in what you think.

"But he could find no opening; had no pretext, and he waited for some fortunate circumstance, with his heart ravaged, and his mind topsy-turvy. The night passed, and the pretty girl still slept, while Morin was meditating his own fall. The day broke and soon the first ray of sunlight appeared in the sky, a long, clear ray which shone on the face of the sleeping girl, and woke her, so she sat up, looked at the country, then at Morin and smiled. She smiled like a happy woman, with an engaging and bright look, and Morin trembled. Certainly that smile was intended for him, it was a discreet invitation, the signal which he was waiting for. That smile meant to say: 'How stupid, what a ninny, what a dolt, what a donkey you are, to have sat there on your seat like a post all night.

" 'Just look at me, am I not charming? And you have sat like that for the whole night, when you have been alone with a pretty woman, you great simpleton!'

"She was still smiling as she looked at him, she even began to laugh; and he lost his head trying to find something suitable to say, no matter what. But he could think of nothing, nothing, and then, seized with a coward's courage, he said to himself: 'So much the worse, I will risk everything,' and suddenly, without the slightest warning, he went toward her, his arms extended, his lips protruding, and seizing her in his arms, kissed her.

"She sprang up with a bound, crying out: 'Help! help!' and screaming with terror; then she opened the carriage door, and waved her arm outside; then mad with terror she was trying to jump out, while Morin, who was almost distracted, and feeling sure that she would throw herself out, held her by her skirt and stammered: 'Oh! Madame! Oh! Madame!'

"The train slackened speed, and then stopped. Two

guards rushed up at the young woman's frantic signals, and she threw herself into their arms, stammering: 'That man wanted—wanted—to—to—' And then she fainted.

"They were at Mauzé station, and the gendarme on duty arrested Morin. When the victim of his brutality had regained her consciousness, she made her charge against him, and the police drew it up. The poor linen-draper did not reach home till night, with a prosecution hanging over him for an outrage on morals in a public place.

II

"At that time I was editor of *Fanal des Charentes*, and I used to meet Morin every day at the Café du Commerce. The day after his adventure he came to see me, as he did not know what to do. I did not hide my opinion from him, but said to him: 'You are no better than a pig. No decent man behaves like that.'

"He cried. His wife had given him a beating, and he foresaw his trade ruined, his name dragged through the mire and dishonored, his friends outraged and taking no more notice of him. In the end he excited my pity, and I sent for my colleague Rivet, a bantering, but very sensible little man, to give us his advice.

"He advised me to see the Public Prosecutor, who was a friend of mine, and so I sent Morin home, and went to call on the magistrate. He told me that the woman who had been insulted was a young lady, Mademoiselle Henriette Bonnel, who had just received her certificate as governess in Paris, and spent her holidays with her uncle and aunt, who were very respectable tradespeople in Mauzé, and what made Morin's case all the more serious was, that the uncle had lodged a complaint. But the public official had consented to let the matter drop if this complaint were withdrawn, so that we must try and get him to do this.

"I went back to Morin's and found him in bed, ill with excitement and distress. His wife, a tall, raw-boned woman with a beard, was abusing him continually, and she showed me into the room, shouting at me: 'So you have come to see that pig of a Morin. Well, there he is, the darling!' And she planted herself in front of the bed, with her hands on her hips. I told him how matters stood, and he begged me to go and see her uncle and aunt. It was a delicate mission, but I undertook it, and the poor devil never ceased repeating: 'I assure you I did not even kiss her, no, not even that. I will take my oath to it!'

"I replied: 'It is all the same; you are nothing but a pig.' And I took a thousand francs which he gave me, to employ them as I thought best, but as I did not care venturing to her uncle's house alone, I begged Rivet to go with me, which he agreed to do, on the condition that we went immediately, for he had some urgent business at La Rochelle that afternoon. So two hours later we rang at the door of a nice countryhouse. A pretty girl came and opened the door to us, who was assuredly the young lady in question, and I said to Rivet in a low voice: 'Confound it! I begin to understand Morin!'

"The uncle, Monsieur Tonnelet subscribed to *Fanal*, and was a fervent political co-religionist of ours. He received us with open arms, and congratulated us and wished us joy; he was delighted at having the two editors in his house, and Rivet whispered to me: 'I think we shall be able to arrange the matter of that pig of a Morin for him.'

"The niece had left the room, and I introduced the delicate subject. I waved the specter of scandal before his eyes; I accentuated the inevitable depreciation which the young lady would suffer if such an affair got known, for nobody would believe in a simple kiss. The good man seemed undecided, but could not make up his mind about anything without his wife, who would not be in until late that evening. But suddenly he uttered an exclamation of triumph: 'Look here, I have an excellent idea. I will keep you here to dine and sleep, and when my wife comes home, I hope we shall be able to arrange matters.'

"Rivet resisted at first, but the wish to extricate that pig of a Morin decided him, and we accepted the invitation. So the uncle got up radiant, called his niece, and proposed that we should take a stroll in his grounds, saying: 'We will leave serious matters until the morning.' Rivet and he began to talk politics, while I soon found myself lagging a little behind with the girl, who was really charming, charming, and with the greatest precaution I began to speak to her about her adventure, and try to make her my ally. She did not, however, appear the least confused, and listened to me like a person who was enjoying the whole thing very much.

"I said to her: 'Just think, Mademoiselle, how unpleasant it will be for you. You will have to appear in court, to encounter malicious looks, to speak before everybody, and to recount that unfortunate occurrence in the railway carriage, in public. Do you not think, between ourselves, that it would have been much better for you to have put that dirty scoundrel back into his place without calling for assistance, and merely to have changed your carriage?' She began to laugh, and replied: 'What you say is quite true! but what could I do? I was frightened, and when one is frightened, one does not stop to reason with oneself. As soon as I realized the situation, I was very

141

sorry that I had called out, but then it was too late. You must also remember that the idiot threw himself upon me like a madman, without saying a word and looking like a lunatic. I did not even know what he wanted of me.'

"She looked me full in the face, without being nervous or intimidated, and I said to myself: 'She is a funny sort of girl, that: I can quite see how that pig Morin came to make a mistake,' and I went on, jokingly: 'Come, Mademoiselle, confess that he was excusable, for after all, a man cannot find himself opposite such a pretty girl as you are, without feeling a legitimate desire to kiss her.'

"She laughed more than ever, and showed her teeth, and said: 'Between the desire and the act, Monsieur, there is room for respect.' It was a funny expression to use, although it was not very clear, and I asked abruptly: 'Well now, supposing I were to kiss you now, what would you do?' She stopped to look at me from head to foot, and then said calmly: 'Oh! you? That is quite another matter.'

"I knew perfectly well, by Jove, that it was not the same thing at all, as everybody in the neighborhood called me 'Handsome Labarbe.' I was thirty years old in those days, but I asked her: 'And why, pray?'

"She shrugged her shoulders, and replied: 'Well! because you are not so stupid as he is.' And then she added, looking at me slyly: 'Nor so ugly, either.'

"Before she could make a movement to avoid me, I had implanted a hearty kiss on her cheek. She sprang aside, but it was too late, and then she said: 'Well, you are not very bashful, either! But don't do that sort of thing again.'

"I put on a humble look and said in a low voice: 'Oh! Mademoiselle, as for me, if I long for one thing more than another, it is to be summoned before a magistrate on the same charge as Morin.'

" 'Why?' she asked.

"Looking steadily at her, I replied: 'Because you are one of the most beautiful creatures living; because it would be an honor and a glory for me to have offered you violence, and because people would have said, after seeing you: "Well, Labarbe has richly deserved what he has got, but he is a lucky fellow, all the same." '

"She began to laugh heartily again, and said: 'How funny you are!' And she had not finished the word *funny,* before I had her in my arms and was kissing her ardently wherever I could find a place, on her forehead, on her eyes, on her lips occasionally, on her cheeks, in fact, all over her head, some part of which she was obliged to leave exposed, in spite of herself, in order to defend the others. At last she managed to release herself, blushing and angry. 'You are very unmannerly, Monsieur,' she said, 'and I am sorry I listened to you.'

"I took her hand in some confusion, and stammered out: 'I beg your pardon—I beg your pardon, Mademoiselle. I have offended you; I have acted like a brute! Do not be angry with me for what I have done. If you knew—'

"I vainly sought for some excuse, and in a few moments she said: 'There is nothing for me to know, Monsieur.' But I had found something to say, and I cried: 'Mademoiselle, I love you!'

"She was really surprised, and raised her eyes to look at me, and I went on: 'Yes, Mademoiselle, and pray listen to me. I do not know Morin, and I do not care anything about him. It does not matter to me the least if he is committed for trial and locked up meanwhile. I saw you here

last year, and I was so taken with you, that the thought of
you has never left me since, and it does not matter to me
whether you believe me or not. I thought you adorable,
and the remembrance of you took such a hold on me that
I longed to see you again, and so I made use of that fool
Morin as a pretext, and here I am. Circumstances have
made me exceed the due limits of respect, and I can only
beg you to pardon me.'

"She read the truth in my looks, and was ready to
smile again; then she murmured: 'You humbug!' But I
raised my hand, and said in a sincere voice (and I really
believe that I was sincere): 'I swear to you that I am
speaking the truth.'

"She replied quite simply: 'Really?'

"We were alone, quite alone, as Rivet and her uncle
had disappeared in a side walk, and I made her a real
declaration of love, while I squeezed and kissed her
hands, and she listened to it as to something new and
agreeable, without exactly knowing how much of it she
was to believe, while in the end I felt agitated, and
at last really myself believed what I said. I was pale,
anxious, and trembling, and I gently put my arm round
her waist, and spoke to her softly, whispering into the
little curls over her ears. She seemed dead, so absorbed in
thought was she.

"Then her hand touched mine, and she pressed it,
and I gently circled her waist with a trembling, and
gradually a firmer, grasp. She did not move now, and I
touched her cheeks with my lips, and suddenly, without
seeking them, mine met hers. It was a long, long kiss, and
it would have lasted longer still, if I had not heard a
Hum! Hum! just behind me. She made her escape
through the bushes, and I turning round saw Rivet
coming toward me, and walking in the middle of the

path. He said without even smiling: 'So that is the way in which you settle the affair of that pig Morin.'

"I replied, conceitedly: 'One does what one can, my dear fellow. But what about the uncle? How have you got on with him? I will answer for the niece.'

" 'I have not been so fortunate with him,' he replied. Whereupon I took his arm, and we went indoors.

III

"Dinner made me lose my head altogether. I sat beside her, and my hand continually met hers under the tablecloth, my foot touched hers, and our looks encountered each other.

"After dinner we took a walk by moonlight, and I whispered all the tender things I could think of to her. I held her close to me, kissed her every moment, moistening my lips against hers, while her uncle and Rivet were disputing as they walked in front of us. We went in, and soon a messenger brought a telegram from her aunt, saying that she would return by the first train the next morning, at seven o'clock.

" 'Very well, Henriette,' her uncle said, 'go and show the gentlemen their rooms.' She showed Rivet his first, and he whispered to me: 'There was no danger of her taking us into yours first.' Then she took me to my room, and as soon as she was alone with me, I took her in my arms again and tried to excite her senses and overcome her resistance, but when she felt that she was near succumbing, she escaped out of the room, and I got between the sheets, very much put out and excited and feeling rather foolish, for I knew that I should not sleep much. I was wondering how I could have committed such a mistake, when there was a gentle knock at my door, and on my asking who was there, a low voice replied: 'I.'

145

"I dressed myself quickly and opened the door, and she came in. 'I forgot to ask you what you take in the morning,' she said, 'chocolate, tea, or coffee?' I put my arms around her impetuously and said, devouring her with kisses: 'I will take—I will take—' But she freed herself from my arms, blew out my candle, and disappeared, and left me alone in the dark, furious, trying to find some matches and not able to do so. At last I got some and I went into the passage, feeling half mad, with my candlestick in my hand.

"What was I going to do? I did not stop to reason, I only wanted to find her, and I would. I went a few steps without reflecting, but then I suddenly thought to myself: 'Suppose I should go into the uncle's room, what should I say?' And I stood still, with my head a void, and my heart beating.

"But in a few moments, I thought of an answer: 'Of course, I shall say that I was looking for Rivet's room, to speak to him about an important matter,' and I began to inspect all the doors, trying to find hers, and at last I took hold of a handle at a venture, turned it and went it. There was Henriette, sitting on her bed and looking at me in tears. So I gently turned the key, and going up to her on tiptoe, I said: 'I forgot to ask you for something to read, Mademoiselle.' I will not tell you the book I read, but it is the most wonderful of romances, the most divine of poems. And when once I had turned the first page, she let me turn over as many leaves as I liked, and I got through so many chapters that our candles were quite burned out.

"Then, after thanking her, I was stealthily returning to my room, when a rough hand seized me, and a voice—it was Rivet's—whispered in my ear: 'So you have not yet quite settled that affair of Morin's?'

"At seven o'clock the next morning, she herself brought me a cup of chocolate. I have never drunk anything like it, soft, velvety, perfumed, delicious. I could scarcely take away my lips from the cup, and she had hardly left the room when Rivet came in. He seemed nervous and irritable like a man who had not slept, and he said to me crossly: 'If you go on like this, you will end by spoiling the affair of that pig of a Morin!'

"At eight o'clock the aunt arrived. Our discussion was very short, for they withdrew their complaint, and I left five hundred francs for the poor of the town. They wanted to keep us for the day, and they arranged an excursion to go and see some ruins. Henriette made signs to me to stay, behind her uncle's back, and I accepted, but Rivet was determined to go, and though I took him aside, and begged and prayed him to do this for me, he appeared quite exasperated and kept saying to me: 'I have had enough of that pig of a Morin's affair, do you hear?'

"Of course I was obliged to go also, and it was one of the hardest moments of my life. I could have gone on arranging that business as long as I lived, and when we were in the railway carriage, after shaking hands with her in silence, I said to Rivet: 'You are a mere brute!' And he replied: 'My dear fellow, you were beginning to excite me confoundedly.'

"On getting to the *Fanal* office, I saw a crowd waiting for us, and as soon as they saw us, they all exclaimed: 'Well, have you settled the affair of that pig of a Morin?' All La Rochelle was excited about it, and Rivet, who had got over his ill humor on the journey, had great difficulty in keeping himself from laughing as he said: 'Yes, we have managed it, thanks to Labarbe.' And we went to Morin's.

"He was sitting in an easy-chair, with mustard plasters on his legs, and cold bandages on his head, nearly dead with misery. He was coughing with the short cough of a dying man, without anyone knowing how he had caught it, and his wife seemed like a tigress ready to eat him. As soon as he saw us he trembled so violently as to make his hands and knees shake, so I said to him immediately: 'It is all settled, you dirty scamp, but don't do such a thing again.'

"He got up, choking, took my hands and kissed them as if they had belonged to a prince, cried, nearly fainted, embraced Rivet, and even kissed Madame Morin, who gave him such a push as to send him staggering back into his chair. But he never got over the blow: his mind had been too much upset. In all the country round, moreover, he was called nothing but that pig of a Morin, and the epithet went through him like a sword-thrust every time he heard it. When a street-boy called after him: 'Pig!' he turned his head instinctively. His friends also overwhelmed him with horrible jokes, and used to chaff him, whenever they were eating ham, by saying: 'It's a bit of you!' He died two years later.

"As for myself, when I was a candidate for the Chamber of Deputies in 1875, I called on the new notary at Foncerre, Monsieur Belloncle, to solicit his vote, and a tall, handsome, and evidently wealthy lady received me. 'You do not know me again?' she said.

"I stammered out: 'But—no, Madame.'

" 'Henriette Bonnel?'

" 'Ah!' And I felt myself turning pale, while she seemed perfectly at her ease, and looked at me with a smile.

"As soon as she had left me alone with her husband, he took both my hands, and squeezing them as if he meant to crush them, he said: 'I have been intending to

148

go and see you for a long time, my dear sir, for my wife has very often talked to me about you. I know under what painful circumstances you made her acquaintance, and I know also how perfectly you behaved, how full of delicacy, tact, and devotion you showed yourself in the affair—' He hesitated, and then said in a lower tone, as if he had been saying something low and coarse: 'In the affair of that pig of a Morin.' "

The Umbrella

MME. OREILLE was a very economical woman; she thoroughly knew the value of a half-penny, and possessed a whole storehouse of strict principles with regard to the multiplication of money, so that her cook found the greatest difficulty in making what the servants call their "market-penny," while her husband was hardly allowed any pocket-money at all. They were, however, very comfortably off, and had no children. It really pained Mme. Oreille to see any money spent; it was like tearing at her heartstrings when she had to take any of those nice crownpieces out of her pocket; and whenever she had to spend anything, no matter how necessary it was, she slept badly the next night.

Oreille was continually saying to his wife:

"You really might be more liberal, as we have no children and never spend our income."

"You don't know what may happen," she used to reply. "It is better to have too much than too little."

She was a little woman of about forty, very active, rather hasty, wrinkled, very neat and tidy, and with a very short temper. Her husband very often used to complain of all the privations she made him endure; some of them were particularly painful to him, as they touched his vanity.

He was one of the upper clerks in the War Office, and only stayed there in obedience to his wife's wish, so as to increase their income, which they did not nearly spend.

For two years he had always come to the office with the same old patched umbrella, to the great amusement

of his fellow-clerks. At last he got tired of their jokes, and
insisted upon his wife buying him a new one. She bought
one for eight francs and a half, one of those cheap things
which large houses sell as an advertisement. When the
others in the office saw the article, which was being sold
in Paris by the thousand, they began their jokes again,
and Oreille had a dreadful time of it with them. They
even made a song about it, which he heard from morning
till night all over the immense building.

Oreille was very angry, and peremptorily told his
wife to get him a new one, a good silk one, for twenty
francs, and to bring him the bill, so that he might see that
it was all right.

She bought him one for eighteen francs, and said,
getting red with anger as she gave it to her husband:

"This will last you for five years at least."

Oreille felt quite triumphant, and obtained a small
ovation at the office with his new acquisition. When he
went home in the evening, his wife said to him, looking
at the umbrella uneasily:

"You should not leave it fastened up with the elastic;
it will very likely cut the silk. You must take care of it, for
I shall not buy you a new one in a hurry."

She took it, unfastened it, and then remained dumfounded with astonishment and rage. In the middle of
the silk there was a hole as big as a six-penny-piece, as if
made with the end of a cigar.

"What is that?" she screamed.

Her husband replied quietly, without looking at it.

"What is it? What do you mean?"

She was choking with rage and could hardly get out
a word.

"You—you—have burned—your umbrella! Why—
you must be—mad! Do you wish to ruin us outright?"

151

He turned round hastily, as if frightened.

"What are you talking about?"

"I say that you have burned your umbrella. Just look here—"

And rushing at him, as if she were going to beat him, she violently thrust the little circular burned hole under his nose.

He was so utterly struck dumb at the sight of it that he could only stammer out:

"What—what is it? How should I know? I have done nothing, I will swear. I don't know what is the matter with the umbrella."

"You have been playing tricks with it at the office; you have been playing the fool and opening it, to show it off!" she screamed.

"I only opened it once, to let them see what a nice one it was, that is all, I declare."

But she shook with rage, and got up one of those conjugal scenes which make a peaceable man dread the domestic hearth more than a battlefield where bullets are raining.

She mended it with a piece of silk cut out of the old umbrella, which was of a different color, and the next day Oreille went off very humbly with the mended article in his hand. He put it into a cupboard, and thought no more of it than of some unpleasant recollection.

But he had scarcely got home that evening when his wife took the umbrella from him, opened it, and nearly had a fit when she saw what had befallen it, for the disaster was now irreparable. It was covered with small holes, which evidently, proceeded from burns, just as if some one had emptied the ashes from a lighted pipe onto it. It was done for utterly, irreparably.

She looked at it without a word, in too great a passion to be able to say anything. He also, when he saw the damage, remained almost dumb, in a state of frightened consternation.

They looked at each other; then he looked onto the floor. The next moment she threw the useless article at his head, screaming out in a transport of the most violent rage, for she had now recovered her voice:

"Oh! you brute! you brute! You did it on purpose, but I will pay you out for it. You shall not have another."

And then the scene began again. After the storm had raged for an hour, he, at last, was enabled to explain himself. He declared that he could not understand it at all, and that it could only proceed from malice or from vengeance.

A ring at the bell saved him; it was a friend whom they were expecting to dinner.

Mme. Oreille submitted the case to him. As for buying a new umbrella, that was out of the question; her husband should not have another. The friend very sensibly said that in that case his clothes would be spoiled, and they were certainly worth more than the umbrella. But the little woman, who was still in a rage, replied:

"Very well, then, when it rains he may have the kitchen umbrella, for I will not give him a new silk one."

Oreille utterly rebelled at such an idea.

"All right," he said; "then I shall resign my post. I am not going to the office with the kitchen umbrella."

The friend interposed:

"Have this one recovered; it will not cost much."

But Mme. Oreille, being in the temper that she was, said:

"It will cost at least eight francs to recover it. Eight and eighteen are twenty-six. Just fancy, twenty-six francs for an umbrella! It is utter madness!"

The Umbrella

The friend, who was only a poor man of the middle classes, had an inspiration:

"Make your fire insurance pay for it. The companies pay for all articles that are burned, as long as the damage has been done in your own house."

On hearing this advice the little woman calmed down immediately, and then, after a moment's reflection, she said to her husband:

"Tomorrow, before going to your office, you will go to the Maternelle Insurance Company, show them the state your umbrella is in, and make them pay for the damage."

M. Oreille fairly jumped, he was so startled at the proposal.

"I would not do it for my life! It is eighteen francs lost, that is all. It will not ruin us."

The next morning he took a walking-stick when he went out, for, luckily, it was a fine day.

Left at home alone, Mme. Oreille could not get over the loss of her eighteen francs by any means. She had put the umbrella on the dining-room table, and she looked at it without being able to come to any decision.

Every moment she thought of the insurance company, but she did not dare to encounter the quizzical looks of the gentlemen who might receive her, for she was very timid before people, and grew red at a mere nothing, feeling embarrassed when she had to speak to strangers.

But regret at the loss of the eighteen francs pained her as if she had been wounded. She tried not to think of it any more, and yet every moment the recollection of the loss struck her painfully. What was she to do, however? Time went on, and she could not decide; but suddenly, like all cowards, she made up her mind.

"I will go, and we will see what will happen."

But first of all she was obliged to prepare the umbrella so that the disaster might be complete, and the reason of it quite evident. She took a match from the mantelpiece, and between the ribs she burned a hole as big as the palm of her hand. Then she rolled it up carefully, fastened it with the elastic band, put on her bonnet and shawl, and went quickly toward the Rue de Rivoli, where the insurance office was.

But the nearer she got the slower she walked. What was she going to say, and what reply would she get?

She looked at the numbers of the houses; there were still twenty-eight. That was all right, she had time to consider, and she walked slower and slower. Suddenly she saw a door on which was a large brass plate with "La Maternelle Fire Insurance Office" engraved on it. Already! She waited for a moment, for she felt nervous and almost ashamed; then she went past, came back, went past again, and came back again.

At last she said to herself:

"I must go in, however, so I may as well do it now as later."

She could not help noticing, however, how her heart beat as she entered. She went into an enormous room with grated wicket openings all round, and a man behind each of them, and as a gentleman, carrying a number of papers, passed her, she stopped him and said, timidly:

"I beg your pardon, Monsieur, but can you tell me where I must apply for payment for anything that has been accidentally burned?"

He replied in a sonorous voice:

"The first door on the left; that is the department you want."

This frightened her still more, and she felt inclined to run away, to make no claim, to sacrifice her eighteen francs. But the idea of that sum revived her courage, and she went upstairs, out of breath, stopping at almost every other step.

She knocked at a door which she saw on the first landing, and a clear voice said, in answer:

"Come in!"

She obeyed mechanically, and found herself in a large room where three solemn gentlemen, each with a decoration in his buttonhole, were standing talking.

One of them asked her: "What do you want, Madame?"

She could hardly get out her words, but stammered: "I have come—I have come on account of an accident, something—"

He very politely pointed out a seat to her.

"If you will kindly sit down I will attend to you in a moment."

And, returning to the other two, he went on with the conversation.

"The company, gentlemen, does not consider that it is under any obligation to you for more than four hundred thousand francs, and we can pay no attention to your claim to the further sum of a hundred thousand, which you wish to make us pay. Besides that, the surveyor's valuation—"

One of the others interrupted him:

"That is quite enough, Monsieur; the law-courts will decide between us, and we have nothing further to do than to take our leave." And they went out after mutual ceremonious bows.

Oh! if she could only have gone away with them, how gladly she would have done it; she would have run away and given up everything. But it was too late, for the gentleman came back, and said, bowing:

"What can I do for you, Madame?"

She could scarcely speak, but at last she managed to say:

"I have come—for this."

The manager looked at the object which she held out to him in mute astonishment. With trembling fingers she tried to undo the elastic, and succeeded, after several attempts, and hastily opened the damaged remains of the umbrella.

"It looks to me to be in a very bad state of health," he said, compassionately.

"It cost me twenty francs," she said, with some hesitation.

He seemed astonished. "Really! As much as that?"

"Yes, it was a capital article, and I wanted you to see the state it is in."

"Very well, I see; very well. But I really do not understand what it can have to do with me."

She began to feel uncomfortable; perhaps this company did not pay for such small articles, and she said:

"But—it is burned."

He could not deny it.

"I see that very well," he replied.

She remained open-mouthed, not knowing what to say next; then suddenly forgetting that she had left out the main thing, she said hastily:

"I am Mme. Oreille; we are insured in La Maternelle, and I have come to claim the value of this damage. I only want you to have it recovered," she added quickly, fearing a positive refusal.

The manager was rather embarrassed, and said:

"But, really, Madame, we do not sell umbrellas; we cannot undertake such kinds of repairs."

The little woman felt her courage reviving; she was

not going to give up without a struggle; she was not even afraid now, so she said:

"I only want you to pay me the cost of repairing it; I can quite well get it done myself."

The gentleman seemed rather confused.

"Really, Madame, it is such a very small matter! We are never asked to give compensation for such trivial losses. You must allow that we cannot make good pocket-handkerchiefs, gloves, brooms, slippers, all the small articles which are every day exposed to the chances of being burned."

She got red, and felt inclined to fly into a rage.

"But, Monsieur, last December one of our chimneys caught fire, and caused at least five hundred francs' damage. M. Oreille made no claim on the company, and so it is only just that it should pay for my umbrella now."

The manager, guessing that she was telling a lie, said, with a smile:

"You must acknowledge, Madame, that it is very surprising that M. Orielle should have asked no compensation for damages amounting to five hundred francs, and should now claim five or six francs for mending an umbrella."

She was not the least put out, and replied:

"I beg your pardon, Monsieur, the five hundred francs affected M. Oreille's pocket, whereas this damage, amounting to eighteen francs, concerns Mme. Oreille's pocket only, which is a totally different matter."

As he saw that he had no chance of getting rid of her, and that he would only be wasting his time, he said, resignedly:

"Will you kindly tell me how the damage was done?"

She felt that she had won the victory, and said:

The Umbrella

"This is how it happened, Monsieur: In our hall there is a bronze stick- and umbrella-stand, and the other day, when I came in, I put my umbrella into it. I must tell you that just above there is a shelf for the candlesticks and matches. I put out my hand, took three or four matches, and struck one, but it missed fire, so I struck another, which ignited, but went out immediately, and a third did the same."

The manager interrupted her, to make a joke.

"I suppose they were Government matches, then?"

She did not understand him, and went on:

"Very likely. At any rate, the fourth caught fire, and I lit my candle, and went into my room to go to bed; but in a quarter-of-an-hour I fancied that I smelled something burning, and I have always been terribly afraid of fire. If ever we have an accident it will not be my fault, I assure you. I am terribly nervous since our chimney was on fire, as I told you; so I got up, and hunted about everywhere, sniffing like a dog after game, and at last I noticed that my umbrella was burning. Most likely a match had fallen between the folds and burned it. You can see how it has damaged it."

The manager had taken his cue, and asked her:

"What do you estimate the damage at?"

She did not know what to say, as she was not certain what amount to put on it, but at last she replied:

"Perhaps you had better get it done yourself. I will leave it to you."

He, however, naturally refused.

"No, Madame, I cannot do that. Tell me the amount of your claim, that is all I want to know."

"Well!—I think that— Look here, Monsieur, I do not want to make any money out of you, so I will tell you

159

The Umbrella

what we will do. I will take my umbrella to the maker, who will recover it in good, durable silk, and I will bring the bill to you. Will that suit you, Monsieur?"

"Perfectly, Madame; we will settle it on that basis. Here is a note for the cashier, who will repay you whatever it costs you."

He gave Mme. Oreille a slip of paper. She took it, got up, and went out, thanking him, for she was in a hurry to escape lest he should change his mind.

She went briskly through the streets, looking out for a really good umbrella-maker, and when she found a shop which appeared to be a first-class one, she went in, and said, confidently:

"I want this umbrella recovered in silk, good silk. Use the very best and strongest you have; I don't mind what it costs."

Was It a Dream?

I HAD loved her madly!

"Why does one love? Why does one love? How queer it is to see only one being in the world, to have only one thought in one's mind, only one desire in the heart, and only one name on the lips—a name which comes up continually, rising, like the water in a spring, from the depths of the soul to the lips, a name which one repeats over and over again, which one whispers ceaselessly, everywhere, like a prayer.

"I am going to tell you our story, for love only has one, which is always the same. I met her and loved her; that is all. And for a whole year I have lived on her tenderness, on her caresses, in her arms, in her dresses, on her words, so completely wrapped up, bound, and absorbed in everything which came from her, that I no longer cared whether it was day or night, or whether I was dead or alive, on this old earth of ours.

"And then she died. How? I do not know; I no longer know anything. But one evening she came home wet, for it was raining heavily, and the next day she coughed, and she coughed for about a week, and took to her bed. What happened I do not remember now, but doctors came, wrote, and went away. Medicines were brought, and some women made her drink them. Her hands were hot, her forehead was burning, and her eyes bright and sad. When I spoke to her, she answered me, but I do not remember what we said. I have forgotten everything, everything, everything! She died, and I very well remember her slight, feeble sigh. The nurse said: 'Ah!' and I understood, I understood!

"I knew nothing more, nothing. I saw a priest, who said: 'Your mistress?' and it seemed to me as if he were insulting her. As she was dead, nobody had the right to say that any longer, and I turned him out. Another came who was very kind and tender, and I shed tears when he spoke to me about her.

"They consulted me about the funeral, but I do not remember anything that they said, though I recollected the coffin, and the sound of the hammer when they nailed her down in it. Oh! God, God!

"She was buried! Buried! She! In that hole! Some people came—female friends. I made my escape and ran away. I ran, and then walked through the streets, went home, and the next day started on a journey.

"Yesterday I returned to Paris, and when I saw my room again—our room, our bed, our furniture, everything that remains of the life of a human being after death—I was seized by such a violent attack of fresh grief, that I felt like opening the window and throwing myself out into the street. I could not remain any longer among these things, between these walls which had inclosed and sheltered her, which retained a thousand atoms of her, of her skin and of her breath, in their imperceptible crevices. I took up my hat to make my escape, and just as I reached the door, I passed the large glass in the hall, which she had put there so that she might look at herself every day from head to foot as she went out, to see if her toilette looked well, and was correct and pretty, from her little boots to her bonnet.

"I stopped short in front of that looking-glass in

which she had so often been reflected—so often, so often, that it must have retained her reflection. I was standing there, trembling, with my eyes fixed on the glass—on that flat, profound, empty glass—which had contained her entirely, and had possessed her as much as I, as my passionate looks had. I felt as if I loved that glass. I touched it; it was cold. Oh! the recollection! sorrowful mirror, burning mirror, horrible mirror, to make men suffer such torments! Happy is the man whose heart forgets everything that it has contained, everything that has passed before it, everything that has looked at itself in it, or has been reflected in its affection, in its love! How I suffer!

"I went out without knowing it, without wishing it, and toward the cemetery. I found her simple grave, a white marble cross, with these few words:

" 'She loved, was loved, and died.'

"She is there, below, decayed! How horrible! I sobbed with my forehead on the ground, and I stopped there for a long time, a long time. Then I saw that it was getting dark, and a strange, mad wish, the wish of a despairing lover, seized me. I wished to pass the night, the last night, in weeping on her grave. But I should be seen and driven out. How was I to manage? I was cunning, and got up and began to roam about in that city of the dead. I walked and walked. How small this city is, in comparison with the other, the city in which we live. And yet, how much more numerous the dead are than the living. We want high houses, wide streets, and much room for the four generations who see the daylight at the same time, drink water from the spring, and wine from the vines, and eat bread from the plains.

"And for all the generations of the dead, for all that

ladder of humanity that has descended down to us, there is scarcely anything, scarcely anything! The earth takes them back, and oblivion effaces them. Adieu!

"At the end of the cemetery, I suddenly perceived that I was in its oldest part, where those who had been dead a long time are mingling with the soil, where the crosses themselves are decayed, where possibly newcomers will be put tomorrow. It is full of untended roses, of strong and dark cypress-trees, a sad and beautiful garden, nourished on human flesh.

"I was alone, perfectly alone. So I crouched in a green tree and hid myself there completely amid the thick and somber branches. I waited, clinging to the stem, like a shipwrecked man does to a plank.

"When it was quite dark, I left my refuge and began to walk softly, slowly, inaudibly, through that ground full of dead people. I wandered about for a long time, but could not find her tomb again. I went on with extended arms, knocking against the tombs with my hands, my feet, my knees, my chest, even with my head, without being able to find her. I groped about like a blind man finding his way, I felt the stones, the crosses, the iron railings, the metal wreaths, and the wreaths of faded flowers! I read the names with my fingers, by passing them over the letters. What a night! What a night! I could not find her again!

"There was no moon. What a night! I was frightened, horribly frightened in these narrow paths, between two rows of graves. Graves! graves! graves! nothing but graves! On my right, on my left, in front of me, around me, everywhere there were graves! I sat down on one of them, for I could not walk any longer, my knees were so weak. I could hear my heart beat! And I heard something else as well. What? A confused, nameless noise. Was the

noise in my head, in the impenetrable night, or beneath
the mysterious earth, the earth sown with human corpses?
I looked all around me, but I cannot say how long I remained there; I was paralyzed with terror, cold with
fright, ready to shout out, ready to die.

"Suddenly, it seemed to me that the slab of marble
on which I was sitting, was moving. Certainly it was moving, as if it were being raised. With a bound, I sprang on
to the neighboring tomb, and I saw, yes, I distinctly saw
the stone which I had just quitted rise upright. Then the
dead person appeared, a naked skeleton, pushing the
stone back with its bent back. I saw it quite clearly, although the night was so dark. On the cross I could read:

" 'Here lies Jacques Olivant, who died at the age of fifty-one.
He loved his family, was kind and honorable, and died in the
grace of the Lord.'

"The dead man also read what was inscribed on his
tombstone; then he picked up a stone off the path, a
little, pointed stone, and began to scrape the letters carefully. He slowly effaced them, and with the hollows of his
eyes he looked at the places where they had been engraved. Then with the tip of the bone that had been his
forefinger, he wrote in luminous letters, like those lines
which boys trace on walls with the tip of a lucifer match:

" 'Here reposes Jacques Olivant, who died at the age of fifty-
one. He hastened his father's death by his unkindness, as he
wished to inherit his fortune, he tortured his wife, tormented
his children, deceived his neighbors, robbed everyone he could,
and died wretched.'

"When he had finished writing, the dead man stood
motionless, looking at his work. On turning round I saw
that all the graves were open, that all the dead bodies had

emerged from them, and that all had effaced the lies inscribed on the gravestones by their relations, substituting the truth instead. And I saw that all had been the tormentors of their neighbors—malicious, dishonest, hypocrites, liars, rogues, calumniators, envious; that they had stolen, deceived, performed every disgraceful, every abominable action, these good fathers, these faithful wives, these devoted sons, these chaste daughters, these honest tradesmen, these men and women who were called irreproachable. They were all writing at the same time, on the threshold of their eternal abode, the truth, the terrible and the holy truth of which everybody was ignorant, or pretended to be ignorant, while they were alive.

"I thought that *she* also must have written something on her tombstone, and now running without any fear among the half-open coffins, among the corpses and skeletons, I went toward her, sure that I should find her immediately. I recognized her at once, without seeing her face, which was covered by the winding-sheet, and on the marble cross, where shortly before I had read:

" 'She loved, was loved, and died.'

I now saw:

" 'Having gone out in the rain one day, in order to deceive her lover, she caught cold and died.'

"It appears that they found me at daybreak, lying on the grave unconscious."

The False Gems

M. LANTIN had met the young woman at a *soirée*, at the home of the assistant chief of his bureau, and at first sight had fallen madly in love with her.

She was the daughter of a country physician who had died some months previously. She had come to live in Paris, with her mother, who visited much among her acquaintances, in the hope of making a favorable marriage for her daughter. They were poor and honest, quiet and unaffected.

The young girl was a perfect type of the virtuous woman whom every sensible young man dreams of one day winning for life. Her simple beauty had the charm of angelic modesty, and the imperceptible smile which constantly hovered about her lips seemed to be the reflection of a pure and lovely soul. Her praises resounded on every side. People never tired of saying: "Happy the man who wins her love! He could not find a better wife."

Now M. Lantin enjoyed a snug little income of $700, and, thinking he could safely assume the responsibilities of matrimony, proposed to this model young girl and was accepted.

He was unspeakably happy with her; she governed his household so cleverly and economically that they seemed to live in luxury. She lavished the most delicate attentions on her husband, coaxed and fondled him, and the charm of her presence was so great that six years after their marriage M. Lantin discovered that he loved his wife even more than during the first days of their honey-moon.

He only felt inclined to blame her for two things: her love of the theater, and a taste for false jewelry. Her friends (she was acquainted with some officers' wives) frequently procured for her a box at the theater, often for the first representations of the new plays; and her husband was obliged to accompany her, whether he willed or not, to these amusements, though they bored him excessively after a day's labor at the office.

After a time, M. Lantin begged his wife to get some lady of her acquaintance to accompany her. She was at first opposed to such an arrangement; but, after much persuasion on his part, she finally consented—to the infinite delight of her husband.

Now, with her love for the theater came also the desire to adorn her person. True, her costumes remained as before, simple, and in the most correct taste; but she soon began to ornament her ears with huge rhinestones which glittered and sparkled like real diamonds. Around her neck she wore strings of false pearls, and on her arms bracelets of imitation gold.

Her husband frequently remonstrated with her, saying:

"My dear, as you cannot afford to buy real diamonds, you ought to appear adorned with your beauty and modesty alone, which are the rarest ornaments of your sex."

But she would smile sweetly, and say:

"What can I do? I am so fond of jewelry. It is my only weakness. We cannot change our natures."

Then she would roll the pearl necklaces around her fingers, and hold up the bright gems for her husband's admiration, gently coaxing him:

"Look! are they not lovely? One would swear they were real."

M. Lantin would then answer, smilingly:
"You have Bohemian tastes, my dear."

Often of an evening, when they were enjoying a tête-à-tête by the fireside, she would place on the tea table the leather box containing the "trash," as M. Lantin called it. She would examine the false gems with a passionate attention as though they were in some way connected with a deep and secret joy; and she often insisted on passing a necklace around her husband's neck, and laughing heartily would exclaim: "How droll you look!" Then she would throw herself into his arms and kiss him affectionately.

One evening in winter she attended the opera, and on her return was chilled through and through. The next morning she coughed, and eight days later she died of inflammation of the lungs.

M. Lantin's despair was so great that his hair became white in one month. He wept unceasingly; his heart was torn with grief, and his mind was haunted by the remembrance, the smile, the voice—by every charm of his beautiful, dead wife.

Time, the healer, did not assuage his grief. Often during office hours, while his colleagues were discussing the topics of the day, his eyes would suddenly fill with tears, and he would give vent to his grief in heartrending sobs. Everything in his wife's room remained as before her decease; and here he was wont to seclude himself daily and think of her who had been his treasure—the joy of his existence.

But life soon became a struggle. His income, which in the hands of his wife had covered all household expenses, was now no longer sufficient for his own immediate wants; and he wondered how she could have man aged to buy such excellent wines, and such rare delicacies, things which he could no longer procure with his modest resources.

He incurred some debts and was soon reduced to absolute poverty. One morning, finding himself without a cent in his pocket, he resolved to sell something, and, immediately, the thought occurred to him of disposing of his wife's paste jewels. He cherished in his heart a sort of rancor against the false gems. They had always irritated him in the past, and the very sight of them spoiled somewhat the memory of his lost darling.

To the last days of her life, she had continued to make purchases; bringing home new gems almost every evening. He decided to sell the heavy necklace which she seemed to prefer, and which, he thought, ought to be worth about six or seven francs; for although paste it was, nevertheless, of very fine workmanship.

He put it in his pocket and started out in search of a jeweler's shop. He entered the first one he saw; feeling a little ashamed to expose his misery, and also to offer such a worthless article for sale.

"Sir," said he to the merchant, "I would like to know what this is worth."

The man took the necklace, examined it, called his clerk and made some remarks in an undertone; then he put the ornament back on the counter, and looked at it from a distance to judge of the effect.

M. Lantin was annoyed by all this detail and was on the point of saying: "Oh! I know well enough it is not worth anything," when the jeweler said: "Sir, that necklace is worth from twelve to fifteen thousand francs; but I could not buy it unless you tell me now whence it comes."

The widower opened his eyes wide and remained

gaping, not comprehending the merchant's meaning. Finally he stammered: "You say—are you sure?" The other replied dryly: "You can search elsewhere and see if anyone will offer you more. I consider it worth fifteen thousand at the most. Come back here if you cannot do better."

M. Lantin, beside himself with astonishment, took up the necklace and left the store. He wished time for reflection.

Once outside, he felt inclined to laugh, and said to himself: "The fool! Had I only taken him at his word! That jeweler cannot distinguish real diamonds from paste."

A few minutes after, he entered another store in the Rue de la Paix. As soon as the proprietor glanced at the necklace, he cried out:

"Ah, *parbleu!* I know it well; it was bought here."

M. Lantin was disturbed, and asked:

"How much is it worth?"

"Well, I sold it for twenty thousand francs. I am willing to take it back for eighteen thousand when you inform me, according to our legal formality, how it comes to be in your possession."

This time M. Lantin was dumfounded. He replied:

"But—but—examine it well. Until this moment I was under the impression that it was paste."

Said the jeweler:

"What is your name, sir?"

"Lantin—I am in the employ of the Minister of the Interior. I live at No. 16 Rue des Martyrs."

The merchant looked through his books, found the entry, and said: "That necklace was sent to Mme. Lantin's address, 16 Rue des Martyrs, July 20, 1876."

The two men looked into each other's eyes—the

widower speechless with astonishment, the jeweler scenting a thief. The latter broke the silence by saying:

"Will you leave this necklace here for twenty-four hours? I will give you a receipt."

"Certainly," answered M. Lantin, hastily. Then, putting the ticket in his pocket, he left the store.

He wandered aimlessly through the streets, his mind in a state of dreadful confusion. He tried to reason, to understand. His wife could not afford to purchase such a costly ornament. Certainly not. But, then, it must have been a present!—a present!—a present from whom? Why was it given her?

He stopped and remained standing in the middle of the street. A horrible doubt entered his mind—she? Then all the other gems must have been presents, too! The earth seemed to tremble beneath him—the tree before him was falling—throwing up his arms, he fell to the ground, unconscious. He recovered his senses in a pharmacy into which the passers-by had taken him, and was then taken to his home. When he arrived he shut himself up in his room and wept until nightfall. Finally, overcome with fatigue, he threw himself on the bed, where he passed an uneasy, restless night.

The following morning he arose and prepared to go to the office. It was hard to work after such a shock. He sent a letter to his employer requesting to be excused. Then he remembered that he had to return to the jeweler's. He did not like the idea; but he could not leave the necklace with that man. So he dressed and went out.

It was a lovely day; a clear blue sky smiled on the busy city below, and men of leisure were strolling about with their hands in their pockets.

Observing them, M. Lantin said to himself: "The rich, indeed, are happy. With money it is possible to forget even the deepest sorrow. One can go where one pleases, and in travel find that distraction which is the surest cure for grief. Oh! if I were only rich!"

He began to feel hungry, but his pocket was empty. He again remembered the necklace. Eighteen thousand francs! Eighteen thousand francs! What a sum!

He soon arrived in the Rue de la Paix, opposite the jeweler's. Eighteen thousand francs! Twenty times he resolved to go in, but shame kept him back. He was hungry, however—very hungry, and had not a cent in his pocket. He decided quickly, ran across the street in order not to have time for reflection, and entered the store.

The proprietor immediately came forward, and politely offered him a chair; the clerks glanced at him knowingly.

"I have made inquiries, M. Lantin," said the jeweler, "and if you are still resolved to dispose of the gems, I am ready to pay you the price I offered."

"Certainly, sir," stammered M. Lantin.

Whereupon the proprietor took from a drawer eighteen large bills, counted and handed them to M. Lantin, who signed a receipt and with a trembling hand put the money into his pocket.

As he was about to leave the store, he turned toward the merchant, who still wore the same knowing smile, and lowering his eyes, said:

"I have—I have other gems which I have received from the same source. Will you buy them also?"

The merchant bowed: "Certainly, sir."

M. Lantin said gravely: "I will bring them to you." An hour later he returned with the gems.

The large diamond earrings were worth twenty thousand francs; the bracelets thirty-five thousand; the rings, sixteen thousand; a set of emeralds and sapphires, fourteen thousand; a gold chain with solitaire pendant, forty thousand—making the sum of one hundred and forty-three thousand francs.

The jeweler remarked, jokingly:

"There was a person who invested all her earnings in precious stones."

M. Lantin replied, seriously:

"It is only another way of investing one's money."

That day he lunched at Voisin's and drank wine worth twenty francs a bottle. Then he hired a carriage and made a tour of the Bois, and as he scanned the various turn-outs with a contemptuous air he could hardly refrain from crying out to the occupants:

"I, too, am rich!—I am worth two hundred thousand francs."

Suddenly he thought of his employer. He drove up to the office, and entered gaily, saying:

"Sir, I have come to resign my position. I have just inherited three hundred thousand francs."

He shook hands with his former colleagues and confided to them some of his projects for the future; then he went off to dine at the Café Anglais.

He seated himself beside a gentleman of aristocratic bearing, and during the meal informed the latter confidentially that he had just inherited a fortune of four hundred thousand francs.

For the first time in his life he was not bored at the theater, and spent the remainder of the night in a gay frolic.

Six months afterward he married again. His second wife was a very virtuous woman, with a violent temper. She caused him much sorrow.

Hautot Senior and Hautot Junior

IN front of the building, half farmhouse, half manor-house, one of those rural habitations of a mixed character which were all but seigneurial, and which are at the present time occupied by large cultivators, the dogs, lashed beside the apple trees in the orchard near the house, kept barking and howling at the sight of the shooting-bags carried by the gamekeepers and the boys. In the spacious dining-room kitchen, Hautot Senior and Hautot Junior, M. Bermont, the tax-collector, and M. Mondaru, the notary, were taking a bite and drinking some wine before going out to shoot, for it was the opening day.

Hautot Senior, proud of all his possessions, talked boastfully beforehand of the game which his guests were going to find on his lands. He was a big Norman, one of those powerful, ruddy, bony men, who can lift wagonloads of apples on their shoulders. Half peasant, half gentleman, rich, respected, influential, invested with authority, he made his son César go as far as the third form at school, so that he might be an educated man, and there he had brought his studies to a stop for fear of his becoming a fine gentleman and paying no attention to the land.

César Hautot, almost as tall as his father, but thinner, was a good son, docile, content with everything, full of admiration, respect, and deference for the wishes and opinions of his sire.

M. Bermont, the tax-collector, a stout little man, who showed on his red cheeks a thin network of violet

175

veins resembling the tributaries and the winding courses
of rivers on maps, asked:

"And hares—are there any hares on it?"

Hautot Senior answered:

"As many as you like, especially in the Puysatier
lands."

"Which direction shall we begin in?" asked the notary,
a jolly notary, fat and pale, big-paunched too, and
strapped up in an entirely new hunting costume bought
at Rouen.

"Well, that way, through these grounds. We will drive
the partridges into the plain, and we will beat there
again."

And Hautot Senior rose up. They all followed his
example, took their guns out of the corners, examined
the locks, stamped with their feet in order to feel themselves firmer in their boots which were rather hard, not
having as yet been rendered flexible by the heat of the
blood. Then they went out; and the dogs, standing erect
at the ends of their leashes, gave vent to piercing howls
while beating the air with their paws.

They set forth for the lands referred to. These consisted of a little glen, or rather a long undulating stretch
of inferior soil, which had on that account remained un-
cultivated, furrowed with mountain-torrents, covered
with ferns, an excellent preserve for game.

The sportsmen took up their positions at some distance from each other, Hautot Senior posting himself at
the right, Hautot Junior at the left, and the two guests
in the middle. The keeper and those who carried the
game-bags followed. It was the anxious moment when the
first shot is awaited, when the heart beats a little, while
the nervous finger keeps feeling at the trigger every second.

Suddenly the shot went off. Hautot Senior had fired. They all stopped, and saw a partridge breaking off from a covey which was rushing along at great speed to fall down into a ravine under a thick growth of brushwood. The sportsman, becoming excited, rushed forward with rapid strides, thrusting aside the briers which stood in his path, and disappeared in his turn into the thicket in quest of his game.

Almost at the same instant, a second shot was heard.

"Ha! ha! the rascal!" exclaimed M. Bermont, "he will unearth a hare down there."

They all waited, with their eyes riveted on the heap of branches through which their gaze failed to penetrate.

The notary, making a speaking-trumpet of his hands, shouted:

"Have you got them?"

Hautot Senior made no response.

Then César, turning toward the keeper, said to him:

"Just go and assist him, Joseph. We must keep walking in a straight line. We'll wait."

And Joseph, an old stump of a man, lean and knotty, all of whose joints formed protuberances, proceeded at an easy pace down the ravine, searching at every opening through which a passage could be effected with the cautiousness of a fox. Then, suddenly, he cried:

"Oh! come! come! an unfortunate thing has occurred."

They all hurried forward, plunging through the briers.

The elder Hautot, who had fallen on his side, in a fainting condition, kept both his hands over his stomach, from which flowed down upon the grass through the linen vest torn by the lead, long streamlets of blood. As he was laying down his gun, in order to seize the partridge within reach of him, he had let the firearm fall, and the second discharge, going off with the shock, had torn open his entrails. They drew him out of the trench; they removed his clothes and they saw a frightful wound, through which the intestines came out. Then, after having bandaged him the best way they could, they brought him back to his own house, and awaited the doctor, who had been sent for, as well as a priest.

When the doctor arrived, he gravely shook his head, and, turning toward young Hautot, who was sobbing on a chair:

"My poor boy," said he, "this does not look well."

But, when the dressing was finished, the wounded man moved his fingers, opened his mouth, then his eyes, cast around him troubled, haggard glances, then appeared to search about in his memory, to recollect, to understand, and ne murmured:

"Ah! good God! this has done for me!"

The doctor held his hand.

"Why, no, why, no, some days of rest merely—it will be nothing."

Hautot returned:

"It has done for me! My stomach is split open! I know it well."

Then, all of a sudden:

"I want to talk to my son, if I have time."

Hautot Junior, in spite of himself, shed tears, and kept repeating like a little boy:

"P'pa, P'pa, poor P'pa!"

But the father, in a firmer tone:

"Come! stop crying—this is not the time for it. I have to talk to you. Sit down there quite close to me. It will be quickly done, and I shall be more calm. As for the rest of you, kindly give me one minute."

They all went out, leaving the father and son face to face.

As soon as they were alone:

"Listen, son! you are twenty-four years; one can say things like this to you. And then there is not such mystery about these matters as we import into them. You know well that your mother has been seven years dead, isn't that so? and that I am not more than forty-five years myself, seeing that I got married at nineteen? Is not that true?"

The son faltered: "Yes, it is true."

"So then your mother has been seven years dead, and I have remained a widower. Well, a man like me cannot remain without a wife at thirty-eight, isn't that true?"

The son replied: "Yes, it is true."

The father, out of breath, quite pale, and his face contracted with suffering, went on:

"God! what pain I feel! Well, you understand. Man is not made to live alone, but I did not want to take a successor to your mother, since I promised her not to do so. Then—you understand?"

"Yes, Father."

"So, I kept a young girl at Rouen, Rue d'Eperlan 18, in the third story, the second door—I tell you all this, don't forget—but a young girl, who has been very nice to me, loving, devoted, a true woman, eh? You comprehend, my lad?"

"Yes, Father."

"So then, if I am carried off, I owe something to her, something substantial, that will place her in a safe position. You understand?"

"Yes, Father."

"I tell you that she is an honest girl, and that, but for you, and the remembrance of your mother, and again but

for the house in which we three lived, I would have
brought her here, and then married her, for certain—listen—listen, my lad. I might have made a will—I haven't
done so. I did not wish to do so—for it is not necessary
to write down things—things of this sort—it is too hurt-
ful to the legitimate children—and then it embroils everything—it ruins everyone! Look you, the stamped
paper, there's no need of it—never make use of it. If I
am rich, it is because I have not made waste of what I
have during my own life. You understand, my son?"

"Yes, Father."

"Listen again—listen well to me! So then, I have
made no will—I did not desire to do so—and then I knew
what you were; you have a good heart; you are not niggardly, not too near, in any way; I said to myself that
when my end approached I would tell you all about it,
and that I would beg of you not to forget the girl. And
then listen again! When I am gone, make your way to
the place at once—and make such arrangements that she
may not blame my memory. You have plenty of means.
I leave it to you—I leave you enough. Listen! You won't
find her at home every day in the week. She works at
Madame Moreau's in the Rue Beauvoisine. Go there on
a Thursday. That is the day she expects me. It has been
my day for the past six years. Poor little thing! she will
weep!—I say all this to you because I have known you
so well, my son. One does not tell these things in public
either to the notary or to the priest. They happen—everyone knows that—but they are not talked about, save in
case of necessity. Then there is no outsider in the secret,
nobody except the family, because the family consists of
one person alone. You understand?"

"Yes, Father."

"Do you promise?"

"Yes, Father."

"Do you swear it?"

"Yes, Father."

"I beg of you, I implore of you, so do not forget. I bind you to it."

"No, Father."

"You will go yourself. I want you to make sure of everything."

"Yes, Father."

"And, then, you will see—you will see what she will explain to you. As for me, I can say no more to you. You have vowed to do it."

"Yes, Father."

"That's good, my son. Embrace me. Farewell. I am going to break up, I'm sure. Tell them they may come in."

Young Hautot embraced his father, groaning while he did so; then, always docile, he opened the door, and the priest appeared in a white surplice, carrying the holy oils.

But the dying man had closed his eyes and he refused to open them again, he refused to answer, he refused to show, even by a sign, that he understood.

He had spoken enough, this man; he could speak no more. Besides he now felt his heart calm; he wanted to die in peace. What need had he to make a confession to the deputy of God, since he had just done so to his son, who constituted his own family?

He received the last rites, was purified and absolved, in the midst of his friends and his servants on their bended knees, without any movement of his face indicating that he still lived.

He expired about midnight, after four hours' convulsive movements, which showed that he must have suffered dreadfully in his last moments.

II

It was on the following Tuesday that they buried him; the shooting had opened on Sunday. On his return home, after having accompanied his father to the cemetery, César Hautot spent the rest of the day weeping. He scarcely slept at all on the following night, and he felt so sad on awakening that he asked himself how he could go on living.

However, he kept thinking until evening that, in order to obey the last wish of his father, he ought to repair to Rouen next day, and see this girl Catholine Donet, who resided in the Rue d'Eperlan in the third story, second door. He had repeated to himself in a whisper, just as a little boy repeats a prayer, this name and address a countless number of times, so that he might not forget them, and he ended by lisping them continually, without being able to stop or to think of what they were, so much were his tongue and his mind possessed by the commission.

Accordingly, on the following day, about eight o'clock, he ordered Graindorge to be yoked to the tilbury, and set forth at the quick trotting pace of the heavy Norman horse, along the highroad from Ainville to Rouen. He wore his black frock-coat, a tall silk hat on his head, and breeches with straps; and he did not, on account of the occasion, dispense with the handsome costume, the blue overalls which swelled in the wind, protecting the cloth from dust and from stains, and which was to be removed quickly the moment he jumped out of the coach.

He entered Rouen accordingly just as it was striking ten o'clock, drew up, as he had usually done, at the Hôtel des Bon-Enfants, in the Rue des Trois-Marcs, submitted to the hugs of the landlord and his wife and their five children, for they had heard the melancholy news. After that, he had to tell them all the particulars about the accident, which caused him to shed tears, to repel all the proffered attentions which they sought to thrust upon him merely because he was wealthy, and to decline even the breakfast they wanted him to partake of, thus wounding their sensibilities.

Then, having wiped the dust off his hat, brushed his coat and removed the mud stains from his boots, he set forth in search of the Rue d'Eperlan, without venturing to make inquiries from anyone, for fear of being recognized and arousing suspicions.

At length, being unable to find the place, he saw a priest passing by, and, trusting to the professional discretion which churchmen possess, he questioned the ecclesiastic.

He had only a hundred steps farther to go; it was exactly the second street to the right.

Then he hesitated. Up to that moment, he had obeyed, like a mere animal, the expressed wish of the deceased. Now he felt quite agitated, confused, humiliated, at the idea of finding himself—the son—in the presence of this woman who had been his father's mistress. All the morality which lies buried in our breasts, heaped up at the bottom of our sensuous emotions by centuries of hereditary instruction, all that he had been taught, since he had learned his catechism, about creatures of evil life, the instinctive contempt which every man entertains for them, even though he may marry one of them, all the narrow honesty of the peasant in his character, was stirred up within him and held him back, making him grow red with shame.

But he said to himself:

"I promised the father, I must not break my promise."

Then he gave a push to the door of the house bearing the number 18, which stood ajar, discovered a gloomy-looking staircase, ascended three flights, perceived a door, then a second door, came upon the string of a bell, and pulled it. The ringing, which resounded in the apartment before which he stood, sent a shiver through his frame. The door was opened, and he found himself facing a young lady very well dressed, a brunette with a fresh complexion, who gazed at him with eyes of astonishment.

He did not know what to say to her, and she, who suspected nothing, and who was waiting for him to speak, did not invite him to come in. They stood looking thus at one another for nearly half a minute, at the end of which she said in a questioning tone:

"You have something to tell me, Monsieur?"

He falteringly replied:

"I am M. Hautot's son."

She gave a start, turned pale, and stammered out as if she had known him for a long time:

"Monsieur César?"

"Yes."

"And what next?"

"I have come to speak to you on the part of my father."

She articulated: "Oh, my God!"

She then drew back so that he might enter. He shut the door and followed her into the interior. Then he saw a little boy of four or five years playing with a cat, seated on the floor in front of a stove, from which rose the steam of dishes which were being kept hot.

"Take a seat," she said.

He sat down.

She asked:

"Well?"

He no longer ventured to speak, keeping his eyes fixed on the table which stood in the center of the room, with three covers laid on it, one of which was for a child. He glanced at the chair which had its back turned to the fire. They had been expecting him. That was his bread which he saw, and which he recognized near the fork, for the crust had been removed on account of Hautot's bad teeth. Then, raising his eyes, he noticed on the wall his father's portrait, the large photograph taken at Paris the year of the exhibition, the same as that which hung above the bed in the sleeping apartment at Ainville.

The young woman again asked:

"Well, Monsieur César?"

He kept staring at her. Her face was livid with anguish; and she waited, her hands trembling with fear.

Then he took courage.

"Well, Mam'zelle, papa died on Sunday last just after he had opened the shooting."

She was so much overwhelmed that she did not move. After a silence of a few seconds, she faltered in an almost inaudible tone:

"Oh! it is not possible!"

Then, on a sudden, tears showed themselves in her eyes, and covering her face with her hands, she burst out sobbing.

At that point the little boy turned round, and, seeing his mother weeping, began to howl. Then, realizing that this sudden trouble was brought about by the stranger, he rushed at César, caught hold of his breeches with one hand and with the other hit him with all his strength on the thigh. And César remained agitated, deeply aflected, with this woman mourning for his father at one side of him, and the little boy defending his mother at the other. He felt their emotion taking possession of himself, and his eyes were beginning to brim over with the same sorrow; so, to recover his self-command, he began to talk:

"Yes," he said, "the accident occurred on Sunday, at eight o'clock—"

And he told, as if she were listening to him, all the facts without forgetting a single detail, mentioning the most trivial matters with the minuteness of a countryman. And the child still kept assailing him, making kicks at his ankles.

When he came to the time at which his father had spoken about her, her attention was caught by hearing her own name, and, uncovering her face, she said:

"Pardon me! I was not following you; I would like to know—if you do not mind beginning over again."

He related everything at great length, with stoppages, breaks, and reflections of his own from time to time. She listened to him eagerly now perceiving with a woman's keen sensibility all the sudden changes of fortune which his narrative indicated, and trembling with horror, every now and then, exclaiming:

"Oh, my God!"

The little fellow, believing that she had calmed down, ceased beating César, in order to catch his mother's hand, and he listened, too, as if he understood.

When the narrative was finished, young Hautot continued:

"Now, we will settle matters together in accordance with his wishes. Listen: I am well off, he has left me plenty of means. I don't want you to have anything to complain about—"

But she quickly interrupted him:

"Oh! Monsieur César, Monsieur César, not today. I am cut to the heart—another time—another day. No, not today. If I accept, listen! 'Tis not for myself—no, no, no, I swear to you. 'Tis for the child. Besides this provision will be put to his account."

Thereupon César scared, divined the truth, and stammering:

"So then—'tis his—the child?"

"Why, yes," she said.

And Hautot Junior gazed at his brother with a confused emotion, intense and painful.

After a lengthened silence, for she had begun to weep afresh, César, quite embarrassed, went on:

"Well, then, Mam'zelle Donet, I am going. When would you wish to talk this over with me?"

She exclaimed: "Oh! no, don't go! don't go! Don't leave me all alone with Emile. I would die of grief. I have no longer anyone, anyone but my child. Oh! what wretchedness, what wretchedness. Monsieur César! Stop! Sit down again. You will say something more to me. You will tell me what he was doing over there all the week."

And César resumed his seat, accustomed to obey.

She drew over another chair for herself in front of the stove, where the dishes had all this time been simmering, took Emile upon her knees, and asked César a thousand questions about his father with reference to matters of an intimate nature, which made him feel, without reasoning on the subject, that she had loved Hautot with all the strength of her frail woman's heart.

And, by the natural concatenation of his ideas—which were rather limited in number—he recurred once more to the accident, and set about telling the story over again with all the same details.

When he said: "He had a hole in his stomach—you could put your two fists into it," she gave vent to a sort of shriek, and the tears gushed forth again from her eyes.

Then, seized by the contagion of her grief, César began to weep, too, and as tears always soften the fibers of the heart, he bent over Emile whose forehead was close to his own mouth and kissed him.

The mother, recovering her breath, murmured: "Poor lad, he is an orphan now!"

"And so am I," said César.

And they ceased to talk.

But suddenly the practical instinct of the housewife, accustomed to be thoughtful about many things, revived in the young woman's breast.

"You have perhaps taken nothing all the morning, Monsieur César."

"No, Mam'zelle."

"Oh! You must be hungry. You will eat a morsel."

"Thanks," he said, "I am not hungry; I have had too much trouble."

She replied:

"In spite of sorrow, we must live. You will not refuse to let me get something for you! And then you will remain a little longer. When you are gone I don't know what will become of me."

He yielded after some further resistance, and, sitting down with his back to the fire, facing her, he ate a plateful of tripe, which had been bubbling in the stove, and drank a glass of red wine. But he would not allow her to uncork the bottle of white wine. He several times wiped the mouth of the little boy, who had smeared all his chin with sauce.

As he was rising up to go, he asked:

"When would you like me to come back to speak about this business to you, Mam'zelle Donet?"

"If it is all the same to you, say next Thursday, Monsieur César. In that way I would lose none of my time, as I always have my Thursdays free."

"That will suit me—next Thursday."

"You will come to lunch. Won't you?"

"Oh! On that point I can't give you a promise."

"The reason I suggested it is that people can chat better when they are eating. One has more time, too."

"Well, be it so. About twelve o'clock, then."

And he took his departure, after he had again kissed little Emile, and pressed Mademoiselle Donet's hand.

III

The week appeared long to César Hautot. He had never before found himself alone, and the isolation seemed to him insupportable. Till now, he had lived at his father's side, just like his shadow, followed him into the fields, superintended the execution of his orders, and, when they had been a short time separated, again met him at dinner. They had spent the evenings smoking their pipes, face to face with one another, chatting about horses, cows, or sheep, and the grip of their hands when they rose up in the morning might have been regarded as a manifestation of deep family affection on both sides.

Now that César was alone, he went vacantly through the process of dressing the soil in autumn, every moment expecting to see the tall gesticulating silhouette of his father rising up at the end of a plain. To kill time, he entered the houses of his neighbors, told about the accident to all who had not heard of it, and sometimes repeated it to the others. Then, after he had finished his occupations and his reflections, he would sit down at the side of the road, asking himself whether this kind of life was going to last forever.

He frequently thought of Mademoiselle Donet. He liked her. He considered her thoroughly respectable, a gentle and honest young woman, as his father had said. Yes, undoubtedly she was an honest girl. He resolved to act handsomely toward her, and to give her two thousand francs a year, settling the capital on the child. He even experienced a certain pleasure in thinking that he was going to see her on the following Thursday and arrange this matter with her. And then the notion of this brother, this little chap of five, who was his father's son, plagued him, annoyed him a little, and at the same time, excited him. He had, as it were, a family in this brat, sprung from a clandestine alliance, who would never bear the name of Hautot, a family which he might take or leave, just as he pleased, but which would recall his father.

And so, when he saw himself on the road to Rouen on Thursday morning, carried along by Graindorge trotting with clattering foot-beats, he felt his heart lighter, more at peace than he had hitherto felt it since his bereavement.

On entering Mademoiselle Donet's apartment, he saw the table laid as on the previous Thursday, with the sole difference that the crust had not been removed from the bread. He pressed the young woman's hand, kissed Emile on the cheeks, and sat down, more or less as if he were in his own house, his heart swelling in the same way. Mademoiselle Donet seemed to him a little thinner and paler. She must have grieved sorely. She wore now an air of constraint in his presence, as if she understood what she had not felt the week before under the first blow of her misfortune, and she exhibited an excessive deference toward him, a mournful humility, and made touching efforts to please him, as if to pay him back by her attentions for the kindness he had manifested toward her. They were a long time at lunch talking over the business which had brought him there. She did not want so much money. It was too much. She earned enough to live on herself, but she only wished that Emile might find a few sous awaiting him when he grew big. César held out, however, and even added a gift of a thousand francs for herself for the expense of mourning.

When he had taken his coffee, she asked:

"Do you smoke?"

"Yes—I have my pipe."

He felt in his pocket. Good God! He had forgotten it! He was becoming quite woe-begone about it when she offered him a pipe of his father's that had been shut up in a cupboard. He accepted it, took it up in his hand, recognized it, smelled it, spoke of its quality in a tone of emotion, filled it with tobacco, and lighted it. Then he set Emile astride on his knee, and made him play the cavalier, while she removed the tablecloth and put the soiled plates at one end of the sideboard in order to wash them as soon as he was gone.

About three o'clock, he rose up with regret, quite annoyed at the thought of having to go.

"Well! Mademoiselle Donet," he said, "I wish you good evening, and am delighted to have found you like this."

She remained standing before him, blushing, much affected, and gazed at him while she thought of the other.

"Shall we not see one another again?" she said.

He replied simply:

191

"Why, yes, Mam'zelle, if it gives you pleasure."

"Certainly, Mònsieur César. Will next Thursday suit you then?"

"Yes, Mademoiselle Donet."

"You will come to lunch, of course?"

"Well—if you are so kind as to invite me, I can't refuse."

"It is understood, then, Monsieur César—next Thursday, at twelve, the same as today."

"Thursday at twelve, Mam'zelle Donet!"

A Family Affair

THE Neuilly steam-tram had just passed the Porte Maillot, and was going along the broad avenue that terminates at the Seine. The small engine that was attached to the car whistled, to warn any obstacle to get out of its way, let off steam, panted like a person out of breath from running, and its pistons made a rapid noise, like iron legs running. The oppressive heat of the end of a July day lay over the whole city, and from the road, although there was not a breath of wind stirring, there arose a white, chalky, opaque, suffocating, and warm dust which stuck to the moist skin, filled the eyes, and got into the lungs. People were standing in the doors of their houses in search of a little air.

The windows of the steam-tram were down, and the curtains fluttered in the wind. There were very few passengers inside, because on such warm days people preferred the top or the platforms. The few inside consisted of stout women in strange toilettes, shopkeepers' wives from the suburbs, who made up for the distinguished looks which they did not possess by ill-assumed dignity; of gentlemen tired of the office, with yellow faces, who stooped with one shoulder higher than the other, in consequence of long hours of work bending over the desk. Their uneasy and melancholy faces also spoke of domestic troubles, of constant want of money, of former hopes that had been finally disappointed. They all belonged to that army of poor, threadbare devils who vegetate economically in mean, plastered houses, with a tiny

piece of neglected garden, in the midst of fields where
night soil is deposited, on the outskirts of Paris.

A short, fat man, with a puffy face and a big stomach,
dressed in black and wearing a decoration in his buttonhole, was talking to a tall, thin man, attired in a dirty,
white linen suit all unbuttoned, and wearing a white
Panama hat. The former spoke so slowly and hesitat-
ingly, that occasionally it almost seemed as if he stammered; it was Monsieur Caravan, chief clerk in the Admiralty. The other, who had formerly been surgeon on
board a merchant ship, had set up in practice in Courbevoie, where he applied the vague remnants of medical
knowledge which he had retained after an adventurous
life, to healing the wretched population of that district.
His name was Chenet, and strange rumors were current
as to his morality.

Monsieur Caravan had always led the normal life
of a man in a government office. Every morning for the
last thirty years he had invariably gone the same way to
his office, had met the same men going to business at the
same time and nearly on the same spot, returned home
every evening the same way, and again met the same
faces, which he had seen growing old. Every morning,
after buying his half-penny paper at the corner of the
Faubourg Saint-Honoré, he bought his two rolls, and
then went into his office, like a culprit giving himself up
to justice. He got to his desk as quickly as possible, always
feeling uneasy, as if expecting a rebuke for some neglect
of duty of which he might have been guilty.

Nothing had ever occurred to change the monotonous order of his existence; no event affected him except
the work of his office, perquisites, gratuities, and promo-
tion. He never spoke of anything but of his duties, either
at the Admiralty or at home, for he had married the

portionless daughter of one of his colleagues. His mind, which was in a state of atrophy from his depressing daily work, had no other thoughts, hopes, or dreams than such as related to the office, and there was a constant source of bitterness that spoiled every pleasure that he might have had, and that was the employment of so many commissioners of the navy, "tinmen," as they were called, because of their silver-lace, as first-class clerks. Every evening at dinner he discussed the matter hotly with his wife, who shared his angry feelings, and proved to their own satisfaction that it was in every way unjust to give places in Paris to men who ought properly to have been employed in the navy.

He was old now, and had scarcely noticed how his life was passing, for school had merely been exchanged, without any transition, for the office, and the ushers at whom he had formerly trembled were replaced by his chiefs, of whom he was terribly afraid. When he had to go into the rooms of these official despots, it made him tremble from head to foot, and that constant fear had given him a very awkward manner in their presence, a humble demeanor, and a kind of nervous stammering.

He knew nothing more about Paris than a blind man could know, who was led to the same spot by his dog every day. If he read the account of any uncommon events, or of scandals, in his half-penny paper, they appeared to him like fantastic tales, which some pressman had made up out of his own head, in order to amuse the inferior employees. He did not read the political news, which his paper frequently altered, as the cause which subsidized them might require, for he was not fond of innovations, and when he went through the Avenue of the Champs-Elysées every evening, he looked at the surging crowd of pedestrians, and at the stream of carriages, like a traveler who has lost his way in a strange country.

As he had completed his thirty years of obligatory service that year, on the first of January, he had had the cross of the Legion of Honor bestowed upon him, which, in the semi-military public offices, is a recompense for the miserable slavery—the official phrase is, "loyal services"—of unfortunate convicts who are riveted to their desks. That unexpected dignity gave him a high and new idea of his own capacities, and altogether altered him. He immediately left off wearing light trousers and fancy waistcoats, and wore black trousers and long coats, on which his "ribbon," which was very broad, showed off better. He got shaved every morning, trimmed his nails more carefully, changed his linen every two days, from a legitimate sense of what was proper, and out of respect for the national Order of which he formed a part. In fact, from that day he was another Caravan, scrupulously clean, majestic, and condescending.

At home, he said, "my cross," at every moment, and he had become so proud of it that he could not bear to see other men wearing any other ribbon in their buttonholes. He got angry when he saw strange orders, which "nobody ought to be allowed to wear in France," and he bore Chenet a particular grudge, as he met him on a tram-car every evening, wearing a decoration of some sort or another, white, blue, orange, or green.

The conversation of the two men, from the Arc de Triomphe to Neuilly, was always the same. One day they discussed, first of all, various local abuses, which disgusted them both, and the mayor of Neuilly received his full share of the blame. Then, as invariably happens in the company of a medical man, Caravan began to enlarge on the subject of illness, as, in that manner, he hoped to obtain a little gratuitous advice. His mother had been causing him no little anxiety for some time; she had frequent and prolonged fainting fits, and, although she was ninety, she would not take care of herself.

Caravan grew quite tender-hearted when he mentioned her great age, and more than once asked Doctor Chenet, emphasizing the word "doctor"—although the latter had no right to the title, being only an *Officier de Santé*, and, as such, not fully qualified—whether he had often met anyone as old as that. And he rubbed his hands with pleasure; not, perhaps, that he cared very much about seeing the good woman last forever here on earth, but because the long duration of his mother's life was, as it were, an earnest of old age for himself. Then he continued:

"In my family, we last long, and I am sure that, unless I meet with an accident, I shall not die until I am very old."

The *medico* looked at him with pity, glancing for a moment at his neighbor's red face, his short, thick neck, his "corporation," as Chenet called it, that hung down between two flaccid, fat legs, and the apoplectic rotundity of the old, flabby official. Lifting the white Panama hat which he wore from his head, he said, with a snigger:

"I am not so sure of that, old fellow; your mother is as tough as nails, and I should say that your life is not a very good one."

This rather upset Caravan, who did not speak again until the tram put them down at their destination. The two friends got out, and Chenet asked his friend to have a glass of vermuth at the *Café du Globe,* opposite, a place which both of them were in the habit of frequenting. The proprietor, who was a friend of theirs, held out two fingers to them, which they shook across the bottles on the counter, and then they joined three of their friends, who were playing at dominoes, and had been there since midday. They exchanged cordial greetings, with the usual inquiry: "Anything fresh?" Then the three players continued their game, and held out their hands without looking up, when the others wished them "Good night" and went home to dinner.

Caravan lived in a small, two-storied house in Courbevoie, near the meeting of the roads; the ground floor was occupied by a hairdresser. Two bedrooms, a dining-room, and a kitchen formed the whole of their apartments, and Madame Caravan spent nearly her whole time in cleaning them up, while her daughter, Marie-Louise, who was twelve, and her son, Philippe-Auguste, were running about with all the little, dirty, mischievous brats of the neighborhood, and playing in the gutters.

Caravan had installed his mother, whose avarice was notorious in the neighborhood, and who was terribly thin, in the room above them. She was always in a bad temper and never passed a day without quarreling and flying into furious tempers. She used to apostrophize the neighbors standing at their own doors, the costermongers, the street-sweepers, and the street-boys, in the most violent language. The latter, to have their revenge, used to follow her at a distance when she went out and call out rude things after her.

A little servant from Normandy, who was incredibly giddy and thoughtless, performed the household work, and slept on the second floor in the same room as the old woman, for fear of anything happening to her in the night.

When Caravan got in, his wife, who suffered from a chronic passion for cleaning, was polishing up the mahogany chairs, that were scattered about the room, with a piece of flannel. She always wore cotton gloves and adorned her head with a cap, ornamented with many colored ribbons, which was always tilted on one ear, and whenever anyone caught her polishing, sweeping, or washing, she used to say:

"I am not rich; everything is very simple in my house, but cleanliness is my luxury, and that is worth quite as much as any other."

As she was gifted with sound, obstinate, practical common sense, she swayed her husband in everything. Every evening during dinner, and afterward, when they were in bed, they talked over the business in the office, and, although she was twenty years younger, he confided everything to her, as if she had had the direction, and followed her advice in every matter.

She had never been pretty, and now had grown ugly; in addition to that, she was short and thin, while her careless and tasteless way of dressing herself hid the few, small feminine attributes which might have been brought out if she had possessed any skill in dress. Her petticoats were always awry, and she frequently scratched herself, no matter on what place, totally indifferent as to who might be there, and so persistently that anybody who saw her would have thought that she was suffering from something like the itch. The only ornaments that she allowed herself were silk ribbons, which she had in great profusion, and of various colors mixed together, in the pretentious caps which she wore at home.

As soon as she saw her husband she got up, and said, as she kissed him:

"Did you remember Potin, my dear?"

He fell into a chair, in consternation, for that was the fourth time he had forgotten a commission that he had promised to do for her.

"It is a fatality," he said; "it is no good for me to

think of it all day long, for I am sure to forget it in the evening."

But as he seemed really so very sorry, she merely said, quietly:

"You will think of it tomorrow, I daresay. Anything fresh at the office?"

"Yes, a great piece of news: another tinman has been appointed senior chief clerk." She became very serious.

"So he succeeds Ramon. That was the very post that I wanted you to have. And what about Ramon?"

"He retires on his pension."

She grew furious, her cap slid down on her shoulder, and she continued:

"There is nothing more to be done in that shop now. And what is the name of the new commissioner?"

"Bonassot."

She took up the "Naval Year Book," which she always kept close at hand, and looked him up:

" 'Bonassot—Toulon. Born in 1851. Student-Commissioner in 1871. Sub-Commissioner in 1875.'

Has he been to sea?" she continued, and at that question Caravan's looks cleared up, and he laughed until his sides shook.

"Just like Balin—just like Balin, his chief." Then he added an old office joke, and laughed more than ever:

"It would not even do to send them by water to inspect the Point-du-Four, for they would be sick on the penny steamboats on the Seine."

But she remained as serious as if she had not heard him, and then she said in a low voice, while she scratched her chin:

"If only we had a deputy to fall back upon. When the

Chamber hears everything that is going on at the Admiralty, the minister will be turned out—"

She was interrupted by a terrible noise on the stairs. Marie-Louise and Philippe-Auguste, who had just come in from the gutter, were giving each other slaps all the way upstairs. Their mother rushed at them furiously, and taking each of them by an arm, she dragged them into the room, shaking them vigorously. But as soon as they saw their father, they rushed up to him. He kissed them affectionately, and taking one of them on each knee, he began to talk to them.

Philippe-Auguste was an ugly, ill-kempt little brat, dirty from head to foot, with the face of an idiot, and Marie-Louise was already like her mother—spoke like her, repeated her words, and even imitated her movements. She also asked him whether there was anything fresh at the office, and he replied merrily:

"Your friend, Ramon, who comes and dines here every Sunday, is going to leave us, little one. There is a new senior head-clerk."

She looked at her father, and with a precocious child's pity, she said:

"So somebody has been put over your head again!"

He stopped laughing and did not reply. Then, in order to create a diversion, he said, addressing his wife, who was cleaning the windows:

"How is mamma, up there?"

Madame Caravan left off rubbing, turned round, pulled her cap up, as it had fallen quite onto her back, and said, with trembling lips:

"Ah! yes; just speak to your mother about this, for she has created a pretty scene. Just think that a short time ago Madame Lebaudin, the hairdresser's wife, came upstairs to borrow a packet of starch of me, and, as I was not at home, your mother called her *a beggar woman,* and turned her out; but I gave it to the old woman. She pretended not to hear, as she always does when one tells her unpleasant truths, but she is no more deaf than I am, as you know. It is all a sham, and the proof of it is that she went up to her own room immediately without saying a word."

Caravan did not utter a word, and at that moment the little servant came in to announce dinner. In order to let his mother know, he took a broom-handle, which always stood in a corner, and rapped loudly on the ceiling three times, and then they went into the dining-room. Madame Caravan, junior, helped the soup, and waited for the old woman. But she did not come, and the soup was getting cold, so they began to eat slowly, and when their plates were empty, they waited again. Then Madame Caravan, who was furious, attacked her husband:

"She does it on purpose, you know that as well as I do. But you always uphold her."

In great perplexity between the two, he sent up Marie-Louise to fetch her grandmother, and sat motionless, with his eyes down, while his wife tapped her glass angrily with her knife. In about a minute the door flew open suddenly, and the child came in again, out of breath, and very pale, and said quickly:

"Grandmamma has fallen down on the ground."

Caravan jumped up, threw his table-napkin down, and rushed upstairs, while his wife, who thought it was some trick of her mother-in-law, followed more slowly, shrugging her shoulders, as if to express her doubt. When they got upstairs, however, they found the old woman lying at full length in the middle of the room, and when they turned her over they saw that she was insensible and motionless. Her skin looked more wrinkled and yellow than usual, her eyes were closed, her teeth clenched, and her thin body was stiff.

Caravan kneeled down by her and began to moan: "My poor mother! my poor mother!" he said. But the other Madame Caravan said:

"Bah! She has only fainted again, that is all, and she has done it to prevent us from dining comfortably, you may be sure of that."

They put her on the bed, undressed her completely, and Caravan, his wife, and the servant began to rub her, but, in spite of their efforts, she did not recover consciousness, so they sent Rosalie, the servant, to fetch "Doctor" Chenet. He lived a long way off, on the quay going toward Suresnes, and so it was a considerable time before he arrived. He came at last, however, and, after having looked at the old woman, felt her pulse, and auscultated her, he said: "It is all over."

Caravan threw himself on the body, sobbing violently. He kissed his mother's rigid face, and wept so that great tears fell on the dead woman's face, like drops of water. Naturally, Madame Caravan, junior, showed a decorous amount of grief, uttered feeble moans as she stood behind her husband, and she rubbed her eyes vigorously.

But, suddenly, Caravan raised himself up, with his thin hair in disorder, and, looking very ugly in his grief, said:

"But, are you sure, doctor? Are you quite sure?"

The medical man stooped over the body, and, handling it with professional dexterity, as a shopkeeper might do, when showing off his goods, he said: "See, my dear friend, look at her eye."

He raised the eyelid and the old woman's look reappeared under his finger, altogether unaltered, unless, per-

haps, the pupil was rather larger, and Caravan felt a severe shock at the sight. Then Monsieur Chenet took her
thin arm, forced the fingers open, and said, angrily, as if
he had been contradicted:

"Just look at her hand; I never make a mistake, you
may be quite sure of that."

Caravan fell on the bed, and almost bellowed, while
his wife, still whimpering, did what was necessary.

She brought the night-table, on which she spread a
table-napkin. Then she placed four wax candles on it,
which she lighted; then took a sprig of box, which was
hanging over the chimney glass, and put it between the
candles, into the plate, which she filled with clean water,
as she had no holy water. After a moment's rapid reflection, she threw a pinch of salt into the water, no doubt
thinking she was performing some sort of act of consecra-
tion by doing that. When she had finished, she remained
standing motionless, and the medical man, who had been
helping her, whispered to her:

"We must take Caravan away."

She nodded assent, and, going up to her husband,
who was still on his knees, sobbing, she raised him up by
one arm, while Chenet took him by the other.

They put him into a chair, and his wife kissed his
forehead and then began to lecture him. Chenet enforced
her words, and preached firmness, courage, and resignation—the very things which are always wanting in such
overwhelming misfortunes—and then both of them took
him by the arms again and led him out.

He was crying like a big child, with convulsive sobs;
his arms were hanging down and his legs seemed useless;
he went downstairs without knowing what he was doing,
and moved his legs mechanically. They put him into the
chair which he always occupied at dinner, in front of

his empty soup-plate. And there he sat, without moving, with his eyes fixed on his glass, so stupefied with grief that he could not even think.

In a corner, Madame Caravan was talking with the doctor, and asking what the necessary formalities were, as she wanted to obtain practical information. At last, Monsieur Chenet, who appeared to be waiting for some-thing, took up his hat and prepared to go, saying that he had not dined yet; whereupon, she exclaimed:

"What! you have not dined? But stop here, doctor; don't go. You shall have whatever we can give you, for, of course, you will understand that we do not fare sump-tuously." However, he made excuses and refused, but she persisted, and said:

"You really must stop; at times like this people like to have friends near them, and, besides that, perhaps you will be able to persuade my husband to take some nourishment; he must keep up his strength."

The doctor bowed, and, putting down his hat, said:

"In that case, I will accept your invitation, Madame."

She gave Rosalie, who seemed to have lost her head, some orders, and then sat down, "to pretend to eat," as she said, "to keep the 'doctor' company."

The soup was brought in again, and Monsieur Chenet took two helpings. Then there came a dish of tripe, which exhaled a smell of onions, and which Mad-ame Caravan made up her mind to taste.

"It is excellent," the doctor said, at which she smiled, and, turning to her husband, she said:

"Do take a little, my poor Alfred, only just to get something into your stomach. Remember that you have got to pass the night watching by her!"

He held out his plate, docilely, just as he would have gone to bed if he had been told to, obeying her in everything without resistance and without reflection, and, therefore, he ate. The doctor helped himself three times, while Madame Caravan, from time to time, fished out a large piece at the end of her fork, and swallowed it with a sort of studied inattention.

When a salad bowl full of macaroni was brought in, the doctor said:

"By Jove! That is what I am very fond of." And this time Madame Caravan helped everybody. She even filled the children's saucers, which they had scraped clean, and who, being left to themselves, had been drinking wine without any water, and were now kicking each other under the table.

Chenet remembered that Rossini, the composer, had been very fond of that Italian dish, and suddenly he exclaimed:

"Why! that rhymes, and one could begin some lines like this:

"The Maestro Rossini
Was fond of macaroni."

Nobody listened to him, however. Madame Caravan, who had suddenly grown thoughtful, was thinking of all the probable consequences of the event, while her husband made bread pellets, which he put on the tablecloth, and looked at with a fixed, idiotic stare. As he was devoured by thirst, he was continually raising his glass to his lips, and the consequence was that his senses, already rather upset by the shock and grief, seemed to dance about vaguely in his head, as if they were going to vanish altogether.

Meanwhile, the doctor, who had been drinking away steadily, was getting visibly drunk, and Madame Caravan herself felt the reaction which follows all nervous shocks. She was agitated and excited, and although she had been drinking nothing but water, she felt her head rather confused.

By and by, Chenet began to relate stories of deaths, that appeared funny to him. In the suburbs of Paris, which are full of people from the provinces, one meets with the indifference toward death, even of a father or a mother, which all peasants show; a want of respect, an unconscious callousness which is common in the country, and rare in Paris. Said he:

"Why, I was sent for last week to the Rue du Puteaux, and when I went, I found the sick person (and there was the whole family calmly sitting near the bed) finishing a bottle of liqueur of aniseed, which had been bought the night before to satisfy the dying man's fancy."

But Madame Caravan was not listening; she was continually thinking of the inheritance, and Caravan was incapable of understanding anything.

Soon Rosalie served coffee, which had been made very strong, and as every cup was well qualified with cognac, it made all their faces red, and confused their ideas still more. To make matters still worse, Chenet suddenly seized the brandy bottle and poured out "a drop just to wash their mouths out with," as he termed it, for each of them. Then, without speaking any more, overcome, in spite of themselves, by that feeling of animal comfort which alcohol affords after dinner, they slowly sipped the sweet cognac, which formed a yellowish syrup at the bottom of their cups.

The children had gone to sleep, and Rosalie carried them off to bed. Then, Caravan, mechanically obeying that wish to forget oneself which possesses all unhappy persons, helped himself to brandy again several times, and his dull eyes grew bright. At last the doctor rose to go, and seizing his friend's arm, he said:

"Come with me; a little fresh air will do you good. When you are in trouble, you must not stick to one spot."

The other obeyed mechanically, put on his hat, took his stick, and went out, and both of them went arm-in-arm toward the Seine, in the starlight night.

The air was warm and sweet, for all the gardens in the neighborhood are full of flowers at that season of the year, and their scent, which is scarcely perceptible during the day, seems to awaken at the approach of night, and mingles with the light breezes which blow upon them in the darkness.

The broad avenue, with its two rows of gas-lamps, which extend as far as the Arc de Triomphe, was deserted and silent, but there was the distant roar of Paris, which seemed to have a reddish vapor hanging over it. It was a kind of continual rumbling, which was at times answered by the whistle of a train at full speed, in the distance, traveling to the ocean through the provinces.

The fresh air on the faces of the two men rather overcame them at first, made the doctor lose his equilibrium a little, and increased Caravan's giddiness, from which he had suffered since dinner. He walked as if he were in a dream; his thoughts were paralyzed, although he felt no great grief, for he was in a state of mental torpor that prevented him from suffering, and he even felt a sense of relief which was increased by the mildness of the night.

When they reached the bridge, they turned to the right and faced the fresh breeze from the river, which rolled along, calm and melancholy, bordered by tall poplar-trees. The stars looked as if they were floating on the water and were moving with the current. A slight, white mist that floated over the opposite banks filled their lungs with a sensation of cold, and Caravan stopped suddenly, for he was struck by that smell from the water, which brought back old memories to his mind. For suddenly, in his mind, he saw his mother again, in Picardy, as he had seen her years before, kneeling in front of their door and washing the heaps of linen, by her side, in the stream that ran through their garden. He almost fancied that he could hear the sound of the wooden beetle with which she beat the linen, in the calm silence of the country, and her voice, as she called out to him: "Alfred, bring me some soap." And he smelled the odor of the trickling water, of the mist rising from the wet ground, of the heap of wet linen which he should never forget, the less that it came back to him on the very evening on which his mother died.

He stopped, with a feeling of despair, feeling heartbroken at that eternal separation. His life seemed cut in half, all his youth gone, swallowed up by that death. All the *former* life was over and done with, all the recollections of his youthful days would vanish; for the future, there would be nobody to talk to him of what had happened in days gone by, of the people he had known of old, of his own part of the country, and of his past life; that was a part of his existence which existed no longer, and the other might as well end now.

And then he saw his mother as she was when younger, wearing well-worn dresses, which he remembered for such a long time that they seemed inseparable from her. He recollected her movements, the different tones of her voice, her habits, her manias, her fits of anger, the wrinkles on her face, the movements of her thin fingers, and all her well-known attitudes, which she would never have again, and clutching hold of the doctor, he began to moan and weep. His lank legs began to tremble, his whole stout body was shaken by his sobs, all he could say was:

"My mother, my poor mother, my poor mother!"

But his companion, who was still drunk, and who intended to finish the evening in certain places of bad repute that he frequented secretly, made him sit down on the grass by the riverside, and left him almost immediately, under the pretext that he had to see a patient.

Caravan went on crying for a long time, and then, when he had got to the end of his tears—when his grief had, so to speak, run out of him—he again felt relief, repose, and sudden tranquillity.

The moon had risen and bathed the horizon in its soft light. The tall poplar-trees had a silvery sheen on them, and the mist on the plain looked like floating snow. The river, in which the stars were reflected, and which looked as if it were covered with mother-of-pearl, was rippled by the wind. The air was soft and sweet, and Caravan inhaled it almost greedily, thinking that he could perceive a feeling of freshness, of calm and of superhuman consolation pervading him.

He really tried to resist that feeling of comfort and relief, and kept on saying to himself: "My mother, my poor mother!" He tried to make himself cry, from a kind of conscientious feeling, but he could not succeed in doing so any longer, and the sad thoughts which had made him sob so bitterly a short time before had almost passed away. In a few moments he rose to go home, and returned slowly, under the influence of that serene night, with a heart soothed in spite of himself.

When he reached the bridge, he saw the last tram-car, ready to start, and the lights through the windows of the *Café du Globe,* and felt a longing to tell somebody of the catastrophe that had happened, to excite pity, to make himself interesting. He put on a woeful face, pushed open the door, and went up to the counter, where the landlord still was. He had counted on creating an effect, and had hoped that everybody would get up and come to him with outstretched hands, and say: "Why, what is the matter with you?" But nobody noticed his disconsolate face, so he rested his two elbows on the counter, and, burying his face in his hands, he murmured: "Good heavens! Good heavens!"

The landlord looked at him and said: "Are you ill, Monsieur Caravan?"

"No, my friend," he replied, "but my mother has just died."

"Ah!" the other exclaimed, and as a customer at the other end of the establishment asked for a glass of Bavarian beer, he went to attend to him, leaving Caravan almost stupefied at his want of sympathy.

The three domino players were sitting at the same table which they had occupied before dinner, totally absorbed in their game, and Caravan went up to them, in search of pity, but as none of them appeared to notice him, he made up his mind to speak.

"A great misfortune has happened to me since I was here," he said.

All three raised their heads slightly at the same instant, but kept their eyes fixed on the pieces which they held in their hands.

"What do you say?"

"My mother has just died."

Whereupon one of them said: "Oh! the devil," with that false air of sorrow which indifferent people assume. Another, who could not find anything to say, emitted a sort of sympathetic whistle, shaking his head at the same time, and the third turned to the game again, as if he were saying to himself: "Is that all!"

Caravan had expected some of those expressions that are said to "come from the heart," and when he saw how his news was received he left the table, indignant at their calmness before a friend's sorrow, although at that moment he was so dazed with grief that he hardly felt it, and went home. When he got in, his wife was waiting for him in her nightgown, sitting in a low chair by the open window, still thinking of the inheritance.

"Undress yourself," she said; "we will talk when we are in bed."

He raised his head, and looking at the ceiling, he said: "But there is nobody up there."

"I beg your pardon, Rosalie is with her, and you can go and take her place at three o'clock in the morning, when you have had some sleep."

He only partially undressed, however, so as to be ready for anything that might happen, and after tying a silk handkerchief round his head, he joined his wife, who had just got in between the sheets. For some time they remained side by side, and neither of them spoke. She was thinking.

Even in bed, her nightcap was adorned with a red bow, and was pushed rather over one ear, as was the way with all the caps that she wore. Presently, she turned toward him and said:

"Do you know whether your mother made a will?"

He hesitated for a moment, and then replied:

"I—I do not think so. No, I am sure that she did not."

His wife looked at him, and she said, in a low, furious voice:

"I call that infamous; here we have been wearing ourselves out for ten years in looking after her, and have boarded and lodged her! Your sister would not have done so much for her, nor I either, if I had known how I was to be rewarded! Yes, it is a disgrace to her memory! I daresay that you will tell me that she paid us, but one cannot pay one's children in ready money for what they do; that obligation is recognized after death; at any rate, that is how honorable people act. So I have had all my worry and trouble for nothing! Oh, that is nice! that is very nice!"

Poor Caravan, who felt nearly distracted, kept on saying:

"My dear, my dear, please, please be quiet."

She grew calmer by degrees, and, resuming her usual voice and manner, she continued:

"We must let your sister know tomorrow."

He started, and said:

"Of course we must; I had forgotten all about it; I will send her a telegram the first thing in the morning."

"No," she replied, like a woman who had foreseen everything, "no, do not send it before ten or eleven o'clock, so that we may have time to turn round before she comes. It does not take more than two hours to get here from Charenton, and we can say that you lost your head from grief. If we let her know in the course of the day that will be soon enough, and will give us time to look round."

But Caravan put his hand to his forehead, and, in the same timid voice in which he always spoke of his chief, the very thought of whom made him tremble, he said:

"I must let them know at the office."

"Why?" she replied. "On such occasions, it is always

excusable to forget. Take my advice, and don't let him know; your chief will not be able to say anything to you, and you will put him into a nice fix."

"Oh! yes, I shall, indeed, and he will be in a terrible rage, too, when he notices my absence. Yes, you are right; it is a capital idea, and when I tell him that my mother is dead, he will be obliged to hold his tongue."

And he rubbed his hands in delight at the joke, when he thought of his chief's face; while the body of the dead old woman lay upstairs, and the servant was asleep close to it.

But Madame Caravan grew thoughtful, as if she were preoccupied by something which she did not care to mention. But at last she said:

"Your mother had given you her clock, had she not; the girl playing at cup and ball?"

He thought for a moment, and then replied:

"Yes, yes; she said to me a long time ago, when she first came here: 'I shall leave the clock to you, if you look after me well.'"

Madame Caravan was reassured, and regained her serenity, and said:

"Well, then, you must go and fetch it out of her room, for if we get your sister here, she will prevent us from having it."

He hesitated: "Do you think so?" That made her angry.

"I certainly think so; as soon as it is in our possession, she will know nothing at all about where it came from; it belongs to us. It is just the same with the chest of drawers with the marble top that is in her room; she gave it to me one day when she was in a good temper. We will bring it down at the same time."

Caravan, however, seemed incredulous, and said:

"But, my dear, it is a great responsibility!"

She turned on him furiously.

"Oh! Indeed! Will you never alter? You would let your children die of hunger, rather than make a move. Does not that chest of drawers belong to us, as she gave it to me? And if your sister is not satisfied, let her tell me so, me! I don't care a straw for your sister. Come, get up, and we will bring down what your mother gave us, immediately."

Trembling and vanquished, he got out of bed, and began to put on his trousers, but she stopped him:

"It is not worth while to dress yourself; your underclothes are quite enough; I mean to go as I am."

They both left the room in their nightclothes, went upstairs quite noiselessly, opened the door, and went into the room, where the four lighted tapers and the plate with the sprig of box alone seemed to be watching the old woman in her rigid repose; for Rosalie, who was lying back in the easy-chair with her legs stretched out, her hands folded in her lap, and her head on one side, was also quite motionless, and snoring with her mouth wide open.

Caravan took the clock, which was one of those grotesque objects that were produced so plentifully under the Empire. A girl in gilt bronze was holding a cup and ball, and the ball formed the pendulum.

"Give that to me," his wife said, "and take the marble top off the chest of drawers."

He put the marble on his shoulder with a considerable effort, and they left the room. Caravan had to stoop in the doorway, and trembled as he went downstairs, while his wife walked backward, so as to light him, holding the candlestick in one hand and the clock under her other arm.

When they were in their own room, she heaved a sigh.

"We have got over the worst part of the job," she said; "so now let us go and fetch the other things."

But the drawers were full of the old woman's wearing apparel which they must manage to hide somewhere, and Madame Caravan soon thought of a plan.

"Go and get that wooden box in the passage; it is hardly worth anything and we may just as well put it here."

And when he had brought it upstairs, the change began. One by one, she took out all the collars, cuffs, chemises, caps, all the well-worn things that had belonged to the poor woman lying there behind them, and arranged them methodically in the wooden box, in such a manner as to deceive Madame Braux, the deceased woman's other child, who would be coming the next day.

When they had finished, they first of all carried the drawers downstairs, and the remaining portion afterward, each of them holding an end. It was some time before they could make up their minds where it would stand best; but at last they settled upon their own room, opposite the bed, between the two windows. As soon as it was in its place, Madame Caravan filled it with her own things. The clock was placed on the chimney-piece in the dining-room. They looked to see what the effect was, and were both delighted with it, agreeing that nothing could be better. Then they got into bed, she blew out the candle, and soon everybody in the house was asleep.

It was broad daylight when Caravan opened his eyes again. His mind was rather confused when he woke up, and he did not clearly remember what had happened for a few minutes; when he did, he felt it painfully, and jumped out of bed, almost ready to cry again.

He very soon went to the room overhead, where

Rosalie was still sleeping in the same position as the night before, for she did not wake up once during the whole time. He sent her to do her work, put fresh tapers in the place of those that had burned out, and then he looked at his mother, revolving in his brain those apparently profound thoughts, those religious and philosophical commonplaces, which trouble people of mediocre minds in the face of death.

But he went downstairs as soon as his wife called him. She had written out a list of what had to be done during the morning, which rather frightened him when he saw it.

1. Give information of the death to the mayor's officer.
2. See the doctor who had attended her.
3. Order the coffin.
4. Give notice at the church.
5. Go to the undertaker.
6. Order the notices of her death at the printer's.
7. Go to the lawyer.
8. Telegraph the news to all the family.

Besides all this, there were a number of small commissions; so he took his hat and went out. As the news had got abroad, Madame Caravan's female friends and neighbors soon began to come in, and begged to be allowed to see the body. There had been a scene at the hairdresser's, on the ground floor, about the matter, between husband and wife, while he was shaving a customer. While busily knitting the woman had said: "Well, there is one less, and one as great a miser as one ever meets with. I certainly was not very fond of her; but, nevertheless, I must go and have a look at her."

The husband, while lathering his customer's chin, said:

"That is another queer fancy! Nobody but a woman

would think of such a thing. It is not enough for them to worry you during life, but they cannot even leave you at peace when you are dead."

But his wife, not put out in the least, replied: "The feeling is stronger than I, and I must go. It has been on me since the morning. If I were not to see her, I should think about it all my life, but when I have had a good look at her, I shall be satisfied."

The knight of the razor shrugged his shoulders, and remarked in a low voice to the gentleman whose cheek he was scraping:

"Now, what sort of ideas do you think these con-founded females have? I should not amuse myself by inspecting a corpse!"

But his wife heard him, and replied very quietly:

"But I do, I do." And then, putting her knitting down on the counter, she went upstairs, to the first floor, where she met two other neighbors. These had just come, and were discussing the event with Madame Caravan, who was giving them the details. Then the four went together to the mortuary chamber. The women went in softly, and, one after the other, sprinkled the bedclothes with the water, kneeled down, made the sign of the cross while they mumbled a prayer, then got up, and, open-mouthed, regarded the corpse for a long time, while the daughter-in-law of the dead woman, with her handkerchief to her face, pretended to be sobbing piteously.

When she turned to walk away, whom should she perceive standing close to the door but Marie-Louise and Philippe-Auguste, who were curiously taking stock of things. Then, forgetting to control her temper, she threw herself upon them with uplifted hands, crying out in a furious voice: "Will you get out of this, you brats."

Ten minutes later, going upstairs again with another

contingent of neighbors, she prayed, wept profusely, performed all her duties, and again caught the children following her upstairs. She boxed their ears soundly, but
the next time she paid no heed to them, and at each fresh
influx of visitors the two urchins followed in the wake,
crowded themselves up in a corner, slavishly imitating
everything they saw their mother do.

When afternoon came round the crowds of curious
people began to diminish, and soon there were no more
visitors. Madame Caravan, returning to her own apartments, began to·make the necessary preparations for the
funeral ceremony, and the defunct was left by herself.

The window of the room was open. A torrid heat
entered along with clouds of dust; the flames of the four
candles were flickering in the direction of the corpse, and
upon the cloth which covered the face, the closed eyes,
the two hands stretched out, small flies alighted, came,
went, and buzzed up and down incessantly, being the
only companions of the old woman during the next hour.

Marie-Louise and Philippe-Auguste, however, had
now left the house, and were running up and down the
street. They were soon surrounded by their playmates,
and by little girls, especially, who were older, and who
were interested in the mysteries of life, and asked questions in the manner of persons of great importance.

"Then your grandmother is dead?"

"Yes, she died yesterday evening."

"How, in what way did she meet her death?"

Then Marie began to explain, telling all about the
candles and the cadaverous face. It was not long before
great curiosity was aroused in the breasts of all the children, and they asked to be allowed to go upstairs to look
at the departed.

Then Marie-Louise arranged a party for the first

visit, consisting of five girls and two boys—the biggest and the most courageous. She made them take off their shoes so that they might not be discovered. The troop filed into the house and mounted the stairs as stealthily as an army of mice.

Once in the chamber, the little girl, imitating her mother, regulated the ceremony. She solemnly walked in advance of her comrades, went down on her knees, made the sign of the cross, moistened the lips of the corpse with a few drops of water, stood up again, sprinkled the bed, and while the children all crowded together were approaching—frightened and curious, and eager to look at the face and hands of the deceased—she began suddenly to simulate sobbing, and to bury her eyes in her little handkerchief. Then, instantly consoled on thinking of the other children who were downstairs waiting at the door, she withdrew in haste, returning in a minute with another group, and then a third; for all the little ruffians of the neighborhood, even to the little beggars in rags, had congregated in order to participate in this new pleasure. Each time she repeated her mother's grimaces with absolute perfection.

At length, however, she tired of it. Some game or another attracted the children away from the house, and the old grandmother was left alone, forgotten suddenly by everybody.

A dismal gloom pervaded the chamber, and upon the dry and rigid features of the corpse the dying flames of the candles cast occasional gleams of light.

Toward eight o'clock, Caravan ascended to the chamber of death, closed the windows, and renewed the candles. On entering now he was quite composed, evidently accustomed to regard the corpse as though it had been there for a month. He even went the length of declaring that, as yet, there were no signs of decomposition, making this remark just at the moment when he and his wife were about to sit down at table. "Pshaw!" she responded, "she is now in wood; she will keep there for a year."

The soup was eaten without a word being uttered by anyone. The children, who had been free all day, were now worn out by fatigue and were sleeping soundly in their chairs, and nobody ventured to break the silence.

Suddenly the flame of the lamp went down. Mme. Caravan immediately turned up the wick, a prolonged, gurgling noise ensued, and the light went out. She had forgotten to buy oil during the day. To send for it now to the grocer's would keep back the dinner, and everybody began to look for candles. But none were to be found except the night lights which had been placed upon the table upstairs, in the death-chamber.

Mme. Caravan, always prompt in her decisions, quickly dispatched Marie-Louise to fetch two, and her return was awaited in total darkness.

The footsteps of the girl who had ascended the stairs were distinctly heard. Then followed silence for a few seconds, and then the child descended precipitately. She threw open the door affrighted, and in a choked voice murmured: "Oh! papa, grandmamma is dressing herself!"

Caravan bounded to his feet with such precipitation that his chair rolled over against another chair. He stammered out: "You say? What do you say?"

But Marie-Louise, gasping with emotion, repeated: "Grand—grand—grandmamma is putting on her clothes, and is coming downstairs."

Caravan rushed boldly up the staircase, followed by his wife, dumbfounded; but he came to a standstill before the door of the room, overcome with terror, not daring to enter. What was he going to see? Mme. Caravan, more courageous, turned the handle of the door and stepped forward into the room.

The room seemed to be darker, and in the middle of it, a tall emaciated figure moved about. The old woman stood upright, and in awakening from her lethargic sleep, before even full consciousness had returned to her, in turning upon her side and raising herself on her elbow, she had extinguished three of the candles which burned near the mortuary bed. Then, recovering her strength, she got out of bed and began to seek for her things. The absence of her chest of drawers had at first given her some trouble, but, after a little, she had succeeded in finding her things at the bottom of the wooden trunk, and was now quietly dressing. She emptied the dishful of salted water, replaced the box which contained the latter behind the looking-glass, arranged the chairs in their places, and was ready to go downstairs when her son and daughter-in-law appeared.

Caravan rushed forward, seized her by the hands, and embraced her with tears in his eyes, while his wife, who was behind him, repeated in a hypocritical tone of voice: "Oh, what a blessing! Oh, what a blessing!"

But the old woman, not at all moved, without even appearing to understand, as rigid as a statue, and with glazed eyes, simply asked: "Will dinner soon be ready?"

He stammered out, not knowing what he said:

"Oh, yes, mother, we have been waiting for you."

And with an alacrity unusual in him he took her arm, while Mme. Caravan the younger seized the candle and lighted them downstairs, walking backward in front of them, step by step, just as she had done the previous night, in front of her husband, when he was carrying the marble.

On reaching the first floor, she ran against people who were ascending. It was the Charenton family, Mme. Braux, followed by her husband.

The wife, tall and fleshy, opened wide her astonished eyes, ready to take flight. The husband, a shoemaker and socialist, a little hairy man, the perfect image of a monkey, murmured, quite unconcerned: "Well, what next? Is she resurrected?"

As soon as Mme. Caravan recognized them, she made despairing signs to them; then speaking aloud, she said: "Mercy! How do you mean! Look there! What a happy surprise!"

But Mme. Braux, dumbfounded, understood nothing. She responded in a low voice: "It was your dispatch which made us come; we believed it was all over."

Her husband, who was behind her, pinched her to make her keep silent. He added with a malignant laugh, which his thick beard concealed: "It was very kind of you to invite us here. We set out in post-haste"—a remark which showed clearly the hostility that for a long time had reigned between the households. Then, just as the old woman had arrived at the last steps, he pushed forward quickly and rubbed against her cheeks the hair which covered his face, bawling out in her ear, on account of her deafness: "How well you look, mother; sturdy as usual, hey!"

Mme. Braux, in her stupor at seeing the old woman whom they all believed to be dead, dared not even embrace her; and her enormous bulk blocked up the passage and hindered the others from advancing. The old woman, uneasy and suspicious, but without speaking, looked at everyone around her. Her little gray eyes, piercing and hard, fixed themselves now on the one and now on the other. So terrible were they in their expression that the children became frightened.

Caravan, to explain matters, said: "She has been somewhat ill, but she is better now—quite well, indeed, are you not, mother?"

Then the good woman, stopping in her walk, responded in a husky voice, as though it came from a distance: "It was catalepsy. I heard you all the while."

An embarrassing silence followed. They entered the dining-room, and in a few minutes sat down to an improvised dinner.

Only M. Braux had retained his self-possession; his gorilla features grinned wickedly, while he let fall some words of double meaning which painfully disconcerted everyone.

But the clock in the dining-room kept on ticking every second; and Rosalie, lost in astonishment, came in for Caravan, who darted a fierce glance at her as she placed his napkin before him. His brother-in-law even asked him whether it was not one of his days for reception, to which he stammered out, in answer: "No, I have only been executing a few commissions; nothing more."

Next, a packet was brought in, which he began to open sadly; from it dropped out unexpectedly a letter with black borders. Reddening up to the very eyes, Caravan picked up the letter hurriedly, and pushed it into his waistcoat pocket.

His mother had not seen it! She was looking intently at her clock, which stood on the mantelpiece, and the embarrassment increased in midst of a glacial silence. Turning her face toward her daughter, the old woman, from whose eyes flashed fierce malice, said:

A Family Affair

"On Monday you must take me away from here, so that I can see your little girl. I want so much to see her."

Madame Braux, her features illuminated, exclaimed: "Yes, mother, that I will," while Mme. Caravan, the younger, became pale, and seemed to be enduring the most excruciating agony. The two men, however, gradually drifted into conversation, and soon became embroiled in a political discussion. Braux maintained the most revolutionary and communistic doctrines, gesticulating and throwing about his arms, his eyes gleaming like a bloodhound's.

"Property, sir," he said, "is a robbery perpetrated on the working classes; the land is the common property of every man; hereditary rights are an infamy and a disgrace." But, hereupon, he suddenly stopped, having all the appearance of a man who has just said something foolish; then, resuming, after a pause, he said in softer tones: "But, I can see quite well that this is not the proper moment to discuss such things."

The door was opened, and Doctor Chenet appeared. For a moment he seemed bewildered, but regaining his usual smirking expression of countenance, he jauntily approached the old woman, and said:

"Ah, ha! mamma, you are better today. Oh! I never had any doubt but you would come round again; in fact, I said to myself as I was mounting the staircase: 'I have an idea that I shall find the old woman on her feet once more.'" Then he tapped her gently on the back: "Ah! she is as solid as the Pont-Neuf, she will see us all out: you will see if she does not."

He sat down, accepted the coffee that was offered him, and soon began to join in the conversation of the two men, backing up Braux, for he himself had been mixed up in the Commune.

Now the old woman, feeling herself fatigued, wished to leave the room, at which Caravan rushed forward. She thereupon looked him in the eyes and said to him:

"You must carry my clock and chest of drawers upstairs again without a moment's delay."

"Yes, mamma," he replied, yawning, "I will do so."

The old woman then took the arm of her daughter and withdrew from the room. The two Caravans remained rooted to the floor, silent, plunged in the deepest despair, while Braux rubbed his hands and sipped his coffee, gleefully.

Suddenly Mme. Caravan, consumed with rage, attacked him, exclaiming: "You are a thief, a foot-pad, a cur. I would spit in your face, if—I would—I—would—" She could find nothing further to say, suffocating as she was with rage, while Braux still sipped his coffee, with a smile.

His wife, returning just then, looked menacingly at her sister-in-law, and both—the one with her enormous bulk, the other, epileptic and spare, voice changed, hands trembling—flew at one another and seized each other by the throat.

Chenet and Braux now interposed, and the latter, taking his better half by the shoulders, pushed her out of the door in front of him, shouting to his sister-in-law:

"Go away, you slut: you are a disgrace to your relations." Then the two were heard in the street bellowing and shouting at the Caravans, until they had disappeared in the distance.

M. Chenet also took his departure, leaving the Caravans alone, face to face. The husband fell back in his chair, and with the cold sweat standing out in beads on his temples murmured: "What shall I say to my chief tomorrow?"

A Normandy Joke

THE procession came in sight in the hollow road which was shaded by the tall trees which grew on the slopes of the farm. The newly-married couple came first, then the relations, then the invited guests, and lastly the poor of the neighborhood, while the village urchins who hovered about the narrow road like flies, ran in and out of the ranks, or climbed up the trees to see it better.

The bridegroom was a good-looking young fellow, Jean Patu, the richest farmer in the neighborhood. Above all things, he was an ardent sportsman who seemed to lose all common sense in order to satisfy that passion, who spent large sums on his dogs, his keepers, his ferrets, and his guns. The bride, Rosalie Roussel, had been courted by all the likely young fellows in the district, for they all thought her prepossessing and they knew that she would have a good dowry, but she had chosen Patu—partly, perhaps, because she liked him better than she did the others, but still more, like a careful Normandy girl, because he had more crown pieces.

When they went in at the white gateway of the husband's farm, forty shots resounded without any one seeing those who fired. The shooters were hidden in the ditches, and the noise seemed to please the men, who were sprawling about heavily in their best clothes. Patu left his wife, and running up to a farm servant whom he perceived behind a tree, he seized his gun, and fired a shot himself, kicking his heels about like a colt. Then they went on, beneath the apple-trees heavy with fruit, through the high grass and through the herd of calves, who looked at them with their great eyes, got up slowly and remained standing with their muzzles turned toward the wedding party.

The men became serious when they came within measurable distance of the wedding-dinner. Some of them, the rich ones, had on tall, shining silk hats, which seemed altogether out of place there; others had old head-coverings with a long nap, which might have been taken for moleskin, while the humbler among them wore caps. All women had on shawls, which they wore as loose wraps, holding the ends daintily under their arms. They were red, parti-colored, flaming shawls, and their brightness seemed to astonish the black fowls on the dung-heap, the ducks on the side of the pond, and the pigeons on the thatched roofs.

The extensive farm-buildings awaited the party at the end of that archway of apple-trees, and a sort of vapor came out of open door and windows, an almost over-whelming smell of eatables, which permeated the vast building, issuing from its openings and even from its very walls. The string of guests extended through the yard; when the foremost of them reached the house, they broke the chain and dispersed, while behind they were still coming in at the open gate. The ditches were now lined with urchins and poor curious people. The shots did not cease, but came from every side at once, injecting a cloud of smoke, and that powdery smell which has the same intoxicating effects as absinthe, into the atmosphere.

The women were shaking their dresses outside the door to get rid of the dust, were undoing their cap strings and folding their shawls over their arms. Then they went into the house to lay them aside altogether for the time. The table was laid in the great kitchen, which could hold a hundred persons; they sat down to dinner at two o'clock and at eight o'clock they were still eating; the men, in their shirt sleeves, with their waistcoats unbuttoned, and with red faces, were swallowing the food and drink as if they were insatiable. The cider sparkled merrily, clear and golden in the large glasses, by the side of the dark, blood-colored wine, and between every dish they made the *trou,* the Normandy *trou,* with a glass of brandy which inflamed the body, and put foolish notions into the head.

From time to time, one of the guests, being as full as a barrel, would go out for a few moments to get a mouthful of fresh air, as they said, and then return with redoubled appetite. The farmers' wives, with scarlet faces and their corsets nearly bursting, did not like to follow their example, until one of them, feeling more uncomfortable than the others, went out. Then all the rest followed her example, and came back quite ready for any fun, and the rough jokes began afresh. Broadsides of doubtful jokes were exchanged across the table, all about the wedding-night, until the whole arsenal of peasant wit was exhausted. For the last hundred years, the same broad jokes had served for similar occasions, and although everyone knew them, they still hit the mark, and made both rows of guests roar with laughter.

At the bottom of the table four young fellows, who were neighbors, were preparing some practical jokes for the newly-married couple, and they seemed to have got hold of a good one, by the way they whispered and laughed. Suddenly, one of them profiting by a moment of silence, exclaimed: "The poachers will have a good time tonight with this moon! I say, Jean, you will not be looking at the moon, will you?" The bridegroom turned to him quickly and replied: "Only let them come, that's all!" But the other young fellow began to laugh, and said: "I do not think you will neglect your duty for them!"

The whole table was convulsed with laughter, so that the glasses shook, but the bridegroom became furious at the thought that anybody should profit by his wedding to come and poach on his land, and repeated: "I only say: just let them come!"

Then there was a flood of talk with a double meaning which made the bride blush somewhat, although she was trembling with expectation, and when they had emptied the kegs of brandy they all went to bed. The young couple went into their own room, which was on the ground floor, as most rooms in farmhouses are. As it was very warm, they opened the window and closed the shutters. A small lamp in bad taste, a present from the bride's father, was burning on the chest of drawers, and the bed stood ready to receive the young people, who did not stand upon all the ceremony which is usual among refined people.

The young woman had already taken off her wreath and her dress, and was in her petticoat, unlacing her boots, while Jean was finishing his cigar, and looking at her out of the corners of his eyes. It was an ardent look, more sensual than tender, for he felt more desire than love for her. Suddenly with a brusque movement, like a man who is going to set to work, he took off his coat. She had already taken off her boots, and was now pulling off her stockings; then she said to him: "Go and hide yourself behind the curtains while I get into bed."

He seemed as if he were going to refuse, but with a cunning look went and hid himself with the exception of his head. She laughed and tried to cover up his eyes, and they romped in an amorous and happy manner, without shame or embarrassment. At last he did as she asked him, and in a moment she unfastened her petticoat which slipped down her legs, fell at her feet and lay on the floor in a circle. She left it there, stepped over it, naked with the exception of her floating chemise, and slipped into the bed, whose springs creaked beneath her weight. He immediately went up to her, without his shoes and in his trousers, and stooping over his wife sought her lips, which she hid beneath the pillow, when a shot was heard in the distance, in the direction of the forest of Râpées, as he thought.

He raised himself anxiously, and running to the window, with his heart beating, he opened the shutters. The full moon flooded the yard with yellow light, and the silhouettes of the apple-trees made black shadows at his feet, while in the distance the fields gleamed, covered with the ripe corn. But as he was leaning out, listening to every sound in the still night, two bare arms were put round his neck, and his wife whispered, trying to pull him back: "Do leave them alone; it has nothing to do with you. Come to bed."

He turned round, put his arms round her, and drew her toward him, feeling her warm skin through the thin material, and lifting her up in his vigorous arms, he carried her toward their couch, but just as he was laying her on the bed, which yielded beneath her weight, they heard another report, considerably nearer this time. Jean, giving way to his tumultuous rage, swore aloud: "Good God! Do you think I shall not go out and see what it is, because of you? Wait, wait a few minutes!" He put on his shoes again, took down his gun, which was always hanging within reach upon the wall, and, as his wife threw herself on her knees in her terror to implore him not to go, he hastily freed himself, ran to the window and jumped into the yard.

A Normandy Joke

She waited one hour, two hours, until daybreak, but her husband did not return. Then she lost her head, aroused the house, related how angry Jean was, and said that he had gone after the poachers, and immediately all the male farm-servants, even the boys, went in search of their master. They found him two leagues from the farm, tied hand and foot, half dead with rage, his gun broken, his trousers turned inside out, three dead hares hanging round his neck, and a placard on his chest, with these words:

"Who goes on the chase, loses his place."

And later on when he used to tell this story of his wedding night, he generally added: "Ah! As far as a joke went, it was a good joke. They caught me in a snare, as if I had been a rabbit, the dirty brutes, and they shoved my head into a bag. But if I can only catch them some day, they had better look out for themselves!"

That is how they amuse themselves in Normandy on a wedding day.

The Diamond Necklace

SHE was one of those pretty, charming young ladies, born, as if through an error of destiny, into a family of clerks. She had no dowry, no hopes, no means of becoming known, appreciated, loved, and married by a man either rich or distinguished; and she allowed herself to marry a petty clerk in the office of the Board of Education.

She was simple, not being able to adorn herself; but she was unhappy, as one out of her class; for women belong to no caste, no race; their grace, their beauty, and their charm serving them in the place of birth and family. Their inborn finesse, their instinctive elegance, their suppleness of wit are their only aristocracy, making some daughters of the people the equal of great ladies.

She suffered incessantly, feeling herself born for all delicacies and luxuries. She suffered from the poverty of her apartment, the shabby walls, the worn chairs, and the faded stuffs. All these things, which another woman of her station would not have noticed, tortured and angered her. The sight of the little Breton, who made this humble home, awoke in her sad regrets and desperate dreams. She thought of quiet antechambers, with their Oriental hangings, lighted by high, bronze torches, and of the two great footmen in short trousers who sleep in the large armchairs, made sleepy by the heavy air from the heating apparatus. She thought of large drawing-rooms, hung in old silks, of graceful pieces of furniture carrying bric-à-brac of inestimable value, and of the little perfumed coquettish apartments, made for five o'clock chats with most intimate friends, men known and sought after, whose attention all women envied and desired.

When she seated herself for dinner, before the round table where the tablecloth had been used three days, opposite her husband who uncovered the tureen with a delighted air, saying: "Oh! the good potpie! I know nothing better than that—" she would think of the elegant dinners, of the shining silver, of the tapestries peopling the walls with ancient personages and rare birds in the midst of fairy forests; she thought of the exquisite food served on marvelous dishes, of the whispered gallantries, listened to with the smile of the sphinx, while eating the rose-colored flesh of the trout or a chicken's wing.

She had neither frocks nor jewels, nothing. And she loved only those things. She felt that she was made for them. She had such a desire to please, to be sought after, to be clever, and courted.

She had a rich friend, a schoolmate at the convent, whom she did not like to visit, she suffered so much when she returned. And she wept for whole days from chagrin, from regret, from despair, and disappointment.

One evening her husband returned elated, bearing in his hand a large envelope.

"Here," said he, "here is something for you."

She quickly tore open the wrapper and drew out a printed card on which were inscribed these words:

"The Minister of Public Instruction and Madame George Ramponneau ask the honor of Mr. and Mrs. Loisel's company Monday evening, January 18, at the Minister's residence."

Instead of being delighted, as her husband had hoped, she threw the invitation spitefully upon the table murmuring:

"What do you suppose I want with that?"

"But, my dearie, I thought it would make you happy. You never go out, and this is an occasion, and a fine one! I had a great deal of trouble to get it. Everybody wishes one, and it is very select; not many are given to employees. You will see the whole official world there."

She looked at him with an irritated eye and declared impatiently:

"What do you suppose I have to wear to such a thing as that?"

He had not thought of that; he stammered:

"Why, the dress you wear when we go to the theater. It seems very pretty to me—"

He was silent, stupefied, in dismay, at the sight of his wife weeping. Two great tears fell slowly from the corners of his eyes toward the corners of his mouth; he stammered:

"What is the matter? What is the matter?"

By a violent effort, she had controlled her vexation and responded in a calm voice, wiping her moist cheeks:

"Nothing. Only I have no dress and consequently I cannot go to this affair. Give your card to some colleague whose wife is better fitted out than I."

He was grieved, but answered:

"Let us see, Matilda. How much would a suitable costume cost, something that would serve for other occasions, something very simple?"

She reflected for some seconds, making estimates and thinking of a sum that she could ask for without bringing with it an immediate refusal and a frightened exclamation from the economical clerk.

Finally she said, in a hesitating voice:

"I cannot tell exactly, but it seems to me that four hundred francs ought to cover it."

He turned a little pale, for he had saved just this sum to buy a gun that he might be able to join some hunting parties the next summer, on the plains at Nanterre, with some friends who went to shoot larks up there on Sunday. Nevertheless, he answered:

"Very well. I will give you four hundred francs. But try to have a pretty dress."

The day of the ball approached and Mme. Loisel seemed sad, disturbed, anxious. Nevertheless, her dress was nearly ready. Her husband said to her one evening:

"What is the matter with you? You have acted strangely for two or three days."

And she responded: "I am vexed not to have a jewel, not one stone, nothing to adorn myself with. I shall have such a poverty-laden look. I would prefer not to go to this party."

He replied: "You can wear some natural flowers. At this season they look very *chic*. For ten francs you can have two or three magnificent roses."

She was not convinced. "No," she replied, "there is nothing more humiliating than to have a shabby air in the midst of rich women."

Then her husband cried out: "How stupid we are! Go and find your friend Mrs. Forestier and ask her to lend you her jewels. You are well enough acquainted with her to do this."

She uttered a cry of joy: "It is true!" she said. "I had not thought of that."

The next day she took herself to her friend's house and related her story of distress. Mrs. Forestier went to her closet with the glass doors, took out a large jewel-case, brought it, opened it, and said: "Choose, my dear."

The Diamond Necklace

She saw at first some bracelets, then a collar of pearls, then a Venetian cross of gold and jewels and of admirable workmanship. She tried the jewels before the glass, hesitated, but could neither decide to take them nor leave them. Then she asked:

"Have you nothing more?"

"Why, yes. Look for yourself. I do not know what will please you."

Suddenly she discovered, in a black satin box, a superb necklace of diamonds, and her heart beat fast with an immoderate desire. Her hands trembled as she took them up. She placed them about her throat against her dress, and remained in ecstasy before them. Then she asked, in a hesitating voice, full of anxiety:

"Could you lend me this? Only this?"

"Why, yes, certainly."

She fell upon the neck of her friend, embraced her with passion, then went away with her treasure.

The day of the ball arrived. Mme Loisel was a great success. She was the prettiest of all, elegant, gracious, smiling, and full of joy. All the men noticed her, asked her name, and wanted to be presented. All the members of the Cabinet wished to waltz with her. The Minister of Education paid her some attention.

She danced with enthusiasm, with passion, intoxicated with pleasure, thinking of nothing, in the triumph of her beauty, in the glory of her success, in a kind of cloud of happiness that came of all this homage, and all this admiration, of all these awakened desires, and this victory so complete and sweet to the heart of woman.

She went home toward four o'clock in the morning.

Her husband had been half asleep in one of the little salons since midnight, with three other gentlemen whose wives were enjoying themselves very much.

He threw around her shoulders the wraps they had carried for the coming home, modest garments of everyday wear, whose poverty clashed with the elegance of the ball costume. She felt this and wished to hurry away in order not to be noticed by the other women who were wrapping themselves in rich furs.

Loisel retained her: "Wait," said he. "You will catch cold out there. I am going to call a cab."

But she would not listen and descended the steps rapidly. When they were in the street, they found no carriage; and they began to seek one, hailing the coachmen whom they saw at a distance.

They walked along toward the Seine, hopeless and shivering. Finally they found on the dock one of those old, nocturnal *coupés* that one sees in Paris after nightfall, as if they were ashamed of their misery by day.

It took them as far as their door in Martyr street, and they went wearily up to their apartment. It was all over for her. And on his part, he remembered that he would have to be at the office by ten o'clock.

She removed the wraps from her shoulders before the glass, for a final view of herself in her glory. Suddenly she uttered a cry. Her necklace was not around her neck.

Her husband, already half undressed, asked: "What is the matter?"

She turned toward him excitedly:

"I have—I have—I no longer have Mrs. Forestier's necklace."

He arose in dismay: "What! How is that? It is not possible."

And they looked in the folds of the dress, in the folds

of the mantle, in the pockets, everywhere. They could not find it.

He asked: "You are sure you still had it when we left the house?"

"Yes, I felt it in the vestibule as we came out."

"But if you had lost it in the street, we should have heard it fall. It must be in the cab."

"Yes. It is probable. Did you take the number?"

"No. And you, did you notice what it was?"

"No."

They looked at each other utterly cast down. Finally, Loisel dressed himself again.

"I am going," said he, "over the track where we went on foot, to see if I can find it."

And he went. She remained in her evening gown, not having the force to go to bed, stretched upon a chair, without ambition or thoughts.

Toward seven o'clock her husband returned. He had found nothing.

He went to the police and to the cab offices, and put an advertisement in the newspapers, offering a reward; he did everything that afforded them a suspicion of hope.

She waited all day in a state of bewilderment before this frightful disaster. Loisel returned at evening with his face harrowed and pale; he had discovered nothing.

"It will be necessary," said he, "to write to your friend that you have broken the clasp of the necklace and that you will have it repaired. That will give us time to turn around."

She wrote as he dictated.

At the end of a week, they had lost all hope. And Loisel, older by five years, declared:

"We must take measures to replace this jewel."

The next day they took the box which had inclosed it, to the jeweler whose name was on the inside. He consulted his books:

"It is not I, Madame," said he, "who sold this necklace; I only furnished the casket."

Then they went from jeweler to jeweler seeking a necklace like the other one, consulting their memories, and ill, both of them, with chagrin and anxiety.

In a shop of the Palais-Royal, they found a chaplet of diamonds which seemed to them exactly like the one they had lost. It was valued at forty thousand francs. They could get it for thirty-six thousand.

They begged the jeweler not to sell it for three days. And they made an arrangement by which they might return it for thirty-four thousand francs if they found the other one before the end of February.

Loisel possessed eighteen thousand francs which his father had left him. He borrowed the rest.

He borrowed it, asking for a thousand francs of one, five hundred of another, five louis of this one, and three louis of that one. He gave notes, made ruinous promises, took money of usurers and the whole race of lenders. He compromised his whole existence, in fact, risked his signature, without even knowing whether he could make it good or not, and, harassed by anxiety for the future, by the black misery which surrounded him, and by the prospect of all physical privations and moral torture, he went to get the new necklace, depositing on the merchant's counter thirty-six thousand francs.

When Mrs. Loisel took back the jewels to Mrs. Forestier, the latter said to her in a frigid tone:

"You should have returned them to me sooner, for I might have needed them."

She did open the jewel-box as her friend feared she would. If she should perceive the substitution, what would she think? What should she say? Would she take her for a robber?

Mrs. Loisel now knew the horrible life of necessity. She did her part, however, completely, heroically. It was necessary to pay this frightful debt. She would pay it. They sent away the maid; they changed their lodgings; they rented some rooms under a mansard roof.

She learned the heavy cares of a household, the odious work of a kitchen. She washed the dishes, using her rosy nails upon the greasy pots and the bottoms of the stewpans. She washed the soiled linen, the chemises and dishcloths, which she hung on the line to dry; she took down the refuse to the street each morning and brought up the water, stopping at each landing to breathe. And, clothed like a woman of the people, she went to the grocer's, the butcher's, and the fruiterer's, with her basket on her arm, shopping, haggling, defending to the last sou her miserable money.

Every month it was necessary to renew some notes, thus obtaining time, and to pay others.

The husband worked evenings, putting the books of some merchants in order, and nights he often did copying at five sous a page.

And this life lasted for ten years.

At the end of ten years, they had restored all, all, with interest of the usurer, and accumulated interest besides.

Mrs. Loisel seemed old now. She had become a strong, hard woman, the crude woman of the poor household. Her hair badly dressed, her skirts awry, her hands red, she spoke in a loud tone, and washed the floors in large pails of water. But sometimes, when her husband was at the office, she would seat herself before the window and think of that evening party of former times, of that ball where she was so beautiful and so flattered.

How would it have been if she had not lost that necklace? Who knows? Who knows? How singular is life, and how full of changes! How small a thing will ruin or save one!

One Sunday, as she was taking a walk in the Champs-Elysées to rid herself of the cares of the week, she suddenly perceived a woman walking with a child. It was Mrs. Forestier, still young, still pretty, still attractive. Mrs. Loisel was affected. Should she speak to her? Yes, certainly. And now that she had paid, she would tell her all. Why not?

She approached her. "Good morning, Jeanne."

Her friend did not recognize her and was astonished to be so familiarly addressed by this common personage. She stammered:

"But, Madame—I do not know—You must be mistaken—"

"No, I am Matilda Loisel."

Her friend uttered a cry of astonishment: "Oh! my poor Matilda! How you have changed—"

"Yes, I have had some hard days since I saw you; and some miserable ones—and all because of you—"

"Because of me? How is that?"

"You recall the diamond necklace that you loaned me to wear to the Commissioner's ball?"

"Yes, very well."

"Well, I lost it."

"How is that, since you returned it to me?"

"I returned another to you exactly like it. And it

has taken us ten years to pay for it. You can understand that it was not easy for us who have nothing. But it is finished and I am decently content."

Madame Forestier stopped short. She said:

"You say that you bought a diamond necklace to replace mine?"

"Yes. You did not perceive it then? They were just alike."

And she smiled with a proud and simple joy. Madame Forestier was touched and took both her hands as she replied:

"Oh! my poor Matilda! Mine were false. They were not worth over five hundred francs!"

In the Moonlight

WELL-MERITED was the name "soldier of God," by the Abbé Marignan. He was a tall, thin priest, fanatical to a degree, but just, and of an exalted soul. All his beliefs were fixed, with never a waver. He thought that he understood God thoroughly, that he penetrated His designs, His wishes, His intentions.

Striding up and down the garden walk of his little country parsonage, sometimes a question rose in his mind: "Why did God make that?" Then in his thoughts, putting himself in God's place, he searched obstinately, and nearly always was satisfied that he found the reason. He was not the man to murmur in transports of pious humility, "O Lord, thy ways are past finding out!" What he said was: "I am the servant of God; I ought to know the reason of what he does, or to divine it if I do not."

Everything in nature seemed to him created with an absolute and admirable logic. The "wherefore" and the "because" were always balanced. The dawns were made to rejoice you on waking, the days to ripen the harvests, the rains to water them, the evenings to prepare for sleeping, and the nights dark for sleep.

The four seasons corresponded perfectly to all the needs of agriculture; and to him the suspicion could never have come that nature has no intention, and that all which lives has accustomed itself, on the contrary, to the hard conditions of different periods, of climates, and of matter.

But he hated women; he hated them unconsciously, and despised them by instinct. He often repeated the

words of Christ, "Woman, what have I to do with thee?"
and he would add, "One would almost say that God himself was ill-pleased with that particular work of his
hands." Woman for him was indeed the "child twelve
times unclean" of whom the poet speaks. She was the
temptress who had ensnared the first man, and who still
continued her damnable work; she was the being who
is feeble, dangerous, mysteriously troublous. And even
more than her poisonous beauty, he hated her loving
soul.

He had often felt women's tenderness attack him,
and though he knew himself to be unassailable, he grew
exasperated at this need of loving which quivers continually in their hearts.

To his mind, God had only created woman to tempt
man and to test him. Man should not approach her without those precautions for defense which he would take,
and the fears he would cherish, near an ambush. Woman,
indeed, was just like a trap, with her arms extended and
her lips open toward a man.

He had toleration only for nuns, rendered harmless
by their vow; but he treated them harshly notwithstanding, because, ever at the bottom of their chained-up
hearts, their chastened hearts, he perceived the eternal
tenderness that constantly went out even to him, although he was a priest.

He had a niece who lived with her mother in a little
house near by. He was bent on making her a sister of
charity. She was pretty and hare-brained, and a great
tease. When the abbé sermonized, she laughed; when he
was angry at her, she kissed him vehemently, pressing
him to her heart, while he would seek involuntarily to
free himself from her embrace. Notwithstanding, it made
him taste a certain sweet joy, awaking deep within him

that sensation of fatherhood which slumbers in every man.

Often he talked to her of God, of his God, walking beside her along the footpaths through the fields. She hardly listened, but looked at the sky, the grass, the flowers, with a joy of living which could be seen in her eyes. Sometimes she rushed forward to catch some flying creature, and bringing it back would cry: "Look, my uncle, how pretty it is; I should like to kiss it." And this necessity to "kiss flies" or sweet flowers worried, irritated, and revolted the priest, who saw, even in that, the ineradicable tenderness which ever springs in the hearts of women.

One day the sacristan's wife, who kept house for the Abbé Marignan, told him, very cautiously, that his niece had a lover!

He experienced a dreadful emotion, and he stood choking, with the soap all over his face, in the act of shaving.

When he found himself able to think and speak once more, he cried: "It is not true; you are lying, Melanie!"

But the peasant woman put her hand on her heart; "May our Lord judge me if I am lying, Monsieur le Curé. I tell you she goes to him every evening as soon as your sister is in bed. They meet each other beside the river. You have only to go there between ten o'clock and midnight, and see for yourself."

He ceased scratching his chin and commenced to pace the room quickly, as he always did in his hours of gravest thought. When he tried to begin his shaving again, he cut himself three times from nose to ear.

All day long, he remained silent, swollen with anger and with rage. To his priestly zeal against the mighty power of love was added the moral indignation of a father, of a teacher, of a keeper of souls, who has been deceived, robbed, played with by a child. He felt the egotistical sorrow that parents feel when their daughter announces that she has chosen a husband without them and in spite of their advice.

After his dinner, he tried to read a little, but he could not attune himself to it; and he grew angrier and angrier. When it struck ten, he took his cane, a formidable oaken club which he always carried when he had to go out at night to visit the sick. Smilingly he regarded the enormous cudgel, holding it in his solid, countryman's fist and cutting threatening circles with it in the air. Then, suddenly, he raised it, and grinding his teeth, he brought it down upon a chair, the back of which, split in two, fell heavily to the ground.

He opened his door to go out; but he stopped upon the threshold, surprised by such a splendor of moonlight as you seldom see.

Endowed as he was with an exalted spirit, such a spirit as must have belonged to those dreamer-poets, the Fathers of the Church, he felt himself suddenly softened and moved by the grand and serene beauty of the pale-faced night.

In his little garden, bathed in the soft brilliance, his fruit-trees, all a-row, were outlining in shadow upon the walk their slender limbs of wood scarce clothed with green; while the giant honeysuckle climbing on the house wall exhaled delicious, sugared breaths, which hovered through the warm, clear night like a perfumed soul.

He began to breathe deep, drinking the air as drunkards drink their wine, and walking slowly, ravished, surprised, and almost oblivious of his niece.

As he stepped into the open country he stopped to

contemplate the whole plain, inundated by this caressing radiance, and drowned in the tender and languishing charm of the serene night. In chorus the frogs threw into space their short, metallic notes, and with the seduction of the moonlight, distant nightingales mingled that fitful music of theirs which brings no thoughts but dreams, a light and vibrant melody which seems attuned to kisses.

The abbé continued his walk, his courage failing, he knew not why. He felt, as it were, enfeebled, and suddenly exhausted; he had a great desire to sit down, to pause right there and praise God in all His works.

Below him, following the bends of the little river, wound a great line of poplars. On and about the banks, wrapping all the tortuous watercourse in a kind of light, transparent wadding, hung suspended a fine mist, a white vapor, which the moon-rays crossed, and silvered, and caused to gleam.

The priest paused yet again, penetrated to the depths of his soul by a strong and growing emotion. And a doubt, a vague uneasiness, seized on him; he felt that one of those questions he sometimes put to himself was now being born.

Why had God done this? Since the night is destined for sleep, for unconsciousness, for repose, for forgetfulness of everything, why, then, make it more charming than the day, sweeter than dawns and sunsets? And this slow, seductive star, more poetical than the sun, and so discreet that it seems designed to light up things too delicate, too mysterious, for the great luminary—why had it come to brighten all the shades? Why did not the sweetest of all songsters go to rest like the others? Why set himself to singing in the vaguely troubling dark? Why this half-veil over the world? Why these quiverings of the heart, this emotion of the soul, this languor of the body?

Why this display of seductions which mankind never sees, since night brings sleep? For whom was this sublime spectacle intended, this flood of poetry poured from heaven to earth? The abbé did not understand it at all.

But then, down there along the edge of the pasture appeared two shadows walking side by side under the arched roof of the trees all soaked in glittering mist.

The man was the taller, and had his arm about his mistress's neck; from time to time he kissed her on the forehead. They animated the lifeless landscape which enveloped them, a divine frame made, as it were, expressly for them. They seemed, these two, a single being, the being for whom this calm and silent night was destined; and they approached the priest like a living answer, the answer vouchsafed by his Master to his question.

He stood stock-still, overwhelmed, and with a beating heart. He likened it to some Bible story, such as the loves of Ruth and Boaz, the accomplishment of the will of the Lord in one of those great scenes talked of in holy writ. Through his head ran the versicles of the Song of Songs, the ardent cries, the calls of the body, all the passionate poetry of that poem which burns with tenderness and love. And he said to himself, "God perhaps has made such nights as this to clothe with his ideals the loves of men."

He withdrew before the couple, who went on arm in arm. It was really his niece; and now he asked himself if he had not been about to disobey God. For does not God indeed permit love, since He surrounds it visibly with splendor such as this?

And he fled, in wonder, almost ashamed, as if he had penetrated into a temple where he had no right to enter.

Love
THREE PAGES FROM A SPORTSMAN'S BOOK

〰〰〰〰〰〰〰〰〰〰〰〰〰〰〰〰〰〰〰〰〰〰〰

I HAVE just read among the general news in one of the papers a drama of passion. He killed her and then he killed himself, so he must have loved her. What matters He or She? Their love alone matters to me; and it does not interest me because it moves me or astonishes me, or because it softens me or makes me think, but because it recalls to my mind a remembrance of my youth, a strange recollection of a hunting adventure where Love appeared to me, as the Cross appeared to the early Christians, in the midst of the heavens.

I was born with all the instincts and the senses of primitive man, tempered by the arguments and the restraints of a civilized being. I am passionately fond of shooting, yet the sight of the wounded animal, of the blood on its feathers and on my hands, affects my heart so as almost to make it stop.

That year the cold weather set in suddenly toward the end of autumn, and I was invited by one of my cousins, Karl de Rauville, to go with him and shoot ducks on the marshes, at daybreak.

My cousin was a jolly fellow of forty, with red hair, very stout and bearded, a country gentleman, an amiable semi-brute, of a happy disposition and endowed with that Gallic wit which makes even mediocrity agreeable. He lived in a house, half farmhouse, half château, situated in a broad valley through which a river ran. The hills right and left were covered with woods, old manorial woods where magnificent trees still remained, and where the rarest feathered game in that part of France was to be found. Eagles were shot there occasionally, and birds of passage, such as rarely venture into our over-populated part of the country, invariably lighted amid these giant oaks, as if they knew or recognized some little corner of a primeval forest which had remained there to serve them as a shelter during their short nocturnal halt.

In the valley there were large meadows watered by trenches and separated by hedges; then, further on, the river, which up to that point had been kept between banks, expanded into a vast marsh. That marsh was the best shooting ground I ever saw. It was my cousin's chief care, and he kept it as a preserve. Through the rushes that covered it, and made it rustling and rough, narrow passages had been cut, through which the flat-bottomed boats, impelled and steered by poles, passed along silently over dead water, brushing up against the reeds and making the swift fish take refuge in the weeds, and the wild fowl, with their pointed, black heads, dive suddenly.

I am passionately fond of the water: of the sea, though it is too vast, too full of movement, impossible to hold; of the rivers which are so beautiful, but which pass on, and flee away; and above all of the marshes, where the whole unknown existence of aquatic animals palpitates. The marsh is an entire world in itself on the world of earth—a different world, which has its own life, its settled inhabitants and its passing travelers, its voices, its noises, and above all its mystery. Nothing is more impressive, nothing more disquieting, more terrifying occasionally, than a fen. Why should a vague terror hang over these low plains covered with water? Is it the low rustling of the rushes, the strange will-o'-the-wisp lights, the silence which prevails on calm nights, the still mists which hang over the surface like a shroud; or is it the almost inaudible splashing, so slight and so gentle, yet sometimes more terrifying than the cannons of men or the thunders of the skies, which make these marshes resemble countries one has dreamed of, terrible countries holding an unknown and dangerous secret?

No, something else belongs to it—another mystery, profounder and graver, floats amid these thick mists, perhaps the mystery of the creation itself! For was it not in stagnant and muddy water, amid the heavy humidity of moist land under the heat of the sun, that the first germ of life pulsated and expanded to the day?

I arrived at my cousin's in the evening. It was freezing hard enough to split the stones.

During dinner, in the large room whose sideboards, walls, and ceiling were covered with stuffed birds, with wings extended or perched on branches to which they were nailed—hawks, herons, owls, nightjars, buzzards, tiercels, vultures, falcons—my cousin who, dressed in a sealskin jacket, himself resembled some strange animal from a cold country, told me what preparations he had made for that same night.

We were to start at half past three in the morning, so as to arrive at the place which he had chosen for our watching-place at about half past four. On that spot a hut had been built of lumps of ice, so as to shelter us somewhat from the trying wind which precedes daybreak, a wind so cold as to tear the flesh like a saw, cut it like the blade of a knife, prick it like a poisoned sting, twist it like a pair of pincers, and burn it like fire.

My cousin rubbed his hands: "I have never known such a frost," he said; "it is already twelve degrees below zero at six o'clock in the evening."

I threw myself on to my bed immediately after we

had finished our meal, and went to sleep by the light of a bright fire burning in the grate.

At three o'clock he woke me. In my turn, I put on a sheepskin, and found my cousin Karl covered with a bearskin. After having each swallowed two cups of scalding coffee, followed by glasses of liqueur brandy, we started, accompanied by a gamekeeper and our dogs, Plongeon and Pierrot.

From the first moment that I got outside, I felt chilled to the very marrow. It was one of those nights on which the earth seems dead with cold. The frozen air becomes resisting and palpable, such pain does it cause; no breath of wind moves it, it is fixed and motionless; it bites you, pierces through you, dries you, kills the trees, the plants, the insects, the small birds themselves, who fall from the branches on to the hard ground, and become stiff themselves under the grip of the cold.

The moon, which was in her last quarter and was inclining all to one side, seemed fainting in the midst of space, so weak that she was unable to wane, forced to stay up yonder, seized and paralyzed by the severity of the weather. She shed a cold, mournful light over the world, that dying and wan light which she gives us every month, at the end of her period.

Karl and I walked side by side, our backs bent, our hands in our pockets and our guns under our arms. Our boots, which were wrapped in wool so that we might be able to walk without slipping on the frozen river, made no sound, and I looked at the white vapor which our dogs' breath made.

We were soon on the edge of the marsh, and entered one of the lanes of dry rushes which ran through the low forest.

Our elbows, which touched the long, ribbonlike

leaves, left a slight noise behind us, and I was seized, as I had never been before, by the powerful and singular emotion which marshes cause in me. This one was dead, dead from cold, since we were walking on it, in the middle of its population of dried rushes.

Suddenly, at the turn of one of the lanes, I perceived the ice-hut which had been constructed to shelter us. I went in, and as we had nearly an hour to wait before the wandering birds would awake, I rolled myself up in my rug in order to try and get warm. Then, lying on my back, I began to look at the misshapen moon, which had four horns through the vaguely transparent walls of this polar house. But the frost of the frozen marshes, the cold of these walls, the cold from the firmament penetrated me so terribly that I began to cough. My cousin Karl became uneasy.

"No matter if we do not kill much today," he said: "I do not want you to catch cold; we will light a fire." And he told the gamekeeper to cut some rushes.

We made a pile in the middle of our hut which had a hole in the middle of the roof to let out the smoke, and when the red flames rose up to the clear, crystal blocks they began to melt, gently, imperceptibly, as if they were sweating. Karl, who had remained outside, called out to me: "Come and look here!" I went out of the hut and remained struck with astonishment. Our hut, in the shape of a cone, looked like an enormous diamond with a heart of fire, which had been suddenly planted there in the midst of the frozen water of the marsh. And inside, we saw two fantastic forms, those of our dogs, who were warming themselves at the fire.

But a peculiar cry, a lost, a wandering cry, passed over our heads, and the light from our hearth showed us the wild birds. Nothing moves one so much as the first clamor of a life which one does not see, which passes through the somber air so quickly and so far off, just before the first streak of a winter's day appears on the horizon. It seems to me, at this glacial hour of dawn, as if that passing cry which is carried away by the wings of a bird is the sigh of a soul from the world!

"Put out the fire," said Karl, "it is getting daylight."

The sky was, in fact, beginning to grow pale, and the flights of ducks made long, rapid streaks which were soon obliterated on the sky.

A stream of light burst out into the night; Karl had fired, and the two dogs ran forward.

And then, nearly every minute, now he, now I, aimed rapidly as soon as the shadow of a flying flock appeared above the rushes. And Pierrot and Plongeon, out of breath but happy, retrieved the bleeding birds, whose eyes still, occasionally, looked at us.

The sun had risen, and it was a bright day with a blue sky, and we were thinking of taking our departure, when two birds with extended necks and outstretched wings, glided rapidly over our heads. I fired, and one of them fell almost at my feet. It was a teal, with a silver breast, and then, in the blue space above me, I heard a voice, the voice of a bird. It was a short, repeated, heart-rending lament; and the bird, the little animal that had been spared began to turn round in the blue sky, over our heads, looking at its dead companion which I was holding in my hand.

Karl was on his knees, his gun to his shoulder watching it eagerly, until it should be within shot. "You have killed the duck," he said, "and the drake will not fly away."

He certainly did not fly away; he circled over our heads continually, and continued his cries. Never have

any groans of suffering pained me so much as that desolate appeal, as that lamentable reproach of this poor bird
which was lost in space.

Occasionally he took flight under the menace of the
gun which followed his movements, and seemed ready to
continue his flight alone, but as he could not make up his
mind to this, he returned to find his mate.

"Leave her on the ground," Karl said to me, "he will
come within shot by and by." And he did indeed come
near us, careless of danger, infatuated by his animal love,
by his affection for his mate, which I had just killed.

Karl fired, and it was as if somebody had cut the
string which held the bird suspended. I saw something
black descend, and I heard the noise of a fall among the
rushes. And Pierrot brought it to me.

I put them—they were already cold—into the same
game-bag, and I returned to Paris the same evening.

The Little Cask

$\mathbf{J}$ULES CHICOT, the innkeeper, who lived at Épreville, pulled up his tilbury in front of Mother Magloire's farmhouse. He was a tall man of about forty, fat and with a red face and was generally said to be a very knowing customer.

He hitched his horse up to the gatepost and went in. He owned some land adjoining that of the old woman. He had been coveting her plot for a long while, and had tried in vain to buy it a score of times, but she had always obstinately refused to part with it.

"I was born here, and here I mean to die," was all she said.

He found her peeling potatoes outside the farmhouse door. She was a woman of about seventy-two, very thin, shriveled and wrinkled, almost dried-up, in fact, and much bent, but as active and untiring as a girl. Chicot patted her on the back in a very friendly fashion, and then sat down by her on a stool.

"Well, Mother, you are always pretty well and hearty, I am glad to see."

"Nothing to complain of, considering, thank you. And how are you, Monsieur Chicot?"

"Oh! pretty well, thank you, except a few rheumatic pains occasionally; otherwise, I should have nothing to complain of."

"That's all the better!"

And she said no more, while Chicot watched her going on with her work. Her crooked, knotty fingers, hard as a lobster's claws, seized the tubers, which were lying in a pail, as if they had been a pair of pincers, and peeled them rapidly, cutting off long strips of skin with an old knife which she held in the other hand, throwing the potatoes into the water as they were done. Three daring fowls jumped one after the other into her lap, seized a bit of peel, and then ran away as fast as their legs would carry them with it in their beaks.

Chicot seemed embarrassed, anxious, with something on the tip of his tongue which he could not get out. At last he said hurriedly:

"I say, Mother Magloire—"

"Well, what is it?"

"You are quite sure that you do not want to sell your farm?"

"Certainly not; you may make up your mind to that. What I have said, I have said, so don't refer to it again."

"Very well; only I fancy I have thought of an arrangement that might suit us both very well."

"What is it?"

"Here you are: You shall sell it to me, and keep it all the same. You don't understand? Very well, so just follow me in what I am going to say."

The old woman left off peeling her potatoes, and looked at the innkeeper attentively from under her bushy eyebrows, and he went on:

"Let me explain myself: Every month I will give you a hundred and fifty francs. You understand me, I suppose? Every month I will come and bring you thirty crowns, and it will not make the slightest difference in your life—not the very slightest. You will have your own home just as you have now, will not trouble yourself about me, and will owe me nothing; all you will have to do will be to take my money. Will that arrangement suit you?"

The Little Cask

He looked at her good-humoredly, one might almost have said benevolently, and the old woman returned his looks distrustfully, as if she suspected a trap, and said:

"It seems all right, as far as I am concerned, but it will not give you the farm."

"Never mind about that," he said, "you will remain here as long as it pleases God Almighty to let you live; it will be your home. Only you will sign a deed before a lawyer making it over to me after your death. You have no children, only nephews and nieces for whom you don't care a straw. Will that suit you? You will keep everything during your life, and I will give you the thirty crowns a month. It is pure gain as far as you are concerned."

The old woman was surprised, rather uneasy, but, nevertheless, very much tempted to agree, and answered:

"I don't say that I will not agree to it, but I must think about it. Come back in a week and we will talk it over again, and I will then give you my definite answer."

And Chicot went off, as happy as a king who had conquered an empire.

Mother Magloire was thoughtful, and did not sleep at all that night; in fact, for four days she was in a fever of hesitation. She *smelled,* so to say, that there was something underneath the offer which was not to her advantage; but then the thought of thirty crowns a month, of all those coins chinking in her apron, falling to her, as it were, from the skies, without her doing anything for it, filled her with covetousness.

She went to the notary and told him about it. He advised her to accept Chicot's offer, but said she ought to ask for a monthly payment of fifty crowns instead of thirty, as her farm was worth sixty thousand francs at the lowest calculation.

"If you live for fifteen years longer," he said, "even

then he will only have paid forty-five thousand francs for it."

The old woman trembled with joy at this prospect of getting fifty crowns a month; but she was still suspicious, fearing some trick, and she remained a long time with the lawyer asking questions without being able to make up her mind to go. At last she gave him instructions to draw up the deed, and returned home with her head in a whirl, just as if she had drunk four jugs of new cider.

When Chicot came again to receive her answer she took a lot of persuading, and declared that she could not make up her mind to agree to his proposal, though she was all the time on tenterhooks lest he should not consent to give the fifty crowns. At last, when he grew urgent, she told him what she expected for her farm.

He looked surprised and disappointed, and refused.

Then, in order to convince him, she began to talk about the probable duration of her life.

"I am certainly not likely to live for more than five or six years longer. I am nearly seventy-three, and far from strong, even considering my age. The other evening I thought I was going to die, and could hardly manage to crawl into bed."

But Chicot was not going to be taken in.

"Come, come, old lady, you are as strong as the church tower, and will live till you are a hundred at least; you will be sure to see me put underground first."

The whole day was spent in discussing the money, and as the old woman would not give way, the landlord consented to give the fifty crowns, and she insisted upon having ten crowns over and above to strike the bargain.

Three years passed by, and the old dame did not seem to have grown a day older. Chicot was in despair. It seemed to him as if he had been paying that annuity for fifty years, that he had been taken in, outwitted, and ruined. From time to time he went to see his annuitant, just as one goes in July to see when the harvest is likely to begin. She always met him with a cunning look, and one would have felt inclined to think that she was congratulating herself on the trick she had played him. Seeing how well and hearty she seemed, he very soon got into his tilbury again, growling to himself:

"Will you never die, you old brute?"

He did not know what to do, and felt inclined to strangle her when he saw her. He hated her with a ferocious, cunning hatred, the hatred of a peasant who has been robbed, and began to cast about for means of getting rid of her.

One day he came to see her again, rubbing his hands as he did the first time when he proposed the bargain, and, after having chatted for a few minutes, he said:

"Why do you never come and have a bit of dinner at my place when you are in Épreville? The people are talking about it and saying that we are not on friendly terms, and that pains me. You know it will cost you nothing if you come, for I don't look at the price of a dinner. Come whenever you feel inclined; I shall be very glad to see you."

Old Mother Magloire did not need to be told twice, and the next day but one—she was going to the town in any case, it being market-day, in her gig, driven by her man—she, without any demur, put her trap up in Chicot's stable, and went in search of her promised dinner.

The publican was delighted, and treated her like a princess, giving her roast fowl, black pudding, leg of mutton, and bacon and cabbage. But she ate next to nothing. She had always been a small eater and had generally lived on a little soup and a crust of bread-and-butter.

Chicot was disappointed, and pressed her to eat

more, but she refused. She would drink next to nothing either, and declined any coffee, so he asked her:

"But surely, you will take a little drop of brandy or liquor?"

"Well, as to that, I don't know that I will refuse." Whereupon he shouted out:

"Rosalie, bring the superfine brandy—*the special*— you know."

The servant appeared, carrying a long bottle ornamented with a paper vine-leaf, and he filled two liquor glasses.

"Just try that; you will find it first-rate."

The good woman drank it slowly in sips, so as to make the pleasure last all the longer, and when she had finished her glass, draining the last drops so as to make sure of all, she said:

"Yes, that is first-rate!"

Almost before she had said it, Chicot had poured her out another glassful. She wished to refuse, but it was too late, and she drank it very slowly, as she had done the first, and he asked her to have a third. She objected, but he persisted.

"It is as mild as milk, you know. I can drink ten or a dozen without any ill effect; it goes down like sugar, and leaves no headache behind; one would think that it evaporated on the tongue. It is the most wholesome thing you can drink."

She took it, for she really wished to have it, but she left half the glass.

Then Chicot, in an excess of generosity, said:

"Look here, as it is so much to your taste, I will give you a small keg of it, just to show that you and I are still excellent friends." Then she took her leave, feeling slightly overcome by the effects of what she had drunk.

The Little Cask

The next day the innkeeper drove into her yard, and took a little iron-hooped keg out of his gig. He insisted on her tasting the contents, to make sure it was the same delicious article, and, when they had each of them drunk three more glasses, he said, as he was going away:

"Well, you know, when it is all gone, there is more left; don't be modest, for I shall not mind. The sooner it is finished the better pleased I shall be."

Four days later he came again. The old woman was outside her door cutting up the bread for her soup.

He went up to her, and put his face close to hers, so that he might smell her breath; and when he smelled the alcohol he felt pleased.

"I suppose you will give me a glass of *the special?*" he said. And they had three glasses each.

Soon, however, it began to be whispered abroad that Mother Magloire was in the habit of getting drunk all by herself. She was picked up in her kitchen, then in her yard, then in the roads in the neighborhood, and was often brought home like a log.

Chicot did not go near her any more, and, when people spoke to him about her, he used to say, putting on a distressed look:

"It is a great pity that she should have taken to drink at her age; but when people get old there is no remedy. It will be the death of her in the long run."

And it certainly was the death of her. She died the next winter. About Christmas time she fell down unconscious in the snow, and was found dead the next morning.

And when Chicot came in for the farm he said:

"It was very stupid of her; if she had not taken to drink she might very well have lived for ten years longer."

Clochette

~~~~~~

ＨOW strange are those old recollections which haunt us, without our being able to get rid of them!

This one is so very old that I cannot understand how it has clung so vividly and tenaciously to my memory. Since then I have seen so many sinister things, either affecting or terrible, that I am astonished at not being able to pass a single day without the face of Mother Clochette recurring to my mind's eye, just as I knew her formerly, long, long ago, when I was ten or twelve years old.

She was an old seamstress who came to my parents' house once a week, every Thursday, to mend the linen. My parents lived in one of those country houses called châteaux, which are merely old houses with pointed roofs, to which are attached three or four adjacent farms.

The village, a large village, almost a small market town, was a few hundred yards off, and nestled round the church, a red brick church, which had become black with age.

Well, every Thursday Mother Clochette came between half past six and seven in the morning, and went immediately into the linen-room and began to work. She was a tall, thin, bearded or rather hairy woman, for she had a beard all over her face, a surprising, an unexpected beard, growing in improbable tufts, in curly bunches which looked as if they had been sown by a madman over that great face, the face of a gendarme in petticoats. She had them on her nose, under her nose, round her nose, on her chin, on her cheeks; and her eyebrows, which were extraordinarily thick and long, and quite gray, bushy and bristling, looked exactly like a pair of mustaches stuck on there by mistake.

She limped, but not as lame people generally do, but like a ship pitching. When she planted her great, bony, vibrant body on her sound leg, she seemed to be preparing to mount some enormous wave, and then suddenly she dipped as if to disappear in an abyss, and buried herself in the ground. Her walk reminded one of a ship in a storm, and her head, which was always covered with an enormous white cap, whose ribbons fluttered down her back, seemed to traverse the horizon from north to south and from south to north, at each limp.

I adored Mother Clochette. As soon as I was up I used to go into the linen-room, where I found her installed at work, with a foot-warmer under her feet. As soon as I arrived, she made me take the foot-warmer and sit upon it, so that I might not catch cold in that large, chilly room under the roof.

"That draws the blood from your head," she would say to me.

She told me stories, while mending the linen with her long, crooked, nimble fingers; behind her magnifying spectacles, for age had impaired her sight, her eyes appeared enormous to me, strangely profound, double.

As far as I can remember from the things which she told me and by which my childish heart was moved, she had the large heart of a poor woman. She told me what had happened in the village, how a cow had escaped from the cowhouse and had been found the next morning in front of Prosper Malet's mill, looking at the sails turning, or about a hen's egg which had been found in the church belfry without anyone being able to understand what creature had been there to lay it, or the queer story of Jean Pila's dog, who had gone ten leagues to bring back his master's breeches which a tramp had stolen while they were hanging up to dry out of doors, after he had been caught in the rain. She told me these simple adventures in such a manner that in my mind they assumed the proportions of never-to-be-forgotten dramas, of grand and mysterious poems; and the ingenious stories invented by the poets, which my mother told me in the evening, had none of the flavor, none of the fullness or of the vigor of the peasant woman's narratives.

Well, one Thursday when I had spent all the morning in listening to Mother Clochette, I wanted to go upstairs to her again during the day, after picking hazelnuts with the manservant in the wood behind the farm. I remember it all as clearly as what happened only yesterday.

On opening the door of the linen-room, I saw the old seamstress lying on the floor by the side of her chair, her face turned down and her arms stretched out, but still holding her needle in one hand and one of my shirts in the other. One of her legs in a blue stocking, the longer one no doubt, was extended under her chair, and her spectacles glistened by the wall, where they had rolled away from her.

I ran away uttering shrill cries. They all came running, and in a few minutes I was told that Mother Clochette was dead.

I cannot describe the profound, poignant, terrible emotion which stirred my childish heart. I went slowly down into the drawing-room and hid myself in a dark corner, in the depths of a great, old armchair, where I knelt and wept. I remained there for a long time no doubt, for night came on. Suddenly some one came in with a lamp—without seeing me, however—and I heard my father and mother talking with the medical man, whose voice I recognized.

He had been sent for immediately, and he was explaining the cause of the accident, of which I understood nothing, however. Then he sat down and had a glass of liqueur and a biscuit.

He went on talking, and what he then said will remain engraved on my mind until I die! I think that I can give the exact words which he used.

"Ah!" said he, "the poor woman! she broke her leg the day of my arrival here. I had not even had time to wash my hands after getting off the diligence before I was sent for in all haste, for it was a bad case, very bad.

"She was seventeen, and a pretty girl, very pretty! Would anyone believe it? I have never told her story before, in fact no one but myself and one other person, who is no longer living in this part of the country, ever knew it. Now that she is dead, I may be less discreet.

"A young assistant teacher had just come to live in the village; he was good-looking and had the bearing of a soldier. All the girls ran after him, but he was disdainful. Besides that, he was very much afraid of his superior, the schoolmaster, old Grabu, who occasionally got out of bed the wrong foot first.

"Old Grabu already employed pretty Hortense, who has just died here, and who was afterward nicknamed Clochette. The assistant master singled out the pretty young girl, who was no doubt flattered at being chosen by this disdainful conqueror; at any rate, she fell in love with him, and he succeeded in persuading her to give him a first meeting in the hayloft behind the school, at night, after she had done her day's sewing.

"She pretended to go home, but instead of going downstairs when she left the Grabus', she went upstairs and hid among the hay, to wait for her lover. He soon joined her, and he was beginning to say pretty things to her, when the door of the hayloft opened and the school-master appeared, and asked: 'What are you doing up there, Sigisbert?' Feeling sure that he would be caught, the young schoolmaster lost his presence of mind and re-plied stupidly: 'I came up here to rest a little among the bundles of hay, Monsieur Grabu.'

"The loft was very large and absolutely dark. Sigis-bert pushed the frightened girl to the further end and said: 'Go there and hide yourself. I shall lose my situa-tion, so get away and hide yourself.'

"When the schoolmaster heard the whispering, he continued: 'Why, you are not by yourself?'

" 'Yes I am, Monsieur Grabu!'

" 'But you are not, for you are talking.'

" 'I swear I am, Monsieur Grabu.'

" 'I will soon find out,' the old man replied, and dou-ble-locking the door, he went down to get a light.

"Then the young man, who was a coward such as one sometimes meets, lost his head, and he repeated, having grown furious all of a sudden: 'Hide yourself, so that he may not find you. You will deprive me of my bread for my whole life; you will ruin my whole career! Do hide yourself!'

"They could hear the key turning in the lock again, and Hortense ran to the window which looked out on to the street, opened it quickly, and then in a low and de-termined voice said: 'You will come and pick me up when he is gone,' and she jumped out.

"Old Grabu found nobody, and went down again in great surprise. A quarter of an hour later, Monsieur Sigis-bert came to me and related his adventure. The girl had remained at the foot of the wall unable to get up, as she had fallen from the second story, and I went with him to fetch her. It was raining in torrents, and I brought the unfortunate girl home with me, for the right leg was broken in three places, and the bones had come out through the flesh. She did not complain, and merely said, with admirable resignation: 'I am punished, well punished!'

"I sent for assistance and for the workgirl's friends and told them a made-up story of a runaway carriage which had knocked her down and lamed her, outside my door. They believed me, and the gendarmes for a whole month tried in vain to find the author of this accident.

"That is all! Now I say that this woman was a heroine, and had the fiber of those who accomplish the grandest deeds in history.

"That was her only love affair, and she died a virgin. She was a martyr, a noble soul, a sublimely devoted woman! And if I did not absolutely admire her, I should not have told you this story, which I would never tell anyone during her life: you understand why."

The doctor ceased; mamma cried and papa said some words which I did not catch; then they left the room, and I remained on my knees in the armchair and sobbed, while I heard a strange noise of heavy footsteps and something knocking against the side of the staircase.

They were carrying away Clochette's body.

A Fishing Excursion

PARIS was blockaded, desolate, famished. The sparrows were few, and anything that was to be had was good to eat.

On a bright morning in January, Mr. Morissot, a watchmaker by trade, but idler through circumstances, was walking along the boulevard, sad, hungry, with his hands in the pockets of his uniform trousers, when he came face to face with a brother-in-arms whom he recognized as an old-time friend.

Before the war, Morissot could be seen at daybreak every Sunday, trudging along with a cane in one hand and a tin box on his back. He would take the train to Colombes and walk from there to the Isle of Marante where he would fish until dark.

It was there he had met Mr. Sauvage who kept a little notion store in the Rue Notre Dame de Lorette, a jovial fellow and passionately fond of fishing like himself. A warm friendship had sprung up between these two and they would fish side by side all day, very often without saying a word. Some days, when everything looked fresh and new and the beautiful spring sun gladdened every heart, Mr. Morissot would exclaim:

"How delightful!" and Mr. Sauvage would answer: "There is nothing to equal it."

Then again on a fall evening, when the glorious setting sun, spreading its golden mantle on the already tinted leaves, would throw strange shadows around the two friends, Sauvage would say:

"What a grand picture!"

270

"It beats the boulevard!" would answer Morissot. But they understood each other quite as well without speaking.

The two friends had greeted each other warmly and had resumed their walk side by side, both thinking deeply of the past and present events. They entered a *café,* and when a glass of absinthe had been placed before each Sauvage sighed:

"What terrible events, my friend!"

"And what weather!" said Morissot sadly; "this is the first nice day we have had this year. Do you remember our fishing excursions?"

"Do I! Alas! when shall we go again!"

After a second absinthe they emerged from the *café,* feeling rather dizzy—that light-headed effect which alcohol has on an empty stomach. The balmy air had made Sauvage exuberant and he exclaimed:

"Suppose we go!"

"Where?"

"Fishing."

"Fishing! Where?"

"To our old spot, to Colombes. The French soldiers are stationed near there and I know Colonel Dumoulin will give us a pass."

"It's a go; I am with you."

An hour after, having supplied themselves with their fishing tackle, they arrived at the colonel's villa. He had smiled at their request and had given them a pass in due form.

At about eleven o'clock they reached the advance-guard, and after presenting their pass, walked through Colombes and found themselves very near their destination. Argenteuil, across the way, and the great plains toward Nanterre were all deserted. Solitary the hills of

Orgemont and Sannois rose clearly above the plains; a splendid point of observation.

"See," said Sauvage pointing to the hills, "the Prussians are there."

Prussians! They had never seen one, but they knew that they were all around Paris, invisible and powerful; plundering, devastating, and slaughtering. To their superstitious terror they added a deep hatred for this unknown and victorious people.

"What if we should meet some?" said Morissot.

"We would ask them to join us," said Sauvage in true Parisian style.

Still they hesitated to advance. The silence frightened them. Finally Sauvage picked up courage.

"Come, let us go on cautiously."

They proceeded slowly, hiding behind bushes, looking anxiously on every side, listening to every sound. A bare strip of land had to be crossed before reaching the river. They started to run. At last, they reached the bank and sank into the bushes, breathless, but relieved.

Morissot thought he heard some one walking. He listened attentively, but no, he heard no sound. They were indeed alone! The little island shielded them from view. The house where the restaurant used to be seemed deserted; feeling reassured, they settled themselves for a good day's sport.

Sauvage caught the first fish, Morissot the second; and every minute they would bring one out which they would place in a net at their feet. It was indeed miraculous! They felt that supreme joy which one feels after having been deprived for months of a pleasant pastime. They had forgotten everything; even the war!

Suddenly, they heard a rumbling sound and the earth shook beneath them. It was the cannon on Mont

Valérien. Morissot looked up and saw a trail of smoke, which was instantly followed by another explosion. Then they followed in quick succession.

"They are at it again," said Sauvage shrugging his shoulders. Morissot, who was naturally peaceful, felt a sudden, uncontrollable anger.

"Stupid fools! What pleasure can they find in killing each other!"

"They are worse than brutes!"

"It will always be thus as long as we have governments."

"Well, such is life!"

"You mean death!" said Morissot laughing.

They continued to discuss the different political problems, while the cannon on Mont Valérien sent death and desolation among the French.

Suddenly they started. They had heard a step behind them. They turned and beheld four big men in dark uniforms, with guns pointed right at them. Their fishing-lines dropped out of their hands and floated away with the current.

In a few minutes, the Prussian soldiers had bound them, cast them into a boat, and rowed across the river to the island which our friends had thought deserted. They soon found out their mistake when they reached the house, behind which stood a score or more of soldiers. A big burly officer, seated astride a chair, smoking an immense pipe, addressed them in excellent French:

"Well, gentlemen, have you made a good haul?"

Just then, a soldier deposited at his feet the net full of fish which he had taken good care to take along with him. The officer smiled and said:

"I see you have done pretty well; but let us change the subject. You are evidently sent to spy upon me. You pretended to fish so as to put me off the scent, but I am not so simple. I have caught you and shall have you shot. I am sorry, but war is war. As you passed the advance-guard you certainly must have the password; give it to me, and I will set you free."

The two friends stood side by side, pale and slightly trembling, but they answered nothing.

"No one will ever know. You will go back home quietly and the secret will disappear with you. If you refuse, it is instant death! Choose!"

They remained motionless, silent. The Prussian officer calmly pointed to the river.

"In five minutes you will be at the bottom of this river! Surely, you have a family, friends waiting for you?"

Still they kept silent. The cannon rumbled incessantly. The officer gave orders in his own tongue, then moved his chair away from the prisoners. A squad of men advanced within twenty feet of them, ready for command.

"I give you one minute; not a second more!"

Suddenly approaching the two Frenchmen, he took Morissot aside and whispered:

"Quick, the password. Your friend will not know; he will think I have changed my mind." Morissot said nothing.

Then taking Sauvage aside he asked him the same thing, but he also was silent. The officer gave further orders and the men leveled their guns. At that moment, Morissot's eyes rested on the net full of fish lying in the grass a few feet away. The sight made him feel faint and, though he struggled against it, his eyes filled with tears. Then turning to his friend:

"Farewell! Mr. Sauvage!"

"Farewell! Mr. Morissot."

They stood for a minute, hand in hand, trembling with emotion which they were unable to control.

"Fire!" commanded the officer.

The squad of men fired as one. Sauvage fell straight on his face. Morissot, who was taller, swayed, pivoted, and fell across his friend's body, his face to the sky; while blood flowed freely from the wound in his breast. The officer gave further orders and his men disappeared. They came back presently with ropes and stones, which they tied to the feet of the two friends, and four of them carried them to the edge of the river. They swung them and threw them in as far as they could. The bodies weighted by stones sank immediately. A splash, a few ripples and the water resumed its usual calmness. The only thing to be seen was a little blood floating on the surface. The officer calmly retraced his steps toward the house muttering:

"The fish will get even now."

He perceived the net full of fish, picked it up, smiled, and called:

"Wilhelm!"

A soldier in a white apron approached. The officer handed him the fish saying:

"Fry these little things while they are still alive. They will make a delicious meal."

And having resumed his position on the chair, he puffed away at his pipe.

Humiliation

THE two young women have the appearance of being buried in a bed of flowers. They are alone in an immense landau filled with bouquets like a giant basket. Upon the seat before them are two small hampers full of Nice violets, and upon the bear-skin which covers their knees is a heap of roses, gillyflowers, marguerites, tuberoses, and orange flowers, bound together with silk ribbons, which seem to crush the two delicate bodies, only allowing to appear above the spread-out, perfumed bed the shoulders, arms, and a little of their bodices, one of which is blue and the other lilac.

The coachman's whip bears a sheath of anemones, the horses' heads are decorated with wallflowers, the spokes of the wheels are clothed in mignonette, and in place of lanterns, there are two round, enormous bouquets, which seem like the two eyes of this strange, rolling, flowery beast.

The landau goes along Antibes street at a brisk trot, preceded, followed, and accompanied by a crowd of other garlanded carriages full of women concealed under a billow of violets. For it is the Flower Festival at Cannes.

They arrived at the Foncière Boulevard where the battle takes place. The whole length of the immense avenue, a double line of bedecked equipages was going and coming, like a ribbon without end. They threw flowers from one to the other. Flowers passed in the air like balls, hit the fair faces, hovered and fell in the dust where an army of street urchins gathered them.

A compact crowd, clamorous but orderly, looked on,

standing in rows upon the sidewalks, and held in place by policemen on horseback who passed along, pushing back the curious brutally with their feet, in order that the villains might not mingle with the rich.

Now, the people in the carriages recognize each other, call to each other, and bombard one another with roses. A chariot full of pretty young women, clothed in red like devils, attracts and holds all eyes. One gentleman, who resembles the portraits of Henry IV, throws repeatedly, with joyous ardor, a huge bouquet retained by an elastic. At the threat of the blow the women lower their heads and hide their eyes, but the gracious projectile only describes a curve and again returns to its master, who immediately throws it again, and with greater joy, to a new face.

The two young women empty their arsenal with full hands and receive a shower of bouquets; then, after an hour of battle, and a little wearied at the last, they order the coachman to take the road to the Juan gulf, which skirts the sea.

The sun disappeared behind the Esterel, outlining in black, upon a background of fire, the lacy silhouette of the stretched-out mountain. The calm sea was spread out blue and clear as far as the horizon, where it mingled with the sky and with the squadron anchored in the middle of the gulf, having the appearance of a troop of monstrous beasts, immovable upon the water, apocalyptic animals, humpbacked and clothed in coats-of-mail, capped with thin masts like plumes, and with eyes that lighted up when night came on.

The young women, stretched out under the fur robe, looked upon it languidly. Finally one of them said:

"How delicious these evenings are! Everything seems good. Is it not so, Margot?"

The other replied: "Yes, it is good. But there is always something lacking."

"What is it? For my part, I am completely happy. I have need of nothing."

"Yes? You think so, perhaps. But whatever well-being surrounds our bodies, we always desire something more —for the heart."

Said the other, smiling: "A little love?"

"Yes."

They were silent, looking straight before them; then the one called Marguerite said: "Life does not seem supportable to me without that. I need to be loved, if only by a dog. And we are all so, whatever you may say, Simone."

"No, no, my dear. I prefer not to be loved at all than to be loved by no one of importance. Do you think, for example, that it would be agreeable to me to be loved by—by—"

She looked for some one by whom she could possibly be loved, casting her eyes over the neighboring country. Her eyes, after having made the tour of the whole horizon, fell upon the two metal buttons shining on the coachman's back, and she continued, laughing, "By my coachman?"

Miss Marguerite scarcely smiled as she replied:

"I can assure you it is very amusing to be loved by a domestic. This has happened to me two or three times. They roll their eyes so queerly that one is dying to laugh. Naturally, the more one is loved, the more severe she becomes, since otherwise, one puts herself in the way of being made ridiculous for some very slight cause, if anyone happened to observe it."

Miss Simone listened, her look fixed straight before her; then she declared:

"No, decidedly, the heart of my valet at my feet would not appear to me sufficient. But tell me how you perceived that you were loved."

"I perceived it in them as I do in other men, they become so stupid!"

"But others do not appear so stupid to me, when they are in love."

"Idiots, my dear, incapable of chatting, of answering, of comprehending anything."

"And you? What effect did it have on you to be loved by a domestic? Were you moved—flattered?"

"Moved? No. Flattered? Yes, a little. One is always flattered by the love of a man, whoever he may be."

"Oh! now, Margot!"

"Yes, my dear. Wait! I will tell you a singular adventure that happened to me. You will see what curious things take place among us in such cases.

"It was four years ago in the autumn, when I found myself without a maid. I had tried five or six, one after the other, all of them incompetent, and almost despaired of finding one, when I read in the advertisements of a newspaper of a young girl, knowing how to sew, embroider, and dress hair, who was seeking a place and could furnish the best of references. She could also speak English.

"I wrote to the address given, and the next day the person in question presented herself. She was rather tall, thin, a little pale, with a very timid air. She had beautiful black eyes, a charming color, and she pleased me at once. I asked for her references; she gave me one written in English, because she had come, she said, from the house of Lady Ryswell, where she had been for ten years.

"The certificate attested that the girl was returning to France of her own will, and that she had nothing to reproach her for during her long service with her, except a little *French coquettishness.*

"The modest turn of the English phrase made me smile a little and I engaged the maid immediately. She came to my house the same day; she called herself Rose.

"At the end of a month, I adored her. She was a treasure, a pearl, a phenomenon.

"She could dress my hair with exquisite taste; she could flute the lace of a cap better than the best of the professionals, and she could make frocks. I was amazed at her ability. Never had I been so well served.

"She dressed me rapidly with an astonishing lightness of hand. I never felt her fingers upon my skin, and nothing is more disagreeable to me than contact with a maid's hand. I immediately got into excessively idle habits, so pleasant was it to let her dress me from head to foot, from chemise to gloves—this tall, timid girl, always blushing a little and never speaking. After my bath, she would rub me and massage me while I slept a little while on my divan; indeed, I came to look upon her more as a friend in poorer circumstances, than a servant.

"One morning the *concierge,* with some show of mystery, said he wished to speak to me. I was surprised but let him enter. He was an old soldier, once orderly for my husband.

"He appeared to hesitate at what he was going to say. Finally, he said stammeringly: 'Madame, the police captain for this district is downstairs.'

"I asked: 'What does he want?'

" 'He wants to search the house.'

"Certainly the police are necessary, but I do detest them. I never can make it seem a noble profession. And I answered, irritated as well as wounded:

" 'Why search here? For what purpose? There has been no burglary.'

"He answered:

" 'He thinks that a criminal is concealed somewhere here.'

"I began to be a little afraid and ordered the police captain to be brought that I might have some explanation. He was a man rather well brought up and decorated with the Legion of Honor. He excused himself, asked my pardon, then asserted that I had among my servants a convict!

"I was thunderstruck, and answered that I could vouch for every one of them and that I would make a review of them for his satisfaction.

" 'There is Peter Courtin, an old soldier.'

"It was not he.

" 'The coachman, Francis Pingau, a peasant, son of my father's farmer.'

"It was not he.

" 'A stable boy, also from Champagne, and also a son of peasants I had known, and no more except the footman whom you have seen.'

"It was not any of them.

" 'Then, sir, you see that you have been deceived.'

" 'Pardon me, Madame, but I am sure I am not deceived. As he has not at all the appearance of a criminal, will you have the goodness to have all your servants appear here before you and me, all of them?'

"I hesitated at first, then I yielded, summoning all my people, men and women.

"He looked at them all for an instant, then declared:

" 'This is not all.'

" 'Your pardon, sir,' I replied; 'this is all except my own maid who could not possibly be confounded with a convict.'

"He asked: 'Could I see her too?'

" 'Certainly.'

"I rang and Rose appeared immediately. Scarcely had she entered when he gave a signal and two men, whom I had not seen, concealed behind the door, threw themselves upon her, seized her hands, and bound them.

"I uttered a cry of fury, and was going to try and defend her. The captain stopped me:

" 'This girl, Madame, is a man who calls himself John Nicholas Lecapet, condemned to death in 1879 for assassination preceded by violation. His sentence was changed to life imprisonment. He escaped four months ago. We have been on the search for him ever since.'

"I was dismayed, struck dumb. I could not believe it. The policeman continued, laughing:

" 'I can only give you one proof. His right arm is tattooed.'

"His sleeve was rolled up. It was true. The policeman added, certainly in bad taste:

" 'Doubtless you will be satisfied without the other proofs.'

"And he led my maid away!

"Well, if you will believe it, the feeling which was uppermost in me was that of anger at having been played with in this way, deceived and made ridiculous; it was not shame at having been dressed, undressed, handled, and touched by this man, but—a—profound humiliation —the humiliation of a woman. Do you understand?"

"No, not exactly."

"Let us see. Think a minute— He had been condemned—for violation, this young man—and that—that humiliated me—there! Now do you understand?"

And Miss Simone did not reply. She looked straight before her, with her eyes singularly fixed upon the two shining buttons of the livery, and with that sphinx's smile that women have sometimes.

Julie Romain

IN the springtime, two years ago, I was walking along the shores of the Mediterranean. What is more charming than to dream while walking over a lonely road? One enjoys the sunlight and the caressing wind when climbing the mountains, or strolling by the sea-shore. And in his day-dreams, what illusions, what love-poems, what adventures pass in two hours through the mind of one who idles along a road. Every possible hope, confused and joyous, penetrates him with the warm, light air; he inhales them with the breeze, and they give birth in his being to an appetite for happiness that increases like the hunger he acquires in walking. Sweet and fleeting thoughts sing in his soul as he comes closer to nature.

I followed the road that leads from Saint Raphael to Italy, or rather, I made my way through that superb and changing scenery which seems made to be celebrated in all the love-poems of the earth. It seemed to me a pity to think that, from Cannes to Monaco, scarcely anyone comes into this part of the country save to make trouble, to juggle with money, or to display, under this delicious sky and in this garden of roses and oranges, base vanities, stupid pretensions, and vile covetousness, and to show the human mind as it is—servile, ignorant, arrogant, and grasping.

Suddenly, in one of the curves of the ravishing bays I saw a group of villas, four or five only, fronting on the sea at the foot of the mountain. Behind them was a wild forest of pines, which covered two great valleys, apparently without roads or outlet. Involuntarily I stopped in

front of the gate of one of these châlets, so pretty was it
—a little white cottage with brown decorations, covered
with roses that climbed to the roof. The garden was filled
with flowers of all colors and every size, coquettishly arranged in studied disorder. The lawn was dotted with
flower-beds; a vase with trailing vines stood on the steps
of the veranda, and over the windows hung clusters of
purple grapes, while the stone balustrade that surrounded this charming dwelling was covered with enormous red morning-glories that looked like spots of blood.
Behind the house stretched a long alley of orange-trees in
flower, which reached as far as the foot of the mountain.

On the door of the villa, in small, gilt letters, I read
this name: "Villa d'Antan." I asked myself what poet or
fairy inhabited the place, what inspired recluse had discovered it and created this dream of a dwelling, that appeared to spring from masses of flowers.

A workman was breaking stones on the road at a
short distance. I asked him the name of the proprietor of
the châlet. He replied that it belonged to the famous
Madame Julie Romain.

Julie Romain! In my childhood I had often heard
her spoken of—the great actress, the rival of Rachel! No
woman had been more applauded, or more loved—more
loved, above all! How many duels had been fought and
how many suicides had been committed because of her,
and how many wild adventures had been undertaken for
her sake! What was her age now, that seductress? Sixty—
no, seventy—seventy-five years. Julie Romain! Here, in
this house! I recalled again the emotion created throughout France (I was twelve years old then) by her flight to
Sicily with one lover, a poet, after her notorious quarrel
with another adorer.

She fled with her new love one evening, after a first-

night representation, during which the audience had applauded her for half an hour and called her out eleven
times in succession. She went away with the poet in a
post-chaise, as was the custom then; they had crossed the
sea in order to love in that antique island, daughter of
Greece, under the immense grove of orange-trees that surrounds Palermo, which is called the "Conque d'Or."

Their ascent of Ætna was gossiped about, and also
how they had hung over the immense crater, arm in arm,
cheek against cheek, as if they desired to throw themselves into the gulf of fire.

He was dead now, the writer of affecting verses, of
poems so brilliant that they dazzled a whole generation,
and so subtle and mysterious that they opened a new
world to other poets.

The other lover was dead also, the abandoned one,
who created for her those musical expressions that remain in all hearts—expressions of triumph and despair
that are at once intoxicating and heartrending.

She lived here, in this house veiled with flowers!

I hesitated no longer. I rang the bell. A domestic
came to open the door, a boy of eighteen years, awkward
and shy, with hands that appeared to be in his way. I
wrote on my card a gallant compliment to the old actress,
and an ardent prayer that she would receive me. Perhaps
she might know my name and allow me to see her.

The young valet disappeared, but soon returned and
asked me to follow him. He showed me into a neat drawing-room, correct in every detail, in the style of Louis
Philippe, with furniture of a cold and cumbersome fashion, the coverings of which were being removed in my
honor by a little maid of about sixteen years, with a slender figure but not much beauty.

Then the servants left me alone. I looked around the

room with interest. On the walls hung three portraits, one was of the actress in a celebrated rôle, another was of the poet-lover, wearing a long frock-coat, tight at the waist, and the ruffled shirt of those days, and the third was of the musician, seated before a clavichord. The lady was blond and charming in her portrait, but her pose was a little affected, as was the fashion of that day. Her charming mouth and blue eyes smiled graciously; and the technique of the painting was of a high degree of excellence. Those three remarkable faces seemed to be looking already at the next generation, and their surroundings had an air of a day that was past and of individualities that were no more.

A door opened and a little woman entered. She was very old, very small, with white eyebrows and bands of white hair. Somehow she reminded me of a white mouse, quick and furtive in her movements. She gave me her hand, and, with a voice that was still fresh, vibrating, and sonorous, she said graciously: "Thank you, Monsieur. It is very kind of the men of today to remember the women of yesterday! Be seated."

I told her that her house had attracted me, that I had tried to learn the name of the proprietor, and, having learned it, I could not resist the desire to ring her bell.

"Your visit gives me the greater pleasure, Monsieur," she said, "as it is the first time such an event has happened. When your card was handed to me, with the gracious compliment it carried, I was as startled as if someone had announced an old friend who had been gone these twenty years. I am forgotten, truly forgotten, no one remembers me, no one will think of me until the day of my death; then, all the papers will talk for three days of Julie Romain, telling anecdotes, giving details, and souvenirs and scandals, and, perhaps, pompous eulogies. Then that will be the end of me!"

She was silent a moment and then resumed: "And that will not be long now. In a few months, in a few days, perhaps, the little woman who is now alive will be nothing but a corpse!"

She raised her eyes to her portrait, which met her gaze as if smiling at that withered caricature of itself; then she looked at the two men, the scornful poet and the inspired musician, both of whom seemed to say: "What does that ruin ask of us?"

An indescribable, keen, irresistible sadness seized my heart, the sadness that overwhelms those whose lives are finished and who struggle still with memories as a drowning man struggles in deep water.

From the place where I sat I could see brilliant and swiftly moving carriages passing along the road, going from Nice to Monte Carlo. And seated inside were beautiful young women, rich and happy, and men, smiling and satisfied. She followed my glance, and, comprehending my thought, murmured with a resigned smile: "It is not possible to be and to have been at the same time."

"How beautiful life must have been for you!" I said.

She sighed deeply: "Yes, beautiful and sweet! It is for that reason that I regret it so much."

I saw that she was disposed to talk of herself; so, softly and with delicate precautions, as one would touch a painful wound, I began to question her. She spoke of her success, of her intoxicating joys, of her friends, of her whole triumphant existence.

"Your greatest joy and your deepest happiness—did you owe them to the theater, Madame?" I asked.

"Oh! no," she replied quickly.

I smiled and she added, raising her eyes, with a sad look, to the portraits of the two men:

"I owed my greatest happiness to them."

I could not refrain from asking her to which one she owed it.

"To both, Monsieur! I even confuse them in my mind sometimes, and besides, I feel remorse toward one of them to this day."

"Then, Madame, it is not to them but to the act of love itself that you owe your gratitude. They have merely been love's instruments."

"That is possible. But, ah! what wonderful instruments!"

"Are you certain that you have not been loved—that you would not have been loved as well, and perhaps better, by a simple man, one who was not great, but who would have offered you his whole life, his whole heart, his whole being, every thought and every hour? With those two you had two formidable rivals—music and poetry."

She cried out with force, with that youthful voice, which could still thrill the soul: "No, Monsieur, no! A simpler man might have loved me better, perhaps, but he would not have loved me as those two did. Ah! but they knew how to sing the music of love, as no other man in the world could have sung it.

"How they intoxicated me! Is it possible that any other man could have found that which they found in words and in sounds? Is it enough to love, if one does not know how to put into love all the poetry and all the music of the sky and the earth? They knew, those two, how to make a woman ecstatic with joy with their songs and their words as well as with their deeds. Yes, there was

288

perhaps more of illusion than reality in our passion; but those illusions lift you to the clouds, whereas realities, alone, always leave you on the earth. If others loved me more, it was through them alone that I learned, felt, and adored love!"

Suddenly she began to weep, noiselessly, tears of bitter sorrow. I appeared not to notice it and looked far away out of the window. After a few moments she went on:

"You see, Monsieur, with most people the heart grows old with the body. With me that has not happened. My poor body is sixty-nine years old, but my heart is only twenty. And that is the reason why I live all alone, with my flowers and my dreams."

Again a long silence fell between us. After a time she calmed herself, and again spoke smilingly:

"How you would laugh at me, Monsieur, if you knew how I pass my evenings when the weather is fine! I am ashamed of my folly and pity myself at the same time."

It was useless for me to beg of her to tell me; she would not do so; then I rose to go, at which she cried, "What! so soon?"

I told her that I had intended to dine at Monte Carlo, and at once she asked, a little timidly: "Would you not like to dine with me? It would give me very much pleasure."

I accepted her invitation immediately. She appeared delighted and rang the bell; then, when she had given a few orders to the little maid, she said she would like to show me her house.

A kind of glass-covered veranda, full of plants, opened from the dining-room, and permitted one to see, from one end to the other, the long alley of orange-trees, extending to the foot of the mountains. A low seat, hidden under the shrubbery, indicated that the aged actress often came to sit there.

Then we went into the garden to look at the flowers. Evening came on softly, one of those calm, warm evenings that bring forth all the perfumes of the earth. It was almost dark when we placed ourselves at the table. The dinner was excellent and we sat long over it. We became quite intimate friends. A profound sympathy for her had sprung up in my heart. She drank a glass of wine and became more friendly and confidential.

"Let us go out and look at the moon," she said at last. "I adore the moon, the lovely moon! It has been the witness of my greatest joys. It seems to me that all my sweetest memories are treasured there, and that I have only to look at it in order to have them come back to me. And sometimes, in the evening, I arrange for myself a pretty scene, so pretty—if you only knew! But no, you would laugh at me too much—I cannot tell you—I don't dare—no—no, I cannot tell you!"

"Ah, Madame, continue, I pray!" I begged of her. "What is your little secret? Tell me! I promise you not to laugh—I swear it!"

She hesitated; I took her hands, her poor little hands, so thin and cold, and kissed them one after the other many times, as her lovers were wont to do in former days. She was moved, though she still hesitated.

"You promise me not to laugh?" she said timidly.

"Yes, I swear it, Madame!"

"Well, then, come!" she said with a smile.

We rose from the table, and as the awkward youth in green livery drew back the chair behind her, she spoke a few low, quick words in his ear.

He replied, respectfully, "Yes, Madame, immediately."

She took my arm and led me upon the veranda. The orange-tree walk was a beautiful sight. The moon cast a slender line of silver among the trees—a long line of light that fell on the yellow sand between the dense and rounded branches. As the trees were in bloom, their delicious and penetrating perfume filled the air, and among the dark foliage were thousands of fireflies, whose tiny flames looked like the seed of stars.

"Oh, what an ideal environment for a scene of love!" I cried.

She smiled. "Is it not? Is it not? You will see presently!"

She made me sit down beside her, and murmured:

"The memory of such scenes is what makes me regret life. But you hardly dream of those things, you men of today. You are merely money-makers, traders, business men. You don't know how to talk to us even. When I say 'us,' I mean women who are young. Love affairs have become merely *liaisons*, which originate often in an unacknowledged bill of the dressmaker. If you find the bill more important than the woman, you disappear; but if you esteem the woman of greater value than the bill, you pay! Nice manners, and charming affections!"

She took my hand. "Look!" she said.

I was astonished and transported with pleasure at the charming picture that appeared. Below us, at the end of the alley and in the full moonlight, a youth and a maiden were coming toward us, clasping each other around the waist. They advanced, their arms entwined, walking slowly in the moon's rays, the soft effulgence of which bathed them completely.

They disappeared in the darkness for a moment, then reappeared farther down the avenue.

The youth was dressed in a white satin costume of the last century, with a broad hat, over which hung an ostrich feather. The maiden wore a skirt with wide hoops, and her head was dressed with the high, powdered coiffure affected by beautiful dames in the days of the Regency.

At last they came to a halt, about a hundred steps away from us, and, standing in the middle of the alley, they embraced, after saluting each other gracefully.

Suddenly I recognized the two little servants! Then I was seized with one of those irresistible desires to laugh that shake one all over. I did not laugh, however. I resisted the impulse, and waited to see the next scene in this extraordinary comedy.

The lovers now returned toward the end of the alley, and distance again made them appear charming. They withdrew farther and farther away, and at last disappeared like figures in a dream. The alley seemed lonely without them.

I took my departure also. I left immediately, so that I should not see them again; for I thought it probable that the spectacle was made to last a long time, in order to recall all the past—that past of love and scenic effect; that fictitious past, deceiving and seductive, falsely yet truly charming—to cause the tender heart to throb again in the romantic breast of the old actress, and to use me as a final instrument.

The Specter

IN speaking of a recent lawsuit, our conversation had turned on sequestration, and each of us, thereupon, had a story to tell—a story affirmed to be true. We were a party of intimate friends, who had passed a pleasant evening, now drawing to a close, in an old family residence in the Rue de Grenelle. The aged Marquis de la Tour-Samuel, bowed 'neath the weight of eighty-two winters, at last rose, and leaning on the mantelpiece, said, in somewhat trembling tones:

"I also know something strange, so strange that it has been a haunting memory all my life. It is now fifty-six years since the incident occurred, and yet not a month has passed in which I have not seen it again in a dream, so great was and is the impression of fear it left on my mind. For ten minutes I experienced such horrible fright that, ever since, a sort of constant terror has made me tremble at unexpected noises, and objects half-seen in the gloom of night inspire me with a mad desire to take flight. In short, I am afraid of the dark!

"Ah, no! I would not have avowed that before having reached my present age! Now I can say anything. I have never receded before real danger. So at eighty-two years of age, I do not feel compelled to be brave over an imaginary danger.

"The affair upset me so completely, and caused me such lasting and mysterious uneasiness, that I never spoke of it to anyone. I will now tell it to you exactly as it happened, without any attempt at explanation.

"In July, 1827, I was in garrison at Rouen. One day,

as I was walking on the quay, I met a man whom I thought I recognized, without being able to recall exactly who he was. Instinctively, I made a movement to stop; the stranger perceived it and at once extended his hand.

"He was a friend to whom I had been deeply attached as a youth. For five years I had not seen him, and he seemed to have aged half a century. His hair was quite white, and he walked with a stoop as though completely worn out. He apparently comprehended my surprise, for he told me of the misfortune which had shattered his life.

"Having fallen madly in love with a young girl he had married her, but, after a year of more than earthly happiness, she died suddenly of heart failure. He had left his château on the very day of her burial and had come to live at Rouen. There he still dwelt, more dead than alive, desperate and solitary, exhausted by grief, and so miserable that he thought constantly of suicide.

"'Now that I have found you again,' said he, 'I will ask you to render me an important service. It is to go to my old home and get for me, from the desk of my bedroom—our bedroom—some papers which I greatly need. I cannot send a servant or an agent, as discretion and absolute silence are necessary. As for myself, nothing on earth would induce me to re-enter that house. I will give you the key of the room, which I myself locked on leaving, and the key of my desk—also a note to my gardener, telling him to open the château for you. But come and breakfast with me tomorrow, and we will arrange all that.'

"I promised to do him the slight favor he asked. For that matter, it was nothing of a trip, his property being but a few miles distant from Rouen and easily reached in an hour on horseback.

The Specter

"At ten o'clock the following day I breakfasted, *tête-à-tête,* with my friend, but he scarcely spoke.

"He begged me to pardon him; the thought of the visit I was about to make to that room, the scene of his dead happiness, overwhelmed him, he said. He, indeed, seemed singularly agitated and preoccupied, as though undergoing some mysterious mental combat.

"At length he explained to me exactly what I had to do. It was very simple. I must take two packages of letters and a roll of papers from the first drawer on the right of the desk of which I had the key. He added, 'I need not beg you to refrain from glancing at them.'

"I was wounded at that remark, and told him so somewhat sharply. He stammered, 'Forgive me, I suffer so,' and tears came to his eyes.

"At about one o'clock I took leave of him to accomplish my mission.

"The weather was glorious, and I cantered over the turf, listening to the songs of the larks and the rhythmical striking of my sword against my boot. Then I entered the forest and walked my horse. Branches of the trees caressed my face as I passed, and, now and then, I caught a leaf with my teeth, from sheer gladness of heart at being alive and strong on such a radiant day.

"As I approached the château, I took from my pocket the letter I had for the gardener, and was astonished at finding it sealed. I was so irritated that I was about to turn back without having fulfilled my promise, but reflected that I should thereby display undue susceptibility. My friend's state of mind might easily have caused him to close the envelope without noticing that he did so.

"The manor seemed to have been abandoned for twenty years. The open gate was dropping from its hinges; the walks were overgrown with grass, and the flower-beds were no longer distinguishable.

"The noise I made by tapping loudly on a shutter brought an old man from out a door near by, who seemed stunned with astonishment at seeing me. On receiving my letter, he read it, reread it, turned it over and over, looked me up and down, put the paper in his pocket, and finally asked:

"'Well! what is it you wish?'

"I replied shortly: 'You ought to know, since you have just read your master's orders. I wish to enter the château.'

"He seemed overcome. 'Then you are going in—in her room?'

"I began to lose patience and said sharply: 'Of course; but is that your affair?'

"He stammered in confusion: 'No—sir—but it is because—that is, it has not been opened since—since the—death. If you will be kind enough to wait five minutes, I will go to—to see if—'

"I interrupted him, angrily: 'Look here, what do you mean with your tricks? You know very well you cannot enter the room, since I have the key!'

"He no longer objected. 'Then, sir, I will show you the way.'

"'Show me the staircase and leave me. I'll find my way without you.'

"'But—sir—indeed—'

"This time I silenced him effectually, pushed him aside, and went into the house.

"I first traversed the kitchen; then two rooms occupied by the servant and his wife; next, by a wide hall, I reached the stairs, which I mounted, and recognized the door indicated by my friend.

"I easily opened it and entered. The apartment was so dark that, at first, I could distinguish nothing. I stopped short, my nostrils penetrated by the disagreeable, mouldy odor of long-unoccupied rooms. Then, as my eyes slowly became accustomed to the darkness, I saw plainly enough, a large and disordered bedroom, the bed without sheets, but still retaining its mattresses and pillows, on one of which was a deep impression, as though an elbow or a head had recently rested there.

"The chairs all seemed out of place. I noticed that a door, doubtless that of a closet, had remained half open.

"I first went to the window, which I opened to let in the light; but the fastenings of the shutters had grown so rusty that I could not move them. I even tried to break them with my sword, but without success. As I was growing irritated over my useless efforts, and could now see fairly well in the semi-obscurity, I renounced the idea of getting more light and went over to the writing-table.

"Seating myself in an armchair and letting down the lid of the desk, I opened the designated drawer. It was full to the top. I needed but three packages, which I knew how to recognize, and began searching for them.

"I was straining my eyes in the effort to read the superscriptions, when I seemed to hear, or rather feel, something rustle back of me. I paid no attention, believing that a draught from the window was moving some drapery. But, in a minute or so, another movement, almost imperceptible, sent a strangely disagreeable little shiver over my skin. It was so stupid to be affected, even slightly, that self-respect prevented my turning around. I had then found the second packet I needed and was about to lay my hand on the third when a long and painful sigh, uttered just over my shoulder, made me bound like a madman from my seat and land several feet away.

As I jumped I had turned about, my hand on the hilt of my sword, and, truly, had I not felt it at my side, I should have taken to my heels like a coward.

"A tall woman, dressed in white, stood gazing at me from the back of the chair where I had been sitting an instant before.

"Such a shudder ran through all my limbs that I nearly fell backward. No one can understand unless he has felt it, that frightful, unreasoning terror! The mind becomes vague; the heart ceases to beat; the entire body grows as limp as a sponge.

"I do not believe in ghosts, nevertheless I completely gave way to a hideous fear of the dead; and I suffered more in those few moments than in all the rest of my life, from the irresistible anguish of supernatural fright. If she had not spoken, I should have died, perhaps! But she spoke, she spoke in a sweet, sad voice, that set my nerves vibrating. I dare not say that I became master of myself and recovered my reason. No! I was so frightened that I scarcely knew what I was doing; but a certain innate pride, a remnant of soldierly instinct, made me, almost in spite of myself, maintain a creditable countenance.

"She said: 'Oh! sir, you can render me a great service.'

"I wanted to reply, but it was impossible for me to pronounce a word. Only a vague sound came from my throat.

"She continued: 'Will you? You can save me, cure me. I suffer frightfully. I suffer, oh! how I suffer!' and she slowly seated herself in the armchair, still looking at me.

" 'Will you?' she said.

"I replied 'Yes' by a nod, my voice still being paralyzed.

"Then she held out to me a tortoise-shell comb, and murmured:

" 'Comb my hair, oh! comb my hair; that will cure me; it must be combed. Look at my head—how I suffer; and my hair pulls so!'

"Her hair, unbound, very long and very black, it seemed to me, hung over the back of the chair and touched the floor.

"Why did I receive that comb with a shudder, and why did I take in my hands the long, black hair which gave to my skin a gruesomely cold sensation, as though I were handling snakes? I cannot tell.

"That sensation has remained in my fingers and I still tremble when I think of it.

"I combed her hair. I handled, I know not how, those icy locks. I twisted, knotted, and plaited, and braided them. She sighed and bowed her head, seeming to be happy. Suddenly she said: 'Thank you!' snatched the comb from my hands, and fled by the door that I had noticed ajar.

"Left alone, I experienced for several seconds the horrible agitation of one who awakens from a nightmare. At length I regained my full senses; I ran to the window, and with a mighty effort burst open the shutters, letting a flood of light into the room. Immediately I sprang to the door by which she had departed. I found it closed and immovable!

"Then a mad desire to flee came on me like a panic, the panic which soldiers know in battle. I seized the three packets of letters on the open secretary; ran from the room, dashed down the stairs, found myself outside, I know not how, and seeing my horse a few steps off, leaped into the saddle and galloped away.

The Specter

"I stopped only when I reached Rouen and my lodgings. There I shut myself into my room to reflect. For an hour I anxiously strove to convince myself that I had been the victim of an hallucination. I was about ready to believe that all I had seen was a vision, an error of my senses, when, as I approached the window, my eyes fell, by chance, upon my chest. Around the buttons of my uniform were entwined a quantity of long, black hairs! One by one, with trembling fingers, I plucked them off and threw them away.

"I then called my orderly, feeling unable to see my friend that day; wishing, also, to reflect more fully upon what I ought to tell him. I had his letters carried to him, for which he gave the messenger a receipt. He asked after me most particularly, and, on being told I was ill—had had a sunstroke—appeared exceedingly anxious. Next morning I went to him, determined to tell him the truth. He had gone out the evening before and not yet returned. I called again during the day; my friend was still absent. After waiting a week longer without news of him, I advised the authorities, and a judicial search was instituted. Not the slightest trace of his whereabouts or manner of disappearance was discovered.

"A minute inspection of the abandoned château revealed nothing of a suspicious character. There was no indication that a woman had been concealed there.

"After these fruitless researches all further efforts were abandoned, and in the fifty-six years that have elapsed since then I have heard nothing more."

My Uncle Sosthenes

M Y uncle Sosthenes was a Freethinker, like many others are, from pure stupidity; people are very often religious in the same way. The mere sight of a priest threw him into a violent rage; he would shake his fist and grimace at him, and touch a piece of iron when the priest's back was turned, forgetting that the latter action showed a belief after all, the belief in the evil eye.

Now when beliefs are unreasonable one should have all or none at all. I myself am a Freethinker; I revolt at all the dogmas which have invented the fear of death, but I feel no anger toward places of worship, be they Catholic Apostolic, Roman, Protestant, Greek, Russian, Buddhist, Jewish, or Mohammedan. I have a peculiar manner of looking at them and explaining them. A place of worship represents the homage paid by man to "The Unknown." The more extended our thoughts and our views become, the more The Unknown diminishes, and the more places of worship will decay. I, however, in the place of church furniture, in the place of pulpits, reading desks, altars, and so on, would fit them up with telescopes, microscopes, and electrical machines; that is all.

My uncle and I differed on nearly every point. He was a patriot, while I was not—for after all patriotism is a kind of religion; it is the egg from which wars are hatched.

My uncle was a Freemason, and I used to declare that they are stupider than old women devotees. That is my opinion, and I maintain it; if we must have any religion at all the old one is good enough for me.

What is their object? Mutual help to be obtained by tickling the palms of each other's hands. I see no harm in it, for they put into practice the Christian precept: "Do unto others as ye would they should do unto you." The only difference consists in the tickling, but it does not seem worth while to make such a fuss about lending a poor devil half-a-crown.

To all my arguments my uncle's reply used to be:

"We are raising up a religion against a religion; Freethought will kill clericalism. Freemasonry is the headquarters of those who are demolishing all deities."

"Very well, my dear uncle," I would reply (in my heart I felt inclined to say, "You old idiot!"); "it is just that which I am blaming you for. Instead of destroying, you are organizing competition; it is only a case of lowering the prices. And then, if you only admitted Freethinkers among you I could understand it, but you admit anybody. You have a number of Catholics among you, even the leaders of the party. Pius IX is said to have been one of you before he became Pope. If you call a society with such an organization a bulwark against clericalism, I think it is an extremely weak one."

"My dear boy," my uncle would reply, with a wink, "our most formidable actions are political; slowly and surely we are everywhere undermining the monarchical spirit."

Then I broke out: "Yes, you are very clever! If you tell me that Freemasonry is an election-machine, I will grant it you. I will never deny that it is used as a machine to control candidates of all shades; if you say that it is only used to hoodwink people, to drill them to go to the voting-urn as soldiers are sent under fire, I agree with you; if you declare that it is indispensable to all political ambitions because it changes all its members into electoral agents, I should say to you, 'That is as clear as the sun.' But when you tell me that it serves to undermine the monarchical spirit, I can only laugh in your face.

"Just consider that vast and democratic association which had Prince Napoleon for its Grand Master under the Empire; which has the Crown Prince for its Grand Master in Germany, the Czar's brother in Russia, and to which the Prince of Wales and King Humbert and nearly all the royalists of the globe belong."

"You are quite right," my uncle said; "but all these persons are serving our projects without guessing it."

I felt inclined to tell him he was talking a pack of nonsense.

It was, however, indeed a sight to see my uncle when he had a Freemason to dinner.

On meeting they shook hands in a manner that was irresistibly funny; one could see that they were going through a series of secret mysterious pressures. When I wished to put my uncle in a rage, I had only to tell him that dogs also have a manner which savors very much of Freemasonry, when they greet one another on meeting.

Then my uncle would take his friend into a corner to tell him something important, and at dinner they had a peculiar way of looking at each other, and of drinking to each other, in a manner as if to say: "We know all about it, don't we?"

And to think that there are millions on the face of the globe who are amused at such monkey tricks! I would sooner be a Jesuit.

Now in our town there really was an old Jesuit who was my uncle's detestation. Every time he met him, or if he only saw him at a distance, he used to say: "Go on, you toad!" And then, taking my arm, he would whisper to me:

My Uncle Sosthenes

"Look here, that fellow will play me a trick some day or other, I feel sure of it."

My uncle spoke quite truly, and this was how it happened, through my fault also.

It was close on Holy Week, and my uncle made up his mind to give a dinner on Good Friday, a real dinner with his favorite chitterlings and black puddings. I resisted as much as I could, and said:

"I shall eat meat on that day, but at home, quite by myself. Your *manifestation,* as you call it, is an idiotic idea. Why should you manifest? What does it matter to you if people do not eat any meat?"

But my uncle would not be persuaded. He asked three of his friends to dine with him at one of the best restaurants in the town, and as he was going to pay the bill, I had certainly, after all, no scruples about *manifesting.*

At four o'clock we took a conspicuous place in the most frequented restaurant in the town, and my uncle ordered dinner in a loud voice, for six o'clock.

We sat down punctually, and at ten o'clock we had not finished. Five of us had drunk eighteen bottles of fine still wines, and four of champagne. Then my uncle proposed what he was in the habit of calling: "The archbishop's feat." Each man put six small glasses in front of him, each of them filled with a different liqueur, and then they had all to be emptied at one gulp, one after another, while one of the waiters counted twenty. It was very stupid, but my uncle thought it was very suitable to the occasion.

At eleven o'clock he was dead drunk. So we had to take him home in a cab and put him to bed, and one could easily foresee that his anti-clerical demonstration would end in a terrible fit of indigestion.

My Uncle Sosthenes

As I was going back to my lodgings, being rather drunk myself, with a cheerful Machiavellian drunkenness which quite satisfied all my instincts of scepticism, an idea struck me.

I arranged my necktie, put on a look of great distress, and went and rang loudly at the old Jesuit's door. As he was deaf he made me wait a longish while, but at length he appeared at his window in a cotton nightcap and asked what I wanted.

I shouted out at the top of my voice:

"Make haste, reverend Sir, and open the door; a poor, despairing, sick man is in need of your spiritual ministra-tions."

The good, kind man put on his trousers as quickly as he could and came down without his cassock. I told him in a breathless voice that my uncle, the Freethinker, had been taken suddenly ill. Fearing it was going to be something serious he had been seized with a sudden fear of death, and wished to see a priest and talk to him; to have his advice and comfort, to make up with the Church, and to confess, so as to be able to cross the dreaded threshold at peace with himself; and I added in a mocking tone:

"At any rate, he wishes it, and if it does him no good it can do him no harm."

The old Jesuit, who was startled, delighted, and almost trembling, said to me:

"Wait a moment, my son, I will come with you."

But I replied: "Pardon me, reverend Father, if I do not go with you; but my convictions will not allow me to do so. I even refused to come and fetch you, so I beg you not to say that you have seen me, but to declare that you had a presentiment—a sort of revelation of his ill-ness."

My Uncle Sosthenes

The priest consented, and went off quickly, knocked at my uncle's door, was soon let in, and I saw the black cassock disappear within that stronghold of Freethought.

I hid under a neighboring gateway to wait for events. Had he been well, my uncle would have half murdered the Jesuit, but I knew that he would scarcely be able to move an arm, and I asked myself, gleefully, what sort of a scene would take place between these antagonists— what explanation would be given, and what would be the issue of this situation, which my uncle's indignation would render more tragic still?

I laughed till I had to hold my sides, and said to myself, half aloud: "Oh! what a joke, what a joke!"

Meanwhile it was getting very cold. I noticed that the Jesuit stayed a long time, and thought: "They are having an explanation, I suppose."

One, two, three hours passed, and still the reverend Father did not come out. What had happened? Had my uncle died in a fit when he saw him, or had he killed the cassocked gentleman? Perhaps they had mutually devoured each other? This last supposition appeared very unlikely, for I fancied that my uncle was quite incapable of swallowing a grain more nourishment at that moment.

At last the day broke. I was very uneasy, and, not venturing to go into the house myself, I went to one of my friends who lived opposite. I roused him, explained matters to him, much to his amusement and astonishment, and took possession of his window.

At nine o'clock he relieved me and I got a little sleep. At two o'clock I, in my turn, replaced him. We were utterly astonished.

At six o'clock the Jesuit left, with a very happy and satisfied look on his face, and we saw him go away with a quiet step.

Then, timid and ashamed, I went and knocked at my uncle's door. When the servant opened it I did not dare to ask her any questions, but went upstairs without saying a word.

My uncle was lying pale, exhausted, with weary, sorrowful eyes and heavy arms, on his bed. A little religious picture was fastened to one of the bed-curtains with a pin.

"Why, uncle," I said, "you in bed still? Are you not well?"

He replied in a feeble voice:

"Oh! my dear boy, I have been very ill; nearly dead."

"How was that, uncle?"

"I don't know; it was most surprising. But what is stranger still is, that the Jesuit priest who has just left—you know, that excellent man whom I have made such fun of—had a divine revelation of my state, and came to see me."

I was seized with an almost uncontrollable desire to laugh, and with difficulty said: "Oh, really!"

"Yes, he came. He heard a Voice telling him to get up and come to me, because I was going to die. It was a revelation."

I pretended to sneeze, so as not to burst out laughing; I felt inclined to roll on the ground with amusement.

In about a minute I managed to say, indignantly: "And you received him, uncle, you? You, a Freethinker, a Freemason? You did not have him thrown out-of-doors?"

He seemed confused, and stammered:

"Listen a moment, it is so astonishing—so astonishing and providential! He also spoke to me about my father; it seems he knew him formerly."

307

My Uncle Sosthenes

"Your father, uncle? But that is no reason for receiving a Jesuit."

"I know that, but I was very ill, and he looked after me most devotedly all night long. He was perfect; no doubt he saved my life; those men are all more or less doctors."

"Oh! he looked after you all night? But you said just now that he had only been gone a very short time."

"That is quite true; I kept him to breakfast after all his kindness. He had it at a table by my bedside while I drank a cup of tea."

"And he ate meat?"

My uncle looked vexed, as if I had said something very much out of place, and then added:

"Don't joke, Gaston; such things are out of place at times. He has shown me more devotion than many a relation would have done and I expect to have his convictions respected."

This rather upset me, but I answered, nevertheless: "Very well, uncle; and what did you do after breakfast?"

"We played a game of bézique, and then he repeated his breviary while I read a little book which he happened to have in his pocket, and which was not by any means badly written."

"A religious book, uncle?"

"Yes, and no, or rather—no. It is the history of their missions in Central Africa, and is rather a book of travels and adventures. What these men have done is very grand."

I began to feel that matters were going badly, so I got up. "Well, good-bye, uncle," I said, "I see you are going to leave Freemasonry for religion; you are a renegade."

He was still rather confused, and stammered:

308

My Uncle Sosthenes

"Well, but religion is a sort of Freemasonry."

"When is your Jesuit coming back?" I asked.

"I don't—I don't know exactly; tomorrow, perhaps; but it is not certain."

I went out, altogether overwhelmed.

My joke turned out very badly for me! My uncle became radically converted, and if that had been all I should not have cared so much. Clerical or Freemason, to me it is all the same; six of one and half-a-dozen of the other; but the worst of it is that he has just made his will—yes, made his will—and has disinherited me in favor of that rascally Jesuit!

The Duel

IN society, they called him "The handsome Signoles." He called himself Viscount Gontran Joseph de
Signoles.

An orphan and master of a sufficient fortune, he
cut something of a figure, as the saying is. He had an attractive form, enough readiness of speech to make some
attempt at wit, a certain natural grace of manner, an air
of nobility and pride, and a mustache which was both
formidable and pleasant to the eye—a thing that pleases
the ladies.

He was in demand in drawing-rooms, sought for by
waltzers, and he inspired in men that smiling enmity
which one has for people of energetic physique. He was
suspected of some love affairs which showed him capable
of much discretion, for a young man. He lived happy,
tranquil, in a state of moral well-being most complete.
It was well known that he was good at handling a sword,
and still better with a pistol.

"If I were to fight," he said, "I should choose a pistol.
With that weapon, I am sure of killing my man."

Now, one evening, having escorted two young
women, friends of his, to the theater, being also accompanied by their husbands, he offered them, after the play,
an ice at Tortoni's. They had been there about ten
minutes, when he perceived that a gentleman, seated at
a neighboring table, gazed persistently at one of the ladies of his party. She seemed troubled and disturbed,
lowering her eyes. Finally, she said to her husband:

"That man is staring me out of countenance. I do not know him; do you?"

The husband, who had seen nothing, raised his eyes but declared:

"No, not at all."

The young woman replied, half laughing, half angry: "It is very annoying; that individual is spoiling my ice."

The husband shrugged his shoulders, replying:

"Pshaw! Pay no attention to him. If we were to notice all the insolent people we meet, there would be no end of it."

But the Viscount arose brusquely. He could not allow this unknown man to spoil an ice he had offered. It was to him that the injury was addressed, as it was through him and for him that his friends had entered this *café*. The affair, then, concerned him only. He advanced toward the man and said to him:

"You have, sir, a manner of looking at these ladies that is not to be tolerated. I beg to ask you to cease this attention."

The other replied: "So you command me to keep the peace, do you?"

With set teeth, the Viscount answered: "Take care, sir, or you will force me to forget myself!"

The gentleman replied with a single word, an obscene word which resounded from one end of the *café* to the other, and made each guest start with a sudden movement as if they were all on springs. Those that were in front turned around; all the others raised their heads; three waiters turned about on their heels as if on pivots; the two ladies at the counter bounded forward, then entirely turned their backs upon the scene, as if they had been two automatons obeying the same manipulation.

There was a great silence. Then, suddenly, a sharp noise rent the air. The Viscount had struck his adversary. Everybody got up to interpose. Cards were exchanged.

After the Viscount had returned home, he walked up and down his room at a lively pace for some minutes. He was too much agitated to reflect upon anything. One idea only hovered over his mind: "a duel"; and yet this idea awoke in him, as yet, no emotion whatever. He had done what he ought to do; he had shown himself what he ought to be. People would talk of it, approve of it, and congratulate him. He said aloud, in a high voice, as one speaks when he is much troubled in thought:

"What a beast that man is."

Then he sat down and began to reflect. He would have to find some seconds in the morning. Whom should he choose? He thought over the people of his acquaintance who were the most celebrated and in the best positions. He took finally, Marquis de la Tour-Noire and Colonel Bourdin, a great lord and a soldier who was very strong. Their names would carry in the journals. He perceived that he was thirsty and he drank, one after the other, three glasses of water; then he began to walk again. He felt himself full of energy. By showing himself hot-brained, resolute in all things, by exacting rigorous, dangerous conditions, and by claiming a serious duel, a very serious one, his adversary would doubtless withdraw and make some excuses.

He took up the card which he had drawn from his pocket and thrown upon the table and re-read it as he had in the *café,* by a glance of the eye, and again in the cab, on returning home, by the light of a gas jet: "George Lamil, 51 Moncey street." That was all.

The Duel

He examined these assembled letters which appeared so mysterious to him, his senses all confused: George Lamil? Who was this man? What had he done? Why had he looked at that woman in such a way? Was it not revolting that a stranger, an unknown should come to trouble his life thus, at a blow, because he had been pleased to fix his insolent gaze upon a woman? And the Viscount repeated again, in a loud voice:

"What a brute!"

Then he remained motionless, standing, thinking, his look ever fixed upon the card. A certain anger against this piece of paper was awakened in him, a hateful anger which was mingled with a strange sentiment of malice. It was stupid, this whole story! He took a penknife which lay open at his hand, and pricked the card through the middle of the printed name, as if he were using a poignard upon some one.

So he must fight! Should he choose the sword or pistol, for he considered himself the insulted one. With the sword he risked less; but with the pistol, there was a chance of his adversary withdrawing. It is rarely that a duel with the sword is mortal, a reciprocal prudence hindering the combatants from keeping near enough to each other for the point to strike very deep; with the pistol he risked his life very seriously; but he could also meet the affair with all the honors of the situation and without arriving at a meeting. He said aloud:

"It is necessary to be firm. He will be afraid."

The sound of his own voice made him tremble and he began to look about him. He felt very nervous. He drank still another glass of water, then commenced to undress, preparatory to retiring.

When he was ready, he put out his light and closed his eyes. Then he thought:

The Duel

"I have all day tomorrow to busy myself with my affairs. I must sleep first, in order to be calm."

He was very warm under the clothes, but he could not succeed in falling asleep. He turned and turned again, remained for five minutes upon his back, then placed himself upon his left side, then rolled over to the right.

He was still thirsty. He got up and drank. Then a kind of disquiet seized him:

"Can it be that I am afraid?" said he.

Why should his heart begin to beat so foolishly at each of the customary noises about his room?—when the clock was going to strike and the spring made that little grinding noise as it raised itself to make the turn? And he found it was necessary for him to open his mouth in order to breathe for some seconds following this start, so great was his feeling of oppression. He began to reason with himself upon the possibilities of the thing:

"What have I to fear?"

No, certainly, he should not fear, since he was resolved to follow it out to the end and since he had fully made up his mind to fight without a qualm. But he felt himself so profoundly troubled that he asked himself:

"Can it be that I am afraid in spite of myself?"

And this doubt invaded him, this disquiet, this fear; if a force more powerful than his will, dominating, irresistible, should conquer him, what would happen to him? Yes, what would happen? Certainly he could walk upon the earth, if he wished to go there. But if he should tremble? And if he should lose consciousness? And he thought of his situation, of his reputation, of his name.

And a singular desire took possession of him to get up and look at himself in the glass. He relighted his candle. When he perceived his face reflected in the polished glass, he scarcely knew himself, and it seemed to him that he had never seen himself before. His eyes appeared enormous; he was pale, certainly; he was pale, very pale.

He remained standing there before the mirror. He put out his tongue as if to examine the state of his health, and suddenly this thought entered his brain after the fashion of a bullet:

"Tomorrow at this time, I shall perhaps be dead."

And his heart began to beat furiously.

"After tomorrow at this time, I shall perhaps be dead. This person opposite me, this being I have so often seen in this glass, will be no more. How can it be! I am here, I see myself, I feel that I am alive, and in twenty-four hours I shall be stretched upon that bed, dead, my eyes closed, cold, inanimate, departed."

He turned around to the bed and distinctly saw himself stretched on his back in the same clothes he had worn on going out. In his face were the lines of death, and a rigidity in the hands that would never stir again.

Then a fear of his bed came over him, and in order to see it no more he passed into his smoking-room. Mechanically he took a cigar, lighted it, and began to walk about. He was cold. He went toward the bell to waken his valet; but he stopped with his hand on the cord:

"This man would perceive at once that I am afraid."

He did not ring, but made a fire. His hands trembled a little from a nervous shiver when they came in contact with any object. His mind wandered; his thoughts from trouble became frightened, hasty, and sorrowful; an intoxication seemed to invade his mind as if he were drunk. And without ceasing he asked:

"What am I going to do? What is going to become of me?"

The Duel

His whole body was vibrating, traversed by a jerking and a trembling; he got up and approached the window, opening the curtains.

The day had dawned, a summer day. A rose-colored sky made the city rosy on roof and wall. A great fall of spread-out light, like a caress from the rising sun, enveloped the waking world; and, with this light, a gay, rapid, brutal hope invaded the heart of the Viscount! He was a fool to allow himself to be thus cast down by fear, even before anything was decided, before his witnesses had seen those of this George Lamil, before he yet knew whether he were going to fight a duel.

He made his toilette, dressed himself, and walked out with firm step.

He repeated constantly, in walking:

"It will be necessary for me to be energetic, very energetic. I must prove that I am not afraid."

His witnesses, the Marquis and the Colonel, placed themselves at his disposal and, after having shaken hands with him energetically, discussed the conditions. The Colonel asked:

"Do you wish it to be a serious duel?"

The Viscount responded: "Very serious."

The Marquis continued: "Will you use a pistol?"

"Yes."

"We leave you free to regulate the rest."

The Viscount enunciated, in a dry, jerky voice:

"Twenty steps at the order, and on raising the arm instead of lowering it. Exchange of bullets until one is grievously wounded."

The Colonel declared, in a satisfied tone:

"These are excellent conditions. You shoot well, all the chances are in your favor."

The Duel

They separated. The Viscount returned home to wait for them. His agitation, appeased for a moment, grew now from minute to minute. He felt along his arms, his legs, and in his breast a kind of trembling, of continued vibration; he could not keep still, either sitting or standing. There was no longer an appearance of saliva in his mouth, and each instant he made a noisy movement with his tongue, as if to unglue it from the roof of his mouth.

He wished to breakfast but he could not eat. Then the idea came to him of drinking to give himself courage and he brought out a small bottle of rum, which he swallowed in six little glasses, one after the other.

A heat, like that of a burning fire, invaded him, followed almost immediately by a numbness of the soul. He thought:

"I have found the remedy. Now all goes well."

But at the end of an hour, he had emptied the bottle and his state of agitation became intolerable. He felt a foolish impulse to roll on the ground, to cry out and bite. Then night fell.

A stroke of the bell gave him such a shock that he had not sufficient strength left to rise and receive his witnesses. He dared not even speak to them to say "Good evening," to pronounce a single word, for fear that they would discover a change in his voice.

The Colonel announced:

"All is arranged according to the conditions that you have fixed upon. Your adversary claimed the privileges of the offended, but he soon yielded and accepted all. His witnesses are two military men."

The Viscount pronounced the word:

"Thanks."

The Marquis continued:

"Excuse us if we only come in and go out, for we have still a thousand things to occupy our attention. A good doctor will be necessary, since the combat is only to cease after a severe wound, and you know that bullets are no trifles. Then, a place must be found, in some proximity to a house, where we may carry the wounded, if necessary, etc., etc.; finally, we have but two or three hours for it."

The Viscount, for the second time, articulated:

"Thanks."

The Colonel asked:

"How is it with you? Are you calm?"

"Yes, very calm, thank you."

The two men then retired.

When he again found himself alone, it seemed to him that he was mad. His domestic having lighted the lamps, he seated himself before his table to write some letters. After having traced, at the top of a page: "This is my testament—" he arose with a shake and put it away from him, feeling himself incapable of forming two ideas, or of sufficient resolution to decide what was to be done.

So he was going to fight a duel! There was no way to avoid it. How could he ever go through with it? He wished to fight, it was his intention and firm resolution so to do; and yet, he felt, that in spite of all his effort of mind and all the tension of his will, he would not be able to preserve even the necessary force to go to the place of meeting. He tried to imagine the combat, his own attitude, and the position of his adversary.

From time to time, his teeth chattered in his mouth with a little hard noise. He tried to read, and took down the Chateauvillard code of dueling. Then he asked himself:

"Has my opponent frequently fought? Is he known? Is he classed? How am I to know?"

He remembered Baron de Vaux's book upon experts with the pistol, and he ran through it from one end to the other. George Lamil was not mentioned. Nevertheless, if this man were not an expert, he would not so readily have accepted this dangerous weapon and these mortal conditions.

He opened, in passing, a box of Gastinne Renettes which stood on a little stand, took out one of the pistols, held it in a position to fire, and raised his arm. But he trembled from head to foot and the gun worked upon all his senses.

Then he said: "It is impossible. I cannot fight in this condition."

He looked at the end of the barrel, at that little black, deep hole that spits out death, he thought of the dishonor, of the whisperings in his circle, of the laughs in the drawing-rooms, of the scorn of the ladies, of the allusions of the journals, of all the insults that cowards would throw at him.

He continued to examine the weapon, and, raising the cock, he suddenly saw a priming glittering underneath like a little red flame. The pistol was loaded then, through a chance forgetfulness. And he found in this discovery a confused, inexplicable joy.

If in the presence of the other man he did not have that calm, noble bearing that he should have, he would be lost forever. He would be spotted, branded with the sign of infamy, hunted from the world! And this calm, heroic bearing he would not have, he knew it, he felt it. However, he was brave, since he did wish to fight! He was brave, since. . . . The thought that budded never took form, even in his own mind; for, opening his mouth wide

The Duel

he brusquely thrust the barrel of his pistol into his throat, and pulled the trigger. . . .

When his valet, hearing the report, hastened to him, he found him dead upon his back. A jet of blood had splashed upon the white paper on the table and made a great red spot upon these four words:

"This is my testament."

A Vagabond

FOR more than a month Randel had been walking, seeking for work everywhere. He had left his native place, Ville-Avary, in the department of La Manche, because there was no work to be had. He was a journeyman carpenter, twenty-seven years old, a steady fellow and good workman, but for two months, he, the eldest son, had been obliged to live on his family, with nothing to do but loaf in the general stoppage of work. Bread was getting scarce with them; the two sisters went out as charwomen, but earned little, and he, Jacques Randel, the strongest of them all, did nothing because he had nothing to do, and ate the others' bread.

Then he went and inquired at the town-hall, and the mayor's secretary told him that he would find work at the Labor-Center. So he started, well provided with papers and certificates, and carrying another pair of shoes, a pair of trousers, and a shirt in a blue handkerchief at the end of his stick.

He had walked almost without stopping, day and night, along interminable roads, in the sun and rain, without ever reaching that mysterious country where workmen find work. At first he had the fixed idea that he must only work at his own trade, but at every carpenter's shop where he applied he was told that they had just dismissed men on account of work being so slack, and finding himself at the end of his resources, he made up his mind to undertake any job that he might come across on the road. And so by turns he was a navvy, stableman, stone-sawyer; he split wood, lopped the branches of trees, dug wells, mixed mortar, tied up faggots, tended goats on a mountain, and all for a few pence, for he only obtained two or three days' work occasionally, by offering himself at a shamefully low price, in order to tempt the avarice of employers and peasants.

And now for a week he had found nothing and he had no money left. He was eating a piece of bread, thanks to the charity of some women from whom he had begged at house-doors, on the road. It was getting dark, and Jacques Randel, jaded, his legs failing him, his stomach empty, and with despair in his heart, was walking barefoot on the grass by the side of the road, for he was taking care of his last pair of shoes, the other pair having already ceased to exist for a long time. It was a Saturday, toward the end of autumn. The heavy gray clouds were being driven rapidly through the sky by gusts of wind that whistled among the trees, and one felt that it would rain soon. The country was deserted at that time of the evening, and on the eve of Sunday. Here and there in the fields there rose up stacks of thrashed-out corn, like huge yellow mushrooms, and the fields looked bare, as they had already been sown for the next year.

Randel was hungry, with the hunger of some wild animal, such a hunger as drives wolves to attack men. Worn out and weakened with fatigue, he took longer strides, so as not to take so many steps, and with heavy head, the blood throbbing in his temples, with red eyes and dry mouth, he grasped his stick tightly in his hand, with a longing to strike the first passerby whom he should meet, and who might be going home to supper, with all his force.

He looked at the sides of the road, with the image of potatoes dug up and lying on the ground, before his eyes; if he had found any, he would have gathered some dead

wood, made a fire in the ditch, and have had a capital
supper off the warm, round tubers, which he would first
of all have held burning hot in his cold hands. But it was
too late in the year and he would have to gnaw a raw
beet-root, as he had done the day before, having picked
one up in a field.

For the last two days he had spoken aloud as he
quickened his steps, under the influence of his thoughts.
He had never done much thinking, hitherto, as he had
given all his mind, all his simple faculties, to his industrial requirements. But now fatigue, and this desperate search for work which he could not get, refusals
and rebuffs, nights spent in the open air lying on the
grass, long fasting, the contempt which he knew people
with a settled abode felt for a vagabond, the question
which he was continually asked: "Why did you not remain at home?" distress at not being able to use his
strong arms which he felt so full of vigor, the recollection
of his relations who had remained at home and who also
had not a half-penny, filled him by degrees with a rage
which was accumulating every day, every hour, every
minute, and which now escaped his lips in spite of himself in short, growling sentences.

As he stumbled over the stones which rolled beneath
his bare feet, he grumbled: "How wretched! how miserable! A set of hogs, to let a man die of hunger, a
carpenter. A set of hogs—not twopence—not twopence.
And now it is raining—a set of hogs!"

He was indignant at the injustice of fate, and cast
the blame on men, on all men, because Nature, that
great, blind mother, is unjust, cruel and perfidious, and
he repeated through his clenched teeth, "A set of hogs,"
as he looked at the thin gray smoke which rose from the
roofs, for it was the dinner hour. And without thinking

about that other injustice, which is human, and which is called robbery and violence, he felt inclined to go into one of those houses to murder the inhabitants, and to sit down to table, in their stead.

He said to himself: "I have a right to live, and they are letting me die of hunger—and yet I only ask for work—a set of hogs!" And the pain in his limbs, the gnawing in his heart, rose to his head like terrible intoxication, and gave rise to this simple thought in his brain: "I have the right to live because I breathe, and because the air is the common property of everybody, and so nobody has the right to leave me without bread!"

A thick, fine, icy cold rain was coming down, and he stopped and murmured: "How miserable! another month of walking before I get home." He was indeed returning home then; for he saw that he should more easily find work in his native town where he was known —and he did not mind what he did—then on the highroads, where everybody suspected him. As the carpentering business was not going well he would turn daylaborer, be a mason's hodman, ditcher, break stones on the road. If he only earned tenpence a day, that would at any rate find him something to eat.

He tied the remains of his last pocket handkerchief round his neck to prevent the cold water from running down his back and chest; but he soon found that it was penetrating the thin material of which his clothes were made, and he glanced round him with the agonized look of a man who does not know where to hide his body and to rest his head, and has no place of shelter in the whole world.

Night came on and wrapped the country in obscurity, and in the distance, in a meadow, he saw a dark spot on the grass; it was a cow, and so he got over the

ditch by the roadside and went up to her, without exactly knowing what he was doing. When he got close to
her, she raised her great head to him, and he thought:
"If I only had a jug, I could get a little milk." He looked
at the cow, and the cow looked at him, and then suddenly giving her a violent kick in the side, he said:
"Get up!"

The animal got up slowly, letting her heavy udder
hang down below her; then the man lay down on his
back between the animal's legs, and drank for a long
time, squeezing the warm swollen teats which tasted of
the cow-stall, with both hands, and drank as long as any
milk remained in that living well. But the icy rain began
to fall more heavily, and he saw no place of shelter on
the whole of that bare plain. He was cold, and he looked
at a light which was shining among the trees, in the
window of a house.

The cow had lain down again, heavily, and he sat
down by her side and stroked her head, grateful for the
nourishment she had given him. The animal's strong,
thick breath, which came out of her nostrils like two
jets of steam in the evening air, blew onto the workman's
face, who said: "You are not cold, inside there!" He put
his hands on to her chest and under her legs, to find
some warmth there, and then the idea struck him that
he might pass the night against that large, warm stomach.
So he found a comfortable place and laid his forehead
against the great udder from which he had quenched his
thirst just previously, and then, as he was worn out with
fatigue, he fell asleep immediately.

He woke up, however, several times, with his back
or his stomach half frozen, according as he put one or the
other to the animal's flank. Then he turned over to warm
and dry that part of his body which had remained ex-

posed to the night air, and he soon went soundly to sleep again.

The crowing of a cock woke him; the day was break-ing, it was no longer raining and the sky was bright. The cow was resting with her muzzle on the ground, and he stooped down, resting on his hands, to kiss those wide nostrils of moist flesh, and said: "Good-bye, my beauty, until next time. You are a nice animal! Good-bye." Then he put on his shoes and went off, and for two hours he walked straight on before him, always following the same road, and then he felt so tired that he sat down on the grass. It was broad daylight by that time, and the church bells were ringing; men in blue blouses, women in white caps, some on foot, some in carts, began to pass along the road, going to the neighboring villages to spend Sunday with friends or relations.

A stout peasant came in sight, driving a score of frightened, bleating sheep in front of him, whom an active dog kept together, so Randel got up and raising his cap, he said: "You do not happen to have any work for a man who is dying of hunger?" But the other, giving an angry look at the vagabond, replied: "I have no work for fellows whom I meet on the road."

And the carpenter went back and sat down by the side of the ditch again. He waited there for a long time, watching the country people pass, and looking for a kind, compassionate face before he renewed his request, and finally selected a man in an overcoat, whose stomach was adorned with a gold chain. "I have been looking for work," he said, "for the last two months and cannot find any, and I have not a half-penny in my pocket."

But the semi-gentleman replied: "You should have read the notice which is stuck up at the beginning of the village: 'Begging is prohibited within the boundaries of this parish.' Let me tell you that I am the mayor, and if you do not get out of here pretty quickly, I shall have you arrested."

Randel, who was getting angry, replied: "Have me arrested if you like; I should prefer it, for at any rate I should not die of hunger." And he went back and sat down by the side of his ditch again, and in about a quarter of an hour two gendarmes appeared on the road. They were walking slowly, side by side, well in sight, glittering in the sun with their shining hats, their yellow accouterments and their metal buttons, as if to frighten evildoers, and to put them to flight at a distance. He knew that they were coming after him, but he did not move, for he was seized with a sudden desire to defy them, to be arrested by them, and to have his revenge later.

They came on without appearing to have seen him, walking with military steps, heavily, and balancing themselves as if they were doing the goose-step; and then suddenly as they passed him, they noticed him and stopped, looking at him angrily and threateningly. The brigadier came up to him and asked: "What are you doing here?"

"I am resting," the man replied, calmly

"Where do you come from?"

"If I had to tell you all the places I have been to, it would take me more than an hour."

"Where are you going to?"

"To Ville-Avary."

"Where is that?"

"In La Manche."

"Is that where you belong to?"

"It is."

"Why did you leave it?"

"To try for work."

A Vagabond

The brigadier turned to his gendarme, and said, in the angry voice of a man who is exasperated at last by the same trick: "They all say that, these scamps. I know all about it." And then he continued: "Have you any papers?"

"Yes, I have some."

"Give them to me."

Randel took his papers out of his pocket, his certificates, those poor, worn-out, dirty papers which were falling to pieces, and gave them to the soldier, who spelled them through, hemming and hawing and then having seen that they were all in order, he gave them back to Randel with the dissatisfied look of a man whom some one cleverer than himself has tricked.

After a few moments further reflection, he asked him: "Have you any money on you?"

"No."

"None whatever?"

"None."

"Not even a sou?"

"Not even a sou!"

"How do you live then?"

"On what people give me."

"Then you beg?"

And Randel answered resolutely: "Yes, when I can."

Then the gendarme said: "I have caught you on the highroad in the act of vagabondage and begging, without any resources or trade, and so I command you to come with me."

The carpenter got up and said: "Wherever you please." And placing himself between the two soldiers, even before he had received the order to do so, he added: "Come, lock me up; that will at any rate put a roof over my head when it rains."

A Vagabond

And they set off toward the village, whose red tiles could be seen through the leafless trees, a quarter of a league off. Service was just going to begin when they went through the village. The square was full of people, who immediately formed two hedges to see the criminal, who was being followed by a crowd of excited children, pass. Male and female peasants looked at the prisoner between the two gendarmes, with hatred in their eyes, and a longing to throw stones at him, to tear his skin with their nails, to trample him under their feet. They asked each other whether he had committed murder or robbery. The butcher, who was an ex-Spahi declared that he was a deserter. The tobacconist thought that he recognized him as the man who had that very morning passed a bad half-franc piece off on him, and the ironmonger declared that he was the murderer of widow Malet, for whom the police had been looking for six months.

In the hall of the municipal council, into which his custodians took him, Randel saw the mayor again, sitting on the magisterial bench, with the schoolmaster by his side.

"Ah! ah!" the magistrate exclaimed, "so here you are again, my fine fellow. I told you I should have you locked up. Well, brigadier, what is he charged with?"

He is a vagabond without house or home, Monsieur le Maire, without any resources or money, so he says, who was arrested in the act of begging, but he is provided with good testimonials, and his papers are all in order."

"Show me his papers," the mayor said. He took them, read them, re-read, returned them, and then said: "Search him"; so they searched him, but found nothing, and the mayor seemed perplexed, and asked the workman:

"What were you doing on the road this morning?"

"I was looking for work."

"Work? On the highroad?"

"How do you expect me to find any if I hide in the woods?"

They looked at each other, with the hatred of two wild beasts which belong to different, hostile species, and the magistrate continued: "I am going to have you set at liberty, but do not be brought up before me again."

To which the carpenter replied: "I would rather you locked me up; I have had enough running about the country."

But the magistrate replied severely: "Be silent." And then he said to the two gendarmes: "You will conduct this man two hundred yards from the village, and let him continue his journey."

"At any rate, give me something to eat," the workman said; but the other grew indignant: "It only remains for us to feed you! Ah! ah! ah! that is rather strong!"

But Randel went on, firmly: "If you let me nearly die of hunger again, you will force me to commit a crime, and then, so much the worse for you other fat fellows."

The mayor had risen, and he repeated: "Take him away immediately, or I shall end by getting angry."

The two gendarmes thereupon seized the carpenter by the arms and dragged him out. He allowed them to do it without resistance, passed through the village again, and found himself on the highroad once more; and when the men had accompanied him two hundred yards beyond the village, the brigader said: "Now off with you, and do not let me catch you about here again, for if I do, you will know it."

Randel went off without replying, or knowing where

he was going. He walked on for a quarter of an hour or twenty miuntes, so stupefied that he no longer thought of anything. But suddenly, as he was passing a· small house, where the window was half open, the smell of the soup and boiled meat stopped him suddenly in front of it, and hunger, fierce, devouring, maddening hunger seized him, and almost drove him against the walls of the house, like a wild beast.

He said aloud, in a grumbling voice: "In Heaven's name! they must give me some, this time." And he began to knock at the door vigorously with his stick, and as nobody came he knocked louder and called out: "Hallo! you people in there, open the door!" And then, as nothing moved, he went up to the window, and pushed it open with his hand, and the close warm air of the kitchen, full of the smell of hot soup, meat, and cabbage escaped into the cold, outer air, and with a bound the carpenter was in the house. Two covers were laid on the table; no doubt the proprietors of the house, on going to church, had left their dinner on the fire, their nice, Sunday boiled beef and vegetable soup, while there was a loaf of new bread on the chimney-piece, between two bottles which seemed full.

Randel seized the bread first of all, and broke it with as much violence as if he were strangling a man, and then he began to eat it voraciously, swallowing great mouthfuls quickly. But almost immediately the smell of the meat attracted him to the fireplace, and having taken off the lid of the saucepan, he plunged a fork into it and brought out a large piece of beef, tied with a string. Then he took more cabbage, carrots, and onions until his plate was full, and having put it on to the table, he sat down before it, cut the meat into four pieces, and dined as if he had been at home. When he had eaten nearly all the meat, besides a quantity of vegetables, he felt thirsty, and took one of the bottles off the mantelpiece.

Scarcely had he poured the liquor into his glass than he saw it was brandy. So much the better; it was warming; it would instill some fire into his veins, and that would be all right, after being so cold; and he drank some. He found it very good, certainly, for he had grown unaccustomed to it, and he poured himself out another glassful, which he drank at two gulps. And then, almost immediately he felt quite merry and light-hearted from the effect of the alcohol, just as if some great happiness were flowing through his system.

He continued to eat, but more slowly, dipping his bread into the soup. His skin had become burning, and especially his forehead, where the veins were throbbing. But suddenly the church bells began to ring. Mass was over, and instinct rather than fear, the instinct of prudence which guides all beings, and makes them clear-sighted in danger, made the carpenter get up. He put the remains of the loaf into one pocket, and the brandy bottle into the other, and he furtively went to the window and looked out into the road. It was still deserted, so he jumped out and set off walking again, but instead of following the highroad, he ran across the fields toward a wood which he saw a little way off.

He felt alert, strong, light-hearted, glad of what he had done, and so nimble that he sprang over the inclosures of the fields, at a single bound, and as soon as he was under the trees, he took the bottle out of his pocket again, and began to drink once more, swallowing it down as he walked, and then his ideas began to get confused, his eyes grew dim, and his legs as elastic as springs, and he started singing the old popular song:

A Vagabond

"Oh! how nice, how nice it is,
To pick the sweet, wild strawberries."

He was now walking on thick, damp, cool moss, and
the soft carpet under his feet made him feel absurdly
inclined to turn head over heels, as he used to do as a
child; so he took a run, turned a somersault, got up, and
began over again. And between each time, he began to
sing again:

"Oh! how nice, how nice it is,
To pick the sweet, wild strawberries."

Suddenly he found himself on the edge of a sunken
road, and in the road he saw a tall girl, a servant who
was returning to the village with two pails of milk. He
watched, stooping down and with his eyes as bright as
those of a dog who scents a quail, but she saw him,
raised her head and said: "Was that you singing like
that?" He did not reply, however, but jumped down into
the road, although it was at least six feet down, and when
she saw him suddenly standing in front of her, she exclaimed: "Oh! dear, how you frightened me!"

But he did not hear her, for he was drunk, he was
mad, excited by another requirement which was more
imperative than hunger, more feverish than alcohol; by
the irresistible fury of the man who has been in want of
everything for two months, and who is drunk; who is
young, ardent, and inflamed by all the appetites which
nature has implanted in the flesh of vigorous men.

The girl started back from him, frightened at his
face, his eyes, his half-open mouth, his outstretched
hands, but he seized her by the shoulders, and without
a word threw her down in the road.

She let her two pails fall, and they rolled over noisily, and all the milk was spilt, and then she screamed, but comprehending that it would be of no use to call for help in that lonely spot, and seeing that he was not going to make an attempt on her life, she yielded without much difficulty, and not very angrily either, for he was a strong, handsome young fellow, and really not rough.

When she got up, the thought of her overturned pails suddenly filled her with fury, and taking off one of her wooden clogs, she threw it, in her turn, at the man to break his head, since he did not pay her for her milk.

But he, mistaking the reason for this sudden violent attack, somewhat sobered, and frightened at what he had done, ran off as fast as he could while she threw stones at him, some of which hit him in the back.

He ran for a long time, very long, until he felt more tired than he had ever been before. His legs were so weak that they could scarcely carry him; all his ideas were confused, he lost the recollection of everything, and could no longer think about anything; and so he sat down at the foot of a tree, and in five minutes was fast asleep. He was soon awakened, however, by a rough shake and, on opening his eyes he saw two cocked hats of polished leather bending over him, and the two gendarmes of the morning, who were holding him and binding his arms.

"I knew I should catch you again," said the brigadier, jeeringly. But Randel got up without replying. The two men shook him, quite ready to ill treat him if he made a movement, for he was their prey now, he had become a jail-bird, caught by hunters of criminals who would not let him go again.

"Now, start!" the brigadier said, and they set off. It was getting evening, and the autumn twilight was settling, heavy and dark, over the land, and in half an hour they reached the village, where every door was open, for the people had heard what had happened. Peasants and peasant women and girls, excited with anger, as if every man had been robbed, and every woman violated, wished to see the wretch brought back, so that they might overwhelm him with abuse. They hooted him from the first house in the village until they reached the mansion-house, where the mayor was waiting for him. Eager to avenge himself on this vagabond as soon as he saw him, he cried:

"Ah! my fine fellow! here we are!" And he rubbed his hands, more pleased than he usually was, and continued: "I said so. I said so, the moment I saw him in the road." And then with increased satisfaction:

"Oh! you blackguard! Oh! you dirty blackguard! You will get your twenty years, my fine fellow!"

Madame Parisse

I WAS seated on the mole of the little port of Obernon, near the hamlet of La Salis, watching Antibes in the setting sun. I have never seen anything so wonderfully beautiful. The little town, inclosed within its heavy fortifications of masonry (constructed by Monsieur de Vauban), was situated in the middle of the Gulf of Nice. The great waves rolled in from afar to throw themselves at its feet, surrounding it with a garland of foam; and, above the ramparts, the houses could be seen, climbing one above another up to the two towers pointing to the sky like two horns on an ancient helmet, and standing out against the milky whiteness of the Alps—an enormous, illimitable wall of snow that appeared to shut off the entire horizon. Between the white foam at the foot of the walls and the white snow on the border of the sky, the little city, sparkling and upright on the blue background of the nearest mountains, shone in the rays of the setting sun, looking like a pyramid of red-roofed houses, the *façades* of which were white, yet of such different shades of white that they seemed to be of many hues.

The sky above the Alps was of a pale blue that was almost white, as if the snow had given to it some of its own frosty whiteness. A few silvery clouds floated near the pale summit; and, on the other side of the gulf, Nice lay on the edge of the water like a white ribbon between the sea and the mountains. Two great lateen sails, forced onward by a strong breeze, appeared to run before the waves. I gazed at the scene, enchanted with its beauty.

It was one of those sights so charming, so rare, so exquisite, which seem to take possession of you, and become one of those moments never to be forgotten, like certain happy memories. We think, we enjoy, we suffer, we are moved, from various causes, but we love by seeing! He that can feel deep emotion through the power of sight experiences the same keen joy, refined and profound, felt by the man with a sensitive and nervous ear when listening to music that stirs the heart.

I said to my companion, Monsieur Martini, a pureblooded southerner, "That is certainly one of the rarest spectacles that it ever has been my good fortune to admire. I have seen Mont-Saint-Michel, that enormous jewel of granite, spring forth from the sands at sunrise. I have seen, in the Sahara, Lake Raianecherqui, fifty kilometers in length, shine under a moon as brilliant as our sun, and exhale toward the clouds a vapor as white as milk. I have seen in the Lipari Islands the fantastic sulphur crater of Volcanello, a giant flower, the center of which is a volcano that smokes and burns with a limitless yellow flame that spreads out over the ocean. But I have seen nothing more impressive than Antibes, standing before the Alps in the setting sun. And I cannot tell why, at this moment, souvenirs of olden days haunt me. Verses of Homer come into my mind. It is a city of the old Orient, Antibes, it is a city of the 'Odyssey,' it is a western Troy—even though Troy was far from the sea."

Monsieur Martini drew from his pocket a Sarty guide, and read:

"The city was originally a colony founded by the Phœnicians of Marseilles, about the year 340 B.C. It received from them the Greek name of Antipolis, that is to say, 'city over against,' 'city in front of another,' because, in reality, it was situated opposite Nice, another colony of Marseilles. After the conquest of the Gauls, the Romans made of Antibes a municipal city, and her inhabitants enjoyed the privileges of a Roman city."

"We know," he continued, "by an epigram of Martial, that in his time—"

I interrupted him, saying: "I don't care what it was! I tell you I have before my eyes a city of the 'Odyssey.' Coast of Asia or coast of Europe—they are alike; and there is nothing on the other shore of the Mediterranean that awakens in me the memory of heroic days as does this."

The sound of an approaching step caused me to turn my head; a tall, dark woman was passing along the road that follows the sea in the direction of the cape.

Monsieur Martini murmured, emphasizing the last words: "It is Madame Parisse—you know!"

No, I did not know, but this name thrown out, the name of the shepherd of Troy, confirmed me in my dream.

I said, however, "Who is this Madame Parisse?"

He appeared surprised that I did not know her story. I reaffirmed that I did not know it, and I looked at the woman, who went on without seeing us, dreaming, walking with a slow, stately step, like the dames of antiquity, without doubt. She was about thirty-five years old, and beautiful yet, very beautiful, though perhaps a trifle too plump.

After she had passed out of sight, Monsieur Martini told me this story.

"Madame Parisse, a Mademoiselle Combelombe, had married, a year before the war of 1870, Monsieur Parisse, an employee of the government. She was then a beautiful young girl, as slender and gay as she has since become stout and sad. She had accepted Monsieur Parisse reluctantly; he was one of those little red-tape men, with short legs, who make a great fuss in a pint measure, which is yet too large for them.

"After the war, Antibes was occupied by a single battalion of line commanded by Monsieur Jean de Carmelin, a young officer who had been decorated during the campaign, and had only recently received the four stripes. As he was greatly bored with the life in that fortress, in that suffocating molehill shut in by enormous double walls, the commander went quite often for a walk on the Cape, a sort of park or forest, where there was a fine, fresh breeze.

"There he met Madame Parisse, who used also to come on summer evenings to breathe the fresh air under the trees. How was it that they loved? Can one tell? They met, they looked at each other, and when they could not meet, they thought of each other, without doubt. The image of the young woman with the brown eyes, black hair, and pale face, the image of that fresh and beautiful southern girl, who showed her pretty white teeth in smiling, remained floating before the eyes of the officer, who would continue his promenade lost in thought, biting his cigar instead of smoking it. And the image of the commander in his close-fitting coat and red trousers, covered with gold lace, whose blond mustache curled on his lip, must have remained before the eyes of Madame Parisse when her husband, unshaved, badly dressed, short of limb, and with pursy stomach, returned home for supper.

"From meeting so often, they smiled at seeing each other, perhaps; and from that they came to think they knew each other. He bowed to her, certainly. She was surprised, and inclined her head slightly, only just enough to escape being impolite. But at the end of two weeks she returned his salutations from afar, before coming face to face.

"He talked to her! Of what? Of the setting sun, without any doubt! And they admired it together, looking deep into each other's eyes more often than at the horizon. And every day during two weeks there was some simple pretext for a little chat of several minutes. Then they dared to take a few steps together in talking of something or other; but their eyes spoke of a thousand things more intimate, of secret and charming things, the reflection of which in the softness and emotion of a look causes the heart to beat, because they reveal the soul better than words. Then he must have taken her hand and murmured those words which a woman divines without appearing to have heard them.

"It was admitted between them that they loved, without submitting their mutual knowledge to the proof of sensuality or passion. She would have been content to remain indefinitely at the stage of romantic tenderness, but not he—he wished to go further. And he pressed her, every day more ardently, to give herself entirely to him. She resisted, did not wish it, and even seemed resolved never to yield.

"One evening, however, she said to him, as if by chance: 'My husband has just gone to Marseilles, and is going to remain there four days.'

"Jean de Carmelin threw himself at her feet, begging her to open her door that very evening near eleven o'clock. But she would not listen to him, and returned home as if angry. The commandant was in a bad humor all the evening; and the next day beginning at daybreak he walked on the ramparts in a rage, going from the drum-school to the platoon-school, and meting out reprimands to officers and men like one throwing stones into a crowd. But on returning for breakfast, he found under his napkin a note containing these four words: 'This evening, ten o'clock.' And he gave five francs, without any apparent reason, to the boy who served him.

"The day seemed long. He passed a part of it in prinking and perfuming himself. At the moment when he placed himself at the table for dinner, another envelope was handed to him. He found inside this telegram:

" 'My darling, business terminated. I return this evening: train at nine.   PARISSE.'

"The commandant gave vent to an oath so violent that the boy let the soup-tureen fall on the floor. What should he do? Certainly, he wanted her, and that very night, too, let it cost what it might, and he would have her. He would have her by some means or another, if he had to arrest and imprison her husband. Suddenly an insane idea crossed his mind. He called for paper and wrote:

" 'MADAME: He will not return this evening. I swear it to you, and I will be at ten o'clock at the place you know. Fear nothing, I guarantee everything on my honor as an officer.
" 'JEAN DE CARMELIN.'

"And, having sent this letter, he dined tranquilly. About eight o'clock he summoned Captain Gribois, who was next in command, and said to him, while rolling between his his fingers the rumpled dispatch of Monsieur Parisse: 'Captain, I have received a telegram of a singular character, which it is impossible for me to communicate to you. You must go immediately and guard the gates of the city, in such a way that no one—you understand, no one—either comes in or goes out before six o'clock tomorrow morning. You must place guards in the streets also, and compel the inhabitants to go into their houses at nine o'clock. Anyone who is found outside after that hour will be conducted to his domicile *manu militari.* If your men meet me during the night they must retire at once with an air of not recognizing me. Do you understand me thoroughly?'

" 'Yes, commandant.'

" 'I make you responsible for the execution of these orders, captain.'

" 'Yes, commandant.'

" 'Would you like a glass of Chartreuse?'

" 'With pleasure, commandant.'

"They touched glasses, drank the yellow liquor, and Captain Gribois departed.

"The train from Marseilles came into the station at exactly nine o'clock, and left on the platform two travelers, then went on its way toward Nice.

"One of the travelers was tall and thin. He was a Monsieur Saribe, merchant in oils. The other passenger was short and stout—it was Monsieur Parisse. They started on their way together, their traveling bags in their hands, to reach the town, a kilometer distant. But on arriving at the gate the sentinels crossed their bayonets and ordered them off.

"Alarmed, amazed, and filled with astonishment they drew aside and deliberated; then, after taking counsel together, they returned with precaution to parley, and to make known their names. But the soldiers must have received peremptory orders, for they threatened to shoot, and the two travelers, greatly frightened, took flight at the top of their speed, leaving behind them their bags, which impeded their flight.

"The two unfortunate travelers made the circle of

the ramparts and presented themselves at the Porte de Cannes. This also was closed and guarded as well by a menacing sentinel. Messieurs Saribe and Parisse, like prudent men, insisted no longer, but returned to the station to find a shelter, for the road around the fortifications was not very safe after sunset.

"The employee at the station, surprised and sleepy, gave them permission to remain until daylight in the waiting-room. They sat there, without light, side by side, on the green velvet-covered bench, too frightened to think of sleeping. The night was long for them.

"Toward half past six they learned that the gates were open and that one could at last enter Antibes. They started for the town, but did not find their bags along the way. When they had passed through the gates, still a little uneasy, the Commandant de Carmelin, with a sly look and his head in the air, came himself to meet and question them. He bowed to them politely, and made excuses for having caused them to pass a bad night, but said he had been obliged to execute orders.

"The people of Antibes were mystified. Some talked of a surprise meditated by the Italians; others of the landing of the imperial prince; and still others imagined an Orléanist plot. The truth was not guessed until later, when they learned that the battalion of the commandant had been sent far away, and that Monsieur de Carmelin had been severely punished."

Monsieur Martini ceased speaking, and soon after Madame Parisse reappeared, her walk being finished. She passed sedately near me, her eyes on the Alps, the summits of which were ruddy with the last rays of the setting sun.

I desired to salute her, that poor, saddened woman who must think always of that one night of love now so far in the past, and of the bold man who had dared, for a kiss from her, to put a whole city in a state of siege and compromise his future. Today he had probably forgotten her, unless sometimes, after drinking, he relates that audacious farce, so comic and so tender.

Had she ever seen him again? Did she love him still? And I thought: Here, indeed, is a trait of modern love, grotesque and yet heroic. The Homer who will sing of this Helen, and of the adventures of her Menelaus, must have the soul of a Merimée. And yet, the captain, this lover of that deserted woman, was valiant, bold, beautiful, strong as Achilles, and more cunning than Ulysses.

One Phase of Love

THE walls of the cell were bare and whitewashed. A narrow, barred window, so high that it could not easily be reached, lighted this little room; the crazy man, seated on a straw chair, looked at us with a fixed eye, vague and haunting. He was thin, with wrinkled cheeks and almost white hair that one would think had grown white in a few months. His clothes seemed too large for his dried-up limbs, his shrunken chest, and hollow body. One felt that this man had been ravaged by his thoughts, by a thought, as fruit is by a worm. His madness, his idea, was there in his head, obstinate, harassing, devouring. It was eating his body, little by little. It, the Invisible, the Impalpable, the Unseizable, the Immaterial Idea gnawed his flesh, drank his blood, and extinguished his life.

What a mystery, that this man should be killed by a Thought! He is an object of fear and pity, this madman! What strange dream, frightful and deadly, can dwell in his forehead, to fold such profound and ever-changing wrinkles in it?

The doctor said to me: "He has terrible paroxysms of rage, and is one of the most singularly demented people I have ever seen. His madness is of an amorous, erotic kind. He is a sort of necrophile. He has written a journal which shows as plainly as daylight the malady of his mind. His madness is visible, so to speak. If you are interested, you may run through this document."

I followed the doctor into his office and he gave me the journal of this miserable man.

"Read it," said he, "and give me your opinion about it."

Here is what the little book contained:

"Up to the age of thirty-two years I lived tranquilly without love. Life appeared to me very simple, very good, and very easy. I was rich. I had a taste for some things, but had never felt a passion for anything. It was good to live! I awoke happy each day, to do things which it pleased me to do, and I went to bed satisfied with calm hope for the next day and a future without care.

"I had had some mistresses without ever having my heart torn by desire or my soul bruised by love after the possession. It is good so to live. It is better to love, but terrible. Still those who love like everybody else should find happiness, less than mine, perhaps, for love has come to me in an unbelievable manner.

"Being rich, I collected ancient furniture and antiques. Often I thought of the unknown hands which had touched these things, of the eyes that had admired them, and the hearts that had loved them—for one does love such things! I often remained for hours and hours looking at a little watch of the last century. It was so dainty, so pretty with its enamel and gold embossing. And it still went, as on the day when some woman had bought it, delighted in the possession of so fine a jewel. It had not ceased to palpitate, to live its mechanical life, but had ever continued its regular ticktock, although a century had passed. Who then had first carried it upon her breast, in the warmth of the dress—the heart of the watch beating against the heart of the woman? What hand had held it at the ends of its warm fingers, then wiped the enameled shepherds, tarnished a little by the moisture of the skin? What eyes had looked upon this flowered dial awaiting the hour, the dear hour, the divine hour?

"How I wished to see her, to know her, the woman who had chosen this rare and exquisite object. But she is dead! I am possessed by a desire for women of former times; I love all those who have loved long ago. The story of past tenderness fills my heart with regrets. Oh! the beauty, the smiles, the caresses of youth, the hopes! These things should be eternal!

"How I have wept, during whole nights, over the women of old, so beautiful, so tender, so sweet, whose lips have opened to the kiss, and who are now dead! The kiss is immortal! It goes from lip to lip, from century to century, from age to age! Men take it and give it and die.

"The past attracts me, the present frightens me, because the future is death. I regret all that which is gone, I weep for those who have lived; I wish to stop the hour, to arrest time. But it goes, it goes, it passes away, and it takes me, from second to second, a little of me for the annihilation of tomorrow. And I shall never live again.

"Adieu, women of yesterday, I love you.

"And yet I have nothing to complain of. I have found her whom I awaited, and I have tasted through her of inconceivable pleasure.

"I was roaming around Paris on a sunny morning, with joyous foot and happy soul, looking in the shops with the vague interest of a stroller. All at once I saw in a shop of antiquities, an Italian piece of furniture of the seventeenth century. It was very beautiful, very rare. I attributed it to a Venetian artist, named Vitelli, who belonged to that epoch. Then I passed along.

"Why did the remembrance of this piece of furniture follow me with so much force that I went back over my steps? I stopped again before the shop to look at it, and felt that it tempted me.

"What a singular thing is temptation! One looks at an object, and, little by little, it seduces you, troubles you, takes possession of you like the face of a woman. Its charm enters into you, a strange charm which comes from its form, its color, and its physiognomy. Already one loves it, wishes it, desires it. A need of possession takes you, a pleasant need at first, because timid, but increasing, becoming violent and irresistible. And the merchants seem to suspect, from the look of the eye, this secret, increasing desire. I bought that piece of furniture and had it carried to my house immediately. I placed it in my room.

"Oh! I pity those who do not know this sweet hobby of the collector with the trinket which he finally buys. He caresses it with his eye and hand as if it were flesh; he returns every moment to it, thinks of it continually, wherever he goes and whatever he may be doing. The thought of it follows him into the street, into the world, everywhere. And when he re-enters his house, before even removing his gloves or his hat, he goes to look at it with the tenderness of a lover.

"Truly, for eight days I adored that piece of furniture. I kept opening its doors and drawers; I handled it with delight and tasted all the intimate joys of possession.

"One evening, in feeling the thickness of a panel, I perceived that there might be a hiding-place there. My heart began to beat and I passed the night in searching out the secret, without being able to discover it.

"I came upon it the next day by forcing a piece of metal into a crevice in the paneling. A shelf slipped, and I saw, exposed upon a lining of black velvet, a marvelous head of hair that had belonged to some woman.

"Yes, a head of hair, an enormous twist of blond hair, almost red, which had been cut off near the skin and tied together with a golden cord.

"I stood there stupefied, trembling and disturbed! An almost insensible perfume, so old that it seemed like the soul of an odor, arose from this mysterious drawer and this most surprising relic.

"I took it gently, almost religiously, and lifted it from its resting-place. Immediately it unwound, spreading out its golden billows upon the floor, where it fell, thick and light, supple and brilliant, like the fiery tail of a comet.

"A strange emotion seized me. To whom had this belonged? When? Under what circumstances? Why had it been shut up in this piece of furniture? What adventure, what drama was connected with this souvenir? Who had cut it off? Some lover, on a day of parting? Some husband, on a day of vengeance? Or, perhaps, some woman herself, who bore on her brow the look of despair? Was it at the hour of entering the cloister that she had thrown there this fortune of love, as a token left to the world of the living? Was it the hour of closing the tomb upon the young and beautiful dead, that he who adored her took this diadem of her head, the only thing he could preserve of her, the only living part of her body that would not perish, the only thing that he could still love and caress and kiss, in the transport of his grief?

"Was it not strange that this hair should remain there thus, when there was no longer any vestige of the body with which she was born?

"It curled about my fingers and touched my skin with a singular caress, the caress of death. I felt myself affected, as if I were going to weep.

"I kept it a long time in my hands, then it seemed to me that it had some effect upon me, as if something of the soul still remained in it. And I laid it upon the velvet again, the velvet blemished by time, then pushed in the drawer, shut the doors of the closet, and betook myself to the street to dream.

"I walked straight ahead, full of sadness, and full of

trouble, of the kind of trouble that remains in the heart after the kiss of love. It seemed to me I had lived in former times, and that I had known this woman.

"And Villon's lines came to my lips, bringing with them a sob:

" 'Tell me in what far-off land
 The Roman beauty, Flora, lives;
Hipparchia, Thaïs' cousin, and
 All the beauty nature gives;
Echo speak, thy voice awake
Over river, stream, and lake,
Where are beauty's smiles and tears?
And where the snows of other years?

" 'Blanche, as fair as lily's chalice,
 Singing sweet, with voice serene,
Bertha Broadfoot, Beatrice, Alice,
 Ermengarde, Le Mayne's dear queen?
Where is Joan, the good Lorraine,
Whom th' English brought to death and fame?
Where are all, O wisest seers,
And where the snows of other years?'

"When I returned to my house I had a strange desire to see my strange treasure again. I took it up and felt it, and in touching it a long shiver ran through my body.

"For some days, however, I remained in my ordinary state, although the thought of this hair never left me. Whenever I came in, it was my first desire to look at it and handle it. I would turn the key of the secretary with the same trembling that one has in opening the door of his well-beloved, for I had in two hands and in my heart a confused, singular, continued, sensual need of burying my fingers in this charming rivulet of dead hair.

"Then, when I had finished caressing it, when I had returned it to its resting-place, I always felt that it was there, as if it were something alive, concealed, imprisoned; I felt it and I still desired it; again I had the imperious need of touching it, of feeling it, of enervating myself to the point of weariness from contact with this cold, glistening, irritating, exciting, delicious hair.

"I lived thus a month or two, I know not how long, with this thing possessing me, haunting me. I was happy and tortured, as in the expectation of love, as one is after the avowal which precedes the embrace.

"I would shut myself up alone with it in order to feel it upon my skin, to bury my lips in it, to kiss it, and bite it. I would roll it around my face, drink it in, drown my eyes in its golden waves, and finally see the blond life beyond it.

"I loved it! Yes, I loved it. I could no longer live away from it, nor be contented an hour without seeing it. I expected—I expected—what? I know not—her!

"One night I was suddenly awakened with a feeling that I was not alone in my room. I was alone, however. But I could not go to sleep again; and, as I was tossing in the fever of insomnia, I rose and went to look at the twist of hair. It appeared to me sweeter than usual, and more animated.

"Could the dead return? The kisses with which I had warmed it failed to give me happiness, and I carried it to my bed and lay down with it, pressing it to my lips, as one does a mistress he hopes to enjoy.

"The dead returned! She came! Yes, I saw her, touched her, possessed her as she was when alive in former times, large, blond, plump, with cool breasts, and with hips in form of a lyre. And I followed that divine, undulating line from the throat to the feet, in all the curves of the flesh with my caresses.

"Yes, I possessed her, every day and every night. She had returned, Death, Death the Beautiful, the Adorable, the Mysterious, the Unknown, and returned every night

One Phase of Love

"My happiness was so great that I could not conceal it. I found near her a superhuman delight, and in possessing this Unseizable, Invisible Death, knew a profound, inexplicable joy. No lover ever tasted joys more ardent or more terrible.

"I knew not how to conceal my happiness. I loved this possession so much that I could not bear to leave it. I carried it with me always, everywhere. I walked with it through the city, as if it were my wife, conducting it to the theater and to restaurants as one would a mistress. But they saw it—and guessed—they took me, and threw me into prison, like a malefactor. They took it away—oh! misery!—"

The manuscript stopped there. And suddenly, as I raised my wondering eyes to the doctor, a frightful cry, a howl of fury and exasperated desire filled the asylum.

"Listen," said the doctor, "it's necessary to douse that obscene maniac with water five times a day. It's only Sergeant Bertrand, the man who fell in love with the dead."

I stammered, moved with astonishment, horror, and pity: "But that hair—did it really exist?"

The doctor got up, opened a closet full of vials and instruments, and threw toward me, across his office, a long thick rope of blond hair, which flew toward me like a bird of gold.

I trembled at feeling upon my hands its caressing, light touch. And I stood there, my heart beating with disgust and desire, the disgust we have in coming in contact with objects connected with crimes, and the desire like that which comes with the temptation to test some infamous and mysterious thing.

Shrugging his shoulders, the doctor added: "The mind of man is capable of anything."

Simon's Papa

NOON had just struck. The schooldoor opened and the youngsters streamed out tumbling over one another in their haste to get out quickly. But instead of promptly dispersing and going home to dinner as was their daily wont, they stopped a few paces off, broke up into knots and set to whispering.

The fact was that that morning Simon, the son of La Blanchotte, had, for the first time, attended school.

They had all of them in their families heard of La Blanchotte; and although in public she was welcome enough, the mothers among themselves treated her with compassion of a somewhat disdainful kind, which the children had caught without in the least knowing why.

As for Simon himself, they did not know him, for he never went abroad, and did not play around with them through the streets of the village or along the banks of the river. So they loved him but little; and it was with a certain delight, mingled with astonishment, that they gathered in groups this morning, repeating to each other this sentence, concocted by a lad of fourteen or fifteen who appeared to know all about it, so sagaciously did he wink: "You know Simon—well, he has no papa."

La Blanchotte's son appeared in his turn upon the threshold of the school.

He was seven or eight years old, rather pale, very neat, with a timid and almost awkward manner.

He was making his way back to his mother's house when the various groups of his schoolfellows, perpetually whispering, and watching him with the mischievous and heartless eyes of children bent upon playing a nasty trick, gradually surrounded him and ended by inclosing him altogether. There he stood amid them, surprised and embarrassed, not understanding what they were going to do with him. But the lad who had brought the news, puffed up with the success he had met with, demanded:

"What do you call yourself?"

He answered: "Simon."

"Simon what?" retorted the other.

The child, altogether bewildered, repeated: "Simon."

The lad shouted at him: "You must be named Simon something! That is not a name—Simon indeed!"

And he, on the brink of tears, replied for the third time:

"I am named Simon."

The urchins began laughing. The lad triumphantly lifted up his voice: "You can see plainly that he has no papa."

A deep silence ensued. The children were dumfounded by this extraordinary, impossibly monstrous thing—a boy who had not a papa; they looked upon him as a phenomenon, an unnatural being, and they felt rising in them the hitherto inexplicable pity of their mothers for La Blanchotte. As for Simon, he had propped himself against a tree to avoid falling, and he stood there as if paralyzed by an irreparable disaster. He sought to explain, but he could think of no answer for them, no way to deny this horrible charge that he had no papa. At last he shouted at them quite recklessly: "Yes, I have one."

"Where is he?" demanded the boy.

Simon was silent, he did not know. The children shrieked, tremendously excited. These sons of toil, nearly

related to animals, experienced the cruel craving which
makes the fowls of a farmyard destroy one of their own
kind as soon as it is wounded. Simon suddenly spied a
little neighbor, the son of a widow, whom he had always
seen, as he himself was to be seen, quite alone with his
mother.

"And no more have you," he said, "no more have
you a papa."

"Yes," replied the other, "I have one."

"Where is he?" rejoined Simon.

"He is dead," declared the brat with superb dignity,
"he is in the cemetery, is my papa."

A murmur of approval rose amid the scapegraces, as
if the fact of possessing a papa dead in a cemetery made
their comrade big enough to crush the other one who had
no papa at all. And these rogues, whose fathers were for
the most part evildoers, drunkards, thieves, and ill-treat-
ers of their wives hustled each other as they pressed closer
and closer to Simon as though they, the legitimate ones,
would stifle in their pressure one who was beyond the
law.

The lad next Simon suddenly put his tongue out at
him with a waggish air and shouted at him:

"No papa! No papa!"

Simon seized him by the hair with both hands and
set to work to demolish his legs with kicks, while he bit
his cheek ferociously. A tremendous struggle ensued between the two boys, and Simon found himself beaten,
torn, bruised, rolled on the ground in the middle of the
ring of applauding little vagabonds. As he arose, mechanically brushing his little blouse all covered with dust with
his hand, some one shouted at him:

"Go and tell your papa."

He then felt a great sinking in his heart. They were

stronger than he, they had beaten him and he had no answer to give them, for he knew it was true that he had no papa. Full of pride he tried for some moments to struggle against the tears which were suffocating him. He had a choking fit, and then without cries he began to weep with great sobs which shook him incessantly. Then a ferocious joy broke out among his enemies, and, just like savages in fearful festivals, they took one another by the hand and danced in a circle about him as they repeated in refrain:

"No papa! No papa!"

But suddenly Simon ceased sobbing. Frenzy overtook him. There were stones under his feet; he picked them up and with all his strength hurled them at his tormentors. Two or three were struck and ran away yelling, and so formidable did he appear that the rest became panic-stricken. Cowards, like a jeering crowd in the presence of an exasperated man, they broke up and fled. Left alone, the little thing without a father set off running toward the fields, for a recollection had been awakened which nerved his soul to a great determination. He made up his mind to drown himself in the river.

He remembered, in fact, that eight days ago a poor devil who begged for his livelihood had thrown himself into the water because he had no more money. Simon had been there when they fished him out again; and the sight of the fellow, who had seemed to him so miserable and ugly, had then impressed him—his pale cheeks, his long drenched beard, and his open eyes being full of calm. The bystanders had said:

"He is dead."

And some one had added:

"He is quite happy now."

So Simon wished to drown himself also because he

had no father, just as the wretched being did who had no money.

He reached the water and watched it flowing. Some fishes were rising briskly in the clear stream and occasionally made little leaps and caught the flies on the surface. He stopped crying in order to watch them, for their feeding interested him vastly. But, at intervals, as in the lulls of a tempest, when tremendous gusts of wind snap off trees and then die away, this thought would return to him with intense pain:

"I am about to drown myself because I have no papa."

It was very warm and fine weather. The pleasant sunshine warmed the grass; the water shone like a mirror; and Simon enjoyed for some minutes the happiness of that languor which follows weeping, desirous even of falling asleep there upon the grass in the warmth of noon.

A little green frog leaped from under his feet. He endeavored to catch it. It escaped him. He pursued it and lost it three times following. At last he caught it by one of its hand legs and began to laugh as he saw the efforts the creature made to escape. It gathered itself up on its large legs and then with a violent spring suddenly stretched them out as stiff as two bars.

Its eyes stared wide open in their round, golden circle, and it beat the air with its front limbs, using them as though they were hands. It reminded him of a toy made with straight slips of wood nailed zigzag one on the other, which by a similar movement regulated the exercise of the little soldiers fastened thereon. Then he thought of his home and of his mother, and overcome by great sorrow he again began to weep. His limbs trembled; and he placed himself on his knees and said his prayers as before going to bed. But he was unable to finish them, for such hurried and violent sobs overtook him that he was completely overwhelmed. He thought no more, he no longer heeded anything around him but was wholly given up to tears.

Suddenly a heavy hand was placed upon his shoulder, and a rough voice asked him:

"What is it that causes you so much grief, my fine fellow?"

Simon turned round. A tall workman, with a black beard and hair all curled, was staring at him good-naturedly. He answered with his eyes and throat full of tears:

"They have beaten me because—I—I have no papa —no papa."

"What!" said the man smiling, "why, everybody has one."

The child answered painfully amid his spasms of grief:

"But I—I—I have none."

Then the workman became serious. He had recognized La Blanchotte's son, and although a recent arrival to the neighborhood he had a vague idea of her history.

"Well," said he, "console yourself, my boy, and come with me home to your mother. She will give you a papa."

And so they started on the way, the big one holding the little one by the hand. The man smiled afresh, for he was not sorry to see this Blanchotte, who by popular report was one of the prettiest girls in the country-side— and, perhaps, he said to himself, at the bottom of his heart, that a lass who had erred once might very well err again.

They arrived in front of a very neat little white house.

"There it is," exclaimed the child, and he cried: "Mamma."

A woman appeared, and the workman instantly left off smiling, for he at once perceived that there was no more fooling to be done with the tall pale girl, who stood austerely at her door as though to defend from one man the threshold of that house where she had already been betrayed by another. Intimidated, his cap in his hand, he stammered out:

"See, Madame, I have brought you back your little boy, who had lost himself near the river."

But Simon flung his arms about his mother's neck and told her, as he again began to cry:

"No, mamma, I wished to drown myself, because the others had beaten me—had beaten me—because I have no papa."

A burning redness covered the young woman's cheeks, and, hurt to the quick, she embraced her child passionately, while the tears coursed down her face. The man, much moved, stood there, not knowing now to get away. But Simon suddenly ran to him and said:

"Will you be my papa?"

A deep silence ensued. La Blanchotte, dumb and tortured with shame, leaned against the wall, her hands upon her heart. The child, seeing that no answer was made him, replied:

"If you do not wish it, I shall return to drown myself."

The workman took the matter as a jest and answered laughing:

"Why, yes, I wish it certainly."

"What is your name, then," went on the child, "so that I may tell the others when they wish to know your name?"

"Philip," answered the man.

Simon was silent a moment so that he might get the

name well into his memory; then he stretched out his arms, quite consoled, and said:

"Well, then, Philip, you are my papa."

The workman, lifting him from the ground, kissed him hastily on both cheeks, and then strode away quickly.

When the child returned to school next day he was received with a spiteful laugh, and at the end of school, when the lads were on the point of recommencing, Simon threw these words at their heads as he would have done a stone: "He is named Philip, my papa."

Yells of delight burst out from all sides.

"Philip who? Philip what? What on earth is Philip? Where did you pick up your Philip?"

Simon answered nothing; and immovable in faith he defied them with his eye, ready to be martyred rather than fly before them. The schoolmaster came to his rescue and he returned home to his mother.

For a space of three months, the tall workman, Philip, frequently passed by La Blanchotte's house, and sometimes made bold to speak to her when he saw her sewing near the window. She answered him civilly, always sedately, never joking with him, nor permitting him to enter her house. Notwithstanding this, being, like all men, a bit of a coxcomb, he imagined that she was often rosier than usual when she chatted with him.

But a fallen reputation is so difficult to recover, and always remains so fragile that, in spite of the shy reserve La Blanchotte maintained, they already gossiped in the neighborhood.

As for Simon, he loved his new papa much, and walked with him nearly every evening when the day's work was done. He went regularly to school and mixed in a dignified way with his schoolfellows without ever answering them back.

One day, however, the lad who had first attacked him said to him:

"You have lied. You have not a papa named Philip."

"Why do you say that?" demanded Simon, much disturbed.

The youth rubbed his hands. He replied:

"Because if you had one he would be your mamma's husband."

Simon was confused by the truth of this reasoning; nevertheless he retorted:

"He is my papa all the same."

"That can very well be," exclaimed the urchin with a sneer, "but that is not being your papa altogether."

La Blanchotte's little one bowed his head and went off dreaming in the direction of the forge belonging to old Loizon, where Philip worked.

This forge was entombed in trees. It was very dark there, the red glare of a formidable furnace alone lit up with great flashes five blacksmiths, who hammered upon their anvils with a terrible din. Standing enveloped in flame, they worked like demons, their eyes fixed on the red-hot iron they were pounding; and their dull ideas rising and falling with their hammers.

Simon entered without being noticed and quietly plucked his friend by the sleeve. Philip turned round. All at once the work came to a standstill and the men looked on very attentively. Then, in the midst of this unaccustomed silence, rose the little slender pipe of Simon:

"Philip, explain to me what the lad at La Michande has just told me, that you are not altogether my papa."

"And why that?" asked the smith.

The child replied in all innocence:

"Because you are not my mamma's husband."

No one laughed. Philip remained standing, leaning

his forehead upon the back of his great hands, which held the handle of his hammer upright upon the anvil. He mused. His four companions watched him, and, like a tiny mite among these giants, Simon anxiously waited. Suddenly, one of the smiths, voicing the sentiment of all, said to Philip:

"All the same La Blanchotte is a good and honest girl, stalwart and steady in spite of her misfortune, and one who would make a worthy wife for an honest man."

"That is true," remarked the three others.

The smith continued:

"Is it the girl's fault if she has fallen? She had been promised marriage, and I know more than one who is much respected today and has sinned every bit as much."

"That is true," responded the three men in chorus.

He resumed:

"How hard she has toiled, poor thing, to educate her lad all alone, and how much she has wept since she no longer goes out, save to church, God only knows."

"That also is true," said the others.

Then no more was heard save the roar of the bellows which fanned the fire of the furnace. Philip hastily bent himself down to Simon:

"Go and tell your mamma that I shall come to speak to her."

Then he pushed the child out by the shoulders. He returned to his work and in unison the five hammers again fell upon their anvils. Thus they wrought the iron until nightfall, strong, powerful, happy, like Vulcans satisfied. But as the great bell of a cathedral resounds upon feast days above the jingling of the other bells, so Philip's hammer, dominating the noise of the others, clanged second after second with a deafening uproar. His eye on the fire, he plied his trade vigorously, erect amid the sparks.

Simon's Papa

The sky was full of stars as he knocked at La Blan-chotte's door. He had his Sunday blouse on, a fresh shirt, and his beard was trimmed. The young woman showed herself upon the threshold and said in a grieved tone:

"It is ill to come thus when night has fallen, Mr. Philip."

He wished to answer, but stammered and stood confused before her.

She resumed:

"And you understand quite well that it will not do that I should be talked about any more."

Then he said all at once:

"What does that matter to me, if you will be my wife!"

No voice replied to him, but he believed that he heard in the shadow of the room the sound of a body falling. He entered very quickly; and Simon, who had gone to his bed, distinguished the sound of a kiss and some words that his mother said very softly. Then he suddenly found himself lifted up by the hands of his friend, who, holding him at the length of his herculean arms, exclaimed to him:

"You will tell your school-fellows that your papa is Philip Remy, the blacksmith, and that he will pull the ears of all who do you any harm."

On the morrow, when the school was full and lessons were about to begin, little Simon stood up quite pale with trembling lips:

"My papa," said he in a clear voice, "is Philip Remy, the blacksmith, and he has promised to box the ears of all who do me any harm."

This time no one laughed any longer, for he was very well known, was Philip Remy, the blacksmith, and he was a papa of whom anyone in the world would be proud.

The Vendetta

THE widow of Paolo Saverini lived alone with her son in a poor little house on the ramparts of Bonifacio. The town, built upon the side of the mountain, suspended in spots above the sea, overlooks, through a defile bristling with rocks, the lowest part of Sardinia. At its foot, on the other side, and almost entirely surrounding it, is a cut in the cliff, which resembles a gigantic corridor and serves as a port; it leads up to the first houses (after a long circuit between the two abrupt walls), the little Italian or Sardinian fishing-boats, and, every two weeks, the old, broken-winded steamer that plies between there and Ajaccio.

Upon the white mountain, the bunch of houses makes a spot whiter still. They have the appearance of nests of wild birds, fastened thus upon this rock, overlooking this terrible passageway where ships scarcely dare venture. The wind, without repose, harasses the sea, harasses the bare coast, which is nibbled by it until it has but little vegetation; it rushes into the defile, whose two sides it strips bare. The track of pale foam, fastened to black points on the innumerable rocks which pierce the waves, has the look of bits of cloth floating and palpitating upon the surface of the water.

The house of the widow Saverini, soldered to the edge of the cliff, had three windows opening upon this wild and desolated horizon.

She lived there alone, with her son Antoine and their dog Semillante, a great, thin beast with long, coarse hair,

364

of a race that watches the herds. This dog served the young man for hunting.

One evening, after a dispute, Antoine Saverini was killed traitorously with a blow of a knife by Nicholas Ravolati who, the same night, went over to Sardinia.

When the old woman received the body of her child, which some passers-by brought to her, she did not weep but remained a long time motionless, looking at him. Then, extending her wrinkled hand upon the dead body, she promised revenge. She did not wish anyone to remain with her, and she shut herself up with the body and the dog.

The dog howled. She howled, this beast, in a continuous fashion, at the foot of the bed, her head extended toward her master, her tail held fast between her legs. She no more stirred than did the mother, who, hanging now upon the body, her eyes fixed, was weeping great tears while gazing at him.

The young man, upon his back, clothed in his coat of gray cloth, torn and bloody about the breast, seemed to be asleep. And there was blood everywhere: on his shirt, drawn up in the first moments, on his waistcoat, his trousers, upon his face, and his hands. Little clots of blood had coagulated in his beard and in his hair.

The old mother began to speak to him. At the sound of her voice, the dog was silent.

"Come, come," she said, "you shall be avenged, my little one, my boy, my poor child. Sleep, sleep, you shall be avenged, do you hear? It is your mother who promises! And she always keeps her word, does your mother, as you know well."

And gently she bent over him, gluing her cold lips to his dead mouth. Then Semillante began to groan again. She uttered a long, plaintive monotone, harrowing and terrible.

There they remained, the corpse, the woman and the beast, until morning.

Antoine Saverini was buried the next day, and soon no one spoke of him more in Bonifacio.

He had left no brother, no near relatives. There was no man to follow up the revenge. Alone, the mother thought of it, the old woman.

On the other side of the defile she saw, each morning and evening, a white spot on the coast. It was the little Sardinian village, Longosardo, where Corsican bandits took refuge when too closely pursued. They almost peopled this hamlet, opposite the shore of their own country, and awaited there the moment of returning, of going back again to the brakes. It was in this village, she knew, that Nicholas Ravolati had taken refuge.

All alone, the whole day long, seated before her window, she would look down there and think of vengeance. How could she do it without anyone to help, infirm as she was and so near death? But she had promised, she had sworn it upon his dead body. She could not forget, she must not delay. How should she accomplish it? She could not sleep at night; she had no repose, no ease; she sought obstinately. The dog slept at her feet, and, sometimes raising her head, howled to the distance. Since her master was no longer there, she often howled thus, as if she were calling him, as if her soul, that of an inconsolable beast, had preserved a remembrance of him that nothing could efface.

One night, as Semillante began to howl in this way, the mother suddenly had an idea, a savage, vindictive, ferocious idea. She meditated upon it until morning;

then, rising at the approach of day, she betook herself to the church. She prayed, prostrate upon the floor, humbled before God, supplicating him to aid her, to sustain her, to give to her poor, spent body force that would be sufficient to avenge the death of her son.

Then she returned. She had in her yard an old barrel with the head knocked in, which caught the rain from the gutters. She emptied it and turned it over, making it fast to the soil by means of some stakes and stones; then she chained Semillante in this niche and went into her house.

Now she walked about constantly in her room, without repose, her eye fixed upon the coast of Sardinia. He was down there, was that assassin.

The dog howled all day and all night. The old woman carried her some water in the morning, in a bowl. But nothing more; no soup, no bread.

The day slipped away. Semillante, weakened from want of food, slept. The next day she had shining eyes and bristling hair; she pulled desperately at her chain.

Still the old woman gave her nothing to eat. The beast became furious, baying with raucous voice. The night passed away thus. Then, at the break of day, Mother Saverini went to the house of a neighbor and begged him to give her two bundles of straw. She took some old clothes that her husband had formerly worn and filled them full of the fodder, to simulate a human body.

Having stuck a stick in the ground before Semillante's niche, she bound the manikin to it, giving him the appearance of standing. Then she formed a head by means of a package of old linen.

The dog, surprised, looked at the straw man and was silent, although devoured with hunger.

Then the old woman went to the butcher's and bought a long piece of black pudding. She returned home, lighted a wood fire in her yard, and cooked this pudding. Semillante, excited, bounded about and frothed at the mouth, her eyes fixed upon the meat, the fumes of which entered her stomach.

Next the woman made a cravat for the straw man of this smoking sausage. She wound it many times about his neck, as if to make it penetrate him. When this was done, she unchained the dog.

With a formidable leap, the beast reached the manikin's throat, and, her paws upon his shoulders, began to tear him to pieces. She fell back, a piece of her prey in her mouth, then leaped upon him again, sinking her teeth in the cords, snatching some particles of nourishment, fell back again, and rebounded enraged. She tore away the face with great blows of the teeth, tearing into shreds the whole neck.

The old woman, mute and motionless, looked on, her eyes lighting up. She rechained the beast, made him fast two days again, and repeated this strange operation.

For three months, she accustomed the dog to this kind of struggle, to a repast conquered by tooth and claw. She did not chain her now, but set her upon the manikin with a gesture.

She taught her to tear him, to devour him, even without anything eatable hung around his throat. She would give her afterward, as a recompense, the pudding she had cooked for her.

Whenever she perceived the manikin, Semillante growled and turned her eyes toward her mistress, who would cry: "Go!" in a whistling tone, at the same time raising her finger.

The Vendetta

When she thought the right time had come, Mother Saverini went to confession and to communion one morning in ecstatic fervor; then, having clothed herself in male attire, so that she looked like a feeble, old man, she went with a Sardinian fisherman, who took her and her dog to the other side of the defile.

She had, in a sack of cloth, a large piece of pudding. Semillante had fasted for two days. Every few moments the old woman made her smell of the pleasant food and endeavored to excite her.

They entered into Longosardo. The Corsican went into a wine-shop. She presented herself at a baker's and asked where Nicholas Ravolati lived. He had taken his old trade, that of a carpenter. He was working alone at the back of his shop.

The old woman opened the door and called:

"Hey, Nicholas!"

He turned around; then, loosing the dog, she cried out:

"Go! go! Devour him! devour him!"

The animal, excited, threw herself upon him and seized him by the throat. The man extended his arms, clinched, and rolled upon the floor. For some minutes he twisted himself, beating the soil with his feet; then he remained motionless, while Semillante dug at his neck until it was in shreds.

Two neighbors, seated before their doors, recalled perfectly having seen an old man go out of the shop, with a black dog at his side, which was eating, as he went along, something brown that his master gave him.

That evening, the old woman returned to her house. She slept well that night.

The Farmer's Wife

ONE day Baron René du Treilles said to me:

"Will you come and open the hunting season with me in my farmhouse at Marinville? By doing so, my dear fellow, you will give me the greatest pleasure. Besides, I am all alone. This will be a hard hunting-bout, to start with, and the house where I sleep is so primitive that I can only bring my most intimate friends there."

I accepted his invitation. So on Saturday we started by the railway-line running into Normandy, and alighted at the station of Alvimare. Baron René, pointing out to me a country jaunting-car drawn by a restive horse, driven by a big peasant with white hair, said to me:

"Here is our equipage, my dear boy."

The man extended his hand to his landlord, and the Baron pressed it warmly, asking:

"Well, Maître Lebrument, how are you?"

"Always the same, M'sieu l' Baron."

We jumped into this hencoop suspended and shaken on two immense wheels. The young horse, after a violent swerve, started into a gallop, flinging us into the air like balls. Every fall backward onto the wooden bench gave me the most dreadful pain.

The peasant kept repeating in his calm, monotonous voice:

"There, there! it's all right, all right, Moutard, all right!"

But Moutard scarcely heard and kept scampering along like a goat.

Our two dogs, behind us, in the empty part of the

hencoop, stood erect and sniffed the air of the plains as if they could smell the game.

The Baron gazed into the distance, with a sad eye. The vast Norman landscape, undulating and melancholy as an immense English park, with farmyards surrounded by two or four rows of trees and full of dwarfed apple-trees which rendered the houses invisible, gave a vista, as far as the eye could see, of old forest-trees, tufts of wood and hedgerows, which artistic gardeners provide for when they are tracing the lines of princely estates.

And René de Treilles suddenly exclaimed:

"I love this soil; I have my very roots in it."

A pure Norman, tall and strong, with the more or less projecting paunch of the old race of adventurers who went to found kingdoms on the shores of every ocean, he was about fifty years of age, ten years less perhaps than the farmer who was driving us. The latter was a lean peasant, all skin and bone, one of those men who live a hundred years.

After two hours' traveling over stony roads, across that green and monotonous plain, the vehicle entered one of those fruit-gardens which adorn the fronts of farm-houses, and drew up before an old structure falling into decay, where an old maid-servant stood waiting at the side of a young fellow who seized the horse's bridle.

We entered the farmhouse. The smoky kitchen was high and spacious. The copper utensils and the earthenware glistened under the reflection of the big fire. A cat lay asleep under the table. Within, you inhaled the odor of milk, of apples, of smoke, that indescribable smell peculiar to old houses where peasants have lived—the odor of the soil, of the walls, of furniture, of stale soup, of washing, and of the old inhabitants, the smell of animals and human beings intermingled, of things and of persons, the odor of time and of things that have passed away.

I went out to have a look at the farmyard. It was big, full of old apple-trees dwarfed and crooked, and laden with fruit which fell on the grass around them. In this farmyard the smell of apples was as strong as that of the orange-trees which blossom on the banks of southern rivers.

Four rows of beeches surrounded this inclosure. They were so tall that they seemed to touch the clouds, at this hour of nightfall, and their summits, through which the night winds passed, shook and sang a sad, interminable song.

I re-entered the house. The Baron was warming his feet at the fire, and was listening to the farmer's talk about country matters. He talked about marriages, births, and deaths, then about the fall in the price of corn and the latest news about the selling value of cattle. The "Veularde" (as he called a cow that had been bought at the fair of Veules) had calved in the middle of June. The cider had not been first-class last year. The apricot-apples were almost disappearing from the country.

Then we had dinner. It was a good rustic meal, simple and abundant, long and tranquil. And while we were dining, I noticed the special kind of friendly familiarity between the Baron and the peasant which had struck me from the start.

Without, the beeches continued sobbing in the night wind, and our two dogs, shut up in a shed, were whining and howling in uncanny fashion. The fire was dying out in the big grate. The maid-servant had gone to bed. Maître Lebrument said in his turn:

"If you don't mind, M'sieu l' Baron, I'm going to bed. I am not used to staying up late."

The Baron extended his hand toward him and said. "Go, my friend," in so cordial a tone that I said, as soon as the man had disappeared:

"He is devoted to you, this farmer?"

"Better than that, my dear fellow! It is a drama, an old drama, simple and very sad, that attaches him to me. Here is the story:

"You know that my father was a colonel in a cavalry regiment. His orderly was this young fellow, now an old man, the son of a farmer. Then, when my father retired from the army, he took this retired soldier, then about forty, as his servant. I was at that time about thirty. We lived then in our old château of Valrenne, near Caude· bec-in-Caux.

"At this period, my mother's chambermaid was one of the prettiest girls you could see, fair-haired, slender, and sprightly in manner, a genuine specimen of the fas· cinating Abigail, such as we scarcely ever find nowadays. Today these creatures spring up into hussies before their time. Paris, with the aid of the railways, attracts them, calls them, takes hold of them, as soon as they are burst- ing into womanhood—these little wenches who, in old times, remained simple maid-servants. Every man passing by, as long ago recruiting sergeants did with conscripts, entices and debauches them—foolish lassies—till now we have only the scum of the female sex for servant-maids, all that is dull, nasty, common, and ill-formed, too ugly even for gallantry.

"Well, this girl was charming, and I often gave her a kiss in dark corners—nothing more, I swear to you! She was virtuous, besides; and I had some respect for my mother's house, which is more than can be said of the blackguards of the present day.

"Now it happened that my father's man-servant, the

ex-soldier, the old farmer you have just seen, fell in love with this girl, but in an unusual sort of way. The first thing we noticed was that his memory was affected; he did not pay attention to anything.

"My father was incessantly saying: 'Look here, Jean! What's the matter with you? Are you unwell?'

" 'No, no, M'sieu l' Baron. There's nothing the matter with me.'

"Jean got thin. Then, when serving at table, he broke glasses and let plates fall. We thought he must have been attacked by some nervous malady, and we sent for the doctor, who thought he could detect symptoms of spinal disease. Then my father, full of anxiety about his faithful man-servant, decided to place him in a private hospital. When the poor fellow heard of my father's intentions, he made a clean breast of it.

" 'M'sieu l' Baron—'

" 'Well, my boy?'

" 'You see, the thing I want is not physic.'

" 'Ha! what is it, then?

" 'It's marriage!'

"My father turned round and stared at him in astonishment.

" 'What's that you say—eh?'

" 'It's marriage.

" 'Marriage? So then, you donkey, you're in love.'

" 'That's how it is, M'sieu l' Baron.'

"And my father began to laugh in such an immoderate fashion that my mother called out through the wall of the next room:

" 'What in the name of goodness is the matter with you, Gontran?'

"My father replied:

" 'Come here, Catherine.'

The Farmer's Wife

"And, when she came in, he told, with tears in his eyes from sheer laughter, that his idiot of a servant-man was love-sick.

"But my mother, instead of laughing, was deeply affected.

" 'Who is it that you have fallen in love with, my poor fellow?' she asked.

"He answered, without hesitation:

" 'With Louise, Madame la Baronne.'

"My mother said, with the utmost gravity: 'We must try to arrange the matter the best way we can.'

"So Louise was sent for, and questioned by my mother. She said in reply that she knew all about Jean's liking for her, that in fact Jean had spoken to her about it several times, but that she did not want him. She refused to say why.

"And two months elapsed during which my father and mother never ceased to urge this girl to marry Jean. As she declared she was not in love with any other man, she could not give any serious reason for her refusal. My father, at last, overcame her resistance by means of a big present of money, and started the pair of them on a farm on the estate—this very farm. At the end of three years, I learned that Louise had died of consumption. But my father and my mother died, too, in their turn, and it was two years more before I found myself face to face with Jean.

"At last, one autumn day, about the end of October, the idea came into my head to go hunting on this part of my estate, which my tenant had told me was full of game.

"So, one evening, one wet evening, I arrived at this house. I was shocked to find the old soldier who had been my father's servant perfectly white-haired, though he was

not more than forty-five or forty-six years of age. I made
him dine with me, at the very table where we're now sitting. It was raining hard. We could hear the rain batter-
ing at the roof, the walls, and the windows, flowing in a
perfect deluge into the farmyard; and my dog was howling in the shed where the other dogs are howling tonight.

"All of a sudden, when the servant-maid had gone to
bed, the man said in a timid voice:

" 'M'sieu l' Baron.'

" 'What is it, my dear Jean?'

" 'I have something to tell you.'

" 'Tell it, my dear Jean.'

" 'You remember Louise, my wife?'

" 'Certainly, I do remember her.'

" 'Well, she left me a message for you.'

" 'What was it?'

" 'A—a—well, it was what you might call a confession.'

" 'Ha! And what was it about?'

" 'It was—it was—I'd rather, all the same, tell you
nothing about it—but I must—I must. Well, it's this—
it wasn't consumption she died of at all. It was grief—
well, that's the long and the short of it. As soon as she
came to live here, after we were married, she grew thin;
she changed so that you wouldn't know her at the end
of six months—no, you wouldn't know her, M'sieu l'
Baron. It was all just as before I married her, but it was
different, too, quite another sort of thing.

" 'I sent for the doctor. He said it was her liver that was
affected—he said it was what he called a "hepatic" complaint—I don't know these big words, M'sieu l'Baron.
Then I bought medicine for her, heaps on heaps of
bottles, that cost about three hundred francs. But she'd
take none of them; she wouldn't have them; she said:
"It's no use, my poor Jean; it wouldn't do me any good."

I saw well that she had some hidden trouble; and then I found her one time crying, and I didn't know what to do —no, I didn't know what to do. I bought caps and dresses and hair-oil and earrings for her. No good! And I saw that she was going to die. And so one night in the end of November, one snowy night, after remaining the whole day without stirring out of the bed, she told me to send for the curé. So I went for him. As soon as he had come, she saw him. Then, she asked him to let me come into the room, and she said to me: "Jean, I'm going to make a confession to you. I owe it to you, Jean. I have never been false to you, never—never, before or after you married me. M'sieu le Curé is there, and can tell it is so, and he knows my soul. Well, listen, Jean. If I am dying, it is because I was not able to console myself for leaving the château—because—I was too—too fond of the young Baron, Monsieur René—too fond of him, mind you, Jean—there was no harm in it! This is the thing that's killing me. When I could see him no more, I felt that I should die. If I could only have seen him, I might have lived; only seen him, nothing more. I wish you'd tell it to him some day, by-and-by, when I am no longer there. You will tell him—swear you will, Jean—swear it in the presence of M'sieu le Curé! It will console me to know that he will know it one day—that this was the cause of my death! Swear it!"

" 'Well, I gave her my promise, M'sieu l' Baron! and, on the faith of an honest man, I have kept my word.'

"And then he ceased speaking, his eyes filling with tears.

"Upon my soul, my dear boy, you can't form any idea of the emotion that filled me when I heard this poor devil, whose wife I had caused the death of without knowing it, telling me this story on that wet night in this very kitchen.

"I exclaimed: 'Ah! my poor Jean! my poor Jean!'

"He murmured: 'Well, that's all, M'sieu l' Baron. I could do nothing, one way or another—and now it's all over!'

"I caught his hand across the table, and I began to cry.

"He asked: 'Will you come and see her grave?' I nodded by way of assent, for I couldn't speak. He rose up, lighted a lantern, and we walked through the blinding rain which, in the light of the lamp, looked like falling arrows.

"He opened a gate, and I saw some crosses of blackwood.

"Suddenly, he said: 'There it is, in front of a marble slab,' and he flashed the lantern close to it so that I could read the inscription:

" 'To Louise-Hortense Marinet,
Wife of *Jean-François Lebrument*, farmer.
She was a faithful Wife! God rest her Soul!'

"We fell on our knees in the damp grass, he and I, with the lantern between us, and I saw the rain beating on the white marble slab. And I thought of the heart of her sleeping there in her grave. Ah! poor heart! poor heart!

"Since then, I have been coming here every year. And I don't know why, but I feel as if I were guilty of some crime in the presence of this man who always shows that he forgives me!"

A Matter of Business

THE name Brument (Cæsar Isidore) and the name Cornu (Prosper Napoleon) appeared before the Court of Assizes of the Lower-Seine under the charge of attempted murder, by immersion, of the Brument woman, legitimate wife of the first of the prisoners. The two accused were seated side by side upon the traditional bench. They were two peasants. The first was short, fat, with short arms and legs and a round, red, blossoming head, planted directly upon his back, which was round also, and short, without any appearance of a neck. He was a pig-raiser and dwelt in Cachville-la-Goupil, district of Criquetot.

Cornu (Prosper Napoleon) was thin, of medium height, with enormous arms. His head was awry, his jaw twisted, and he squinted. A blue blouse as long as a chemise fell about his knees, and his yellow hair, thin and pasted to his cranium, gave to his features a worn-out, dirty appearance, and an expression altogether frightful. He was nicknamed "The Curate" because he knew how to imitate to perfection the chants of the church, and even the noise of the serpent. This talent attracted people to his bar, for he was a tavern-keeper at Criquetot, a large number preferring "Cornu's mass" to the Mass of the Good God.

Mrs. Brument, seated on the witness bench, was a thin peasant woman who always seemed half asleep. She remained motionless, her hands crossed upon her knees, with fixed look and stupid appearance.

The President continued the questioning:

"So then, Mrs. Brument, they entered your house and

threw you into a barrel of water? State the facts in detail. Rise."

She rose and seemed as tall as a mast, with her bonnet, which was only a stiff white skullcap. She made her explanations in a drawling voice:

"I was shelling some beans when they came in. I said to myself: 'What is the matter with them. They are not natural; there is some mischief.' They watched me, like this, crosswise, especially Cornu, seeing that he squints. I never like to see them together, because it means no good to the neighborhood. I said to them: 'What's the matter with you?' They did not answer. I had almost a suspicion—"

The prisoner Brument interrupted the deposition with vivacity, declaring:

"I was drunk."

Then Cornu, turning toward his accomplice, said in a deep voice with the tone of an organ:

"Say that I was drunk, too, and you will not lie."

The President [with severity]: "You wish to state that you were drunk?"

Brument: "That is not demanded."

Cornu: "That can happen to anybody."

The President [to the victim]: "Continue your deposition, Mrs. Brument."

"Then up steps Brument and says to me: 'Do you want to earn a hundred sous?' 'Yes,' said I, seeing that a hundred sous are not found in every footprint of a horse. Then he said to me: 'Open your eye and do like me.' And he went for the big barrel that is under the gutter at the corner of the house; and then he turned it over and brought it into my kitchen and planted it right in the middle of the floor, and then he said to me: 'You go and bring water enough to make this full.'

"Then you might see me going to the pond with two buckets bringing water, and still bringing water, for the good part of an hour, seeing that this barrel was as large as a vat, saving your presence, Mr. President.

"During this time, Brument and Cornu they drank a glass and still another glass and still another. They had finished their talk, when I said to them: 'You two are full, as full as this barrel.' And it was Brument that answered: 'Don't you worry, go your way; your turn will come; each to his own count.' As for me, I paid no attention to his talk, seeing that he was drunk.

"When the barrel was full up I said: 'There, it is done.'

"And then Cornu gave me a hundred sous. Not Brument, but Cornu; it was Cornu that gave them to me. And Brument says to me: 'Do you want to earn another hundred sous?' 'Yes,' I said, seeing that I am not accustomed to finds like that. Then he said to me: 'Undress yourself.'

" 'Why undress myself?'

" 'Yes,' he says to me.

" 'Just how much shall I undress myself?'

"He said to me: 'If that troubles you, keep on your chemise, we make no objection to that.'

"A hundred sous are a hundred sous, and so I began to undress myself, although I would not undress before those two for nothing. I took off my cap, and then my bodice, and then my skirt, and then my shoes. Brument said to me: 'Look out, now, what you do; we're good children.'

"And Cornu answered: 'Yes, we're good children.'

"Then there I was, almost like our mother Eve. And they got up, as well as they could, for they were drunk, saving your presence, Mr. President.

"I said to myself: 'What are these two contriving?'

"And Brument said: 'Is it all right now?'

"Cornu said: 'All right!'

"And then they took me. Brument by the head and Cornu by the feet, as they would take, we might say, a piece of cloth to the bleach. As for me, I bawled.

"And Brument said to me: 'Keep still, poor thing!'

"And they took me under their arms, and threw me into the barrel which was full of water, till I had a turn of the blood and a coldness to my very insides.

"And Brument said: 'Is that all?'

"Cornu said: 'That's all!'

"Brument said: 'The head is not in; that counts.'

"Cornu said: 'Put the head in, then.'

"And then Brument pushed my head down until I nearly was drowned, the water came so into my nose, and I saw paradise already. Then he gave me one more push and I disappeared. And then it was that they had a fear, and they pulled me out and said to me: 'Go, dry yourself, quick, carcass.'

"I escaped and began to run as fast as I could to the house of the curate, who lent me one of his servant's petticoats, seeing I was almost as nature made me, and he went to find master Chicot the officer, who would get some policeman from Criquetot to take me home. There I found Brument and Cornu quarreling like two rams.

"Brument bellowed: 'It's not true; I tell you that it is at least a cubic meter. It was not a good way, anyhow.'

"Cornu bellowed, then: 'Four buckets, that makes just about half a cubic meter. There's no more to be said about it.'

"Then the officer put his hand on them, and that's all I know of it."

A *Matter of Business*

She was seated. The audience laughed. The jury looked at each other in amazement. The judge said:

"Prisoner Cornu, you seem to be the instigator of this infamous business, explain yourself."

And Cornu, in his turn, stood up:

"Mr. President, I was drunk."

The President replied, gravely: "I know that; continue."

"I'm going to. Now, Brument came to my place about nine o'clock, and called for two drinks, and he said to me: 'Here's one for you, Cornu.' And I sat down opposite him, and I drank, out of politeness, and then I offered him another. Then he responded, and I too, so that, turn and turn about, toward midnight we got tipsy.

"Then Brument began to cry. I noticed it and asked him what the matter was. He told me he must have a thousand francs by Thursday. Then I got a little cold, you understand. And as quickly as hay burns, he proposed to me: 'I'll sell you my wife.'

"I was drunk, and I'm a widower. You can understand, the idea struck me. I did not know her, but a woman is a woman, isn't that so? And I asked him: 'How much will you sell her for?'

"He thought, or seemed to be thinking over it some time. When a man is drunk, he is not clear, but he finally said: 'I'll sell her to you by the cubic measure.'

"I was not astonished at that, seeing I was as drunk as he was and that cubic measure was known to me in my trade. 'That's the same as a thousand liters,' said I. 'It is agreed.'

"Now only the price remained to be settled. All depends on the quality. So I asked: 'How much a cubic measure?'"

383

"He answered: 'Two thousand francs.'

"I made a jump like a rabbit, and then I reflected that a woman would not likely measure more than three hundred liters. All the same, I said: 'That's too dear.'

"He replied: 'I couldn't trade for less, I should lose.'

"You understand; a man is not in the hog business for nothing. He knows his trade. But if it comes to strings, or just lard, I am keen myself, seeing that it is just in my line— Ha! ha! ha! Then I said to him: 'If she was new, I'd have nothing to say; but she has served you, and this is second hand. I will give you five hundred francs a cubic measure, and not a sou more— Does it go?'

"He answered: 'It goes. A drink on it!'

"I drink with him and we go out arm in arm. It is a good thing for a man to have a helpmeet in life. But one fear comes to me: How were we to measure her in liquid measure?

"Then he explained his idea to me, with some trouble, seeing he was drunk. Said he: 'I take a barrel and I fill it up with water. Then I put her in. All of the water that goes out I measure, and that makes the count.'

"I said to him: 'I see that; and understand it. But when the water has gone out it runs away; how will you be able to get it again?'

"Then he took me by the shirt front and explained to me that it would only be necessary to refill the barrel of the deficit that the woman had displaced. The amount put in would be the measure. I suppose ten buckets, that is a cubic meter. Oh, he is no fool, even when he is drunk, that donkey there!

"In short, we went to his house, and I looked at her particularly. As for her being a pretty woman, she is not a pretty woman; everybody can see that, since she is here. I said to myself: 'Done again, but that doesn't matter, it all counts; beautiful or plain, she is nevertheless just as useful,' not so, Mr. President? And then I take note that she is thin as a pole and I say to myself: 'There aren't above four hundred liters there.' I knew that, being in liquids.

"The operation she has described to you. I even left the stockings and the chemise on, to my disadvantage. When it was over we found she had gone. I said: 'Look here, Brument, she has escaped.'

"He replied: 'Have no fear, I can always catch her again. She will have to come home to sleep. Let's measure the deficit—'

"We measured. Not quite four buckets. Ha! ha! ha!"

The prisoner began to laugh with so much persistence that an officer was obliged to touch him on the shoulder. Calming himself, he continued:

"Briefly, Brument then declared: 'That is not right. It's not enough.' As for me, I howled and howled and howled again. He struck and I hit back. This might have lasted until the last judgment, as I was drunk, you see. But then came the policeman! He swore at us and took advantage of us. Then prison! I demand damages."

He was seated.

Brument declared the statement of his accomplice true on all points. The jury, in consternation, retired to deliberate. They returned at the end of an hour and acquitted the prisoners, with a severe reprimand based upon the majesty of marriage, and establishing the precise limitations of commercial transactions.

Brument went his way toward the conjugal abode with his wife. Cornu returned to his business.

The Signal

$\mathbf{T}$HE little Marchioness de Rennedon was still asleep in her dark and perfumed bedroom.

In her soft, low bed, between sheets of delicate cambric, fine as lace and caressing as a kiss, she was sleeping alone and tranquil, the happy and profound sleep of divorced women.

She was awakened by loud voices in the little blue drawing-room, and she recognized her dear friend, the little Baroness de Grangerie, who was disputing with the lady's maid, because the latter would not allow her to go into the Marchioness's room. So the little Marchioness got up, opened the door, drew back the door-hangings and showed her head, nothing but her fair head, hidden under a cloud of hair.

"What is the matter with you that you have come so early?" she asked. "It is not nine o'clock yet."

The little Baroness, who was very pale, nervous, and feverish, replied: "I must speak to you. Something horrible has happened to me."

"Come in, my dear."

She went in, they kissed each other and the little Marchioness got back into her bed, while the lady's maid opened the windows to let in light and air. Then when she had left the room, Madame de Rennedon went on: "Well, tell me what it is."

Madame de Grangerie began to cry, shedding those pretty bright tears which make women more charming. She sobbed out, without wiping her eyes, so as not to make them red: "Oh! my dear, what has happened to me

386

is abominable, abominable. I have not slept all night, not a minute; do you hear, not a minute. Here, just feel my heart, how it is beating."

And taking her friend's hand, she put it on her breast, on that firm, round covering of women's hearts which often suffices men, and prevents them from seeking beneath. But her heart was really beating violently.

She continued: "It happened to me yesterday during the day, at about four o'clock—or half past four; I cannot say exactly. You know my apartments, and you know that my little drawing-room, where I always sit, looks on to the Rue Saint-Lazare, and that I have a mania for sitting at the window to look at the people passing. The neighborhood of the railway station is very gay; so full of motion and lively—just what I like! So, yesterday, I was sitting in the low chair which I have placed in my window recess; the window was open and I was not thinking of anything, simply breathing the fresh air. You remember how fine it was yesterday!

"Suddenly, I remarked a woman sitting at the window opposite—a woman in red. I was in mauve, you know, my pretty mauve costume. I did not know the woman, a new lodger, who had been there a month, and as it has been raining for a month, I had not yet seen her, but I saw immediately that she was a bad girl. At first I was very much shocked and disgusted that she should be at the window just as I was; and then by degrees, it amused me to watch her. She was resting her elbows on the window ledge, and looking at the men, and the men looked at her also, all or nearly all. One might have said that they knew of her presence by some means as they got near the house, that they scented her, as dogs scent game, for they suddenly raised their heads, and exchanged a swift look with her, a sort of freemason's look. Hers said: 'Will you?'

Theirs replied: 'I have no time,' or else: 'Another day'; or else: 'I have not got a sou'; or else: 'Hide yourself, you wretch!'

"You cannot imagine how funny it was to see her carrying on such a piece of work, though after all it is her regular business.

"Occasionally she shut the window suddenly, and I saw a gentleman go in. She had caught him like a fisherman hooks a gudgeon. Then I looked at my watch, and I found that they never stopped longer than from twelve to twenty minutes. In the end she really infatuated me, the spider! And then the creature is so ugly.

"I asked myself: 'How does she manage to make herself understood so quickly, so well and so completely? Does she add a sign of the head or a motion of the hands to her looks?' And I took my opera-glasses to watch her proceedings. Oh! they were very simple: first of all a glance, then a smile, then a slight sign with the head which meant: 'Are you coming up?' But it was so slight, so vague, so discreet, that it required a great deal of knack to succeed as she did. And I asked myself: 'I wonder if I could do that little movement, from below upward, which was at the same time bold and pretty, as well as she does,' for her gesture was very pretty.

"I went and tried it before the looking-glass, and my dear, I did it better than she, a great deal better! I was enchanted, and resumed my place at the window.

"She caught nobody more then, poor girl, nobody. She certainly had no luck. It must really be very terrible to earn one's bread in that way, terrible and amusing occasionally, for really some of these men one meets in the street are rather nice.

"After that they all came on my side of the road and none on hers; the sun had turned. They came one after

the other, young, old, dark, fair, gray, white. I saw some
who looked very nice, really very nice, my dear, far better
than my husband or than yours—I mean than your late
husband, as you have got a divorce. Now you can choose.

"I said to myself: 'If I give them the sign, will they
understand me, who am a respectable woman?' And I was
seized with a mad longing to make that sign to them. I
had a longing, a terrible longing; you know, one of those
longings which one cannot resist! I have some like that
occasionally. How silly such things are, don't you think
so? I believe that we women have the souls of monkeys. I
have been told (and it was a physician who told me) that
the brain of a monkey is very like ours. Of course we must
imitate some one or other. We imitate our husbands
when we love them, during the first months after our
marriage, and then our lovers, our female friends, our
confessors when they are nice. We assume their ways of
thought, their manners of speech, their words, their gestures, everything. It is very foolish.

"However, as for me, when I am much tempted to do
a thing I always do it, and so I said to myself: 'I will try it
once, on one man only, just to see. What can happen to
me? Nothing whatever! We shall exchange a smile and
that will be all and I shall deny it, most certainly.'

"So I began to make my choice, I wanted some one
nice, very nice, and suddenly I saw a tall, fair, very good-
looking fellow coming along. I like fair men, as you
know. I looked at him, he looked at me; I smiled, he
smiled, I made the movement, oh! so faintly; he replied
yes with his head, and there he was, my dear! He came in
at the large door of the house.

"You cannot imagine what passed through my mind
then! I thought I should go mad. Oh! how frightened I
was. Just think, he will speak to the servants! To Joseph

who is devoted to my husband! Joseph would certainly think that I had known that gentleman for a long time.

"What could I do, just tell me? And he would ring in a moment. What could I do, tell me? I thought I would go and meet him, and tell him he had made a mistake, and beg him to go away. He would have pity on a woman, on a poor woman: So I rushed to the door and opened it, just at the moment when he was going to ring the bell, and I stammered out, quite stupidly: 'Go away, Monsieur, go away; you have made a mistake, a terrible mistake; I took you for one of my friends whom you are very like. Have pity on me, Monsieur.'

"But he only began to laugh, my dear, and replied: 'Good morning, my dear, I know all about your little story, you may be sure. You are married, and so you want forty francs instead of twenty, and you shall have them, so just show the way.'

"And he pushed me in, closed the door, and as I remained standing before him, horror-struck, he kissed me, put his arm round my waist and made me go back into the drawing-room the door of which had remained open. Then he began to look at everything like an auctioneer, and continued: 'By Jove, it is very nice in your rooms, very nice. You must be very down on your luck just now, to do the window business!'

"Then I began to beg him again: 'Oh! Monsieur, go away, please go away! My husband will be coming in soon, it is just his time. I swear that you have made a mistake!' But he answered quite coolly: 'Come, my beauty, I have had enough of this nonsense, and if your husband comes in, I will give him five francs to go and have a drink at the *café* opposite.' And then seeing Raoul's photograph on the chimney-piece, he asked me: 'Is that your—your husband?'

" 'Yes, that is he.'

" 'He looks like a nice, disagreeable sort of fellow. And who is this? One of your friends?'

"It was your photograph, my dear, you know, the one in ball dress. I did not know any longer what I was saying and I stammered: 'Yes, it is one of my friends.'

" 'She is very nice; you shall introduce me to her.'

"Just then the clock struck five, and Raoul comes home every day at half past! Suppose he were to come home before the other had gone, just fancy what would have happened! Then—then—I completely lost my head —altogether—I thought—I thought—that—that—the best thing would be—to get rid—of—of this man—as quickly as possible— The sooner it was over—you under-stand."

The little Marchioness de Rennedon had begun to laugh, to laugh madly, with her head buried in her pil-low, so that the whole bed shook, and when she was a little calmer she asked:

"And—and—was he good-looking?"

"Yes."

"And yet you complain?"

"But—but—don't you see, my dear, he said—he said —he should come again tomorrow—at the same time— and I—I am terribly frightened— You have no idea how tenacious he is and obstinate— What can I do—tell me— what can I do?"

The little Marchioness sat up in bed to reflect, and then she suddenly said: "Have him arrested!"

The little Baroness looked stupefied, and stammered out: "What do you say? What are you thinking of? Have him arrested? Under what pretext?"

"That is very simple. Go to the Commissary of Police

and say that a gentleman has been following you about for three months; that he had the insolence to go up to your apartments yesterday; that he has threatened you with another visit tomorrow, and that you demand the protection of the law, and they will give you two police officers who will arrest him."

"But, my dear, suppose he tells—"

"They will not believe him, you silly thing, if you have told your tale cleverly to the commissary, but they will believe you, who are an irreproachable woman, and in society."

"Oh! I shall never dare to do it."

"You must dare, my dear, or you are lost."

"But think that he will—he will insult me if he is arrested."

"Very well, you will have witnesses, and he will be sentenced."

"Sentenced to what?"

"To pay damages. In such cases, one must be pitiless!"

"Ah! speaking of damages—there is one thing that worries me very much—very much indeed. He left me two twenty-franc pieces on the mantelpiece."

"Two twenty-franc pieces?"

"Yes."

"No more?"

"No."

"That is very little. It would have humiliated me. Well?"

"Well! What am I to do with that money?"

The little Marchioness hesitated for a few seconds, and then she replied in a serious voice:

"My dear—you must make—you must make your husband a little present with it. That will be only fair!"

Love's Awakening

N<small>O</small> one was surprised at the marriage of Mr. Simon Lebrument and Miss Jean Cordier. Mr. Lebrument came to buy out the office of Mr. Papillon; he needed, it was understood, money with which to pay for it; and Miss Jean Cordier had three hundred thousand francs clear, in stocks and bonds.

Mr. Lebrument was a handsome bachelor, who had style, the style of a notary, a provincial style, but, after all, some style, which was a rare thing at Boutigny-le-Rebours.

Miss Cordier had grace and freshness, grace a little awkward and freshness a little mixed up; but she was nevertheless, a pretty girl, desirable and entertaining.

The wedding ceremonies turned Boutigny topsy-turvy. The married couple was much admired when they returned to the conjugal domicile to conceal their happiness, having resolved to make a little, simple journey to Paris, after they had spent a few days together.

It was charming, these few days together, as Mr. Lebrument knew how to manage his early relations with his wife with a delicacy, a directness, and sense of fitness that was remarkable. He took for his motto: "Everything comes to him who waits." He knew how to be patient and energetic at the same time. His success was rapid and complete.

At the end of four days Mrs. Lebrument adored her husband. She could not bear to be a moment away from him. He must be near her all day long, that she might caress his hands, his beard, his nose, etc. She would sit upon his knees and, taking him by the ears, would say: "Open your mouth and shut your eyes." He opened his mouth with confidence, shut his eyes halfway, and then would receive a very long, sweet kiss that made great shivers in his back. And in his turn, he never had enough caresses, enough lips, enough hands, enough of anything with which to enjoy his wife from morning until evening, and from evening until morning.

As soon as the first week had slipped away he said to his young companion:

"If you wish, we might leave for Paris Tuesday of next week. We shall be like lovers who are not married; go about to the theaters, the restaurants, the concert *cafés,* and everywhere, everywhere."

She jumped for joy. "Oh! yes, yes," she replied, "let us go as soon as possible."

"And, as we must not forget anything, you might ask your father to have your dowry ready; I will take it with me, and at the same time pay Mr. Papillon."

She answered: "I will speak to him about it tomorrow morning."

Then he seized her in his arms and began again the little tendernesses she loved so much, and had reveled in now for eight days.

The Tuesday following, the father-in-law and the mother-in-law accompanied their daughter and son-in-law to the station, whence they set out for the capital. The father-in-law remarked:

"I tell you it is imprudent to carry so much money in your pocketbook." And the young notary smiled.

"Do not be disturbed, father-in-law," he answered, "I am accustomed to these things. You know that in my profession it often happens that I have nearly a million about me. By carrying it with me, we escape a lot of formalities and delays, to say the least. Do not give yourself any uneasiness."

Then the trainman cried out, "All aboard!" and they hurried into a compartment where they found themselves with two old ladies.

Lebrument murmured in his wife's ear: "How annoying! Now I cannot smoke."

She answered in a low tone: "I am sorry too, but not on account of your cigar."

The engine puffed and started. The journey lasted an hour, during which they could not say anything of importance, because the two old ladies did not go to sleep.

When they were in the Saint-Lazare station, in Paris, Mr. Lebrument said to his wife:

"If you wish, my dear, we will first go and breakfast on the Boulevard, then return at our leisure to find our trunk and give it to the porter of some hotel."

She consented immediately: "Oh! yes," said she, "let us breakfast in some restaurant. Is it far from here?"

"Yes, rather far, but we will take an omnibus."

She was astonished: "Why not a cab?" she asked.

He groaned as he said smilingly: "And you are economical! A cab for five minutes' ride, at six sous per minute! You do not deprive yourself of anything!"

"That is true," said she, a little confused.

A large omnibus was passing, with three horses at a trot. Lebrument hailed it: "Conductor! Eh, conductor!"

The heavy carriage stopped. The young notary pushed his wife inside, saying hurriedly, in a low voice:

"You get in while I climb up on the outside to smoke at least a cigarette before breakfast."

She had not time for any answer. The conductor

who had seized her by the arm to aid her in mounting the steps, pushed her into the 'bus, where she landed, half-frightened, upon a seat, and in a sort of stupor watched the feet of her husband through the windows at the back, as he climbed to the top of the imperial.

There she remained immovable between a large gentleman who smelled of a pipe and an old woman who smelled of a dog. All the other travelers, in two mute lines—a grocer's boy, a workman, a sergeant of infantry, a gentleman with gold-rimmed spectacles and a silk cap with enormous visors, like gutters, and two ladies with an important, mincing air, which seemed to say: We are here, although we should be in a better place. Then there were two good sisters, a little girl in long hair, and an undertaker.

The assemblage had the appearance of a collection of caricatures in a freak museum, a series of expressions of the human countenance, like a row of grotesque puppets which one knocks down at a fair.

The jolts of the carriage made them toss their heads a little, and as they shook, the flesh of their cheeks trembled; and the disturbance of the rolling wheels gave them an idiotic or sleepy look.

The young woman remained inert: "Why did he not come with me?" she asked herself. A vague sadness oppressed her. He might, indeed, have deprived himself of his cigar!

The good sisters gave the signal to stop. They alighted, one after the other, leaving an odor of old and faded skirts.

Soon after they were gone another stopped the 'bus. A cook came in, red and out of breath. She sat down and placed her basket of provisions upon her knees. A strong odor of dishwater pervaded the omnibus.

"It is further than I thought," said the young woman to herself.

The undertaker got out and was replaced by a coach-man who smelled of a stable. The girl in long hair was succeeded by an errand-boy who exhaled the perfume of his walks.

The notary's wife perceived all these things, ill at ease and so disheartened that she was ready to weep without knowing why.

Some others got out, still others came in. The omnibus went on through the interminable streets, stopped at the stations, and began its route again.

"How far it is!" said Jean. "Especially when one has nothing for diversion and cannot sleep!" She had not been so much fatigued for many days.

Little by little all the travelers got out. She remained alone, all alone. The conductor shouted:

"Vaugirard!"

As she blushed, he again repeated: "Vaugirard!"

She looked at him, not understanding that this must be addressed to her as all her neighbors had gone. For the third time the man said: "Vaugirard!"

Then she asked: "Where are we?"

He answered in a gruff voice: "We are at Vaugirard, Miss; I've told you twenty times already."

"Is it far from the Boulevard?" she asked.

"What Boulevard?"

"The Italian Boulevard."

"We passed that a long time ago."

"Ah! Will you be kind enough to tell my husband?"

"Your husband? Where is he?"

"On the outside."

"On the outside! It has been a long time since there was anybody there."

397

She made a terrified gesture. Then she said:

"How can it be? It is not possible. He got up there when I entered the omnibus. Look again; he must be there."

The conductor became rude: "Come, little one, this is talk enough. If there is one man lost, there are ten to be found. Scamper out, now! You will find another in the street."

The tears sprung to her eyes. She insisted: "But, sir, you are mistaken, I assure you that you are mistaken. He had a large pocketbook in his hand."

The employee began to laugh: "A large pocketbook? I remember. Yes, he got out at the Madeleine. That's right! He's left you behind! Ha! ha!"

The carriage was standing still. She got down and looked up, in spite of herself to the roof, with an instinctive movement of the eye. It was totally deserted.

Then she began to weep aloud, without thinking that anyone was looking at or listening to her. Finally she said:

"What is going to become of me?"

The inspector came up and inquired: "What's the matter?"

The conductor answered in a jocose fashion:

"This lady's husband has left her on the way."

The other replied: "Now, now, that is nothing. I am at your service." And he turned on his heels.

Then she began to walk ahead, too much frightened, too much excited to think even where she was going. Where was she going? What should she do? How could such an error have occurred? Such an act of carelessness, of disregard, of unheard-of distraction!

She had two francs in her pocket. To whom could

she apply? Suddenly she remembered her cousin **Barral,** who was a clerk in the office of Naval Affairs.

She had just enough to hire a cab; she would go to him. And she met him just as he was starting for his office. Like Lebrument, he carried a large pocketbook under his arm.

She leaned out of the carriage and called: "Henry!"

He stopped, much surprised.

"Jeanne," said he, "here?—and alone? Where do you come from? What are you doing?"

She stammered, with her eyes full of tears: "My husband is lost somewhere—"

"Lost? where?"

"On the omnibus."

"On the omnibus! Oh!"

And she related to him the whole story, weeping much over the adventure.

He listened reflectively, and then asked:

"This morning? And was his head perfectly clear?"

"Oh! yes! And he had my dowry."

"Your dowry? The whole of it?"

"Yes, the whole of it—in order to pay for his office."

"Well, my dear cousin, your husband, whoever he is, is probably watching the wheel—this minute."

She did not yet comprehend. She stammered: "My husband—you say—"

"I say that he has run off with your—your capital—and that's all about it."

She remained standing there, suffocated with grief, murmuring:

"Then he is—he is—is a wretch!"

Then, overcome with emotion, she fell on her cousin's shoulder, sobbing violently.

As people were stopping to look at them, he guided

her gently into the entrance of his house, supporting her body. They mounted the steps, and as the maid came to open the door he ordered her:

"Sophie, run to the restaurant and bring breakfast for two persons. I shall not go to the office this morning."

The Olive Grove

WHEN the longshoremen of Garandou, a little
port of Provence, situated in the bay of Pisca, between
Marseilles and Toulon, perceived the boat of the Abbé
Vilbois entering the harbor, they went down to the beach
to help him pull her ashore.

The priest was alone in the boat. In spite of his
fifty-eight years, he rowed with all the energy of a real
sailor. He had placed his hat on the bench beside him,
his sleeves were rolled up, disclosing his powerful arms,
his cassock was open at the neck and turned over his
knees, and he wore a round hat of heavy, white canvas.
His whole appearance bespoke an odd and strenuous
priest of southern climes, better fitted for adventures
than for clerical duties.

He rowed with strong and measured strokes, as
if to show the southern sailors how the men of the north
handle the oars, and from time to time he turned around
to look at the landing point.

The skiff struck the beach and slid far up, the bow
plowing through the sand; then it stopped abruptly. The
five men watching for the abbé drew near, jovial and
smiling.

"Well!" said one, with the strong accent of Provence,
"have you been successful, Monsieur le Curé?"

The abbé drew in the oars, removed his canvas head-
covering, put on his hat, pulled down his sleeves, and
buttoned his coat. Then having assumed the usual appearance of a village priest, he replied proudly: "Yes, I

have caught three red-snappers, two eels, and five sun-fish."

The fishermen gathered around the boat to examine, with the air of experts, the dead fish, the fat red-snappers, the flat-headed eels, those hideous sea-serpents, and the violet sunfish, streaked with bright orange-colored stripes.

Said one: "I'll carry them up to your house, Monsieur le Curé."

"Thank you, my friend."

Having shaken hands all around, the priest started homeward, followed by the man with the fish; the others took charge of the boat.

The Abbé Vilbois walked along slowly with an air of dignity. The exertion of rowing had brought beads of perspiration to his brow and he uncovered his head each time that he passed through the shade of an olive grove. The warm evening air, freshened by a slight breeze from the sea, cooled his high forehead covered with short, white hair, a forehead far more suggestive of an officer than of a priest.

The village appeared, built on a hill rising from a large valley which descended toward the sea.

It was a summer evening. The dazzling sun, traveling toward the ragged crests of the distant hills, outlined on the white, dusty road the figure of the priest, the shadow of whose three-cornered hat bobbed merrily over the fields, sometimes apparently climbing the trunks of the olive-trees, only to fall immediately to the ground and creep among them.

With every step he took, he raised a cloud of fine, white dust, the invisible powder which, in summer, covers the roads of Provence; it clung to the edge of his cassock turning it grayish white. Completely refreshed, his hands deep in his pockets, he strode along slowly and ponderously, like a mountaineer. His eyes were fixed on the distant village where he had lived twenty years, and where he hoped to die. Its church—his church—rose above the houses clustered around it; the square turrets of gray stone, of unequal proportions and quaint design, stood outlined against the beautiful southern valley; and their architecture suggested the fortifications of some old château rather than the steeples of a place of worship.

The abbé was happy; for he had caught three red-snappers, two eels, and five sunfish. It would enable him to triumph again over his flock, which respected him, no doubt, because he was one of the most powerful men of the place, despite his years. These little innocent vanities were his greatest pleasures. He was a fine marksman; sometimes he practiced with his neighbor, a retired army provost who kept a tobacco shop; he could also swim better than anyone along the coast.

In his day he had been a well-known society man, the Baron de Vilbois, but had entered the priesthood after an unfortunate love-affair. Being the scion of an old family of Picardy, devout and royalistic, whose sons for centuries had entered the army, the magistracy, or the Church, his first thought was to follow his mother's advice and become a priest. But he yielded to his father's suggestion that he should study law in Paris and seek some high office.

While he was completing his studies his father was carried off by pneumonia; his mother, who was greatly affected by the loss, died soon afterward. He came into a fortune, and consequently gave up the idea of following a profession to live a life of idleness. He was handsome and intelligent, but somewhat prejudiced by the traditions and principles which he had inherited, along with his muscular frame, from a long line of ancestors.

Society gladly welcomed him and he enjoyed himself after the fashion of a well-to-do and seriously inclined young man. But it happened that a friend introduced him to a young actress, a pupil of the Conservatoire, who was appearing with great success at the Odéon. It was a case of love at first sight.

His sentiment had all the violence, the passion of a man born to believe in absolute ideas. He saw her act the romantic rôle in which she had achieved a triumph the first night of her appearance. She was pretty, and, though naturally perverse, possessed the face of an angel.

She conquered him completely; she transformed him into a delirious fool, into one of those ecstatic idiots whom a woman's look will forever chain to the pyre of fatal passions. She became his mistress and left the stage. They lived together four years, his love for her increasing during the time. He would have married her in spite of his proud name and family traditions, had he not discovered that for a long time she had been unfaithful to him with the friend who had introduced them.

The awakening was terrible, for she was about to become a mother, and he was awaiting the birth of the child to make her his wife.

When he held the proof of her transgressions—some letters found in a drawer—he confronted her with his knowledge and reproached her with all the savageness of his uncouth nature for her unfaithfulness and deceit. But she, a child of the people, being as sure of this man as of the other, braved and insulted him with the inherited daring of those women, who, in times of war, mounted with the men on the barricades.

He would have struck her to the ground—but she

showed him her form. As white as death, he checked himself, remembering that a child of his would soon be born
to this vile, polluted creature. He rushed at her to crush
them both, to obliterate this double shame. Reeling
under his blows, and seeing that he was about to stamp
out the life of her unborn babe, she realized that she was
lost. Throwing out her hands to parry the blows, she
cried:

"Do not kill me! It is his, not yours!"

He fell back, so stunned with surprise that for a
moment his rage subsided. He stammered:

"What? What did you say?"

Crazed with fright, having read her doom in his
eyes and gestures, she repeated: "It's not yours, it's his."

Through his clenched teeth he stammered:

"The child?"

"Yes."

"You lie!"

And again he lifted his foot as if to crush her, while
she struggled to her knees in a vain attempt to rise. "I
tell you it's his. If it was yours, wouldn't it have come
much sooner?"

He was struck by the truth of this argument. In a
moment of strange lucidity, his mind evolved precise,
conclusive, irresistible reasons to disclaim the child of
this miserable woman, and he felt so appeased, so happy
at the thought, that he decided to let her live.

He then spoke in a calmer voice: "Get up and leave,
and never let me see you again."

Quite cowed, she obeyed him and went. He never
saw her again.

Then he left Paris and came south. He stopped in a
village situated in a valley, near the coast of the Mediterranean. Selecting for his abode an inn facing the sea,

he lived there eighteen months in complete seclusion,
nursing his sorrow and despair. The memory of the unfaithful one tortured him; her grace, her charm, her
perversity haunted him, and withal came the regret of
her caresses.

He wandered aimlessly in those beautiful vales of
Provence, baring his head, filled with the thoughts of
that woman, to the sun that filtered through the grayish-
green leaves of the olive-trees.

His former ideas of religion, the abated ardor of his
faith, returned to him during his sorrowful retreat. Religion had formerly seemed a refuge from the unknown
temptations of life, now it appeared as a refuge from its
snares and tortures. He had never given up the habit of
prayer. In his sorrow, he turned anew to its consolations,
and often at dusk he would wander into the little village
church, where in the darkness gleamed the light of the
lamp hung above the altar, to guard the sanctuary and
symbolize the Divine Presence.

He confided his sorrow to his God, told Him of his
misery, asking advice, pity, help, and consolation. Each
day, his fervid prayers disclosed stronger faith.

The bleeding heart of this man, crushed by love for
a woman, still longed for affection; and soon his prayers,
his seclusion, his constant communion with the Savior
who consoles and cheers the weary, wrought a change in
him, and the mystic love of God entered his soul, casting
out the love of the flesh.

He then decided to take up his former plans and to
devote his life to the Church.

He became a priest. Through family connections he
succeeded in obtaining a call to the parish of this village
which he had come across by chance. Devoting a large
part of his fortune to the maintenance of charitable in-

stitutions, and keeping only enough to enable him to help the poor as long as he lived, he sought refuge in a quiet life filled with prayer and acts of kindness toward his fellow-men.

Narrow-minded but kind-hearted, a priest with a soldier's temperament, he guided his blind, erring flock forcibly through the mazes of this life in which every taste, instinct, and desire is a pitfall. But the old man in him never disappeared entirely. He continued to love out-of-door exercise and noble sports, but he hated every woman, having an almost childish fear of their dangerous fascination.

II

The sailor who followed the priest, being a southerner, found it difficult to refrain from talking. But he did not dare start a conversation, for the abbé exerted a great prestige over his flock. At last he ventured a remark: "So you like your lodge, do you, Monsieur le Curé?"

This lodge was one of the tiny constructions that are inhabited during the summer by the villagers and the town people alike. It was situated in a field not far from the parish-home, and the abbé had hired it because the latter was very small and built in the heart of the village next to the church.

During the summer time, he did not live altogether at the lodge, but would remain a few days at a time to practice pistol-shooting and be close to nature.

"Yes, my friend," said the priest, "I like it very well."

The low structure could now be seen; it was painted pink, and the walls were almost hidden under the leaves and branches of the olive-trees that grew in the open field. A tall woman was passing in and out of the door, setting a small table at which she placed, at each trip, a knife and fork, a glass, a plate, a napkin, and a piece of bread. She wore the small cap of the women of Arles, a pointed cone of silk or black velvet, decorated with a white rosette.

When the abbé was near enough to make himself heard, he shouted:

"Eh! Marguerite!"

She stopped to ascertain whence the voice came, and recognizing her master: "Oh! it's you, Monsieur le Curé!"

"Yes. I have caught some fine fish, and want you to broil this sunfish immediately, do you hear?"

The servant examined, with a critical and approving glance, the fish that the sailor carried.

"Yes, but we are going to have a chicken for dinner," she said.

"Well, it cannot be helped. Tomorrow the fish will not be as fresh as it is now. I mean to enjoy a little feast —it does not happen often—and the sin is not great."

The woman picked out a sunfish and prepared to go into the house. "Ah!" she said, "a man came to see you three times while you were out, Monsieur le Curé."

Indifferently he inquired: "A man! What kind of man?"

"Why, a man whose appearance was not in his favor."

"What! a beggar?"

"Perhaps—I don't know. But I think he is more of a 'maoufatan.'"

The abbé smiled at this word, which, in the language of Provence means a highwayman, a tramp, for he was well aware of Marguerite's timidity, and knew that every day and especially every night she fancied they would be murdered.

He handed a few sous to the sailor, who departed.

And just as he was saying: "I am going to wash my hands"—for his past dainty habits still clung to him—Marguerite called to him from the kitchen where she was scraping the fish with a knife, thereby detaching its blood-stained, silvery scales:

"There he comes!"

The abbé looked down the road and saw a man coming slowly toward the house; he seemed poorly dressed, indeed, so far as he could distinguish. He could not help smiling at his servant's anxiety, and thought, while he waited for the stranger: "I think, after all, she is right; he does look like a 'maoufatan.'"

The man walked slowly, with his eyes on the priest and his hands buried deep in his pockets. He was young and wore a full, blond beard; strands of curly hair escaped from his soft felt hat, which was so dirty and battered that it was impossible to imagine its former color and appearance. He was clothed in a long, dark overcoat, from which emerged the frayed edge of his trousers; on his feet were bathing shoes that deadened his steps, giving him the stealthy walk of a sneak thief.

When he had come within a few steps of the priest, he doffed, with a sweeping motion, the ragged hat that shaded his brow. He was not bad-looking, though his face showed signs of dissipation and the top of his head was bald, an indication of premature fatigue and debauch, for he certainly was not over twenty-five years old.

The priest responded at once to his bow, feeling that this fellow was not an ordinary tramp, a mechanic out of work, or a jail-bird, hardly able to speak any other tongue but the mysterious language of prisons.

"How do you do, Monsieur le Curé?" said the man. The priest answered simply, "I salute you," unwilling to address this ragged stranger as "Monsieur." They considered each other attentively; the abbé felt uncomfortable under the gaze of the tramp, invaded by a feeling of unrest unknown to him.

At last the vagabond continued: "Well, do you recognize me?"

Greatly surprised, the priest answered: "Why, no, you are a stranger to me."

"Ah! you do not know me? Look at me well."

"I have never seen you before."

"Well, that may be true," replied the man sarcastically, "but let me show you some one whom you will know better."

He put on his hat and unbuttoned his coat, revealing his bare chest. A red sash wound around his spare frame held his trousers in place. He drew an envelope from his coat pocket, one of those soiled wrappers destined to protect the sundry papers of the tramp, whether they be stolen or legitimate property, those papers which he guards jealously and uses to protect himself against the too zealous gendarmes. He pulled out a photograph about the size of a folded letter, one of those pictures which were popular long ago; it was yellow and dim with age, for he had carried it around with him everywhere and the heat of his body had faded it.

Pushing it under the abbé's eyes, he demanded:

"Do you know him?"

The priest took a step forward to look and grew pale, for it was his own likeness that he had given Her years ago.

Failing to grasp the meaning of the situation he remained silent.

The tramp repeated:

"Do you recognize him?"

And the priest stammered: "Yes."

"Who is it?"

"It is I."

"It is you?"

"Yes."

"Well, then, look at us both—at me and at your picture!"

Already the unhappy man had seen that these two beings, the one in the picture and the one by his side, resembled each other like brothers; yet he did not understand, and muttered: "Well, what is it you wish?"

Then in an ugly voice, the tramp replied: "What do I wish? Why, first I wish you to recognize me."

"Who are you?"

"Who am I? Ask anybody by the roadside, ask your servant, let's go and ask the mayor and show him this; and he will laugh, I tell you that! Ah! you will not recognize me as your son, papa curé?"

The old man raised his arms above his head, with a patriarchal gesture, and muttered despairingly: "It cannot be true!"

The young fellow drew quite close to him.

"Ah! It cannot be true, you say! You must stop lying, do you hear?" His clenched fists and threatening face, and the violence with which he spoke, made the priest retreat a few steps, while he asked himself anxiously which one of them was laboring under a mistake.

Again he asserted: "I never had a child."

The other man replied: "And no mistress, either?"

The aged priest resolutely uttered one word, a proud admission:

"Yes."

"And was not this mistress about to give birth to a child when you left her?"

Suddenly the anger which had been quelled twenty-five years ago, not quelled, but buried in the heart of the lover, burst through the wall of faith, resignation, and renunciation he had built around it. Almost beside himself, he shouted:

"I left her because she was unfaithful to me and was carrying the child of another man; had it not been for this, I should have killed both you and her, sir!"

The young man hesitated, taken aback at the sincerity of this outburst. Then he replied in a gentler voice:

"Who told you that it was another man's child?"

"She told me herself and braved me."

Without contesting this assertion the vagabond assumed the indifferent tone of a loafer judging a case:

"Well, then, mother made a mistake, that's all!"

After his outburst of rage, the priest had succeeded in mastering himself sufficiently to be able to inquire:

"And who told you that you were my son?"

"My mother, on her deathbed, M'sieur le Curé. And then—this!" And he held the picture under the eyes of the priest.

The old man took it from him; and slowly, with a heart bursting with anguish, he compared this stranger with his faded likeness and doubted no longer—it was his son.

An awful distress wrung his very soul, a terrible, inexpressible emotion invaded him; it was like the remorse of some ancient crime. He began to understand a little, he guessed the rest. He lived over the brutal scene of the parting. It was to save her life, then, that the wretched and deceitful woman had lied to him, her outraged lover. And he had believed her. And a son of his had been brought into the world and had grown up to be this sordid tramp, who exhaled the very odor of vice as a goat exhales its animal smell.

He whispered: "Will you take a little walk with me, so that we can discuss these matters?"

The young man sneered: "Why, certainly! Isn't that what I came for?"

They walked side by side through the olive grove. The sun had gone down and the coolness of southern twilights spread an invisible cloak over the country. The priest shivered, and raising his eyes with a familiar motion, perceived the trembling gray foliage of the holy tree which had spread its frail shadow over the Son of Man in His great trouble and despondency.

A short, despairing prayer rose within him, uttered by his soul's voice, a prayer by which Christians implore the Savior's aid: "O Lord! have mercy on me."

Turning to his son he said: "So your mother is dead?"

These words, "Your mother is dead," awakened a new sorrow; it was the torment of the flesh which cannot forget, the cruel echo of past sufferings; but mostly the thrill of the fleeting, delirious bliss of his youthful passion.

The young man replied: "Yes, Monsieur le Curé, my mother is dead."

"Has she been dead a long while?"

"Yes, three years."

A new doubt entered the priest's mind. "And why did you not find me out before?"

The other man hesitated.

"I was unable to, I was prevented. But excuse me for interrupting these recollections—I will enter into more details later—for I have not had anything to eat since yesterday morning."

A tremor of pity shook the old man and holding forth both hands: "Oh! my poor child!" he said.

The young fellow took those big, powerful hands in his own slender and feverish palms.

Then he replied, with that air of sarcasm which hardly ever left his lips: "Ah! I'm beginning to think that we shall get along very well together, after all!"

The curé started toward the lodge.

"Let us go to dinner," he said.

He suddenly remembered, with a vague and instinctive pleasure, the fine fish he had caught, which, with the chicken, would make a good meal for the poor fellow.

The servant was in front of the door, watching their approach with an anxious and forbidding face.

"Marguerite," shouted the abbé, "take the table and put it into the dining-room, right away; and set two places, as quick as you can."

The woman seemed stunned at the idea that her master was going to dine with this tramp.

But the abbé, without waiting for her, removed the plate and napkin and carried the little table into the dining-room.

A few minutes later he was sitting opposite the beggar, in front of a soup-tureen filled with savory cabbage soup, which sent up a cloud of fragrant steam.

III

When the plates were filled, the tramp fell to with ravenous avidity. The abbé had lost his appetite and ate slowly, leaving the bread in the bottom of his plate. Suddenly he inquired:

"What is your name?"

The man smiled; he was delighted to satisfy his hunger.

"Father unknown," he said, "and no other name but my mother's, which you probably remember. But I possess two Christian names, which, by the way, are quite unsuited to me—Philippe-Auguste."

The priest whitened.

"Why were you named thus?" he asked.

The tramp shrugged his shoulders. "I fancy you ought to know. After mother left you, she wished to make your rival believe that I was his child. He did believe it until I was about fifteen. Then I began to look too much like you. And he disclaimed me, the scoundrel. I had been christened Philippe-Auguste; now, if I had not resembled a soul, or if I had been the son of a third person, who had stayed in the background, today I should be the Vicomte Philippe-Auguste de Pravallon, son of the count and senator bearing this name. I have christened myself 'No-luck.'"

"How did you learn all this?"

"They discussed it before me, you know; pretty lively discussions they were, too. I tell you, that's what shows you the seamy side of life!"

Something more distressing than all he had suffered during the last half hour now oppressed the priest. It was a sort of suffocation which seemed as if it would grow and grow till it killed him; it was not due so much to the things he heard as to the manner in which they were uttered by this wayside tramp. Between himself and this beggar, between his son and himself, he was discovering the existence of those moral divergencies which are as fatal poisons to certain souls. Was this his son? He could not yet believe it. He wanted all the proofs, every one of them. He wanted to hear all, to listen to all. Again he thought of the olive-trees that shaded his little lodge, and for the second time he prayed: "O Lord! have mercy upon me."

Philippe-Auguste had finished his soup. He inquired: "Is there nothing else, abbé?"

The kitchen was built in an annex. Marguerite could not hear her master's voice. He always called her by striking a Chinese gong hung on the wall behind his chair. He took the brass hammer and struck the round metal plate. It gave a feeble sound, which grew and vibrated, becoming sharper and louder till it finally died away on the evening breeze.

The servant appeared with a frowning face and cast angry glances at the tramp, as if her faithful instinct had warned her of the misfortune that had befallen her master. She held a platter on which was the sunfish, spreading a savory odor of melted butter through the room. The abbé divided the fish lengthwise, helping his son to the better half: "I caught it a little while ago," he said, with a touch of pride in spite of his keen distress.

Marguerite had not left the room.

The priest added: "Bring us some wine, the white wine of Cape Corse."

She almost rebelled, and the priest, assuming a severe expression was obliged to repeat: "Now, go, and bring two bottles, remember," for, when he drank with anybody, a very rare pleasure, indeed, he always opened one bottle for himself.

Beaming, Philippe-Auguste remarked: "Fine! A splendid idea! It has been a long time since I've had such a dinner." The servant came back after a few minutes. The abbé thought it an eternity, for now a thirst for information burned his blood like infernal fire.

After the bottles had been opened, the woman still remained, her eyes glued on the tramp.

"Leave us," said the curé.

She intentionally ignored his command.

He repeated almost roughly: "I have ordered you to leave us."

Then she left the room.

Philippe-Auguste devoured the fish voraciously, while his father sat watching him, more and more surprised and saddened at all the baseness stamped on the face that was so like his own. The morsels the abbé raised to his lips remained in his mouth, for his throat could not swallow; so he ate slowly, trying to choose, from the host of questions which besieged his mind, the one he wished his son to answer first. At last he spoke:

"What was the cause of her death?"

"Consumption."

"Was she ill a long time?"

"About eighteen months."

"How did she contract it?"

"We could not tell."

Both men were silent. The priest was reflecting. He was oppressed by the multitude of things he wished to know and to hear, for since the rupture, since the day he had tried to kill her, he had heard nothing. Certainly, he had not cared to know, because he had buried her, along with his happiest days, in forgetfulness; but now, knowing that she was dead and gone, he felt within himself the almost jealous desire of a lover to hear all.

He continued: "She was not alone, was she?"

"No, she lived with him."

The old man started: "With him? With Pravallon?"

"Why, yes."

And the betrayed man rapidly calculated that the

woman who had deceived him, had lived over thirty years with his rival.

Almost unconsciously he asked: "Were they happy?"

The young man sneered. "Why, yes, with ups and downs! It would have been better had I not been there. I always spoiled everything."

"How, and why?" inquired the priest.

"I have already told you. Because he thought I was his son up to my fifteenth year. But the old fellow wasn't a fool, and soon discovered the likeness. That created scenes. I used to listen behind the door. He accused mother of having deceived him. Mother would answer: 'Is it my fault? you knew quite well when you took me that I was the mistress of that other man.' You were that other man."

"Ah! They spoke of me sometimes?"

"Yes, but never mentioned your name before me, excepting toward the end, when mother knew she was lost. I think they distrusted me."

"And you—and you learned quite early the irregularity of your mother's position?"

"Why, certainly. I am not innocent and I never was. Those things are easy to guess as soon as one begins to know life."

Philippe-Auguste had been filling his glass repeatedly. His eyes now were beginning to sparkle, for his long fast was favorable to the intoxicating effects of the wine. The priest noticed it and wished to caution him. But suddenly the thought that a drunkard is imprudent and loquacious flashed through him, and lifting the bottle he again filled the young man's glass.

Meanwhile Marguerite had brought the chicken. Having set it on the table, she again fastened her eyes on the tramp, saying in an indignant voice: "Can't you see that he's drunk, Monsieur le Curé?"

"Leave us," replied the priest, "and return to the kitchen."

She went out, slamming the door.

He then inquired: "What did your mother say about me?"

"Why, what a woman usually says of a man she has jilted: that you were hard to get along with, very strange, and that you would have made her life miserable with your peculiar ideas."

"Did she say that often?"

"Yes, but sometimes only in allusions, for fear I would understand; but nevertheless I guessed all."

"And how did they treat you in that house?"

"Me? They treated me very well at first and very badly afterward. When mother saw that I was interfering with her, she shook me."

"How?"

"How? very easily. When I was about sixteen years old, I got into various scrapes, and those blackguards put me into a reformatory to get rid of me." He put his elbows on the table and rested his cheeks in his palms. He was hopelessly intoxicated, and felt the unconquerable desire of all drunkards to talk and boast about themselves.

He smiled sweetly, with a feminine grace, an arch grace the priest knew and recognized as the hated charm that had won him long ago, and had also wrought his undoing. Now it was his mother whom the boy resembled, not so much because of his features, but because of his fascinating and deceptive glance, and the seductiveness of the false smile that played around his lips, the outlet of his inner ignominy.

Philippe-Auguste began to relate: "Ah! Ah! Ah!— I've had a fine life since I left the reformatory! A great writer would pay a large sum for it! Why, old Père

Dumas's Monte Cristo has had no stranger adventures than mine."

He paused to reflect with the philosophical gravity of the drunkard, then he continued slowly:

"When you wish a boy to turn out well, no matter what he has done, never send him to a reformatory. The associations are too bad. Now, I got into a bad scrape. One night about nine o'clock, I, with three companions —we were all a little drunk—was walking along the road near the ford of Folac. All at once a wagon hove in sight, with the driver and his family asleep in it. They were people from Martinon on their way home from town. I caught hold of the bridle, led the horse to the ferryboat, made him walk into it, and pushed the boat into the middle of the stream. This created some noise and the driver awoke. He could not see in the dark, but whipped up the horse, which started on a run and landed in the water with the whole load. All were drowned! My companions denounced me to the authorities, though they thought it was a good joke when they saw me do it. Really, we didn't think that it would turn out that way. We only wanted to give the people a ducking, just for fun. After that I committed worse offenses to revenge myself for the first one, which did not, on my honor, warrant the reformatory. But what's the use of telling them? I will speak only of the latest one, because I am sure it will please you. Papa, I avenged you!"

The abbé was watching his son with terrified eyes; he had stopped eating.

Philippe-Auguste was preparing to begin. "No, not yet," said the priest, "in a little while."

And he turned to strike the Chinese gong.

Marguerite appeared almost instantly. Her master addressed her in such a rough tone that she hung her

head, thoroughly frightened and obedient: "Bring in
the lamp and the dessert, and then do not appear until
I summon you."

She went out and returned with a porcelain lamp
covered with a green shade, and bringing also a large
piece of cheese and some fruit.

After she had gone, the abbé turned resolutely to
his son.

"Now I am ready to hear you."

Philippe-Auguste calmly filled his plate with dessert
and poured wine into his glass. The second bottle was
nearly empty, though the priest had not touched it.

His mouth and tongue, thick with food and wine,
the man stuttered: "Well, now for the last job. And it's
a good one. I was home again—stayed there in spite of
them, because they feared me—yes, feared me. Ah! you
can't fool with me, you know—I'll do anything, when
I'm roused. They lived together on and off. The old man
had two residences. One official, for the senator, the
other clandestine, for the lover. Still, he lived more in
the latter than in the former, as he could not get along
without mother. Mother was a sharp one—she knew how
to hold a man! She had taken him body and soul, and
kept him to the last! Well, I had come back and I kept
them down by fright. I am resourceful at times—nobody
can match me for sharpness and for strength, too—I'm
afraid of no one. Well, mother got sick and the old man
took her to a fine place in the country, near Meulan,
situated in a park as big as a wood. She lasted about
eighteen months, as I told you. Then we felt the end to
be near. He came from Paris every day—he was very
miserable—really.

"One morning they chatted a long time, over an
hour, I think, and I could not imagine what they were

talking about. Suddenly mother called me in and said:

" 'I am going to die, and there is something I want to tell you beforehand, in spite of the Count's advice.' In speaking of him she always said 'the Count.' 'It is the name of your father, who is alive.' I had asked her this more than fifty times—more than fifty times—my father's name—more than fifty times—and she always refused to tell. I think I even beat her one day to make her talk, but it was of no use. Then, to get rid of me, she told me that you had died penniless, that you were worthless and that she had made a mistake in her youth, an innocent girl's mistake. She lied so well, I really believed you had died.

"Finally she said: 'It is your father's name.'

"The old man, who was sitting in an armchair, repeated three times, like this: 'You do wrong, you do wrong, you do wrong, Rosette.'

"Mother sat up in bed. I can see her now, with her flushed cheeks and shining eyes; she loved me, in spite of everything; and she said: 'Then you do something for him, Philippe!' In speaking to him she called him 'Philippe' and me 'Auguste.'

"He began to shout like a madman: 'Do something for that loafer—that blackguard, that convict? Never!'

"And he continued to call me names, as if he had done nothing else all his life but collect them.

"I was angry, but mother told me to hold my tongue, and she resumed: 'Then you must want him to starve, for you know that I leave no money.'

"Without being deterred, he continued: 'Rosette, I have given you thirty-five thousand francs a year for thirty years—that makes more than a million. I have enabled you to live like a wealthy, a beloved, and I may say, a happy woman. I owe nothing to that fellow, who has spoiled our late years, and he will not get a cent from me. It is useless to insist. Tell him the name of his father, if you wish. I am sorry, but I wash my hands of him.'

"Then mother turned toward me. I thought: 'Good! now I'm going to find my real father—if he has money, I'm saved.'

"She went on: 'Your father, the Baron de Vilbois, is today the Abbé Vilbois, curé of Garandou, near Toulon. He was my lover before I left him for the Count!'

"And she told me all, except that she had deceived you about her pregnancy. But women, you know, never tell the whole truth."

Sneeringly, unconsciously, he was revealing the depths of his foul nature. With beaming face he raised the glass to his lips and continued:

"Mother died two days—two days later. We followed her remains to the grave, he and I—say—wasn't it funny? —he and I—and three servants—that was all. He cried like a calf—we were side by side—we looked like father and son.

"Then he went back to the house alone. I was thinking to myself: 'I'll have to clear out now and without a penny, too.' I owned only fifty francs. What could I do to revenge myself?

"He touched me on the arm and said: 'I wish to speak to you.' I followed him into his office. He sat down in front of the desk and, wiping away his tears, he told me that he would not be as hard on me as he had said he would to mother. He begged me to leave you alone. That —that concerns only you and me. He offered me a thousand-franc note—a thousand—a thousand francs. What could a fellow like me do with a thousand francs?—I saw that there were very many bills in the drawer. The sight of the money made me wild. I put out my hand as if to take the note he offered me, but instead of doing so, I sprang at him, threw him to the ground and choked him till he grew purple. When I saw that he was going to give up the ghost, I gagged and bound him. Then I undressed him, laid him on his stomach and—ah! ah! ah!—I avenged you in a funny way!"

He stopped to cough, for he was choking with merriment. His ferocious, mirthful smile reminded the priest once more of the woman who had wrought his undoing.

"And then?" he inquired.

"Then—ah! ah! ah!—There was a bright fire in the fireplace—it was in the winter—in December—mother died—a bright coal fire—I took the poker—I let it get red-hot—and I made crosses on his back, eight or more, I cannot remember how many—then I turned him over and repeated them on his stomach. Say, wasn't it funny, papa? Formerly they marked convicts in this way. He wriggled like an eel—but I had gagged him so that he couldn't scream. I gathered up the bills—twelve in all—with mine it made thirteen—an unlucky number. I left the house, after telling the servants not to bother their master until dinner-time, because he was asleep. I thought that he would hush the matter up because he was a senator and would fear the scandal. I was mistaken. Four days later I was arrested in a Paris restaurant. I got three years for the job. That is the reason why I did not come to you sooner." He drank again, and stuttering so as to render his words almost unintelligible, continued:

"Now—papa—isn't it funny to have one's papa a curé? You must be nice to me, very nice, because, you know, I am not commonplace—and I did a good job—didn't I—on the old man?"

The anger which years ago had driven the Abbé Vilbois to desperation rose within him at the sight of this miserable man.

He, who in the name of the Lord, had so often pardoned the infamous secrets whispered to him under the seal of confession, was now merciless in his own behalf. No longer did he implore the help of a merciful God, for he realized that no power on earth or in the sky could save those who had been visited by such a terrible disaster.

All the ardor of his passionate heart and of his violent blood, which long years of resignation had tempered, awoke against the miserable creature who was his son. He protested against the likeness he bore to him and to his mother, the wretched mother who had formed him so like herself; and he rebelled against the destiny that had chained this criminal to him, like an iron ball to a galley-slave.

The shock roused him from the peaceful and pious slumber which had lasted twenty-five years; with a wonderful lucidity he saw all that would inevitably ensue.

Convinced that he must talk loud so as to intimidate this man from the first, he spoke with his teeth clenched with fury:

"Now that you have told all, listen to me. You will leave here tomorrow morning. You will go to a country that I shall designate, and never leave it without my permission. I will give you a small income, for I am poor. If you disobey me once, it will be withdrawn and you will learn to know me."

Though Philippe-Auguste was half dazed with wine, he understood the threat. Instantly the criminal within him rebelled. Between hiccoughs he sputtered: "Ah! papa, be careful what you say—you're a curé, remember —I hold you—and you have to walk straight, like the rest!"

The abbé started. Through his whole muscular

frame crept the unconquerable desire to seize this monster, to bend him like a twig, so as to show him that he
would have to yield.

Shaking the table, he shouted: "Take care, take care
—I am afraid of nobody."

The drunkard lost his balance and seeing that he
was going to fall and would forthwith be in the priest's
power, he reached with a murderous look for one of the
knives lying on the table. The abbé perceived his motion,
and he gave the table a terrible shove; his son toppled
over and landed on his back. The lamp fell with a crash
and went out.

During a moment the clinking of broken glass was
heard in the darkness, then the muffled sound of a soft
body creeping on the floor, and then all was silent.

With the crashing of the lamp a complete darkness
spread over them; it was so prompt and unexpected that
they were stunned by it as by some terrible event. The
drunkard, pressed against the wall, did not move; the
priest remained on his chair in the midst of the night
which had quelled his rage. The somber veil that had
descended so rapidly, arresting his anger, also quieted the
furious impulses of his soul; new ideas, as dark and
dreary as the obscurity, beset him.

The room was perfectly silent, like a tomb where
nothing draws the breath of life. Not a sound came from
outside, neither the rumbling of a distant wagon, nor the
bark of a dog, nor even the sigh of the wind passing
through the trees.

This lasted a long time, perhaps an hour. Then suddenly the gong vibrated! It rang once, as if it had been
struck a short, sharp blow, and was instantly followed by
the noise of a falling body and an overturned chair.

Marguerite came running out of the kitchen, but as soon as she opened the door she fell back, frightened by the intense darkness. Trembling, her heart beating as if it would burst, she called in a low, hoarse voice: "M'sieur le Curé! M'sieur le Curé!"

Nobody answered, nothing stirred.

"Mon Dieu, mon Dieu," she thought, "what has happened, what have they done?"

She did not dare enter the room, yet feared to go back to fetch a light. She felt as if she would like to run away, to screech at the top of her voice, though she knew her legs would refuse to carry her. She repeated: "M'sieur le Curé! M'sieur le Curé! it is me, Marguerite."

But, notwithstanding her terror, the instinctive desire of helping her master and a woman's courage, which is sometimes heroic, filled her soul with a terrified audacity, and running back to the kitchen she fetched a lamp.

She stopped at the doorsill. First, she caught sight of the tramp lying against the wall, asleep, or simulating slumber; then she saw the broken lamp, and then, under the table, the feet and black-stockinged legs of the priest, who must have fallen backward, striking his head on the gong.

Her teeth chattering and her hands trembling with fright, she kept on repeating: "My God! My God! what is this?"

She advanced slowly, taking small steps, till she slid on something slimy and almost fell.

Stooping, she saw that the floor was red and that a red liquid was spreading around her feet toward the door. She guessed that it was blood. She threw down her light so as to hide the sight of it, and fled from the room out into the fields, running half crazed toward the village. She ran screaming at the top of her voice, and bumping against the trees she did not heed, her eyes fastened on the gleaming lights of the distant town.

Her shrill voice rang out like the gloomy cry of the night-owl, repeating continuously, "The maoufatan—the maoufatan—the maoufatan"—

When she reached the first house, some excited men came out and surrounded her; but she could not answer them and struggled to escape, for the fright had turned her head.

After a while they guessed that something must have happened to the curé, and a little rescuing party started for the lodge.

The little pink house standing in the middle of the olive grove had grown black and invisible in the dark, silent night. Since the gleam of the solitary window had faded, the cabin was plunged in darkness, lost in the grove, and unrecognizable for anyone but a native of the place.

Soon lights began to gleam near the ground, between the trees, streaking the dried grass with long, yellow reflections. The twisted trunks of the olive-trees assumed fantastic shapes under the moving lights, looking like monsters or infernal serpents. The projected reflections suddenly revealed a vague, white mass, and soon the low, square wall of the lodge grew pink from the light of the lanterns. Several peasants were carrying the lamps, escorting two gendarmes with revolvers, the mayor, the *garde-champêtre,* and Marguerite, supported by the men, for she was almost unable to walk.

The rescuing party hesitated a moment in front of the open, grewsome door. But the brigadier, snatching a lantern from one of the men, entered, followed by the rest.

The Olive Grove

The servant had not lied, blood covered the floor like a carpet. It had spread to the place where the tramp was lying, bathing one of his hands and legs.

The father and son were asleep, the one with a severed throat, the other in a drunken stupor. The two gendarmes seized the latter and before he awoke they had him handcuffed. He rubbed his eyes, stunned, stupefied with liquor, and when he saw the body of the priest, he appeared terrified, unable to understand what had happened.

"Why did he not escape?" said the mayor.

"He was too drunk," replied the officer.

And every man agreed with him, for nobody ever thought that perhaps the Abbé Vilbois had taken his own life.

Saved

THE little Marquise de Rennedon came rushing in like a ball through the window. She began to laugh before she spoke, to laugh till she cried, just as she had done a month previously, when she had told her friend that she had betrayed the Marquis in order to have her revenge, but only once, just because he was really too stupid and too jealous.

The little Baroness de Grangerie had thrown the book which she was reading onto the sofa, and looked at Annette, curiously. She was already laughing herself, and at last she asked:

"What have you been doing now?"

"Oh! my dear!—my dear! it is too funny—too funny. Just fancy—I am saved!—saved!—saved!"

"How do you mean, saved?"

"Yes, saved!"

"From what?"

"From my husband, my dear, saved! Delivered! Free! Free! Free!"

"How free? In what?"

"In what? Divorce! Yes a divorce! I have my divorce!"

"You are divorced?"

"No, not yet; how stupid you are! One does not get divorced in three hours! But I have my proofs that he has deceived me—caught in the very act—just think!—in the very act. I have got him tight."

"Oh! do tell me all about it! So he deceived you?"

"Yes, that is to say no—yes and no—I do not know. At any rate, I have proofs, and that is the chief thing."

"How did you manage it?"

"How did I manage it? This is how! I have been energetic, very energetic. For the last three months he has been odious, altogether odious, brutal, coarse, a despot —in one word, vile. So I said to myself: This cannot last, I must have a divorce! But how?—for it is not very easy. I tried to make him beat me, but he would not. He vexed me from morning till night, made me go out when I did not wish to, and to remain at home when I wanted to dine out; he made my life unbearable for me from one week's end to the other, but he never struck me.

"Then I tried to find out whether he had a mistress. Yes, he had one, but he took a thousand precautions in going to see her, and they could never be caught together. Guess what I did then?"

"I cannot guess."

"Oh! you could never guess. I asked my brother to procure me a photograph of the creature."

"Of your husband's mistress?"

"Yes. It cost Jacques fifteen louis, the price of an evening, from seven o'clock till midnight, including a dinner, at three louis an hour, and he obtained the photograph into the bargain."

"It appears to me that he might have obtained it anyhow by means of some artifice and without—without— without being obliged to take the original at the same time."

"Oh! she is pretty, and Jacques did not mind the least. And then, I wanted some details about her, physical details about her figure, her breast, her complexion, a thousand things, in fact."

"I do not understand you."

"You shall see. When I had learned all that I wanted to know, I went to a—how shall I put it—to a man of business—you know—one of those men who transact business of all sorts—agents of—of—of publicity and complicity—one of those men—well, you understand what I mean."

"Pretty nearly, I think. And what did you say to him?"

"I said to him, showing the photograph of Clarisse (her name is Clarisse): 'Monsieur, I want a lady's maid who resembles this photograph. I require one who is pretty, elegant, neat, and sharp. I will pay her whatever is necessary, and if it costs me ten thousand francs so much the worse. I shall not require her for more than three months.'

"The man looked extremely astonished, and said: 'Do you require a maid of an irreproachable character, Madame?' I blushed, and stammered: 'Yes of course, for honesty.' He continued: 'And—then—as regards morals?' I did not venture to reply, so I only made a sign with my head which signified *No*. Then suddenly, I comprehended that he had a horrible suspicion and losing my presence of mind, I exclaimed: 'Oh! Monsieur—it is for my husband, in order that I may surprise him.'

"Then the man began to laugh, and from his looks I gathered that I had regained his esteem. He even thought I was brave, and I would willingly have made a bet that at that moment he was longing to shake hands with me. However, he said to me: 'In a week, Madame, I shall have what you require; I will answer for my success, and you shall not pay me until I have succeeded. So this is a photograph of your husband's mistress?'

" 'Yes, Monsieur.'

" 'A handsome woman, and not too stout. And what scent?'

"I did not understand, and repeated: 'What scent?'

"He smiled: 'Yes, Madame, perfume is essential in tempting a man, for it unconsciously brings to his mind certain reminiscences which dispose him to action; the perfume creates an obscure confusion in his mind, and disturbs and energizes him by recalling his pleasures to him. You must also try to find out what your husband is in the habit of eating when he dines with his lady, and you might give him the same dishes the day you catch him. Oh! we have got him, Madame, we have got him.'

"I went away delighted, for here I had lighted on a very intelligent man.

"Three days later, I saw a tall, dark girl arrive at my house; she was very handsome, and her looks were modest and bold at the same time, the peculiar look of a female rake. She behaved very properly toward me, and as I did not exactly know what she was, I called her Mademoiselle, but she said immediately: 'Oh! pray, Madame, only call me Rose.' And she began to talk.

" 'Well, Rose, you know why you have come here?'

" 'I can guess it, Madame.'

" 'Very good, my girl—and that will not be too much bother for you?'

" 'Oh! Madame, this will be the eighth divorce that I shall have caused; I am used to it.'

" 'Why, that is capital. Will it take you long to succeed?'

" 'Oh? Madame, that depends entirely on Monsieur's temperament. When I have seen Monsieur for five minutes alone, I shall be able to tell you exactly.'

" 'You will see him soon, my child, but I must tell you that he is not handsome.'

" 'That does not matter to me, Madame. I have already

separated some very ugly ones. But I must ask you, Madame, whether you have discovered his favorite perfume?'

" 'Yes, Rose—verbena.'

" 'So much the better, Madame, for I am also very fond of that scent! Can you also tell me, Madame, whether Monsieur's mistress wears silk underclothing and night-dresses?'

" 'No, my child, cambric and lace.'

" 'Oh! then she is altogether of superior station, for silk underclothing is getting quite common.'

" 'What you say is quite true!'

" 'Well, Madame, I will enter your service.' And so as a matter of fact she did immediately, and as if she had done nothing else all her life.

"An hour later my husband came home. Rose did not even raise her eyes to him, but he raised his eyes to her. She already smelled strongly of verbena. In five minutes she left the room, and he immediately asked me: 'Who is that girl?'

" 'Why—my new lady's maid.'

" 'Where did you pick her up?'

" 'Baroness de Grangerie got her for me with the best references.'

" 'Ah! she is rather pretty!'

" 'Do you think so?'

" 'Why, yes—for a lady's maid.'

"I was delighted, for I felt that he was already biting, and that same evening Rose said to me: 'I can now promise you that it will not take more than a fortnight, Monsieur is very easily caught!'

" 'Ah! you have tried already?'

" 'No, Madame, he only asked what my name was, so that he might hear what my voice was like.'

" 'Very well, my dear Rose. Get on as quick as you can.'

434

" 'Do not be alarmed, Madame; I shall only resist long enough not to make myself depreciated.'

"At the end of a week, my husband scarcely ever went out; I saw him roaming about the house the whole afternoon, and what was most significant in the matter was that he no longer prevented me from going out. And I, I was out of doors nearly the whole day long—in order—in order to leave him at liberty.

"On the ninth day, while Rose was undressing me, she said to me with a timid air: 'It happened this morning, Madame.'

"I was rather surprised, or rather overcome even, not at the part itself, but at the way in which she told me, and I stammered out: 'And—and—it went off well?'

" 'Oh! yes, very well, Madame. For the last three days he has been pressing me, but I did not wish matters to proceed too quickly. You will tell me when you want us to be caught, Madame.'

" 'Yes, certainly. Here! let us say Thursday.'

" 'Very well, Madame, I shall grant nothing more till then, so as to keep Monsieur on the alert.'

" 'You are sure not to fail?'

" 'Oh! quite sure, Madame. I will excite him, so as to make him be there at the very moment which you may appoint.'

" 'Let us say five o'clock then.'

" 'Very well, Madame, and where?'

" 'Well—in my bedroom.'

" 'Very good, Madame, in your bedroom.'

" 'You will understand what I did then, my dear. I went and fetched mamma and papa first of all, and then my uncle d'Orvelin, the President, and Monsieur Raplet, the Judge, my husband's friend. I had not told them what I was going to show them, but I made them all go

on tiptoe as far as the door of my room. I waited till five
o'clock exactly, and oh! how my heart beat! I had made
the porter come upstairs as well, so as to have an addi-
tional witness! And then—and then at the moment when
the clock began to strike, I opened the door wide. Ah!
ah! ah! Here he was evidently—it was quite evident, my
dear. Oh! what a head! If you had only seen his head!
And he turned round, the idiot! Oh! how funny he
looked—I laughed, I laughed. And papa was angry and
wanted to give my husband a beating. And the porter, a
good servant helped him to dress himself before us—
before us. He buttoned his braces for him—what a joke
it was! As for Rose, she was perfect, absolutely perfect.
She cried—oh! she cried very well. She is an invaluable
girl. If you ever want her, don't forget!

"And here I am. I came immediately to tell you of
the affair directly. I am free. Long live divorce!"

And she began to dance in the middle of the drawing-room, while the little Baroness, who was thoughtful
and put out, said:

"Why did you not invite me to see it?"

A Country Excursion

FOR five months they had been talking of going to lunch at some country restaurant in the neighborhood of Paris, on Madame Dufour's birthday, and as they were looking forward very impatiently to the outing, they had risen very early that morning. Monsieur Dufour had borrowed the milkman's tilted cart, and drove himself. It was a very neat, two-wheeled conveyance, with a hood, and in it Madame Dufour, resplendent in a wonderful, sherry-colored silk dress, sat by the side of her husband.

The old grandmother and the daughter were accommodated with two chairs, and a yellow-haired youth, of whom, however, nothing was to be seen except his head, lay at the bottom of the trap.

When they got to the bridge of Neuilly, Monsieur Dufour said: "Here we are in the country at last!" At that warning, his wife grew sentimental about the beauties of nature. When they got to the crossroads at Courbevoie, they were seized with admiration for the tremendous view down there: on the right was the spire of Argenteuil church, above it rose the hills of Sannois and the mill of Orgemont, while on the left, the aqueduct of Marly stood out against the clear morning sky. In the distance they could see the terrace of Saint-Germain, and opposite to them, at the end of a low chain of hills, the new fort of Cormeilles. Afar—a very long way off, beyond the plains and villages—one could see the somber green of the forests.

The sun was beginning to shine in their faces, the dust got into their eyes, and on either side of the road there stretched an interminable tract of bare, ugly country, which smelled unpleasantly. You would have thought that it had been ravaged by a pestilence which had even attacked the buildings, for skeletons of dilapidated and deserted houses, or small cottages left in an unfinished state, as if the contractors had not been paid, reared their four roofless walls on each side.

Here and there tall factory-chimneys rose up from the barren soil, the only vegetation on that putrid land, where the spring breezes wafted an odor of petroleum and soot, mingled with another smell that was even still less agreeable. At last, however, they crossed the Seine a second time. It was delightful on the bridge; the river sparkled in the sun, and they had a feeling of quiet satisfaction and enjoyment in drinking in purer air, not impregnated by the black smoke of factories, nor by the miasma from the deposits of night-soil. A man whom they met told them that the name of the place was Bézons; so Monsieur Dufour pulled up, and read the attractive announcement outside an eating-house:

"Restaurant Poulin, stews and fried fish, private rooms, arbors, and swings."

"Well! Madame Dufour, will this suit you? Will you make up your mind at last?"

She read the announcement in her turn, and then looked at the house for a time.

It was a white country inn, built by the roadside, and through the open door she could see the bright zinc of the counter, at which two workmen out for the day were sitting. At last she made up her mind, and said:

"Yes, this will do; and, besides, there is a view."

So they drove into a large yard studded with trees, behind the inn, which was only separated from the river by the towing-path, and got out. The husband sprang out first, and held out his arms for his wife. As the step was very high, Madame Dufour, in order to reach him, had to show the lower part of her limbs, whose former slenderness had disappeared in fat. Monsieur Dufour, who was already getting excited by the country air, pinched her calf, and then, taking her in his arms, set her on to the ground, as if she had been some enormous bundle. She shook the dust out of the silk dress, and then looked round, to see in what sort of a place she was.

She was a stout woman, of about thirty-six, full-blown and delightful to look at. She could hardly breathe, as she was laced too tightly, which forced the heaving mass of her superabundant bosom up to her double chin. Next, the girl put her hand on to her father's shoulder, and jumped lightly down. The youth with the yellow hair had got down by stepping on the wheel, and he helped Monsieur Dufour to get the grandmother out. Then they unharnessed the horse, which they tied up to a tree, and the carriage fell back, with both shafts in the air. The man and boy took off their coats, washed their hands in a pail of water, and then joined the ladies, who had already taken possession of the swings.

Mademoiselle Dufour was trying to swing herself standing up, but she could not succeed in getting a start. She was a pretty girl of about eighteen; one of those women who suddenly excite your desire when you meet them in the street, and who leave you with a vague feeling of uneasiness and of excited senses. She was tall, had a small waist and large hips, with a dark skin, very large eyes, and very black hair. Her dress clearly marked the outlines of her firm, full figure, which was accentuated by the motion of her hips as she tried to swing herself higher. Her arms were stretched over her head to hold the rope, so that her bosom rose at every movement she made. Her hat, which a gust of wind had blown off, was hanging behind her, and as the swing gradually rose higher and higher, she showed her delicate limbs up to the knees each time, and the wind from the perfumed petticoats, more heady than the fumes of wine, blew into the faces of her father and friend, who were looking at her in admiration.

Sitting in the other swing, Madame Dufour kept saying in a monotonous voice:

"Cyprian, come and swing me; do come and swing me, Cyprian!"

At last he complied, and turning up his shirt-sleeves, as if he intended to work very hard, with much difficulty he set his wife in motion. She clutched the two ropes, and held her legs out straight, so as not to touch the ground. She enjoyed feeling giddy from the motion of the swing, and her whole figure shook like a jelly on a dish, but as she went higher and higher, she grew too giddy and got frightened. Every time she was coming back, she uttered a shriek, which made all the little urchins come round, and, down below, beneath the garden hedge, she vaguely saw a row of mischievous heads, making various grimaces as they laughed.

When a servant girl came out, they ordered lunch.

"Some fried fish, a stewed rabbit, salad, and dessert," Madame Dufour said, with an important air.

"Bring two quarts of beer and a bottle of claret," her husband said.

"We will have lunch on the grass," the girl added.

The grandmother, who had an affection for cats, had been petting one that belonged to the house, and had been bestowing the most affectionate words on it, for the last ten minutes. The animal, no doubt secretly pleased

by her attentions, kept close to the good woman, but just
out of reach of her hand, and quietly walked round the
trees, against which she rubbed herself, with her tail up,
purring with pleasure.

"Hallo!" exclaimed the youth with the yellow hair,
who was ferreting about, "here are two swell boats!"
They all went to look at them, and saw two beautiful
skiffs in a wooden boathouse, which were as beautifully
finished as if they had been objects of luxury. They were
moored side by side, like two tall, slender girls, in their
narrow shining length, and aroused in one a wish to float
in them on warm summer mornings and evenings, along
flower-covered banks of the river, where the trees dip
their branches into the water, where the rushes are continually rustling in the breeze, and where the swift king-
fishers dart about like flashes of blue lightning.

The whole family looked at them with great respect.
"They are indeed two swell boats," Monsieur Dufour
repeated gravely, and he examined them closely, com-
menting on them like a connoisseur. He had been in the
habit of rowing in his younger days, he said, and when
he had that in his hands—and he went through the action of pulling the oars—he did not care a fig for anybody. He had beaten more than one Englishman formerly at the Joinville regattas. He grew quite excited at
last, and offered to make a bet that in a boat like that
he could row six miles an hour, without exerting himself.

"Lunch is ready," said the waitress, appearing at the
entrance to the boathouse. They all hurried off, but two
young men were already lunching at the best place,
which Madame Dufour had chosen in her mind as her
seat. No doubt they were the owners of the skiffs, for they
were dressed in boating costume. They were stretched
out, almost lying on chairs, and were sunburned, and

had on flannel trousers and thin cotton jerseys, with short sleeves, which showed their bare arms, which were as strong as blacksmiths'. They were two strong young fellows, who thought a great deal of their vigor, and who showed in all their movements that elasticity and grace of limb which can only be acquired by exercise, and which is so different to the awkwardness with which the same continual work stamps the mechanic.

They exchanged a rapid smile when they saw the mother, and then a look on seeing the daughter.

"Let us give up our place," one of them said; "it will make us acquainted with them."

The other got up immediately, and holding his black and red boating-cap in his hand, he politely offered the ladies the only shady place in the garden. With many excuses they accepted, and so that it might be more rural, they sat on the grass, without either tables or chairs.

The two young men took their plates, knives, forks, etc., to a table a little way off, and began to eat again. Their bare arms, which they showed continually, rather embarrassed the young girl, who even pretended to turn her head aside, and not to see them. But Madame Dufour, who was rather bolder, tempted by feminine curiosity, looked at them every moment, and no doubt compared them with the secret unsightliness of her husband. She had squatted herself on the ground with her legs tucked under her, after the manner of tailors, and kept wriggling about continually, under the pretext that ants were crawling about her somewhere. Monsieur Dufour, whom the politeness of the strangers had put into rather a bad temper, was trying to find a comfortable position, which he did not, however, succeed in doing, while the youth with the yellow hair was eating as silently as an ogre.

"It is lovely weather, Monsieur," the stout lady said

to one of the boating-men. She wished to be friendly, because they had given up their place.

"It is, indeed, Madame," he replied; "do you often go into the country?"

"Oh! Only once or twice a year, to get a little fresh air; and you, Monsieur?"

"I come and sleep here every night."

"Oh! That must be very nice?"

"Certainly it is, Madame." And he gave them such a practical account of his daily life, that in the hearts of these shopkeepers, who were deprived of the meadows, and who longed for country walks, it roused that innate love of nature, which they all felt so strongly the whole year round, behind the counter in their shop.

The girl raised her eyes and looked at the oarsman with emotion, and Monsieur Dufour spoke for the first time.

"It is indeed a happy life," he said. And then he added: "A little more rabbit, my dear?"

"No, thank you," she replied, and turning to the young men again, and pointing to their arms, asked: "Do you never feel cold like that?"

They both laughed, and amazed the family by telling of the enormous fatigue they could endure, of bathing while in a state of tremendous perspiration, of rowing in the fog at night, and they struck their chests violently, to show how they sounded.

"Ah! You look very strong," the husband said, and he did not talk any more of the time when he used to beat the English. The girl was looking at them askance now, and the young fellow with the yellow hair, as he had swallowed some wine the wrong way, and was coughing violently, bespattered Madame Dufour's sherry-colored silk dress. Madame got angry, and sent for some water to wash the spots.

Meanwhile it had grown unbearably hot, the sparkling river looked looked. like a blaze of fire and the fumes of the wine were getting into their heads. Monsieur Dufour, who had a violent hiccough, had unbuttoned his waistcoat and the top of his trousers, while his wife, who felt choking, was gradually unfastening her dress. The youth was shaking his yellow hair in a happy frame of mind, and kept helping himself to wine, and as the old grandmother felt drunk, she endeavored to be very stiff and dignified. As for the girl, she showed nothing except a peculiar brightness in her eyes, while the brown skin on the cheeks became more rosy.

The coffee finished them off; they spoke of singing, and each of them sang, or repeated a couplet, which the others repeated enthusiastically. Then they got up with some difficulty, and while the two women, who were rather dizzy, were getting some fresh air, the two males, who were altogether drunk, were performing gymnastic tricks. Heavy, limp, and with scarlet faces, they hung awkwardly on to the iron rings, unable to raise themselves, while their shirts continually threatened to part company with their trousers, and to flap in the wind like flags.

Meanwhile, the two boating-men had got their skiffs into the water. They came back, and politely asked the ladies whether they would like a row.

"Would you like one, Monsieur Dufour?" his wife exclaimed. "Please come!"

He merely gave her a drunken look, without understanding what she said. Then one of the rowers came up, with two fishing-rods in his hand; and the hope of catching a gudgeon, that great aim of the Parisian shopkeeper, made Dufour's dull eyes gleam. He politely allowed them to do whatever they liked, while he sat in the shade, under the bridge, with his feet dangling over the river, by

the side of the young man with the yellow hair, who was
sleeping soundly close to him.

One of the boating-men made a martyr of himself,
and took the mother.

"Let us go to the little wood on the Île aux Anglais!"
he called out, as he rowed off. The other skiff went
slower, for the rower was looking at his companion so
intently, that he thought of nothing else. His emotion
paralyzed his strength, while the girl, who was sitting on
the steerer's seat, gave herself up to the enjoyment of
being on the water. She felt disinclined to think, felt a
lassitude in her limbs, a complete self-relaxation, as if
she were intoxicated. She had become very flushed, and
breathed pantingly. The effect of the wine, increased by
the extreme heat, made all the trees on the bank seem to
bow, as she passed. A vague wish for enjoyment, a fer-
mentation of her blood, seemed to pervade her whole
body, and she was also a little agitated by this *tête-à-tête*
on the water, in a place which seemed depopulated by
the heat, with this young man, who thought her so pretty,
whose looks seemed to caress her skin, and whose eyes
were as penetrating and exciting as the sun's rays.

Their inability to speak increased their emotion,
and they looked about them. At last he made an effort
and asked her name.

"Henriette," she said.

"Why! My name is Henri," he replied. The sound of
their voices calmed them, and they looked at the banks.
The other skiff had gone ahead of them, and seemed to
be waiting for them. The rower called out:

"We will meet you in the wood; we are going as far
as Robinson's,* because Madame Dufour is thirsty."

---

* A well-known restaurant on the banks of the Seine, much frequented by the bourgeoisie.

Then he bent over his oars again and rowed off so quickly that he was soon out of sight.

Meanwhile, a continual roar, which they had heard for some time, came nearer, and the river itself seemed to shiver, as if the dull noise were rising from its depths.

"What is that noise?" she asked. It was the noise of the weir, which cut the river in two, at the island. He was explaining it to her, when above the noise of the waterfall they heard the song of a bird, which seemed a long way off.

"Listen!" he said; "the nightingales are singing during the day, so the females must be sitting."

A nightingale! She had never heard one before, and the idea of listening to one roused visions of poetic tenderness in her heart. A nightingale! That is to say, the invisible witness of the lover's interview which Juliet invoked on her balcony; that celestial music which is attuned to human kisses; that eternal inspirer of all those languorous romances which open idealized visions to the poor, tender, little hearts of sensitive girls!

She wanted to hear a nightingale.

"We must not make a noise," her companion said, "and then we can go into the wood, and sit down close to it."

The skiff seemed to glide. They saw the trees on the island, the banks of which were so low that they could look into the depths of the thickets. They stopped, he made the boat fast, Henriette took hold of Henri's arm, and they went beneath the trees.

"Stoop," he said, so she bent down, and they went into an inextricable thicket of creepers, leaves, and reedgrass, which formed an impenetrable retreat, and which the young man laughingly called "his private room."

Just above their heads, perched in one of the trees

which hid them, the bird was still singing. He uttered shakes and *roulades,* and then long, vibrating sounds that filled the air and seemed to lose themselves in the distance, across the level country, through that burning silence which hung low upon the whole country round. They did not speak for fear of frightening the bird away. They were sitting close together, and slowly Henri's arm stole round the girl's waist and squeezed it gently. She took that daring hand, but without anger, and kept removing it whenever he put it round her; not, however, feeling at all embarrassed by this caress, just as if it had been something quite natural which she was resisting just as naturally.

She was listening to the bird in ecstasy. She felt an infinite longing for happiness, for some sudden demonstration of tenderness, for a revelation of divine poesy. She felt such a softening at her heart, and such a relaxation of her nerves, that she began to cry, without knowing why. The young man was now straining her close to him, and she did not remove his arm; she did not think of it. Suddenly the nightingale stopped, and a voice called out in the distance:

"Henriette!"

"Do not reply," he said in a low voice, "you will drive the bird away."

But she had no idea of doing so, and they remained in the same position for some time. Madame Dufour had sat down somewhere or other, for from time to time they heard the stout lady break out into little bursts of laughter.

The girl was still crying; she was filled with strange sensations. Henri's head was on her shoulder, and suddenly he kissed her on the lips. She was surprised and angry, and, to avoid him, she stood up.

They were both very pale when they quitted their grassy retreat. The blue sky looked dull to them, the ardent sun was clouded over to their eyes, they perceived not the solitude and the silence. They walked quickly side by side, without speaking or touching each other, appearing to be irreconcilable enemies, as if disgust had sprung up between them, and hatred between their souls. From time to time Henriette called out:

"Mamma!"

By and by they heard a noise in a thicket, and Madame Dufour appeared, looking rather confused, and her companion's face was wrinkled with smiles that he could not check.

Madame Dufour took his arm, and they returned to the boats. Henri went on first, still without speaking, by the girl's side, and at last they got back to Bézons. Monsieur Dufour, who had sobered up, was waiting for them very impatiently, while the youth with the yellow hair was having a mouthful of something to eat before leaving the inn. The carriage was in the yard, with the horse in, and the grandmother, who had already got in, was frightened at the thought of being overtaken by night, before they got back to Paris, the outskirts not being safe.

The young men shook hands with them, and the Dufour family drove off.

"Good-bye, until we meet again!" the oarsmen cried, and the answers they got were a sigh and a tear.

Two months later, as Henri was going along the Rue des Martyrs, he saw "Dufour, Ironmonger," over a door. So he went in, and saw the stout lady sitting at the counter. They recognized each other immediately, and after an interchange of polite greetings, he inquired after them all.

"And how is Mademoiselle Henriette?" he inquired, specially.

"Very well, thank you; she is married."

"Ah!" Mastering his feelings, he added: "To whom was she married?"

"To that young man who went with us, you know; he has joined us in business."

"I remember him, perfectly."

He was going out, feeling unhappy, though scarcely knowing why, when Madame called him back.

"And how is your friend?" she asked, rather shyly.

"He is very well, thank you."

"Please give him our compliments, and beg him to come and call when he is in the neighborhood." She then added: "Tell him it will give me great pleasure."

"I will be sure to do so. Adieu!"

"I will not say that; come again, very soon."

The next year, one very hot Sunday, all the details of that memorable adventure suddenly came back to him so clearly that he revisited the "private room" in the wood, and was overwhelmed with astonishment when he went in. She was sitting on the grass, looking very sad, while by her side, again in his shirt-sleeves, the young man with the yellow hair was sleeping soundly, like some brute.

She grew so pale when she saw Henri, that at first he thought she was going to faint; then, however, they began to talk quite naturally. But when he told her that he was very fond of that spot, and went there very often on Sundays, she looked into his eyes for a long time. "I, too, often think of it," she replied.

"Come, my dear," her husband said, with a yawn; "I think it is time for us to be going."

The Diary of a Madman

HE was dead—the head of a high tribunal, the upright magistrate, whose irreproachable life was a proverb in all the courts of France. Advocates, young counselors, judges had saluted, bowing low in token of profound respect, remembering that grand face, pale and thin, illumined by two bright, deep-set eyes.

He had passed his life in pursuing crime and in protecting the weak. Swindlers and murderers had no more redoubtable enemy, for he seemed to read in the recesses of their souls their most secret thoughts.

He was dead, now, at the age of eighty-two, honored by the homage and followed by the regrets of a whole people. Soldiers in red breeches had escorted him to the tomb, and men in white cravats had shed on his grave tears that seemed to be real.

But listen to the strange paper found by the dismayed notary in the desk where the judge had kept filed the records of great criminals! It was entitled:

WHY?

June 20, 1851. I have just left court. I have condemned Blondel to death! Now, why did this man kill his five children? Frequently one meets with people to whom killing is a pleasure. Yes, yes, it should be a pleasure—the greatest of all, perhaps, for is not killing most like creating? To make and to destroy! These two words contain the history of the universe, the history of all worlds, all that is, all! Why is it not intoxicating to kill?

June 25. To think that there is a being who lives,

450

who walks, who runs. A being? What is a being? An animated thing which bears in it the principle of motion, and a will ruling that principle. It clings to nothing, this thing. Its feet are independent of the ground. It is a grain of life that moves on the earth, and this grain of life, coming I know not whence, one can destroy at one's will. Then nothing—nothing more. It perishes; it is finished.

June 26. Why, then, is it a crime to kill? Yes, why? On the contrary, it is the law of nature. Every being has the mission to kill; he kills to live, and he lives to kill. The beast kills without ceasing, all day, every instant of its existence. Man kills without ceasing, to nourish himself; but since in addition he needs to kill for pleasure, he has invented the chase! The child kills the insects he finds, the little birds, all the little animals that come in his way. But this does not suffice for the irresistible need of massacre that is in us. It is not enough to kill beasts; we must kill man too. Long ago this need was satisfied by human sacrifice. Now, the necessity of living in society has made murder a crime. We condemn and punish the assassin! But as we cannot live without yielding to this natural and imperious instinct of death, we relieve ourselves, from time to time, by wars. Then a whole nation slaughters another nation. It is a feast of blood, a feast that maddens armies and intoxicates the civilians, women and children, who read, by lamplight at night, the feverish story of massacre.

And do we despise those picked out to accomplish these butcheries of men? No, they are loaded with honors. They are clad in gold and in resplendent stuffs; they wear plumes on their heads and ornaments on their breasts; and they are given crosses, rewards, titles of every kind. They are proud, respected, loved by women, cheered by the crowd, solely because their mission is to shed human blood! They drag through the streets their instruments of death, and the passer-by, clad in black, looks on with envy. For to kill is the great law put by nature in the heart of existence! There is nothing more beautiful and honorable than killing!

June 30. To kill is the law, because Nature loves eternal youth. She seems to cry in all her unconscious acts: "Quick! quick! quick!" The more she destroys, the more she renews herself.

July 3. It must be a pleasure, unique and full of zest, to kill: to place before you a living, thinking being; to make therein a little hole, nothing but a little hole, and to see that red liquid flow which is the blood, which is the life; and then to have before you only a heap of limp flesh, cold, inert, void of thought!

August 5. I, who have passed my life in judging, condemning, killing by words pronounced, killing by the guillotine those who had killed by the knife, if I should do as all the assassins whom I have smitten have done, I, I—who would know it?

August 10. Who would ever know? Who would ever suspect me, especially if I should choose a being I had no interest in doing away with?

August 22. I could resist no longer. I have killed a little creature as an experiment, as a beginning. Jean, my servant, had a goldfinch in a cage hung in the office window. I sent him on an errand, and I took the little bird in my hand, in my hand where I felt its heart beat. It was warm. I went up to my room. From time to time I squeezed it tighter; its heart beat faster; it was atrocious and delicious. I was nearly choking it. But I could not see the blood.

Then I took scissors, short nail scissors, and I cut its throat in three strokes, quite gently. It opened its bill, it struggled to escape me, but I held it, oh! I held it—I even could have held a mad dog—and I saw the blood trickle.

And then I did as assassins do—real ones. I washed the scissors and washed my hands. I sprinkled water, and took the body, the corpse, to the garden to hide it. I buried it under a strawberry-plant. It will never be found. Every day I can eat a strawberry from that plant. How one can enjoy life, when one knows how!

My servant cried; he thought his bird flown. How could he suspect me? Ah!

August 25. I must kill a man! I must!

August 30. It is done. But what a little thing! I had gone for a walk in the forest of Vernes. I was thinking of nothing, literally nothing. See! a child on the road, a little child eating a slice of bread and butter. He stops to see me pass and says, "Good day, Mr. President."

And the thought enters my head: "Shall I kill him?"

I answer: "You are alone, my boy?"

"Yes, sir."

"All alone in the wood?"

"Yes, sir."

The wish to kill him intoxicated me like wine. I approached him quite softly, persuaded that he was going to run away. And suddenly I seized him by the throat. He held my wrists in his little hands, and his body writhed like a feather on the fire. Then he moved no more. I threw the body in the ditch, then some weeds on top of it. I returned home and dined well. What a little thing it was! In the evening I was very gay, light, rejuvenated, and passed the evening at the Prefect's. They found me witty. But I have not seen blood! I am not tranquil.

August 31. The body has been discovered. They are hunting for the assassin. Ah!

September 1. Two tramps have been arrested. Proofs are lacking.

September 2. The parents have been to see me. They wept! Ah!

October 6. Nothing has been discovered. Some strolling vagabond must have done the deed. Ah! If I had seen the blood flow it seems to me I should be tranquil now!

October 10. Yet another. I was walking by the river, after breakfast. And I saw, under a willow, a fisherman asleep. It was noon. A spade, as if expressly put there for me, was standing in a potato-field near by.

I took it. I returned; I raised it like a club, and with one blow of the edge I cleft the fisherman's head. Oh! he bled, this one!—rose-colored blood. It flowed into the water quite gently. And I went away with a grave step. If I had been seen! Ah! I should have made an excellent assassin.

October 25. The affair of the fisherman makes a great noise. His nephew, who fished with him, is charged with the murder.

October 26. The examining magistrate affirms that the nephew is guilty. Everybody in town believes it. Ah! ah!

October 27. The nephew defends himself badly. He had gone to the village to buy bread and cheese, he declares. He swears that his uncle had been killed in his absence! Who would believe him?

October 28. The nephew has all but confessed, so much have they made him lose his head! Ah! Justice!

November 15. There are overwhelming proofs against the nephew, who was his uncle's heir. I shall preside at the sessions.

January 25, 1852. To death! to death! to death! I have had him condemned to death! The advocate-general spoke like an angel! Ah! Yet another! I shall go to see him executed!

March 10. It is done. They guillotined him this morning. He died very well! very well! That gave me pleasure! How fine it is to see a man's head cut off!

Now, I shall wait, I can wait. It would take such a little thing to let myself be caught.

The manuscript contained more pages, but told of no new crime.

Alienist physicians to whom the awful story has been submitted declare that there are in the world many unknown madmen, as adroit and as terrible as this monstrous lunatic.

Two Little Soldiers

EVERY Sunday, the moment they were dismissed, the two little soldiers made off. Once outside the barracks, they struck out to the right through Courbevoie, walking with long rapid strides, as though they were on a march.

When they were beyond the last of the houses, they slackened pace along the bare, dusty roadway which goes toward Bézons.

They were both small and thin, and looked quite lost in their coats, which were too big and too long. Their sleeves hung down over their hands, and they found their enormous red breeches, which compelled them to waddle, very much in the way. Under their stiff, high helmets their faces had little character—two poor, sallow Breton faces, simple with an almost animal simplicity, and with gentle and quiet blue eyes.

They never conversed during these walks, but went straight on, each with the same thought in his head. This thought atoned for the lack of conversation; it was this, that just inside the little wood near Les Champioux they had found a place which reminded them of their own country, where they could feel happy again.

When they arrived under the trees where the roads from Colombes and from Chatou cross, they would take off their heavy helmets and wipe their foreheads. They always halted on the Bézons bridge to look at the Seine, and would remain there two or three minutes, bent double, leaning on the parapet.

Sometimes they would gaze out over the great basin

of Argenteuil, where the skiffs might be seen scudding, with their white, careening sails, recalling perhaps the look of the Breton waters, the harbor of Vanne, near which they lived, and the fishing-boats standing out across the Morbihan to the open sea.

Just beyond the Seine they bought their provisions from a sausage merchant, a baker, and a wine-seller. A piece of blood-pudding, four sous' worth of bread, and a liter of "petit bleu" constituted the provisions, which they carried off in their handkerchiefs. After they had left Bézons they traveled slowly and began to talk.

In front of them a barren plain studded with clumps of trees led to the wood, to the little wood which had seemed to them to resemble the one at Kermarivan. Grainfields and hayfields bordered the narrow path, which lost itself in the young greenness of the crops, and Jean Kerderen would always say to Luc le Ganidec:

"It looks like it does near Plounivon."

"Yes; exactly."

Side by side they strolled, their souls filled with vague memories of their own country, with awakened images as naïve as the pictures on the colored broadsheets which you buy for a penny. They kept on recognizing, as it were, now a corner of a field, a hedge, a bit of moorland, now a crossroad, now a granite cross. Then, too, they would always stop beside a certain landmark, a great stone, because it looked something like the cromlech at Locneuven.

Every Sunday on arriving at the first clump of trees Luc le Ganidec would cut a switch, a hazel switch, and begin gently to peel off the bark, thinking meanwhile of the folk at home. Jean Kerderen carried the provisions.

From time to time Luc would mention a name, or recall some deed of their childhood in a few brief words, which caused long thoughts. And their own country, their dear, distant country, recaptured them little by little, seizing on their imaginations, and sending to them from afar her shapes, her sounds, her well-known prospects, her odors—odors of the green lands where the salt sea-air was blowing.

No longer conscious of the exhalations of the Parisian stables, on which the earth of the *banlieue* fattens, they scented the perfume of the flowering broom, which the salt breeze of the open sea plucks and bears away. And the sails of the boats from the river banks seemed like the white wings of the coasting vessels seen beyond the great plain which extended from their homes to the very margin of the sea.

They walked with short steps, Luc le Ganidec and Jean Kerderen, content and sad, haunted by a sweet melancholy, by the lingering, ever-present sorrow of a caged animal who remembers his liberty.

By the time that Luc had stripped the slender wand of its bark they reached the corner of the wood where every Sunday they took breakfast. They found the two bricks which they kept hidden in the thicket, and kindled a little fire of twigs, over which to roast the bloodpudding at the end of a bayonet.

When they had breakfasted, eaten their bread to the last crumb, and drunk their wine to the last drop, they remained seated side by side upon the grass, saying nothing, their eyes on the distance, their eyelids drooping, their fingers crossed as at mass, their red legs stretched out beside the poppies of the field. And the leather of their helmets and the brass of their buttons glittered in the ardent sun, making the larks, which sang and hovered above their heads, cease in mid-song.

Toward noon they began to turn their eyes from

time to time in the direction of the village of Bézons, because the girl with the cow was coming. She passed by them every Sunday on her way to milk and change the pasture of her cow—the only cow in this district which ever went out of the stable to grass. It was pastured in a narrow field along the edge of the wood a little farther on.

They soon perceived the girl, the only human being within vision, and were gladdened by the brilliant reflections thrown off by the tin milk-pail under the rays of the sun. They never talked about her. They were simply glad to see her, without understanding why.

She was a big strong wench with red hair, burned by the heat of sunny days, a sturdy product of the environs of Paris.

Once, finding them seated in the same place, she said:

"Good morning. You two are always here, aren't you?"

Luc le Ganidec, the bolder, stammered:

"Yes, we come to rest."

That was all. But the next Sunday she laughed on seeing them, laughed with a protecting benevolence and a feminine keenness which knew well enough that they were bashful. And she asked:

"What are you doing there? Are you trying to see the grass grow?"

Luc was cheered up by this, and smiled likewise: "Maybe we are."

"That's pretty slow work," said she.

He answered, still laughing: "Well, yes, it is."

She went on. But coming back with a milk-pail full of milk, she stopped again before them, and said:

"Would you like a little? It will taste like home."

459

With the instinctive feeling that they were of the same peasant race as she, being herself perhaps also far away from home, she had divined and touched the spot.

They were both touched. Then with some difficulty, she managed to make a little milk run into the neck of the glass bottle in which they carried their wine. And Luc drank first, with little swallows, stopping every minute to see whether he had drunk more than his half. Then he handed the bottle to Jean.

She stood upright before them, her hands on her hips, her pail on the ground at her feet, glad at the pleasure which she had given.

Then she departed, shouting: *"Allons,* adieu! Till next Sunday!"

And as long as they could see her at all, they followed with their eyes her tall silhouette, which faded, growing smaller and smaller, seeming to sink into the verdure of the fields.

When they were leaving the barracks the week after, Jean said to Luc:

"Oughtn't we to buy her something good?"

They were in great embarrassment before the problem of the choice of a delicacy for the girl with the cow. Luc was of the opinion that a little tripe would be the best, but Jean preferred some *berlingots* because he was fond of sweets. His choice fairly made him enthusiastic, and they bought at a grocer's two sous' worth of white and red candies.

They ate their breakfast more rapidly than usual, being nervous with expectation.

Jean saw her first. "There she is!" he cried. Luc added: "Yes, there she is."

While yet some distance off she laughed at seeing them. Then she cried:

Two Little Soldiers

"Is everything going as you like it?"

And in unison they asked:

"Are you getting on all right?"

Then she conversed, talked to them of simple things in which they felt an interest—of the weather, of the crops, and of her master.

They were afraid to offer her the candies, which were slowly melting away in Jean's pocket.

At last Luc grew bold, and murmured:

"We have brought you something."

She demanded, "What is it? Tell me!"

Then Jean, blushing up to his ears, managed to get at the little paper cornucopia, and held it out.

She began to eat the little bonbons, rolling them from one cheek to the other where they made little round lumps. The two soldiers, seated before her, gazed at her with emotion and delight.

Then she went to milk her cow, and once more gave them some milk on coming back.

They thought of her all the week; several times they even spoke of her. The next Sunday she sat down with them for a little longer talk; and all three, seated side by side, their eyes lost in the distance, clasping their knees with their hands, told the small doings, the minute details of life in the villages where they had been born, while over there the cow, seeing that the milkmaid had stopped on her way, stretched out toward her its heavy head with its dripping nostrils, and gave a long low to call her.

Soon the girl consented to eat a bit of bread with them and drink a mouthful of wine. She often brought them plums in her pocket, for the season of plums had come. Her presence sharpened the wits of the two little Breton soldiers, and they chattered like two birds.

But, one Tuesday, Luc le Ganidec asked for leave—a thing which had never happened before—and he did not return until ten o'clock at night. Jean racked his brains uneasily for a reason for his comrade's going out in this way.

The next Thursday Luc, having borrowed ten sous from his bedfellow, again asked and obtained permission to leave the barracks for several hours. When he set off with Jean on their Sunday walk his manner was very queer, quite restless, and quite changed. Kerderen did not understand, but he vaguely suspected something without divining what it could be.

They did not say a word to one another until they reached their usual halting-place, where, from their constant sitting in the same spot the grass was quite worn away. They ate their breakfast slowly. Neither of them felt hungry.

Before long the girl appeared. As on every Sunday, they watched her coming. When she was quite near, Luc rose and made two steps forward. She put her milk-pail on the ground and kissed him. She kissed him passionately, throwing her arms about his neck, without noticing Jean, without remembering that he was there, without even seeing him.

And he sat there desperate, poor Jean, so desperate that he did not understand, his soul quite overwhelmed, but heart bursting, but not yet understanding himself. Then the girl seated herself beside Luc, and they began to chatter.

Jean did not look at them. He now divined why his comrade had gone out twice during the week, and he felt within him a burning grief, a kind of wound, that sense of rending which is caused by treason.

Luc and the girl went off together to change the

position of the cow. Jean followed them with his eyes. He saw them departing side by side. The red breeches of his comrade made a bright spot on the road. It was Luc who picked up the mallet and hammered down the stake to which they tied the beast.

The girl stooped to milk her, while he stroked the cow's sharp spine with a careless hand. Then they left the milk-pail on the grass, and went deep into the wood.

Jean saw nothing but the wall of leaves where they had entered; and he felt himself so troubled that if he had tried to rise he would certainly have fallen. He sat motionless, stupefied by astonishment and suffering, with an agony which was simple but deep. He wanted to cry, to run away, to hide himself, never to see anybody any more.

Soon he saw them issuing from the thicket. They returned slowly, holding each other's hands as in the villages do those who are promised. It was Luc who carried the pail.

They kissed one another again before they separated, and the girl went off after having thrown Jean a friendly "Good evening" and a smile which was full of meaning. Today she no longer thought of offering him any milk.

The two little soldiers sat side by side, motionless as usual, silent and calm, their placid faces betraying nothing of all which troubled their hearts. The sun fell on them. Sometimes the cow lowed, looking at them from afar.

At their usual hour they rose to go back. Luc cut a switch. Jean carried the empty bottle to return it to the wine-seller at Bézons. Then they sallied out upon the bridge, and, as they did every Sunday, stopped several minutes in the middle to watch the water flowing.

Two Little Soldiers

Jean leaned, leaned more and more, over the iron railing, as though he saw in the current something which attracted him. Luc said: "Are you trying to drink?" Just as he uttered the last word Jean's head overbalanced his body, his legs described a circle in the air, and the little blue and red soldier fell in a heap, struck the water, and disappeared.

Luc, his tongue paralyzed with anguish, tried in vain to shout. Farther down he saw something stir; then the head of his comrade rose to the surface of the river and sank immediately. Farther still he again perceived a hand, a single hand, which issued from the stream and then disappeared. That was all.

The bargemen who dragged the river did not find the body that day.

Luc set out alone for the barracks, going at a run, his soul filled with despair. He told of the accident, with tears in his eyes, and a husky voice, blowing his nose again and again: "He leaned over—he—he leaned over —so far—so far that his head turned a somersault; and —and—so he fell—he fell—"

Choked with emotion, he could say no more. If he had only known!

The White Wolf

THIS is the story the old Marquis d'Arville told us after a dinner in honor of Saint-Hubert, at the house of Baron des Ravels. They had run down a stag that day. The Marquis was the only one of the guests who had not taken part in the chase. He never hunted.

During the whole of the long repast, they had talked of scarcely anything but the massacre of animals. Even the ladies interested themselves in the sanguinary and often unlikely stories, while the orators mimicked the attacks and combats between man and beast, raising their arms and speaking in thunderous tones.

M. d'Arville talked much, with a certain poesy, a little flourish, but full of effect. He must have repeated this story often, it ran so smoothly, never halting at a choice of words in which to clothe an image.

"Gentlemen, I never hunt, nor did my father, nor my grandfather, nor my great-great-grandfather. The last named was the son of a man who hunted more than all of you. He died in 1764. I will tell you how. He was named John, and was married, and became the father of the man who was my great-great-grandfather. He lived with his younger brother, Francis d'Arville, in our castle, in the midst of a deep forest in Lorraine.

"Francis d'Arville always remained a boy through his love for hunting. They both hunted from one end of the year to the other without cessation or weariness. They loved nothing else, understood nothing else, talked only of this, and lived for this alone.

"They were possessed by this terrible, inexorable passion. It consumed them, having taken entire control of them, leaving no place for anything else. They had agreed not to put off the chase for any reason whatsoever. My great-great-grandfather was born while his father was following a fox, but John d'Arville did not interrupt his sport, and swore that the little beggar might have waited until after the death-cry! His brother Francis showed himself still more hot-headed than he. The first thing on rising, he would go to see the dogs, then the horses; then he would shoot some birds about the place, even when about to set out hunting big game.

"They were called in the country Monsieur the Marquis and Monsieur the Cadet, noblemen then not acting as do those of our time, who wish to establish in their titles a descending scale of rank, for the son of a marquis is no more a count, or the son of a viscount a baron, than the son of a general is a colonel by birth. But the niggardly vanity of the day finds profit in this arrangement. To return to my ancestors:

"They were, it appears, immoderately large, bony, hairy, violent, and vigorous. The younger one was taller than the elder, and had such a voice that, according to a legend he was very proud of, all the leaves of the forest moved when he shouted.

"And when mounted, ready for the chase, it must have been a superb sight to see these two giants astride their great horses.

"Toward the middle of the winter of that year, 1764, the cold was excessive and the wolves became ferocious.

"They even attacked belated peasants, roamed around houses at night, howled from sunset to sunrise, and ravaged the stables.

"At one time a rumor was circulated. It was said that

a colossal wolf, of grayish-white color, which had eaten two children, devoured the arm of a woman, strangled all the watchdogs of the country, was now coming without fear into the house inclosures and smelling around the doors. Many inhabitants affirmed that they had felt his breath, which made the lights flicker. Shortly a panic ran through all the province. No one dared to go out after nightfall. The very shadows seemed haunted by the image of this beast.

"The brothers D'Arville resolved to find and slay him. So they called together for a grand chase all the gentlemen of the country.

"It was in vain. They had beaten the forests and scoured the thickets, but had seen nothing of him. They killed wolves, but not that one. And each night after such a chase, the beast, as if to avenge himself, attacked some traveler, or devoured some cattle, always far from the place where they had sought him.

"Finally, one night he found a way into the swine-house of the castle D'Arville and ate two beauties of the best breed.

"The two brothers were furious, interpreting the attack as one of bravado on the part of the monster—a direct injury, a defiance. Therefore, taking all their best-trained hounds, they set out to run down the beast, with courage excited by anger.

"From dawn until the sun descended behind the great nut-trees, they beat about the forests with no result.

"At last, both of them, angry and disheartened, turned their horses' steps into a bypath bordered by brushwood. They were marveling at the baffling power of this wolf, when suddenly they were seized with a mysterious fear.

The White Wolf

"The elder said:

" 'This can be no ordinary beast. One might say he can think like a man.'

"The younger replied:

" 'Perhaps we should get our cousin, the Bishop, to bless a bullet for him, or ask a priest to pronounce some words to help us.'

"Then they were silent.

"John continued: 'Look at the sun, how red it is. The great wolf will do mischief tonight.'

"He had scarcely finished speaking when his horse reared. Francis's horse started to run at the same time. A large bush covered with dead leaves rose before them, and a colossal beast, grayish white, sprang out, scampering away through the wood.

"Both gave a grunt of satisfaction, and bending to the necks of their heavy horses, they urged them on with the weight of their bodies, exciting them, hastening with voice and spur, until these strong riders seemed to carry the weight of their beasts between their knees, carrying them by force as if they were flying.

"Thus they rode, crashing through forests, crossing ravines, climbing up the sides of steep gorges, and sounding the horn, at frequent intervals, to arouse the people and the dogs of the neighborhood.

"But suddenly, in the course of this breakneck ride, my ancestor struck his forehead against a large branch and fractured his skull. He fell to the ground as if dead, while his frightened horse disappeared in the surrounding thicket.

"The younger D'Arville stopped short, sprang to the ground, seized his brother in his arms, and saw that he had lost consciousness.

"He sat down beside him, took his disfigured head

upon his knees, looking earnestly at the lifeless face. Little by little a fear crept over him, a strange fear that he had never before felt, fear of the shadows, of the solitude, of the lonely woods, and also of the chimerical wolf, which had now come to be the death of his brother.

"The shadows deepened, the branches of the trees crackled in the sharp cold. Francis arose shivering, incapable of remaining there longer, and already feeling his strength fail. There was nothing to be heard, neither the voices of dogs nor the sound of a horn; all within this invisible horizon was mute. And in this gloomy silence and the chill of evening there was something strange and frightful.

"With his powerful hands he seized John's body and laid it across the saddle to take it home; then mounted gently behind it, his mind troubled by horrible, supernatural images, as if he were possessed.

"Suddenly, in the midst of these fears, a great form passed. It was the wolf. A violent fit of terror seized upon the hunter; something cold, like a stream of ice-water seemed to glide through his veins, and he made the sign of the cross, like a monk haunted with devils, so dismayed was he by the reappearance of the frightful wanderer. Then, his eyes falling upon the the inert body before him, his fear was quickly changed to anger, and he trembled with inordinate rage.

"He pricked his horse and darted after him.

"He followed him through copses, over ravines, and around great forest trees, traversing woods that he no longer recognized, his eye fixed upon a white spot, which was ever flying from him as night covered the earth.

"His horse also seemed moved by an unknown force. He galloped on with neck extended, crashing over small trees and rocks, with the body of the dead stretched across him on the saddle. Brambles caught in his mane; his head, where it had struck the trunks of trees, was spattered with blood; the marks of the spurs were over his flanks.

"Suddenly the animal and its rider came out of the forest, rushing through a valley as the moon appeared above the hills. This valley was stony and shut in by enormous rocks, over which it was impossible to pass; there was no other way for the wolf but to turn on his steps.

"Francis gave such a shout of joy and revenge that the echo of it was like the roll of thunder. He leaped from his horse, knife in hand.

"The bristling beast, with rounded back, was awaiting him; his eyes shining like two stars. But before joining in battle, the strong hunter, grasping his brother, seated him upon a rock, supporting his head, which was now but a mass of blood, with stones, and cried aloud to him, as to one deaf: 'Look, John! Look here!'

"Then he threw himself upon the monster. He felt himself strong enough to overthrow a mountain, to crush the very rocks in his hands. The beast meant to kill him by sinking his claws in his vitals; but the man had seized him by the throat, without even making use of his weapon, and strangled him gently, waiting until his breath stopped and he could hear the death-rattle at his heart. And he laughed, with the joy of dismay, clutching more and more with a terrible hold, and crying out in his delirium: 'Look, John! Look!' All resistance ceased. The body of the wolf was limp. He was dead.

"Then Francis, taking him in his arms, threw him down at the feet of his elder brother, crying out in expectant voice: 'Here, here, my little John, here he is!'

"Then he placed upon the saddle the two bodies, the one above the other, and started on his way.

"He returned to the castle laughing and weeping, like Gargantua at the birth of Pantagruel, shouting in triumph and stamping with delight in relating the death of the beast, and moaning and tearing at his beard in calling the name of his brother.

"Often, later, when he recalled this day, he would declare, with tears in his eyes: 'If only poor John had seen me strangle the beast, he would have died content, I am sure!'

"The widow of my ancestor inspired in her son a horror of the chase, which was transmitted from father to son down to myself."

The Marquis d'Arville was silent. Some one asked: "Is the story a legend or not?"

And the narrator replied:

"I swear to you it is true from beginning to end."

Then a lady, in a sweet little voice, declared:

"It is beautiful to have passions like that."

The Devil

THE peasant was standing opposite the doctor, by the bedside of the dying old woman, and she, calmly resigned and quite lucid, looked at them and listened to their talking. She was going to die, and she did not rebel at it, for her life was over—she was ninety-two.

The July sun streamed in at the window and through the open door and cast its hot flames onto the uneven brown clay floor, which had been stamped down by four generations of clodhoppers. The smell of the fields came in also, driven by the brisk wind, and parched by the noontide heat. The grasshoppers chirped themselves hoarse, filling the air with their shrill noise, like that of the wooden crickets which are sold to children at fair time.

The doctor raised his voice and said: "Honoré, you cannot leave your mother in this state; she may die at any moment." And the peasant, in great distress, replied: "But I must get in my wheat, for it has been lying on the ground a long time, and the weather is just right for it; what do you say about it, mother?" And the dying woman, still possessed by her Norman avariciousness, replied *yes* with her eyes and her forehead, and so urged her son to get in his wheat, and to leave her to die alone. But the doctor got angry, and stamping his foot he said: "You are no better than a brute, do you hear, and I will not allow you to do it. Do you understand? And if you must get in your wheat today, go and fetch Rapet's wife and make her look after your mother. I *will* have it.

And if you do not obey me, I will let you die like a dog, when you are ill in your turn; do you hear me?"

The peasant, a tall, thin fellow with slow movements, who was tormented by indecision, by his fear of the doctor and his keen love of saving, hesitated, calculated, and stammered out: "How much does La Rapet charge for attending sick people?"

"How should I know?" the doctor cried. "That depends upon how long she is wanted for. Settle it with her, by Jove! But I want her to be here within an hour, do you hear."

So the man made up his mind. "I will go for her," he replied; "don't get angry, doctor." And the latter left, calling out as he went: "Take care, you know, for I do not joke when I am angry!" And as soon as they were alone, the peasant turned to his mother, and said in a resigned voice: "I will go and fetch La Rapet, as the man will have it. Don't go off while I am away."

And he went out in his turn.

La Rapet, who was an old washerwoman, watched the dead and the dying of the neighborhood, and then, as soon as she had sewn her customers into that linen cloth from which they would emerge no more, she went and took up her irons to smooth the linen of the living. Wrinkled like a last year's apple, spiteful, envious, avaricious with a phenomenal avarice, bent double, as if she had been broken in half across the loins, by the constant movement of the iron over the linen, one might have said that she had a kind of monstrous and cynical affection for a death struggle. She never spoke of anything but of the people she had seen die, of the various kinds of deaths at which she had been present, and she related, with the greatest minuteness, details which were always the same, just like a sportsman talks of his shots.

When Honoré Bontemps entered her cottage, he found her preparing the starch for the collars of the village woman, and he said: "Good evening; I hope you are pretty well, Mother Rapet."

She turned her head round to look at him and said: "Fairly well, fairly well, and you?"

"Oh! as for me, I am as well as I could wish, but my mother is very sick."

"Your mother?"

"Yes, my mother!"

"What's the matter with her?"

"She is going to turn up her toes, that's what's the matter with her!"

The old woman took her hands out of the water and asked with sudden sympathy: "Is she as bad as all that?"

"The doctor says she will not last till morning."

"Then she certainly is very bad!" Honoré hesitated, for he wanted to make a few preliminary remarks before coming to his proposal, but as he could hit upon nothing, he made up his mind suddenly.

"How much are you going to ask to stop with her till the end? You know that I am not rich, and I cannot even afford to keep a servant-girl. It is just that which has brought my poor mother to this state, too much work and fatigue! She used to work for ten, in spite of her ninety-two years. You don't find any made of that stuff nowadays!"

La Rapet answered gravely: "There are two prices: Forty sous by day and three francs by night for the rich, and twenty sous by day, and forty by night for the others. You shall pay me the twenty and forty." But the peasant reflected, for he knew his mother well. He knew how tenacious of life, how vigorous and unyielding she was. He knew, too, that she might last another week, in spite of the doctor's opinion, and so he said resolutely: "No, I would rather you would fix a price until the end. I will take my chance, one way or the other. The doctors says she will die very soon. If that happens, so much the better for you, and so much the worse for me, but if she holds out till tomorrow or longer, so much the better for me and so much the worse for you!"

The nurse looked at the man in astonishment, for she had never treated a death as a speculative job, and she hesitated, tempted by the idea of the possible gain. But almost immediately she suspected that he wanted to juggle her. "I can say nothing until I have seen your mother," she replied.

"Then come with me and see her."

She washed her hands, and went with him immediately. They did not speak on the road; she walked with short, hasty steps, while he strode on with his long legs, as if he were crossing a brook at every step. The cows lying down in the fields, overcome by the heat, raised their heads heavily and lowed feebly at the two passers-by, as if to ask them for some green grass.

When they got near the house, Honoré Bontemps murmured: "Suppose it is all over?" And the unconscious wish that it might be so showed itself in the sound of his voice.

But the old woman was not dead. She was lying on her back, on her wretched bed, her hands covered with a pink cotton counterpane, horribly thin, knotty paws, like some strange animal's, or like crabs' claws, hands closed by rheumatism, fatigue, and the work of nearly a century which she had accomplished.

La Rapet went up to the bed and looked at the

dying woman, felt her pulse, tapped her on the chest, listened to her breathing, and asked her questions, so as to hear her speak: then, having looked at her for some time longer, she went out of the room, followed by Honoré. His decided opinion was, that the old woman would not last out the night, and he asked: "Well?" And the sick-nurse replied: "Well, she may last two days, perhaps three. You will have to give me six francs, everything included."

"Six francs! six francs!" he shouted. "Are you out of your mind? I tell you that she cannot last more than five or six hours!" And they disputed angrily for some time, but as the nurse said she would go home, as the time was slipping away, and as his wheat would not come to the farmyard of its own accord, he agreed to her terms at last:

"Very well, then, that is settled; six francs including every thing, until the corpse is taken out."

"That is settled, six francs."

And he went away, with long strides, to his wheat, which was lying on the ground under the hot sun which ripens the grain, while the sick-nurse returned to the house.

She had brought some work with her, for she worked without stopping by the side of the dead and dying, sometimes for herself, sometimes for the family, who employed her as seamstress also, paying her rather more in that capacity. Suddenly she asked:

"Have you received the last sacrament, Mother Bontemps?"

The old peasant woman said "No" with her head, and La Rapet, who was very devout, got up quickly: "Good heavens, is it possible? I will go and fetch the curé"; and she rushed off to the parsonage so quickly, that the urchins in the street thought some accident had happened, when they saw her trotting off like that.

The priest came immediately in his surplice, preceded by a choir-boy, who rang a bell to announce the passage of the Host through the parched and quiet country. Some men, working at a distance, took off their large hats and remained motionless until the white vestment had disappeared behind some farm buildings; the women who were making up the sheaves stood up to make the sign of the cross; the frightened black hens ran away along the ditch until they reached a well-known hole through which they suddenly disappeared, while a foal, which was tied up in a meadow, took fright at the sight of the surplice and began to gallop round at the length of its rope, kicking violently. The choir-boy, in his red cassock, walked quickly, and the priest, the square biretta on his bowed head, followed him, muttering some prayers. Last of all came La Rapet, bent almost double, as if she wished to prostrate herself; she walked with folded hands, as if she were in church.

Honoré saw them pass in the distance, and he asked: "Where is our priest going to?" And his man, who was more acute, replied: "He is taking the sacrament to your mother, of course!"

The peasant was not surprised and said: "That is quite possible," and went on with his work.

Mother Bontemps confessed, received absolution and extreme unction, and the priest took his departure, leaving the two women alone in the suffocating cottage. La Rapet began to look at the dying woman, and to ask herself whether it could last much longer.

The day was on the wane, and a cooler air came in stronger puffs, making a view of Epinal, which was fastened to the wall by two pins, flap up and down. The scanty window curtains, which had formerly been white, but were now yellow and covered with fly-specks, looked as if they were going to fly off, and seemed to struggle to get away, like the old woman's soul.

Lying motionless, with her eyes open, the old mother seemed to await the death which was so near, and which yet delayed its coming, with perfect indifference. Her short breath whistled in her throat. It would stop altogether soon, and there would be one woman less in the world, one whom nobody would regret.

At nightfall Honoré returned, and when he went up to the bed and saw that his mother was still alive he asked: "How is she?" just as he had done formerly, when she had been sick. Then he sent La Rapet away, saying to her: "Tomorrow morning at five o'clock, without fail." And she replied: "Tomorrow at five o'clock."

She came at daybreak, and found Honoré eating his soup, which he had made himself, before going to work.

"Well, is your mother dead?" asked the nurse.

"She is rather better, on the contrary," he replied, with a malignant look out of the corner of his eyes. Then he went out.

La Rapet was seized with anxiety, and went up to the dying woman, who was in the same state, lethargic and impassive, her eyes open and her hands clutching the counterpane. The nurse perceived that this might go on thus for two days, four days, eight days, even, and her avaricious mind was seized with fear. She was excited to fury against the cunning fellow who had tricked her, and against the woman who would not die.

Nevertheless, she began to sew and waited with her eyes fixed on the wrinkled face of Mother Bontemps. When Honoré returned to breakfast he seemed quite satisfied, and even in a bantering humor, for he was carrying in his wheat under very favorable circumstances.

La Rapet was getting exasperated; every passing minute now seemed to her so much time and money stolen from her. She felt a mad inclination to choke this old ass, this headstrong old fool, this obstinate old wretch —to stop that short, rapid breath, which was robbing her of her time and money, by squeezing her throat a little. But then she reflected on the danger of doing so, and other thoughts came into her head, so she went up to the bed and said to her: "Have you ever seen the Devil?"

Mother Bontemps whispered: "No."

Then the sick-nurse began to talk and to tell her tales likely to terrify her weak and dying mind. "Some minutes before one dies the Devil appears," she said, "to all. He has a broom in his hand, a saucepan on his head and he utters loud cries. When anybody had seen him, all was over, and that person had only a few moments longer to live"; and she enumerated all those to whom the Devil had appeared that year: Josephine Loisel, Eulalie Ratier, Sophie Padagnau, Séraphine Grospied.

Mother Bontemps, who was at last most disturbed in mind, moved about, wrung her hands, and tried to turn her head to look at the other end of the room. Suddenly La Rapet disappeared at the foot of the bed. She took a sheet out of the cupboard and wrapped herself up in it; then she put the iron pot on to her head, so that its three short bent feet rose up like horns, took a broom in her right hand and a tin pail in her left, which she threw up suddenly, so that it might fall to the ground noisily.

The Devil

Certainly when it came down, it made a terrible noise. Then, climbing on to a chair, the nurse showed herself, gesticulating and uttering shrill cries into the pot which covered her face, while she menaced the old peasant woman, who was nearly dead, with her broom.

Terrified, with a mad look on her face, the dying woman made a superhuman effort to get up and escape; she even got her shoulders and chest out of bed; then she fell back with a deep sigh. All was over, and La Rapet calmly put everything back into its place; the broom into the corner by the cupboard, the sheet inside it, the pot onto the hearth, the pail onto the floor, and the chair against the wall. Then with a professional air, she closed the dead woman's enormous eyes, put a plate on the bed and poured some holy water into it, dipped the twig of boxwood into it, and kneeling down, she fervently repeated the prayers for the dead, which she knew by heart, as a matter of business.

When Honoré returned in the evening, he found her praying. He calculated immediately that she had made twenty sous out of him, for she had only spent three days and one night there, which made five francs altogether, instead of the six which he owed her.

480

A Lucky Burglar

THEY were seated in the dining-room of a hotel in Barbizon.

"I tell you, you will not believe it."

"Well, tell it anyhow."

"All right, here goes. But first I must tell you that my story is absolutely true in every respect; even if it does sound improbable." And the old artist commenced:

"We had dined at Soriel's that night. When I say dined, that means that we were all pretty tipsy. We were three young madcaps. Soriel (poor fellow! he is dead now), Le Poittevin, the marine painter, and myself. Le Poittevin is dead, also.

"We had stretched ourselves on the floor of the little room adjoining the studio and the only one in the crowd who was rational was Le Poittevin. Soriel, who was always the maddest, lay flat on his back, with his feet propped up on a chair, discussing war and the uniforms of the Empire, when, suddenly, he got up, took out of the big wardrobe where he kept his accessories a complete hussar's uniform and put it on. He then took out a grenadier's uniform and told Le Poittevin to put it on; but he objected, so we forced him into it. It was so big for him that he was completely lost in it. I arrayed myself as a cuirassier. After we were ready, Soriel made us go through a complicated drill. Then he exclaimed: 'As long as we are troopers let us drink like troopers.'

"The punch-bowl had been brought out and filled for the second time. We were bawling some old camp songs at the top of our voice, when Le Poittevin, who in spite of all the punch had retained his self-control, held up his hand and said: 'Hush! I am sure I heard some one walking in the studio.'

" 'A burglar!' said Soriel, staggering to his feet. 'Good luck!' And he began the 'Marseillaise':

" 'To arms, citizens!'

"Then he seized several weapons from the wall and equipped us according to our uniforms. I received a musket and a saber. Le Poittevin was handed an enormous gun with a bayonet attached. Soriel, not finding just what he wanted, seized a pistol, stuck it in his belt, and brandishing a battle-axe in one hand, he opened the studio door cautiously. The army advanced. Having reached the middle of the room Soriel said:

" 'I am general. You [pointing to me], the cuirassiers, will keep the enemy from retreating—that is, lock the door. You [pointing to Le Poittevin], the grenadiers, will be my escort.'

"I executed my orders and rejoined the troops, who were behind a large screen reconnoitering. Just as I reached it I heard a terrible noise. I rushed up with the candle to investigate the cause of it and this is what I saw. Le Poittevin was piercing the dummy's breast with his bayonet and Soriel was splitting his head open with his axe! When the mistake had been discovered the General commanded: 'Be cautious!'

"We had explored every nook and corner of the studio for the past twenty minutes without success, when Le Poittevin thought he would look in the cupboard. As it was quite deep and very dark, I advanced with the candle and looked in. I drew back stupefied. A man, a real live man this time, stood there looking at me! I quickly recovered myself, however, and locked the cupboard door. We then retired a few paces to hold a council.

"Opinions were divided. Soriel wanted to smoke the burglar out; Le Poittevin suggested starvation, and I proposed to blow him up with dynamite. Le Poittevin's idea being finally accepted as the best, we proceed to bring the punch and pipes into the studio, while Le Poittevin kept guard with his big gun on his shoulder, and settling ourselves in front of the cupboard we drank the prisoner's health. We had done this repeatedly, when Soriel suggested that we bring out the prisoner and take a look at him.

" 'Hooray!' cried I. We picked up our weapons and made a mad rush for the cupboard door. It was finally opened, and Soriel, cocking his pistol which was not loaded, rushed in first. Le Poittevin and I followed yelling like lunatics and, after a mad scramble in the dark, we at last brought out the burglar. He was a haggard-looking, white-haired old bandit, with shabby, ragged clothes. We bound him hand and foot and dropped him in an armchair. He said nothing.

" 'We will try this wretch' said Soriel, whom the punch had made very solemn. I was so far gone that it seemed to me quite a natural thing. Le Poittevin was named for the defense and I for the prosecution. The prisoner was condemned to death by all except his counsel.

" 'We will now execute him,' said Soriel. 'Still, this man cannot die without repenting,' he added, feeling somewhat scrupulous. 'Let us send for a priest.'

"I objected that it was too late, so he proposed that I officiate and forthwith told the prisoner to confess his sins to me. The old man was terrified. He wondered what kind of wretches we were and for the first time he spoke. His voice was hollow and cracked:

" 'Say, you don't mean it, do you?'

"Soriel forced him to his knees, and for fear he had not been baptized, poured a glass of rum over his head, saying: 'Confess your sins; your last hour has come!'

" 'Help! Help!' screamed the old man rolling himself on the floor and kicking everything that came his way. For fear he should wake the neighbors we gagged him.

" 'Come, let us end this'; said Soriel impatiently. He pointed his pistol at the old man and pressed the trigger. I followed his example, but as neither of our guns was loaded we made very little noise. Le Poittevin, who had been looking on said:

" 'Have we really the right to kill this man?'

" 'We have condemned him to death!' said Soriel.

" 'Yes, but we have no right to shoot a civilian. Let us take him to the station-house.'

"We agreed with him, and as the old man could not walk we tied him to a board, and Le Poittevin and I carried him, while Soriel kept guard in the rear. We arrived at the station-house. The chief, who knew us and was well acquainted with our manner of joking, thought it was a great lark and laughingly refused to take our prisoner in. Soriel insisted, but the chief told us very sternly to quit our fooling and go home and be quiet. There was nothing else to do but to take him back to Soriel's.

" 'What are we going to do with him?' I asked.

" 'The poor man must be awfully tired!' said Le Poittevin, sympathizingly.

"He did look half dead, and in my turn I felt a sudden pity for him (the punch, no doubt), and I relieved him of his gag.

" 'How do you feel old man?' I asked.

" 'By Jingo! I have enough of this,' he groaned.

"Then Soriel softened. He unbound him and treated him as a long-lost friend. The three of us immediately brewed a fresh bowl of punch. As soon as it was ready we handed a glass to the prisoner, who quaffed it without flinching. Toast followed toast. The old man could drink more than the three of us put together; but as daylight appeared, he got up and calmly said: 'I shall be obliged to leave you; I must get home now.'

"We begged him not to go, but he positively refused to stay any longer. We were awfully sorry and took him to the door, while Soriel held the candle above his head saying: 'Look out for the last step.' "

Moonlight

~~~~~~

MADAME JULIE ROUBÉRE was awaiting her elder sister, Madame Henriette Letore, who had just returned after a trip to Switzerland.

The Letore household had left nearly five weeks ago. Madame Henriette had allowed her husband to return alone to their estate in Calvados, where some matters of business required his attention, and came to spend a few days in Paris with her sister. Night came on. In the quiet parlor darkened by twilight shadows, Madame Roubère was reading in an absent-minded fashion, raising her eyes whenever she heard a sound.

At last she heard a ring at the door, and presently her sister appeared, wrapped in a traveling cloak. And immediately, without any formal greeting, they clasped each other ardently, only desisting for a moment to begin embracing each other over again. Then they talked, asking questions about each other's health, about their respective families, and a thousand other things, gossiping, jerking out hurried, broken sentences, and rushing about while Madame Henriette was removing her hat and veil.

It was now quite dark. Madame Roubère rang for a lamp, and as soon as it was brought in, she scanned her sister's face, and was on the point of embracing her once more. But she held back, scared and astonished at the other's appearance. Around her temples, Madame Letore had two long locks of white hair. All the rest of her hair was of a glossy, raven-black hue; but there alone, at each side of her head, ran, as it were, two silvery streams which were immediately lost in the black mass surrounding

them. She was, nevertheless, only twenty-four years old
and this change had come on suddenly since her departure for Switzerland.

Without moving, Madame Roubère gazed at her in
amazement, tears rising to her eyes, as she thought that
some mysterious and terrible calamity must have fallen
on her sister. She asked:

"What is the matter with you, Henriette?"

Smiling with a sad smile, the smile of one who is
heartsick, the other replied:

"Why, nothing, I assure you. Were you noticing my
white hair?"

But Madame Roubère impetuously seized her by the
shoulders, and with a searching glance at her, repeated:

"What is the matter with you? Tell me what is the
matter with you. And if you tell me a falsehood, I'll soon
find it out."

They remained face to face, and Madame Henriette,
who became so pale that she was near fainting, had two
pearly tears at each corner of her drooping eyes.

Her sister went on asking:

"What has happened to you? What is the matter with
you? Answer me!"

Then, in a subdued voice, the other murmured:

"I have—I have a lover."

And, hiding her forehead on the shoulder of her
younger sister, she sobbed.

Then, when she had grown a little calmer, when the
heaving of her breast had subsided, she commenced to
unbosom herself, as if to cast forth this secret from herself, to empty this sorrow of hers into a sympathetic
heart.

Thereupon, holding each other's hands tightly
grasped, the two women went over to a sofa in a dark

corner of the room, into which they sank, and the younger sister, passing her arm over the elder one's neck and drawing her close to her heart, listened.

"Oh! I recognize that there was no excuse for one; I do not understand myself, and since that day I feel as if I were mad. Be careful, my child, about yourself—be careful! If you only knew how weak we are, how quickly we yield, we fall! All it needs is a nothing, so little, so little, a moment of tenderness, one of those sudden fits of melancholy which steal into your soul, one of those longings to open your arms, to love, to embrace, which we all have at certain moments.

"You know my husband, and you know how fond of him I am; but he is mature and sensible, and cannot even comprehend the tender vibrations of a woman's heart. He is always, always the same, always good, always smiling, always kind, always perfect. Oh! how I sometimes have wished that he would roughly clasp me in his arms, that he would embrace me with those slow, sweet kisses which make two beings intermingle, which are like mute confidences! How I wished that he was self-abandoned and even weak, so that he should have need of me, of my caresses, of my tears!

"This all seems very silly; but we women are made like that. How can we help it?

"And yet the thought of deceiving never came near me. Today, it has happened, without love, without reason, without anything, simply because the moon shone one night on the Lake of Lucerne.

"During the month when we were traveling together, my husband, with his calm indifference, paralyzed my enthusiasm, extinguished my poetic ardor. When we were descending the mountain paths at sunrise, when as

488

the four horses galloped along with the diligence, we saw, in the transparent morning haze, valleys, woods, streams, and villages, I clasped my hands with delight, and said to him: 'What a beautiful scene, darling! Kiss me now!' he only answered, with a smile of chilling kindliness, 'There is no reason why we should kiss each other because you like the landscape.'

"And his words froze me to the heart. It seems to me that when people love each other, they ought to feel more moved by love than ever in the presence of beautiful scenes.

"Indeed, he prevented the effervescent poetry that bubbled up within me from gushing out. How can I express it? I was almost like a boiler, filled with steam, and hermetically sealed.

"One evening (we had been for four days staying in the Hotel de Fluelen), Robert, having got one of his sick headaches, went to bed immediately after dinner, and I went to take a walk all alone along the edge of the lake.

"It was a night such as one might read of in a fairy tale. The full moon showed itself in the middle of the sky; the tall mountains, with their snowy crests, seemed to wear silver crowns; the waters of the lake glittered with tiny rippling motions. The air was mild, with that kind of penetrating freshness which softens us till we seem to be swooning, to be deeply affected without any apparent cause. But how sensitive, how vibrating, the heart is at such moments! How quickly it leaps up, and how intense are its emotions!

"I sat down on the grass, and gazed at that vast lake so melancholy and so fascinating; and a strange thing passed into me; I became possessed with an insatiable need of love, a revolt against the gloomy dullness of my life. What, would it never be my fate to be clasped in the arms of a man whom I loved on a bank like this under the glowing moonlight? Was I never then, to feel on my lips those kisses so deep, delicious, and intoxicating which lovers exchange on nights that seem to have been made by God for passionate embraces? Was I never to know such ardent, feverish love in the moonlit shadows of a summer's night?

"And I burst out weeping like a woman who has lost her reason. I heard some person stirring behind me. A man was intently gazing at me. When I turned my head round, he recognized me, and, advancing, said:

" 'You are weeping, Madame?'

"It was a young barrister who was traveling with his mother, and whom we had often met. His eyes had frequently followed me.

"I was so much confused that I did not know what answer to give or what to think of the situation. I told him I felt ill.

"He walked on by my side in a natural and respectful fashion, and began talking to me about what we had seen during our trip. All that I had felt he translated into words; everything that made me thrill he understood perfectly, better even than I did myself. And all of a sudden he recited some verses of Alfred de Musset. I felt myself choking, seized with indescribable emotion. It seemed to me that the mountains themselves, the lake, the moonlight, were singing to me about things ineffably sweet.

"And it happened, I don't know how, I don't know why, in a sort of hallucination.

"As for him, I did not see him again till the morning of his departure.

"He gave me his card!"

Moonlight

And, sinking into her sister's arms, Madame Letore broke into groans—almost into shrieks.

Then Madame Roubère, with a self-contained and serious air, said very gently:

"You see, sister, very often it is not a man that we love, but love. And your real lover that night was the moonlight."

The Mad Woman

"I CAN tell you a terrible story about the Franco-Prussian war," Monsieur d'Endolin said to some friends assembled in the smoking-room of Baron de Ravot's château. "You know my house in the Faubourg de Cormeil. I was living there when the Prussians came, and I had for a neighbor a kind of mad woman, who had lost her senses in consequence of a series of misfortunes. At the age of seven and twenty she had lost her father, her husband, and her newly born child, all in the space of a month.

"When death has once entered into a house, it almost invariably returns immediately, as if it knew the way, and the young woman, overwhelmed with grief, took to her bed and was delirious for six weeks. Then a species of calm lassitude succeeded that violent crisis, and she remained motionless, eating next to nothing, and only moving her eyes. Every time they tried to make her get up, she screamed as if they were about to kill her, and so they ended by leaving her continually in bed, and only taking her out to wash her, to change her linen, and to turn her mattress.

"An old servant remained with her, to give her something to drink, or a little cold meat, from time to time. What passed in that despairing mind? No one ever knew, for she did not speak at all now. Was she thinking of the dead? Was she dreaming sadly, without any precise recollection of anything that had happened? Or was her memory as stagnant as water without any current? But

492

however this may have been, for fifteen years she remained thus inert and secluded.

"The war broke out, and in the beginning of December the Germans came to Cormeil. I can remember it as if it were but yesterday. It was freezing hard enough to split the stones, and I myself was lying back in an armchair, being unable to move on account of the gout, when I heard their heavy and regular tread, and could see them pass from my window.

"They filed past interminably, with that peculiar motion of a puppet on wires, which belongs to them. Then the officers billeted their men on the inhabitants, and I had seventeen of them. My neighbor, the crazy woman, had a dozen, one of whom was the Commandant, a regular violent, surly swashbuckler.

"During the first few days, everything went on as usual. The officers next door had been told that the lady was ill, and they did not trouble themselves about that in the least, but soon that woman whom they never saw irritated them. They asked what her illness was, and were told that she had been in bed for fifteen years, in consequence of terrible grief. No doubt they did not believe it, and thought that the poor mad creature would not leave her bed out of pride, so that she might not come near the Prussians, or speak to them or even see them.

"The Commandant insisted upon her receiving him. He was shown into the room and said to her roughly: 'I must beg you to get up, Madame, and to come downstairs so that we may all see you.' But she merely turned her vague eyes on him, without replying, and so he continued: 'I do not intend to tolerate any insolence, and if you do not get up of your own accord, I can easily find means to make you walk without any assistance.'

"But she did not give any signs of having heard him, and remained quite motionless. Then he got furious, taking that calm silence for a mark of supreme contempt; so he added: 'If you do not come downstairs to-morrow—' And then he left the room.

"The next day the terrified old servant wished to dress her, but the mad woman began to scream violently, and resisted with all her might. The officer ran upstairs quickly, and the servant threw herself at his feet and cried: 'She will not come down, Monsieur, she will not. Forgive her, for she is so unhappy.'

"The soldier was embarrassed, as in spite of his anger, he did not venture to order his soldiers to drag her out. But suddenly he began to laugh, and gave some orders in German, and soon a party of soldiers was seen coming out supporting a mattress as if they were carrying a wounded man. On that bed, which had not been un-made, the mad woman, who was still silent, was lying quite quietly, for she was quite indifferent to anything that went on, as long as they let her lie. Behind her, a soldier was carrying a parcel of feminine attire, and the officer said, rubbing his hands: 'We will just see whether you cannot dress yourself alone, and take a little walk.'

"And then the procession went off in the direction of the forest of Imauville; in two hours the soldiers came back alone, and nothing more was seen of the mad woman. What had they done with her? Where had they taken her to? No one knew.

"The snow was falling day and night, and enveloped the plain and the woods in a shroud of frozen foam, and the wolves came and howled at our very doors.

"The thought of that poor lost woman haunted me,

and I made several applications to the Prussian authorities in order to obtain some information, and was nearly shot for doing so. When spring returned, the army of occupation withdrew, but my neighbor's house remained closed, and the grass grew thick in the garden walks. The old servant had died during the winter, and nobody troubled any longer about the occurrence; I alone thought about it constantly. What had they done with the woman? Had she escaped through the forest? Had somebody found her, and taken her to a hospital, without being able to obtain any information from her? Nothing happened to relieve my doubts; but by degrees, time assuaged my fears.

"Well, in the following autumn the woodcocks were very plentiful, and as my gout had left me for a time, I dragged myself as far as the forest. I had already killed four or five of the long-billed birds, when I knocked over one which fell into a ditch full of branches, and I was obliged to get into it, in order to pick it up, and I found that it had fallen close to a dead, human body. Immediately the recollection of the mad woman struck me like a blow in the chest. Many other people had perhaps died in the wood during that disastrous year, but though I do not know why, I was sure, sure, I tell you, that I should see the head of that wretched maniac.

"And suddenly I understood, I guessed everything. They had abandoned her on that mattress in the cold, deserted wood; and, faithful to her fixed idea, she had allowed herself to perish under that thick and light counterpane of snow, without moving either arms or legs.

"Then the wolves had devoured her, and the birds had built their nests with the wool from her torn bed, and I took charge of her bones. I only pray that our sons may never see any wars again."

A Costly Outing

HECTOR DE GRIBELIN, descendant of an old provincial family, had spent his early years in his ancestral home and had finished his studies under the guidance of an old abbé. The family was far from rich, but they kept up appearances the best way they could. At the age of twenty a position was procured for him at the Navy administration, at one thousand five hundred francs a year, but like a great many, not being prepared for the battle, his first three years of office life had been exceedingly hard.

He had renewed acquaintance with a few old friends of his family, poor like himself, but living in the secluded Faubourg St.-Germain, keeping up appearances at any cost, sacrificing everything in order to hold their rank.

It was there he had met and married a young girl, titled but penniless. Two children had blessed their union. Hector and his wife struggled constantly to make both ends meet and for the past four years they had known no other distractions than a walk on Sunday to the Champs-Elysées, and a few evenings at the theater, a friend giving them tickets.

His chief had just intrusted him with some extra work and he received the extra compensation of three hundred francs. Coming home that night he said to his wife:

"My dear Henriette, we ought to do something with this money; a little outing in the country for the children for instance."

A Costly Outing

They had a lengthy discussion, and finally decided on a family picnic.

"We have had so very few outings," said Hector, "that we may as well do things right. We will hire a rig for you and the little ones, and I will hire a horse; it will do me good."

They talked of nothing else all week. Each night, he would dance his elder son up and down on his foot and say:

"This is the way papa will ride next Sunday." And the boy would ride chairs all day screaming:

"This is papa on horseback." Even the servant marveled when she heard Hector tell of his feats on horseback when he was home and how he would ride at the side of the carriage.

"When once on a horse I am afraid of nothing," he would say. "If they could give me a frisky animal I would like it all the better. You will see how I ride, and, if you like, we can come back by the Champs-Elysées when everybody is coming home. We shall cut quite a figure, and I should not be sorry to meet some one from the office; there is nothing like it to inspire respect."

At last Sunday came. The carriage and the horse were at the door, and Hector came down immediately, holding a newly-bought riding-whip, to look the horse over. He examined him from head to foot, opened his mouth, told his age, and as the family was coming out at that moment, he discoursed on horses in general and that one in particular, which he declared to be an excellent animal.

When everyone was comfortably placed in the carriage, Hector examined the saddle, and mounting with a spring, dropped on the horse with such force that he

497

immediately set up a dance which almost threw his rider. Hector became flustered and tried to calm him, saying: "Come, old fellow, be quiet." And having succeeded in calming him a little he asked:

"Is everybody ready?"

Everybody said yes and the party proceeded. All eyes were turned on Hector, who affected the English seat and leaped up and down on his saddle in an exaggerated manner. He looked straight before him, contracting his brow and looking very pale. His wife and the servant each held one of the boys and every minute they would say:

"Look at papa!" And the boys, overcome with joy, uttered piercing screams.

The horse, frightened at so much noise, started off at a gallop and while Hector tried to stop him his hat fell off. The driver had to come down and pick it up, and having recovered it, Hector shouted to his wife:

"Make the children stop screaming, will you? They will make the horse run away."

They arrived at last. The baskets having been opened they lunched on the grass. Although the driver looked after the horses, Hector went every minute to see if his horse wanted anything. He patted him and fed him bread, cake, and sugar.

"He is a great trotter," he said to his wife. "He shook me at first, but you saw how quick I subdued him. He knows his master now."

They came back by the Champs-Elysées as agreed. The weather being beautiful, the avenue was crowded with carriages and the sidewalks lined with pedestrians. The horse, scenting the stable, suddenly took to his heels. He dashed between carriages like a whirlwind and Hector's efforts to stop him were unavailing. The carriage containing his family was far behind. In front of the Palais de l'Industrie, the horse turned to the right at a gallop. An old woman was at that moment leisurely crossing the street, and Hector, who was unable to stop the horse shouted: "Hey there, hey!" But the old woman was deaf, perhaps, for she slowly kept on until the horse struck her with such force that she turned a triple somersault and landed ten feet away. Several people shouted: "Stop him."

Hector was distracted and held on desperately to the horse's mane, crying: "Help, help!" A terrible shock sent him over the horse's head like a bomb, and he landed in the arms of a policeman who was running toward him. An angry crowd gathered. An old gentleman wearing a decoration was especially angry.

"Confound it, sir!" he said, "if you cannot ride a horse why do you not stay at home instead of running over people!"

Four men were carrying the old woman, who to all appearances was dead.

"Take this woman to a drug-store," said the old gentleman, "and let us go to the station-house."

A crowd followed Hector, who walked between two policemen, while a third led his horse. At that moment the carriage appeared, and his wife taking in the situation at a glance, ran toward him; the servant and the children came behind crying. He explained that his horse had knocked a woman down, but it was nothing, he would be home very soon.

Arrived at the station-house, he gave his name, his place of employment, and awaited news of the injured woman. A policeman came back with the information that the woman's name was Mme. Simon, and that she was a charwoman sixty-five years old. She had regained consciousness, but she suffered internally, she claimed. When Hector found that she was not dead, he recovered his spirits and promised to defray the expenses of her illness. He went to the drug-store where they had taken the old woman. An immense crowd blocked the doorway. The old woman was whining and groaning pitifully. Two doctors were examining her.

"There are no bones broken," they said, "but we are afraid she is hurt internally."

"Do you suffer much?" asked Hector.

"Oh, yes."

"Where?"

"I feel as if my inside was on fire."

"Then you are the cause of the accident?" said a doctor approaching.

"Yes, sir," said Hector.

"This woman must go to a sanitarium. I know one where they will take her for six francs a day; shall I fix it for you?"

Hector thanked him gratefully and went home relieved. He found his wife in tears, and he comforted her saying:

"Don't worry, she is much better already. I sent her to a sanitarium, and in three days she will be all right."

After his work the next day he went to see Mme. Simon. She was eating some beef soup which she seemed to relish.

"Well," said Hector, "how do you feel?"

"No better, my poor man," she answered. "I feel as good as dead!"

The doctor advised waiting; complications might arise. He waited three days, then went to see the old woman again. Her skin was clear, her eyes bright, but as soon as she saw Hector she commenced to whine:

"I can't move any more, my poor man; I'll be like this for the rest of my days!"

A Costly Outing

Hector felt a shiver running up and down his back. He asked for the doctor and inquired about the patient.

"I am puzzled," the doctor said. "Every time we try to lift her up or change her position, she utters heart-rending screams; still, I am forced to believe her. I cannot say that she shams until I have seen her walk."

The old woman listened attentively; a sly look on her face. A week, two, then a month passed and still Mme. Simon did not leave her chair. Her appetite was excellent, she gained flesh and joked with the other patients. She seemed to accept her lot as a well-earned rest after fifty years of labor as a charwoman.

Hector came every day and found her the same; always repeating:

"I can't move, my poor man, I can't!"

When Hector came home, his wife would ask with anxiety:

"How is Mme. Simon?"

"Just the same; absolutely no change," answered Hector dejectedly.

They dismissed the servant and economized more than ever. The money received from his chief had been spent. Hector was desperate and one day he called four doctors to hold a consultation. They examined Mme. Simon thoroughly, while she watched them slyly.

"We must make her walk," said one of the doctors.

"I can't, gentlemen; I can't!"

They took hold of her and dragged her a few steps, but she freed herself, and sank to the floor emitting such piercing screams, that they carried her back to her chair very gently.

They reserved their opinion, but concluded, however, that she was incapacitated for work.

A Costly Outing

When Hector brought the news to his wife, she collapsed.

"We had much better take her here, it would cost us less."

"In our own house! What are you thinking of?"

"What else can we do, dear? I am sure it is no fault of mine!"

Ball-of-Fat

F OR many days now the fag-end of the army had been straggling through the town. They were not troops, but a disbanded horde. The beards of the men were long and filthy, their uniforms in tatters, and they advanced at an easy pace without flag or regiment. All seemed worn-out and back-broken, incapable of a thought or a resolution, marching by habit solely, and falling from fatigue as soon as they stopped. In short, they were a mobilized, pacific people, bending under the weight of the gun; some little squads on the alert, easy to take alarm and prompt in enthusiasm, ready to attack or to flee; and in the midst of them, some red breeches, the remains of a division broken up in a great battle; some somber artillery men in line with these varied kinds of foot soldiers; and, sometimes the brilliant helmet of a dragoon on foot who followed with difficulty the shortest march of the lines.

Some legions of free-shooters, under the heroic names of "Avengers of the Defeat," "Citizens of the Tomb," "Partakers of Death," passed in their turn with the air of bandits.

Their leaders were former cloth or grain merchants, ex-merchants in tallow or soap, warriors of circumstance, elected officers on account of their escutcheons and the length of their mustaches, covered with arms and with braid, speaking in constrained voices, discussing plans of campaign, and pretending to carry agonized France alone on their swaggering shoulders, but sometimes fearing their own soldiers, prison-birds, that were often brave at first and later proved to be plunderers and debauchees.

It was said that the Prussians were going to enter Rouen.

The National Guard who for two months had been carefully reconnoitering in the neighboring woods, shooting sometimes their own sentinels, and ready for a combat whenever a little wolf stirred in the thicket, had now returned to their firesides. Their arms, their uniforms, all the murderous accoutrements with which they had lately struck fear into the national heart for three leagues in every direction, had suddenly disappeared.

The last French soldiers finally came across the Seine to reach the Audemer bridge through Saint-Sever and Bourg-Achard; and, marching behind, on foot, between two officers of ordnance, the General, in despair, unable to do anything with these incongruous tatters, himself lost in the breaking-up of a people accustomed to conquer, and disastrously beaten, in spite of his legendary bravery.

A profound calm, a frightful, silent expectancy had spread over the city. Many of the heavy citizens, emasculated by commerce, anxiously awaited the conquerors, trembling lest their roasting spits or kitchen knives be considered arms.

All life seemed stopped; shops were closed, the streets dumb. Sometimes an inhabitant, intimidated by this silence, moved rapidly along next the walls. The agony of waiting made them wish the enemy would come.

In the afternoon of the day which followed the departure of the French troops, some uhlans, coming from one knows not where, crossed the town with celerity. Then, a little later, a black mass descended the side of St. Catharine, while two other invading bands appeared by the way of Darnetal and Boisguillaume. The advance guard of the three bodies joined one another at the same moment in Hotel de Ville square and, by all the neighboring streets, the German army continued to arrive, spreading out its battalions, making the pavement resound under their hard, rhythmic step.

Some orders of the commander, in a foreign, guttural voice, reached the houses which seemed dead and deserted, while behind closed shutters, eyes were watching these victorious men, masters of the city, of fortunes, of lives, through the "rights of war." The inhabitants, shut up in their rooms, were visited with the kind of excitement that a cataclysm, or some fatal upheaval of the earth, brings to us, against which all wisdom, all force is useless. For the same sensation is produced each time that the established order of things is overturned, when security no longer exists, and all that protect the laws of man and of nature find themselves at the mercy of unreasoning, ferocious brutality. The trembling of the earth crushing the houses and burying an entire people; a river overflowing its banks and carrying in its course the drowned peasants, carcasses of beeves, and girders snatched from roofs, or a glorious army massacring those trying to defend themselves, leading others prisoners, pillaging in the name of the Sword and thanking God to the sound of the cannon, all are alike frightful scourges which disconcert all belief in eternal justice, all the confidence that we have in the protection of Heaven and the reason of man.

Some detachments rapped at each door, then disappeared into the houses. It was occupation after invasion. Then the duty commences for the conquered to show themselves gracious toward the conquerors.

After some time, as soon as the first terror disappears, a new calm is established. In many families, the Prussian officer eats at the table. He is sometimes well bred and, through politeness, pities France, and speaks of his repugnance in taking part in this affair. One is grateful to him for this sentiment; then, one may be, some day or other, in need of his protection. By treating him well, one has, perhaps, a less number of men to feed And why should we wound anyone on whom we are entirely dependent? To act thus would be less bravery than temerity. And temerity is no longer a fault of the commoner of Rouen, as it was at the time of the heroic defense, when their city became famous. Finally, each told himself that the highest judgment of French urbanity required that they be allowed to be polite to the strange soldier in the house, provided they did not show themselves familiar with him in public. Outside they would not make themselves known to each other, but at home they could chat freely, and the German might remain longer each evening warming his feet at their hearthstones.

The town even took on, little by little, its ordinary aspect. The French scarcely went out, but the Prussian soldiers grumbled in the streets. In short, the officers of the Blue Hussars, who dragged with arrogance their great weapons of death up and down the pavement, seemed to have no more grievous scorn for the simple citizens than the officers or the sportsmen who, the year before, drank in the same *cafés*.

There was nevertheless, something in the air, something subtle and unknown, a strange, intolerable atmosphere, like a penetrating odor, the odor of invasion. It filled the dwellings and the public places, changed the taste of the food, gave the impression of being on a journey, far away, among barbarous and dangerous tribes.

The conquerors exacted money, much money. The inhabitants always paid and they were rich enough to do

it. But the richer a trading Norman becomes the more he
suffers at every outlay, at each part of his fortune that he
sees pass from his hands into those of another.

Therefore, two or three leagues below the town, following the course of the river toward Croisset, Dieppe-
dalle, or Biessart, mariners and fishermen often picked
up the swollen corpse of a German in uniform from the
bottom of the river, killed by the blow of a knife, the
head crushed with a stone, or perhaps thrown into the
water by a push from the high bridge. The slime of the
river bed buried these obscure vengeances, savage, but
legitimate, unknown heroisms, mute attacks more peril-
ous than the battles of broad day, and without the
echoing sound of glory.

For hatred of the foreigner always arouses some
intrepid ones, who are ready to die for an idea.

Finally, as soon as the invaders had brought the town
quite under subjection with their inflexible discipline,
without having been guilty of any of the horrors for
which they were famous along their triumphal line of
march, people began to take courage, and the need of
trade put new heart into the commerce of the country.
Some had large interests at Havre, which the French army
occupied, and they wished to try and reach this port by
going to Dieppe by land and there embarking.

They used their influence with the German soldiers
with whom they had an acquaintance, and finally, an
authorization of departure was obtained from the General-in-chief.

Then, a large diligence, with four horses, having
been engaged for this journey, and ten persons having
engaged seats in it, it was resolved to set out on Tuesday
morning before daylight, in order to escape observation.

For some time before, the frost had been hardening

the earth and on Monday, toward three o'clock, great black clouds coming from the north brought the snow which fell without interruption during the evening and all night.

At half past four in the morning, the travelers met in the courtyard of Hotel Normandie, where they were to take the carriage.

They were still full of sleep, and shivering with cold under their wraps. They could only see each other dimly in the obscure light, and the accumulation of heavy winter garments made them all resemble fat curates in long cassocks. Only two of the men were acquainted; a third accosted them and they chatted: "I'm going to take my wife," said one. "I too," said another. "And I," said the third. The first added: "We shall not return to Rouen, and if the Prussians approach Havre, we shall go over to England." All had the same projects, being of the same mind.

As yet the horses were not harnessed. A little lantern, carried by a stable boy, went out one door from time to time, to appear immediately at another. The feet of the horses striking the floor could be heard, although deadened by the straw and litter, and the voice of a man talking to the beasts, sometimes swearing, came from the end of the building. A light tinkling of bells announced that they were taking down the harness; this murmur soon became a clear and continuous rhythm by the movement of the animal, stopping sometimes, then breaking into a brusque shake which was accompanied by the dull stamp of a sabot upon the hard earth.

The door suddenly closed. All noise ceased. The frozen citizens were silent; they remained immovable and stiff.

A curtain of uninterrupted white flakes constantly

sparkled in its descent to the ground. It effaced forms, and powdered everything with a downy moss. And nothing could be heard in the great silence. The town was calm, and buried under the wintry frost, as this fall of snow, unnamable and floating, a sensation rather than a sound (trembling atoms which only seem to fill all space), came to cover the earth.

The man reappeared with his lantern, pulling at the end of a rope a sad horse which would not come willingly. He placed him against the pole, fastened the traces, walked about a long time adjusting the harness, for he had the use of but one hand, the other carrying the lantern. As he went for the second horse, he noticed the travelers, motionless, already white with snow, and said to them: "Why not get into the carriage? You will be under cover, at least."

They had evidently not thought of it, and they hastened to do so. The three men installed their wives at the back and then followed them. Then the other forms, undecided and veiled, took in their turn the last places without exchanging a word.

The floor was covered with straw, in which the feet ensconced themselves. The ladies at the back having brought little copper foot stoves, with a carbon fire, lighted them and, for some time, in low voices, enumerated the advantages of the appliances, repeating things that they had known for a long time.

Finally, the carriage was harnessed with six horses instead of four, because the traveling was very bad, and a voice called out:

"Is everybody aboard?"

And a voice within answered: "Yes."

They were off. The carriage moved slowly, slowly for a little way. The wheels were imbedded in the snow; the whole body groaned with heavy cracking sounds; the horses glistened, puffed, and smoked; and the great whip of the driver snapped without ceasing, hovering about on all sides, knotting and unrolling itself like a thin serpent, lashing brusquely some horse on the rebound, which then put forth its most violent effort.

Now the day was imperceptibly dawning. The light flakes, which one of the travelers, a Rouenese by birth, said looked like a shower of cotton, no longer fell. A faint light filtered through the great, dull clouds, which rendered more brilliant the white of the fields, where appeared a line of great trees clothed in whiteness, or a chimney with a cap of snow.

In the carriage, each looked at the others curiously, in the sad light of this dawn.

At the back, in the best places, Mr. Loiseau, wholesale merchant of wine, of Grand-Pont street, and Mrs. Loiseau were sleeping opposite each other. Loiseau had bought out his former patron who failed in business, and made his fortune. He sold bad wine at a good price to small retailers in the country, and passed among his friends and acquaintances as a knavish wag, a true Norman full of deceit and joviality.

His reputation as a sharper was so well established that one evening at the residence of the prefect, Mr. Tournel, author of some fables and songs, of keen, satirical mind, a local celebrity, having proposed to some ladies, who seemed to be getting a little sleepy, that they make up a game of "Loiseau tricks," the joke traversed the rooms of the prefect, reached those of the town, and then, in the months to come, made many a face in the province expand with laughter.

Loiseau was especially known for his love of farce of every kind, for his jokes, good and bad; and no one could

510

ever talk with him without thinking: "He is invaluable, this Loiseau." Of tall figure, his balloon-shaped front was surmounted by a ruddy face surrounded by gray whiskers.

His wife, large, strong, and resolute, with a quick, decisive manner, was the order and arithmetic of this house of commerce, while he was the life of it through his joyous activity.

Beside them, Mr. Carré-Lamadon held himself with great dignity, as if belonging to a superior caste; a considerable man, in cottons, proprietor of three mills, officer of the Legion of Honor, and member of the General Council. He had remained, during the Empire, chief of the friendly opposition, famous for making the Emperor pay more dear for rallying to the cause that if he had combated it with blunted arms, according to his own story. Madame Carré-Lamadon, much younger than her husband, was the consolation of officers of good family sent to Rouen in garrison. She sat opposite her husband, very dainty, petite, and pretty, wrapped closely in furs and looking with sad eyes at the interior of the carriage.

Her neighbors, the Count and Countess Hubert de Breville, bore the name of one of the most ancient and noble families of Normandy. The Count, an old gentleman of good figure, accentuated, by the artifices of his toilette, his resemblance to King Henry IV, who, following a glorious legend of the family, had impregnated one of the De Breville ladies, whose husband, for this reason, was made a count and governor of the province.

A colleague of Mr. Carré-Lamadon in the General Council, Count Hubert represented the Orléans party in the Department.

The story of his marriage with the daughter of a little captain of a privateer had always remained a mystery. But as the Countess had a grand air, received better than anyone, and passed for having been loved by the son of Louis Philippe, all the nobility did her honor, and her salon remained the first in the country, the only one which preserved the old gallantry, and to which the *entrée* was difficult. The fortune of the Brevilles amounted, it was said, to five hundred thousand francs in income, all in good securities.

These six persons formed the foundation of the carriage company, the society side, serene and strong, honest, established people, who had both religion and principles.

By a strange chance, all the women were upon the same seat; and the Countess had for neighbors two sisters who picked at long strings of beads and muttered some *Paters* and *Aves*. One was old and as pitted with smallpox as if she had received a broadside of grapeshot full in the face. The other, very sad, had a pretty face and a disease of the lungs, which, added to their devoted faith, illumined them and made them appear like martyrs.

Opposite these two devotees were a man and a woman who attracted the notice of all. The man, well known, was Cornudet the democrat, the terror of respectable people. For twenty years he had soaked his great red beard in the *bocks* of all the democratic *cafés*. He had consumed with his friends and *confrères* a rather pretty fortune left him by his father, an old confectioner, and he awaited the establishing of the Republic with impatience, that he might have the position he merited by his great expenditures. On the fourth of September, by some joke perhaps, he believed himself elected prefect, but when he went to assume the duties, the clerks of the office were masters of the place and refused to recognize him, obliging him to retreat. Rather a good bachelor, on the whole, inoffensive and serviceable, he had busied himself, with incomparable ardor, in organizing the defense against the Prussians. He had dug holes in all the plains, cut down young trees from the neighboring forests, sown snares over all routes and, at the approach of the enemy, took himself quickly back to the town. He now thought he could be of more use in Havre where more entrenchments would be necessary.

The woman, one of those called a coquette, was celebrated for her *embonpoint,* which had given her the nickname of "Ball-of-Fat." Small, round, and fat as lard, with puffy fingers choked at the phalanges, like chaplets of short sausages; with a stretched and shining skin, an enormous bosom which shook under her dress, she was, nevertheless, pleasing and sought after, on account of a certain freshness and breeziness of disposition. Her face was a round apple, a peony bud ready to pop into bloom, and inside that opened two great black eyes, shaded with thick brows that cast a shadow within; and below, a charming mouth, humid for kissing, furnished with shining, microscopic baby teeth. She was, it was said, full of admirable qualities.

As soon as she was recognized, a whisper went around among the honest women, and the words "prostitute" and "public shame" were whispered so loud that she raised her head. Then she threw at her neighbors such a provoking, courageous look that a great silence reigned, and everybody looked down except Loiseau, who watched her with an exhilarated air.

And immediately conversation began among the three ladies, whom the presence of this girl had suddenly rendered friendly, almost intimate. It seeemed to them they should bring their married dignity into union in opposition to that sold without shame; for legal love always takes on a tone of contempt for its free *confrère.*

The three men, also drawn together by an instinct

of preservation at the sight of Cornudet, talked money with a certain high tone of disdain for the poor. Count Hubert talked of the havoc which the Prussians had caused, the losses which resulted from being robbed of cattle and from destroyed crops, with the assurance of a great lord, ten times millionaire whom these ravages would scarcely cramp for a year. Mr. Carré-Lamadon, largely experienced in the cotton industry, had had need of sending six hundred thousand francs to England, as a trifle in reserve if it should be needed. As for Loiseau, he had arranged with the French administration to sell them all the wines that remained in his cellars, on account of which the State owed him a formidable sum, which he counted on collecting at Havre.

And all three threw toward each other swift and amicable glances.

Although in different conditions, they felt themselves to be brothers through money, that grand freemasonry of those who possess it, and make the gold rattle by putting their hands in their trousers' pockets.

The carriage went so slowly that at ten o'clock in the morning they had not gone four leagues. The men had got down three times to climb hills on foot. They began to be disturbed, because they should be now taking breakfast at Tôtes and they despaired now of reaching there before night. Each one had begun to watch for an inn along the route, when the carriage foundered in a snow-drift, and it took two hours to extricate it.

Growing appetites troubled their minds; and no eating-house, no wine shop showed itself, the approach of the Prussians and the passage of the troops having frightened away all these industries.

The gentlemen ran to the farms along the way for provisions, but they did not even find bread, for the defiant peasant had concealed his stores for fear of being pillaged by the soldiers who, having nothing to put between their teeth, took by force whatever they discovered.

Toward one o'clock in the afternoon, Loiseau announced that there was a decided hollow in his stomach. Everybody suffered with him, and the violent need of eating, ever increasing, had killed conversation.

From time to time some one yawned; another immediately imitated him; and each, in his turn, in accordance with his character, his knowledge of life, and his social position, opened his mouth with carelessness or modesty, placing his hand quickly before the yawning hole from whence issued a vapor.

Ball-of-Fat, after many attempts, bent down as if seeking something under her skirts. She hesitated a second, looked at her neighbors, then sat up again tranquilly. The faces were pale and drawn. Loiseau affirmed that he would give a thousand francs for a small ham. His wife made a gesture, as if in protest; but she kept quiet. She was always troubled when anyone spoke of squandering money, and could not comprehend any pleasantry on the subject. "The fact is," said the Count, "I cannot understand why I did not think to bring some provisions with me." Each reproached himself in the same way.

However, Cornudet had a flask full of rum. He offered it; it was refused coldly. Loiseau alone accepted two swallows, and then passed back the flask saying, by way of thanks: "It is good all the same; it is warming and checks the appetite." The alcohol put him in good-humor and he proposed that they do as they did on the little ship in the song, eat the fattest of the passengers. This indirect allusion to Ball-of-Fat choked the well-bred people. They said nothing. Cornudet alone laughed. The two good sisters had ceased to mumble their rosaries and, with their hands enfolded in their great sleeves held themselves immovable, obstinately lowering their eyes, without doubt offering to Heaven the suffering it had brought upon them.

Finally, at three o'clock, when they found themselves in the midst of an interminable plain, without a single village in sight, Ball-of-Fat bending down quickly drew from under the seat a large basket covered with a white napkin.

At first she brought out a little china plate and a silver cup; then a large dish in which there were two whole chickens, cut up and imbedded in their own jelly. And one could still see in the basket other good things, some *pâtés*, fruits, and sweetmeats, provisions for three days if they should not see the kitchen of an inn. Four necks of bottles were seen among the packages of food. She took a wing of a chicken and began to eat it delicately, with one of those little biscuits called "Regence" in Normandy.

All looks were turned in her direction. Then the odor spread, enlarging the nostrils and making the mouth water, besides causing a painful contraction of the jaw behind the ears. The scorn of the women for this girl became ferocious, as if they had a desire to kill her and throw her out of the carriage into the snow, her, her silver cup, her basket, provisions and all.

But Loiseau with his eyes devoured the dish of chicken. He said: "Fortunately, Madame had more precaution than we. There are some people who know how to think ahead always."

She turned toward him, saying: "If you would like some of it, sir? It is hard to go without breakfast so long."

He saluted her and replied: "Faith, I frankly cannot refuse; I can stand it no longer. Everything goes in time of war, does it not, Madame?" And then casting a comprehensive glance around, he added: "In moments like this, one can but be pleased to find people who are obliging."

He had a newspaper which he spread out on his knees, that no spot might come to his pantaloons, and upon the point of a knife that he always carried in his pocket, he took up a leg all glistening with jelly, put it between his teeth and masticated it with a satisfaction so evident that there ran through the carriage a great sigh of distress.

Then Ball-of-Fat, in a sweet and humble voice, proposed that the two sisters partake of her collation. They both accepted instantly and, without raising their eyes, began to eat very quickly, after stammering their thanks. Cornudet no longer refused the offers of his neighbor, and they formed with the sisters a sort of table, by spreading out some newspapers upon their knees.

The mouths opened and shut without ceasing, they masticated, swallowed, gulping ferociously. Loiseau in his corner was working hard and, in a low voice, was trying to induce his wife to follow his example. She resisted for a long time; then, when a drawn sensation ran through her body, she yielded. Her husband, rounding his phrase, asked their "charming companion" if he might be allowed to offer a little piece to Madame Loiseau.

She replied: "Why, yes, certainly, sir," with an amiable smile, as she passed the dish.

An embarrassing thing confronted them when they opened the first bottle of Bordeaux: they had but one cup. Each passed it after having tasted. Cornudet alone, for politeness without doubt, placed his lips at the spot left humid by his fair neighbor.

Then, surrounded by people eating, suffocated by the odors of the food, the Count and Countess de Breville, as well as Madame and M. Carré-Lamadon, were suffering that odious torment which has preserved the name of Tantalus. Suddenly the young wife of the manufacturer gave forth such a sigh that all heads were turned in her direction; she was white as the snow without; her eyes closed, her head drooped; she had lost consciousness. Her husband, much excited, implored the help of everybody. Each lost his head completely, until the elder of the two sisters, holding the head of the sufferer, slipped Ball-of-Fat's cup between her lips and forced her to swallow a few drops of wine. The pretty little lady revived, opened her eyes, smiled, and declared in a dying voice that she felt very well now. But, in order that the attack might not return, the sister urged her to drink a full glass of Bordeaux, and added: "It is just hunger, nothing more."

Then Ball-of-Fat, blushing and embarrassed, looked at the four travelers who had fasted and stammered: "Goodness knows! if I dared to offer anything to these gentlemen and ladies, I would—" Then she was silent, as if fearing an insult. Loiseau took up the word: "Ah! certainly, in times like these all the world are brothers and ought to aid each other. Come, ladies, without ceremony; why the devil not accept? We do not know whether we shall even find a house where we can pass the night. At the pace we are going now, we shall not reach Tôtes before noon tomorrow—"

They still hesitated, no one daring to assume the responsibility of a "Yes." The Count decided the question. He turned toward the fat, intimidated girl and, taking on a grand air of condescension, he said to her:

"We accept with gratitude, Madame."

It is the first step that counts. The Rubicon passed.

one lends himself to the occasion squarely. The basket was stripped. It still contained a *pâté de foie gras,* a *pâté* of larks, a piece of smoked tongue, some preserved pears, a loaf of hard bread, some wafers, and a full cup of pickled gherkins and onions, of which crudities Ball-of-Fat, like all women, was extremely fond.

They could not eat this girl's provisions without speaking to her. And so they chatted, with reserve at first; then, as she carried herself well, with more abandon. The ladies De Breville and Carré-Lamadon, who were acquainted with all the ins and outs of good-breeding, were gracious with a certain delicacy. The Countess, especially, showed that amiable condescension of very noble ladies who do not fear being soiled by contact with anyone, and was charming. But the great Madame Loiseau, who had the soul of a plebeian, remained crabbed, saying little and eating much.

The conversation was about the war, naturally. They related the horrible deeds of the Prussians, the brave acts of the French; and all of them, although running away, did homage to those who stayed behind. Then personal stories began to be told, and Ball-of-Fat related, with sincere emotion, and in the heated words that such girls sometimes use in expressing their natural feelings, how she had left Rouen:

"I believed at first that I could remain," said she. "I had my house full of provisions, and I preferred to feed a few soldiers rather than expatriate myself, to go I knew not where. But as soon as I saw them, those Prussians, that was too much for me! They made my blood boil with anger, and I wept for very shame all day long. Oh! if I were only a man! I watched them from my windows, the great porkers with their pointed helmets, and my maid held my hands to keep me from throwing the furniture down upon them. Then one of them came to lodge at my house; I sprang at his throat the first thing; they are no more difficult to strangle than other people. And I should have put an end to that one then and there had they not pulled me away by the hair. After that, it was necessary to keep out of sight. And finally, when I found an opportunity, I left town and—here I am!"

They congratulated her. She grew in the estimation of her companions, who had not shown themselves so hot-brained, and Cornudet, while listening to her, took on the approving, benevolent smile of an apostle, as a priest would if he heard a devotee praise God, for the long-bearded democrats have a monopoly of patriotism, as the men in cassocks have of religion. In his turn he spoke, in a doctrinal tone, with the emphasis of a proclamation such as we see pasted on the walls about town, and finished by a bit of eloquence whereby he gave that "scamp of a Badinguet" a good lashing.

Then Ball-of-Fat was angry, for she was a Bona-partist. She grew redder than a cherry and, stammering with indignation, said:

"I would like to have seen you in his place, you other people. Then everything would have been quite right; oh, yes! It is you who have betrayed this man! One would never have had to leave France if it had been governed by blackguards like you!"

Cornudet, undisturbed, preserved a disdainful, supe-rior smile, but all felt that the high note had been struck, until the Count, not without some difficulty, calmed the exasperated girl and proclaimed with a manner of au-thority that all sincere opinions should be respected. But the Countess and the manufacturer's wife, who had in their souls an unreasonable hatred for the people that favor a Republic, and the same instinctive tenderness that all women have for a decorative, despotic government, felt themselves drawn, in spite of themselves, toward this prostitute so full of dignity, whose sentiments so strongly resembled their own.

The basket was empty. By ten o'clock they had easily exhausted the contents and regretted that there was not more. Conversation continued for some time, but a little more coldly since they had finished eating.

The night fell, the darkness little by little became profound, and the cold, felt more during digestion, made Ball-of-Fat shiver in spite of her plumpness. Then Madame de Breville offered her the little footstove, in which the fuel had been renewed many times since morning; she accepted it immediately, for her feet were becoming numb with cold. The ladies Carré-Lamadon and Loiseau gave theirs to the two religious sisters.

The driver had lighted his lanterns. They shone out with a lively glimmer showing a cloud of foam beyond, the sweat of the horses; and, on both sides of the way, the snow seemed to roll itself along under the moving reflection of the lights.

Inside the carriage one could distinguish nothing. But a sudden movement seemed to be made between Ball-of-Fat and Cornudet; and Loiseau, whose eye penetrated the shadow, believed that he saw the big-bearded man start back quickly as if he had received a swift, noiseless blow.

Then some twinkling points of fire appeared in the distance along the road. It was Tôtes. They had traveled eleven hours, which, with the two hours given to resting and feeding the horses, made thirteen. They entered the town and stopped before the Hotel Commerce.

The carriage door opened! A well-known sound gave the travelers a start; it was the scabbard of a sword hitting the ground. Immediately a German voice was heard in the darkness.

Although the diligence was not moving, no one offered to alight, fearing some one might be waiting to murder them as they stepped out. Then the conductor appeared, holding in his hand one of the lanterns which lighted the carriage to its depth, and showed the two rows of frightened faces, whose mouths were open and whose eyes were wide with surprise and fear.

Outside beside the driver, in plain sight, stood a German officer, an excessively tall young man, thin and blond, squeezed into his uniform like a girl in a corset, and wearing on his head a flat, oilcloth cap which made him resemble the porter of an English hotel. His enormous mustache, of long straight hairs, growing gradually thin at each side and terminating in a single blond thread so fine that one could not perceive where it ended, seemed to weigh heavily on the corners of his mouth and, drawing down the cheeks, left a decided wrinkle about the lips.

In Alsatian French, he invited the travelers to come in, saying in a suave tone: "Will you descend, gentlemen and ladies?"

The two good sisters were the first to obey, with the docility of saints accustomed ever to submission. The Count and Countess then appeared, followed by the manufacturer and his wife; then Loiseau, pushing ahead of him his larger half. The last-named, as he set foot on the earth, said to the officer: "Good evening, sir," more as a measure of prudence than politeness. The officer, insolent as all-powerful people usually are, looked at him without a word.

Ball-of-Fat and Cornudet, although nearest the door, were the last to descend, grave and haughty before the enemy. The fat girl tried to control herself and be calm. The democrat waved a tragic hand and his long beard seemed to tremble a little and grow redder. They wished to preserve their dignity, comprehending that in such meetings as these they represented in some degree their great country, and somewhat disgusted with the docility of her companions, the fat girl tried to show more pride than her neighbors, the honest women, and, as she felt that some one should set an example, she continued her attitude of resistance assumed at the beginning of the journey.

They entered the vast kitchen of the inn, and the German, having demanded their traveling papers signed by the General-in-chief (in which the name, the description, and profession of each traveler was mentioned), and having examined them all critically, comparing the people and their signatures, said: "It is quite right," and went out.

Then they breathed. They were still hungry and supper was ordered. A half hour was necessary to prepare it, and while two servants were attending to this they went to their rooms. They found them along a corridor which terminated in a large glazed door.

Finally, they sat down at table, when the proprietor of the inn himself appeared. He was a former horse merchant, a large, asthmatic man, with a constant wheezing and rattling in his throat. His father had left him the name of Follenvie. He asked:

"Is Miss Elizabeth Rousset here?"

Ball-of-Fat started as she answered: "It is I."

"The Prussian officer wishes to speak with you immediately."

"With me?"

"Yes, that is, if you are Miss Elizabeth Rousset."

She was disturbed, and reflecting for an instant, declared flatly:

"That is my name, but I shall not go."

A stir was felt around her; each discussed and tried to think of the cause of this order. The Count approached her, saying:

"You are wrong, Madame, for your refusal may lead to considerable difficulty, not only for yourself, but for all your companions. It is never worth while to resist those in power. This request cannot assuredly bring any danger; it is, without doubt, about some forgotten formality."

Everybody agreed with him, asking, begging, beseeching her to go, and at last they convinced her that it was best; they all feared the complications that might result from disobedience. She finally said:

"It is for you that I do this, you understand."

The Countess took her by the hand, saying: "And we are grateful to you for it."

She went out. They waited before sitting down at table.

Each one regretted not having been sent for in the place of this violent, irascible girl, and mentally prepared some platitudes, in case they should be called in their turn.

But at the end of ten minutes she reappeared, out of breath, red to suffocation, and exasperated. She stammered: "Oh! the rascal! the rascal!"

All gathered around to learn something, but she said nothing; and when the Count insisted, she responded with great dignity: "No, it does not concern you; I can say nothing."

Then they all seated themselves around a high soup tureen whence came the odor of cabbage. In spite of alarm, the supper was gay. The cider was good, the beverage Loiseau and the good sisters took as a means of economy. The others called for wine; Cornudet demanded beer. He had a special fashion of uncorking the bottle, making froth on the liquid, carefully filling the glass and then holding it before the light to better appreciate the color. When he drank, his great beard, which still kept some of the foam of his beloved beverage, seemed to tremble with tenderness; his eyes were squinted, in order not to lose sight of his tipple, and he had the unique air of fulfilling the function for which he was born. One would say that there was in his mind a meeting, like that of affinities, between the two great passions that occupied his life—Pale Ale and Revolutions; and assuredly he could not taste the one without thinking of the other.

Mr. and Mrs. Follenvie dined at the end of the table. The man, rattling like a cracked locomotive, had too much trouble in breathing to talk while eating, but his wife was never silent. She told all her impressions at the arrival of the Prussians, what they did, what they said, reviling them because they cost her some money, and because she had two sons in the army. She addressed herself especially to the Countess, flattered by being able to talk with a lady of quality.

When she lowered her voice to say some delicate thing, her husband would interrupt, from time to time, with: "You had better keep silent, Madame Follenvie." But she paid no attention, continuing in this fashion:

"Yes, Madame, those people there not only eat our potatoes and pork, but our pork and potatoes. And it must not be believed that they are at all proper—oh, no! such filthy things they do, saving the respect I owe to you! And if you could see them exercise for hours in the day! They are all there in the field, marching ahead, then marching back, turning here and turning there. They might be cultivating the land, or at least working on the roads of their own country! But no, Madame, these military men are profitable to no one. Poor people have to feed them, or perhaps be murdered! I am only an old woman without education, it is true, but when I see some endangering their constitutions by raging from morning to night, I say: When there are so many people found to be useless, how unnecessary it is for others to take so much trouble to be nuisances! Truly, is it not an abomination to kill people, whether they be Prussian, or English, or Polish, or French? If one man revenges himself upon another who has done him some injury, it is wicked and he is punished; but when they exterminate our boys, as if they were game, with guns, they give decorations, indeed, to the one who destroys the most! Now, you see, I can never understand that, never!"

Cornudet raised his voice: "War is a barbarity when one attacks a peaceable neighbor, but a sacred duty when one defends his country."

The old woman lowered her head:

"Yes, when one defends himself, it is another thing; but why not make it a duty to kill all the kings who make these wars for their pleasure?"

Cornudet's eyes flashed. "Bravo, my country-woman!" said he.

Mr. Carré-Lamadon reflected profoundly. Although he was prejudiced as a Captain of Industry, the good sense of this peasant woman made him think of the opulence that would be brought into the country were the idle and consequently mischievous hands, and the troops which were now maintained in unproductiveness, employed in some great industrial work that it would require centuries to achieve.

Loiseau, leaving his place, went to speak with the innkeeper in a low tone of voice. The great man laughed, shook, and squeaked, his corpulence quivered with joy at the jokes of his neighbor, and he bought of him six cases of wine for spring, after the Prussians had gone.

As soon as supper was finished, as they were worn out with fatigue, they retired.

However, Loiseau, who had observed things, after getting his wife to bed, glued his eye and then his ear to a hole in the wall, to try and discover what are known as "the mysteries of the corridor."

At the end of about an hour, he heard a groping, and, looking quickly, he perceived Ball-of-Fat, who appeared still more plump in a blue cashmere negligée trimmed with white lace. She had a candle in her hand and was directing her steps toward the great door at the end of the corridor. But a door at the side opened, and when she returned at the end of some minutes Cornudet, in his suspenders, followed her. They spoke low, then they stopped. Ball-of-Fat seemed to be defending the entrance to her room with energy. Loiseau, unfortunately, could not hear all their words, but, finally, as they raised their voices, he was able to catch a few. Cornudet insisted with vivacity. He said:

"Come, now, you are a silly woman; what harm can be done?"

She had an indignant air in responding: "No, my dear, there are moments when such things are out of place. Here it would be a shame."

He doubtless did not comprehend and asked why, Then she cried out, raising her voice still more:

"Why? You do not see why? When there are Prussians in the house, in the very next room, perhaps?"

He was silent. This patriotic shame of the harlot, who would not suffer his caress so near the enemy, must have awakened the latent dignity in his heart, for after simply kissing her, he went back to his own door with a bound.

Loiseau, much excited, left the aperture, cut a caper in his room, put on his pajamas, turned back the clothes that covered the bony carcass of his companion, whom he awakened with a kiss, murmuring: "Do you love me, dearie?"

Then all the house was still. And immediately there arose somewhere, from an uncertain quarter, which might be the cellar but was quite as likely to be the garret, a powerful snoring, monotonous and regular, a heavy, prolonged sound, like a great kettle under pressure. Mr. Follenvie was asleep.

As they had decided that they would set out at eight o'clock the next morning, they all collected in the kitchen. But the carriage, the roof of which was covered with snow, stood undisturbed in the courtyard, without horses and without a conductor. They sought him in vain in the stables, in the hay, and in the coach-house. Then they resolved to scour the town, and started out. They found themselves in a square, with a church at one end and some low houses on either side, where they perceived some Prussian soldiers. The first one they saw was paring potatoes. The second, further off, was cleaning the hair-dresser's shop. Another, bearded to the eyes, was tending a troublesome brat, cradling it and trying to appease it; and the great peasant women, whose husbands were "away in the army," indicated by signs to their obedient conquerors the work they wished to have done: cutting wood, cooking the soup, grinding the coffee, or what not. One of them even washed the linen of his hostess, an impotent old grandmother.

The Count, astonished, asked questions of the beadle who came out of the rectory. The old man responded:

"Oh! those men are not wicked; they are not the Prussians we hear about. They are from far off, I know not where; and they have left wives and children in their country; it is not amusing to them, this war, I can tell you! I am sure they also weep for their homes, and that it makes as much sorrow among them as it does among us. Here, now, there is not so much unhappiness for the moment, because the soldiers do no harm and they work as if they were in their own homes. You see, sir, among poor people it is necessary that they aid one another. These are the great traits which war develops."

Cornudet, indignant at the cordial relations between the conquerors and the conquered, preferred to shut himself up in the inn. Loiseau had a joke for the occasion: "They will repeople the land."

Mr. Carré-Lamadon had a serious word: "They try to make amends."

But they did not find the driver. Finally, they discovered him in a *café* of the village, sitting at table fraternally with the officer of ordnance. The Count called out to him:

"Were you not ordered to be ready at eight o'clock?"

"Well, yes; but another order has been given me since."

"By whom?"

"Faith! the Prussian commander."

"What was it?"

"Not to harness at all."

"Why?"

"I know nothing about it. Go and ask him. They tell me not to harness, and I don't harness. That's all."

"Did he give you the order himself?"

"No, sir, the innkeeper gave the order for him."

"When was that?"

"Last evening, as I was going to bed."

The three men returned, much disturbed. They asked for Mr. Follenvie, but the servant answered that that gentleman, because of his asthma, never rose before ten o'clock. And he had given strict orders not to be wakened before that, except in case of fire.

They wished to see the officer, but that was absolutely impossible, since, while he lodged at the inn, Mr. Follenvie alone was authorized to speak to him upon civil affairs. So they waited. The women went up to their rooms again and occupied themselves with futile tasks.

Cornudet installed himself near the great chimney in the kitchen, where there was a good fire burning. He ordered one of the little tables to be brought from the *café*, then a can of beer, he then drew out his pipe, which plays among democrats a part almost equal to his own, because in serving Cornudet it was serving its country. It was a superb pipe, an admirably colored meerschaum, as black as the teeth of its master, but perfumed, curved, glistening, easy to the hand, completing his physiognomy. And he remained motionless, his eyes as much fixed upon the flame of the fire as upon his favorite tipple and its frothy crown; and each time that he drank, he passed his long, thin fingers through his scanty, gray hair, with an air of satisfaction, after which he sucked in his mustache fringed with foam.

Loiseau, under the pretext of stretching his legs, went to place some wine among the retailers of the coun-

try. The Count and the manufacturer began to talk politics. They could foresee the future of France. One of them believed in an Orléans, the other in some unknown savior for the country, a hero who would reveal himself when all were in despair: a Guesclin, or a Joan of Arc, perhaps, or would it be another Napoleon First? Ah! if the Prince Imperial were not so young!

Cornudet listened to them and smiled like one who holds the word of destiny. His pipe perfumed the kitchen.

As ten o'clock struck, Mr. Follenvie appeared. They asked him hurried questions; but he could only repeat two or three times without variation, these words:

"The officer said to me: 'Mr. Follenvie, you see to it that the carriage is not harnessed for those travelers to-morrow. I do not wish them to leave without my order. That is sufficient.'"

Then they wished to see the officer. The Count sent him his card, on which Mr. Carré-Lamadon wrote his name and all his titles. The Prussian sent back word that he would meet the two gentlemen after he had breakfasted, that is to say, about one o'clock.

The ladies reappeared and ate a little something, despite their disquiet. Ball-of-Fat seemed ill and prodigiously troubled.

They were finishing their coffee when the word came that the officer was ready to meet the gentlemen. Loiseau joined them; but when they tried to enlist Cornudet, to give more solemnity to their proceedings, he declared proudly that he would have nothing to do with the Germans; and he betook himself to his chimney corner and ordered another liter of beer.

The three men mounted the staircase and were introduced to the best room of the inn, where the officer

received them, stretched out in an armchair, his feet on the mantelpiece, smoking a long, porcelain pipe, and enveloped in a flamboyant dressing-gown, appropriated, without doubt, from some dwelling belonging to a common citizen of bad taste. He did not rise, nor greet them in any way, not even looking at them. It was a magnificent display of natural blackguardism transformed into the military victor.

At the expiration of some moments, he asked: "What is it you wish?"

The Count became spokesman: "We desire to go on our way, sir."

"No."

"May I ask the cause of this refusal?"

"Because I do not wish it."

"But, I would respectfully observe to you, sir, that your General-in-chief gave us permission to go to Dieppe; and I know of nothing we have done to merit your severity."

"I do not wish it—that is all; you can go."

All three having bowed, retired.

The afternoon was lamentable. They could not understand this caprice of the German; and the most singular ideas would come into their heads to trouble them. Everybody stayed in the kitchen and discussed the situation endlessly, imagining all sorts of unlikely things. Perhaps they would be retained as hostages—but to what end?—or taken prisoners—or rather a considerable ransom might be demanded. At this thought a panic prevailed. The richest were the most frightened, already seeing themselves constrained to pay for their lives with sacks of gold poured into the hands of this insolent soldier. They racked their brains to think of some acceptable falsehoods to conceal their riches and make

them pass themselves off for poor people, very poor people. Loiseau took off the chain to his watch and hid it away in his pocket. The falling night increased their apprehensions. The lamp was lighted, and as there was still two hours before dinner, Madame Loiseau proposed a game of Thirty-one. It would be a diversion. They accepted. Cornudet himself, having smoked out his pipe, took part for politeness.

The Count shuffled the cards, dealt, and Ball-of-Fat had thirty-one at the outset; and immediately the interest was great enough to appease the fear that haunted their minds. Then Cornudet perceived that the house of Loiseau was given to tricks.

As they were going to the dinner table, Mr. Follenvie again appeared, and, in wheezing, rattling voice, announced:

"The Prussian officer orders me to ask Miss Elizabeth Rousset if she has yet changed her mind."

Ball-of-Fat remained standing and was pale; then suddenly becoming crimson, such a stifling anger took possession of her that she could not speak. But finally she flashed out: "You may say to the dirty beast, that idiot, that carrion of a Prussian, that I shall never change it; you understand, never, never, never!"

The great innkeeper went out. Then Ball-of-Fat was immediately surrounded, questioned, and solicited by all to disclose the mystery of his visit. She resisted, at first, but soon becoming exasperated, she said: "What does he want? You really want to know what he wants? He wants to sleep with me."

Everybody was choked for words, and indignation was rife. Cornudet broke his glass, so violently did he bring his fist down upon the table. There was a clamor of censure against this ignoble soldier, a blast of anger, a union of all for resistance, as if a demand had been made on each one of the party for the sacrifice exacted of her. The Count declared with disgust that those people conducted themselves after the fashion of the ancient barbarians. The women, especially, showed to Ball-of-Fat a most energetic and tender commiseration. The good sisters who only showed themselves at meal-time, lowered their heads and said nothing.

They all dined, nevertheless, when the first *furore* had abated. But there was little conversation; they were thinking.

The ladies retired early, and the men, all smoking, organized a game of cards to which Mr. Follenvie was invited, as they intended to put a few casual questions to him on the subject of conquering the resistance of this officer. But he thought of nothing but the cards and, without listening or answering, would keep repeating: "To the game, sirs, to the game." His attention was so taken that he even forgot to expectorate, which must have put him some points to the good with the organ in his breast. His whistling lungs ran the whole asthmatic scale, from deep, profound tones to the sharp rustiness of a young cock essaying to crow.

He even refused to retire when his wife, who had fallen asleep previously, came to look for him. She went away alone, for she was an "early bird," always up with the sun, while her husband was a "night owl," always ready to pass the night with his friends. He cried out to her: "Leave my creamed chicken before the fire!" and then went on with his game. When they saw that they could get nothing from him, they declared that it was time to stop, and each sought his bed.

They all rose rather early the next day, with an un-defined hope of getting away, which desire the terror of passing another day in that horrible inn greatly increased.

Alas! the horses remained in the stable and the driver was invisible. For want of better employment, they went out and walked around the carriage.

The breakfast was very doleful; and it became apparent that a coldness had arisen toward Ball-of-Fat, and that the night, which brings counsel, had slightly modified their judgments. They almost wished now that the Prussian had secretly found this girl, in order to give her companions a pleasant surprise in the morning. What could be more simple? Besides, who would know anything about it? She could save appearances by telling the officer that she took pity on their distress. To her, it would make so little difference!

No one had avowed these thoughts yet.

In the afternoon, as they were almost perishing from *ennui,* the Count proposed that they take a walk around the village. Each wrapped up warmly and the little party set out, with the exception of Cornudet, who preferred to remain near the fire, and the good sisters, who passed their time in the church or at the curate's.

The cold, growing more intense every day, cruelly pinched their noses and ears; their feet became so numb that each step was torture; and when they came to a field it seemed to them frightfully sad under this limitless white, so that everybody returned immediately, with hearts hard pressed and souls congealed.

The four women walked ahead, the three gentlemen followed just behind. Loiseau, who understood the situation, asked suddenly if they thought that girl there was going to keep them long in such a place as this. The Count, always courteous, said that they could not exact from a woman a sacrifice so hard, unless it should come of her own will. Mr. Carré-Lamadon remarked that if the French made their return through Dieppe, as they were likely to, a battle would surely take place at Tôtes. This reflection made the two others anxious.

"If we could only get away on foot," said Loiseau.

The Count shrugged his shoulders: "How can we think of it in this snow? and with our wives?" he said. "And then, we should be pursued and caught in ten minutes and led back prisoners at the mercy of these soldiers."

It was true, and they were silent.

The ladies talked of their clothes, but a certain constraint seemed to disunite them. Suddenly at the end of the street, the officer appeared. His tall, wasp-like figure in uniform was outlined upon the horizon formed by the snow, and he was marching with knees apart, a gait particularly military, which is affected that they may not spot their carefully blackened boots.

He bowed in passing near the ladies and looked disdainfully at the men, who preserved their dignity by not seeing him, except Loiseau, who made a motion toward raising his hat.

Ball-of-Fat reddened to the ears, and the three married women resented the great humiliation of being thus met by this soldier in the company of this girl whom he had treated so cavalierly.

But they spoke of him, of his figure and his face. Madame Carré-Lamadon, who had known many officers and considered herself a connoisseur of them, found this one not at all bad; she regretted even that he was not French, because he would make such a pretty hussar, one all the women would rave over.

Again in the house, no one knew what to do. Some sharp words, even, were said about things very insignificant. The dinner was silent, and almost immediately after it, each one went to his room to kill time in sleep.

They descended the next morning with weary faces and exasperated hearts. The women scarcely spoke to Ball-of-Fat.

A bell began to ring. It was for a baptism. The fat girl had a child being brought up among the peasants of Yvetot. She had not seen it for a year, or thought of it; but now the idea of a child being baptized threw into her heart a sudden and violent tenderness for her own, and she strongly wished to be present at the ceremony.

As soon as she was gone, everybody looked at each other, then pulled their chairs together, for they thought that finally something should be decided upon. Loiseau had an inspiration: it was to hold Ball-of-Fat alone and let the others go.

Mr. Follenvie was charged with the commission, but he returned almost immediately, for the German, who understood human nature, had put him out. He pretended that he would retain everybody so long as his desire was not satisfied.

Then the commonplace nature of Mrs. Loiseau burst out with:

"Well, we are not going to stay here to die of old age. Since it is the trade of this creature to accommodate herself to all kinds, I fail to see how she has the right to refuse one more than another. I can tell you she has received all she could find in Rouen, even the coachmen! Yes, Madame, the prefect's coachman! I know him very well, for he bought his wine at our house. And to think that today we should be drawn into this embarrassment by this affected woman, this minx! For my part, I find that this officer conducts himself very well. He has perhaps suffered privations for a long time; and doubtless he would have preferred us three; but no, he is contented with common property. He respects married women. And we must remember too that he is master. He has only to say 'I wish,' and he could take us by force with his soldiers."

The two women had a cold shiver. Pretty Mrs. Carré-Lamadon's eyes grew brilliant and she became a little pale, as if she saw herself already taken by force by the officer.

The men met and discussed the situation. Loiseau, furious, was for delivering "the wretch" bound hand and foot to the enemy. But the Count, descended through three generations of ambassadors, and endowed with the temperament of a diplomatist, was the advocate of ingenuity.

"It is best to decide upon something," said he. Then they conspired.

The women kept together, the tone of their voices was lowered, each gave advice and the discussion was general. Everything was very harmonious. The ladies especially found delicate shades and charming subtleties of expression for saying the most unusual things. A stranger would have understood nothing, so great was the precaution of language observed. But the light edge of modesty, with which every woman of the world is barbed, only covers the surface; they blossom out in a scandalous adventure of this kind, being deeply amused and feeling themselves in their element, mixing love with sensuality as a greedy cook prepares supper for his master.

Even gaiety returned, so funny did the whole story seem to them at last. The Count found some of the jokes a little off color, but they were so well told that he was forced to smile. In his turn, Loiseau came out with some still bolder tales, and yet nobody was wounded. The brutal thought, expressed by his wife, dominated all minds: "Since it is her trade, why should she refuse this one more than another?" The genteel Mrs. Carré-Lamadon seemed to think that in her place, she would refuse this one less than some others.

They prepared the blockade at length, as if they were about to surround a fortress. Each took some rôle to play, some arguments he would bring to bear, some maneuvers that he would endeavor to put into execution. They decided on the plan of attack, the ruse to employ, the surprise of assault, that should force this living citadel to receive the enemy in her room.

Cornudet remained apart from the rest, and was a stranger to the whole affair.

So entirely were their minds distracted that they did not hear Ball-of-Fat enter. The Count uttered a light "Ssh!" which turned all eyes in her direction. There she was. The abrupt silence and a certain embarrassment hindered them from speaking to her at first. The Countess, more accustomed to the duplicity of society than the others, finally inquired:

"Was it very amusing, that baptism?"

The fat girl, filled with emotion, told them all about it, the faces, the attitudes, and even the appearance of the church. She added: "It is good to pray sometimes."

And up to the time for luncheon these ladies continued to be amiable toward her, in order to increase her docility and her confidence in their counsel. At the table they commenced the approach. This was in the shape of a vague conversation upon devotion. They cited ancient examples: Judith and Holophernes, then, without reason, Lucrece and Sextus, and Cleopatra obliging all the generals of the enemy to pass by her couch and reducing them in servility to slaves. Then they brought out a fantastic story, hatched in the imagination of these ignorant millionaires, where the women of Rome went to Capua for the purpose of lulling Hannibal to sleep in their arms, and his lieutenants and phalanxes of mercenaries as well. They cited all the women who have been taken by conquering armies, making a battlefield of their bodies, making them also a weapon, and a means of success; and all those hideous and detestable beings who have conquered by their heroic caresses, and sacrificed their chastity to vengeance or a beloved cause. They even spoke in veiled terms of that great English family which allowed one of its women to be inoculated with a horrible and contagious disease in order to transmit it to Bonaparte, who was miraculously saved by a sudden illness at the hour of the fatal rendezvous.

And all this was related in an agreeable, temperate fashion, except as it was enlivened by the enthusiasm deemed proper to excite emulation.

One might finally have believed that the sole duty of woman here below was a sacrifice of her person, and a continual abandonment to soldierly caprices.

The two good sisters seemed not to hear, lost as they were in profound thought. Ball-of-Fat said nothing.

During the whole afternoon they let her reflect. But, in the place of calling her "Madame" as they had up to this time, they simply called her "Mademoiselle" without knowing exactly why, as if they had a desire to put her down a degree in their esteem, which she had taken by storm, and make her feel her shameful situation.

The moment supper was served, Mr. Follenvie appeared with his old phrase: "The Prussian officer orders me to ask if Miss Elizabeth Rousset has yet changed her mind."

Ball-of-Fat responded dryly: "No, sir."

But at dinner the coalition weakened. Loiseau made three unhappy remarks. Each one beat his wits for new examples but found nothing; when the Countess, without premeditation, perhaps feeling some vague need of rendering homage to religion, asked the elder of the good sisters to tell them some great deeds in the lives of the saints. It appeared that many of their acts would have been considered crimes in our eyes; but the Church gave absolution of them readily, since they were done for the glory of God, or for the good of all. It was a powerful argument; the Countess made the most of it.

Thus it may be by one of those tacit understandings, or the veiled complacency in which anyone who wears the ecclesiastical garb excels, it may be simply from the effect of a happy unintelligence, a helpful stupidity, but in fact the religious sister lent a formidable support to the conspiracy. They had thought her timid, but she showed herself courageous, verbose, even violent. She was not troubled by the chatter of the casuist; her doctrine seemed a bar of iron; her faith never hesitated; her conscience had no scruples. She found the sacrifice of Abraham perfectly simple, for she would immediately kill father or mother on an order from on high. And nothing, in her opinion, could displease the Lord, if the intention was laudable. The Countess put to use the authority of her unwitting accomplice, and added to it the edifying paraphrase and axiom of Jesuit morals: "The end justifies the means."

Then she asked her: "Then, my sister, do you think that God accepts intentions, and pardons the deed when the motive is pure?"

"Who could doubt it, Madame? An action blamable in itself often becomes meritorious by the thought it springs from."

And they continued thus, unraveling the will of God, foreseeing his decisions, making themselves interested in things that, in truth, they would never think of noticing. All this was guarded, skillful, discreet. But each word of the saintly sister in a cap helped to break down the resistance of the unworthy courtesan. Then the conversation changed a little, the woman of the chaplet speaking of the houses of her order, of her Superior, of herself, of her dainty neighbor, the dear sister Saint-Nicephore. They had been called to the hospitals of Havre to care for the hundreds of soldiers stricken with smallpox. They depicted these miserable creatures, giving details of the malady. And while they were stopped, *en route,* by the caprice of this Prussian officer, a great number of Frenchmen might die, whom perhaps they could have saved! It was a specialty with her, caring for soldiers. She had been in Crimea, in Italy, in Austria, and, in telling of her campaigns, she revealed herself as one of those religious aids to drums and trumpets, who seem made to follow camps, pick up the wounded in the thick of battle, and, better than an officer, subdue with a word great bands of undisciplined recruits. A true, good sister of the rataplan, whose ravaged face, marked with innumerable scars, appeared the image of the devastation of war.

No one could speak after her, so excellent seemed the effect of her words.

As soon as the repast was ended they quickly went up to their rooms, with the purpose of not coming down the next day until late in the morning.

The luncheon was quiet. They had given the grain

of seed time to germinate and bear fruit. The Countess proposed that they take a walk in the afternoon. The Count, being agreeably inclined, gave an arm to Ball-of-Fat and walked behind the others with her. He talked to her in a familiar, paternal tone, a little disdainful, after the manner of men having girls in their employ, calling her "my dear child," from the height of his social position, of his undisputed honor. He reached the vital part of the question at once:

"Then you prefer to leave us here, exposed to the violences which follow a defeat, rather than consent to a favor which you have so often given in your life?"

Ball-of-Fat answered nothing.

Then he tried to reach her through gentleness, reason, and then the sentiments. He knew how to remain "The Count," even while showing himself gallant or complimentary, or very amiable if it became necessary. He exalted the service that she would render them, and spoke of their appreciation; then suddenly became gaily familiar, and said:

"And you know, my dear, it would be something for him to boast of that he had known a pretty girl; something it is difficult to find in his country."

Ball-of-Fat did not answer but joined the rest of the party. As soon as they entered the house she went to her room and did not appear again. The disquiet was extreme. What were they to do? If she continued to resist, what an embarrassment!

The dinner hour struck. They waited in vain. Mr. Follenvie finally entered and said that Miss Rousset was indisposed, and would not be at the table. Everybody pricked up his ears. The Count went to the innkeeper and said in a low voice:

"Is he in there?"

"Yes."

For convenience, he said nothing to his companions, but made a slight sign with his head. Immediately a great sigh of relief went up from every breast and a light appeared in their faces. Loiseau cried out:

"Holy Christopher! I pay for the champagne, if there is any to be found in the establishment." And Mrs. Loiseau was pained to see the proprietor return with four quart bottles in his hands.

Each one had suddenly become communicative and buoyant. A wanton joy filled their hearts. The Count suddenly perceived that Mrs. Carré-Lamadon was charming, the manufacturer paid compliments to the Countess. The conversation was lively, gay, full of touches.

Suddenly Loiseau, with anxious face and hand upraised, called out: "Silence!" Everybody was silent, surprised, already frightened. Then he listened intently and said: "S-s-sh!" his two eyes and his hands raised toward the ceiling, listening, and then continuing, in his natural voice: "All right! All goes well!"

They failed to comprehend at first, but soon all laughed. At the end of a quarter of an hour he began the same farce again, renewing it occasionally during the whole afternoon. And he pretended to call to some one in the story above, giving him advice in a double meaning, drawn from the fountainhead—the mind of a commercial traveler. For some moments he would assume a sad air, breathing in a whisper: "Poor girl!" Then he would murmur between his teeth, with an appearance of rage: "Ugh! That scamp of a Prussian." Sometimes, at a moment when no more was thought about it, he would say, in an affected voice, many times over: "Enough! Enough!" and add, as if speaking to himself: "If we could only see her again, it isn't necessary that he should kill her, the wretch!"

Although these jokes were in deplorable taste, they amused all and wounded no one, for indignation, like other things, depends upon its surroundings, and the atmosphere which had been gradually created around them was charged with sensual thoughts.

At the dessert the women themselves made some delicate and discreet allusions. Their eyes glistened; they had drunk much. The Count, who preserved, even in his flights, his grand appearance of gravity, made a comparison, much relished, upon the subject of those wintering at the pole, and the joy of shipwrecked sailors who saw an opening toward the south.

Loiseau suddenly arose, a glass of champagne in his hand, and said: "I drink to our deliverance." Everybody was on his feet; they shouted in agreement. Even the two good sisters consented to touch their lips to the froth of the wine which they had never before tasted. They declared that it tasted like charged lemonade, only much nicer.

Loiseau resumed: "It is unfortunate that we have no piano, for we might make up a quadrille."

Cornudet had not said a word, nor made a gesture; he appeared plunged in very grave thoughts, and made sometimes a furious motion, so that his great beard seemed to wish to free itself. Finally, toward midnight, as they were separating, Loiseau, who was staggering, touched him suddenly on the stomach and said to him in a stammer: "You are not very funny, this evening; you have said nothing, citizen!" Then Cornudet raised his head brusquely and, casting a brilliant, terrible glance around the company, said: "I tell you all that you have been guilty of infamy!" He rose, went to the door, and again repeated: "Infamy, I say!" and disappeared.

This made a coldness at first. Loiseau the interlocutor was stupefied; but he recovered immediately and laughed heartily as he said: "He is very green, my friends. He is very green." And then, as they did not comprehend, he told them about the "mysteries of the corridor." Then there was a return of gaiety. The women behaved like lunatics. The Count and Mr. Carré-Lamadon wept from the force of their laughter. They could not believe it.

"How is that? Are you sure?"

"I tell you I saw it."

"And she refused—"

"Yes, because the Prussian officer was in the next room."

"Impossible!"

"I swear it!"

The Count was stifled with laughter. The industrial gentleman held his sides with both hands. Loiseau continued:

"And now you understand why he saw nothing funny this evening! No, nothing at all!" And the three started out half ill, suffocated.

They separated. But Mrs. Loiseau, who was of a spiteful nature, remarked to her husband as they were getting into bed, that "that *grisette* of a little Carré-Lamadon was yellow with envy all the evening. "You know," she continued, "how some women will take to a uniform, whether it be French or Prussian! It is all the same to them! Oh! what a pity!"

And all night, in the darkness of the corridor, there were to be heard light noises, like whisperings and walking in bare feet, and imperceptible creakings. They did

not go to sleep until late, that is sure, for there wer
threads of light shining under the doors for a long time.
The champagne had its effect; they say it troubles sleep.

The next day a clear winter's sun made the snow
very brilliant. The diligence, already harnessed, waited
before the door, while an army of white pigeons, in their
thick plumage, with rose-colored eyes, with a black spot
in the center, walked up and down gravely among the
legs of the six horses, seeking their livelihood in the
manure scattered there.

The driver, enveloped in his sheepskin, had a
lighted pipe under the seat, and all the travelers, radiant,
were rapidly packing some provisions for the rest of the
journey. They were only waiting for Ball-of-Fat. Finally
she appeared.

She seemed a little troubled, ashamed. And she advanced timidly toward her companions, who all, with one
motion, turned as if they had not seen her. The Count,
with dignity, took the arm of his wife and removed her
from this impure contact.

The fat girl stopped, half stupefied; then, plucking
up courage, she approached the manufacturer's wife with
"Good morning, Madame," humbly murmured. The lady
made a slight bow of the head which she accompanied
with a look of outraged virtue. Everybody seemed busy,
and kept themselves as far from her as if she had had
some infectious disease in her skirts. Then they hurried
into the carriage, where she came last, alone, and where
she took the place she had occupied during the first part
of the journey.

They seemed not to see her or know her; although
Madame Loiseau, looking at her from afar, said to her
husband in a half-tone: "Happily, I don't have to sit beside her."

Ball-of-Fat

The heavy carriage began to move and the remainder of the journey commenced. No one spoke at first. Ball-of-Fat dared not raise her eyes. She felt indignant toward all her neighbors, and at the same time humiliated at having yielded to the foul kisses of this Prussian, into whose arms they had hypocritically thrown her.

Then the Countess, turning toward Mrs. Carré-Lamadon, broke the difficult silence:

"I believe you know Madame d'Etrelles?"

"Yes, she is one of my friends."

"What a charming woman!"

"Delightful! A very gentle nature, and well educated, besides; then she is an artist to the tips of her fingers, sings beautifully, and draws to perfection."

The manufacturer chatted with the Count, and in the midst of the rattling of the glass, an occasional word escaped such as "coupon—premium—limit—expiration."

Loiseau, who had pilfered the old pack of cards from the inn, greasy through five years of contact with tables badly cleaned, began a game of bezique with his wife.

The good sisters took from their belt the long rosary which hung there, made together the sign of the cross, and suddenly began to move their lips in a lively manner, hurrying more and more, hastening their vague murmur, as if they were going through the whole of the "Oremus." And from time to time they kissed a medal, made the sign anew, then recommenced their muttering, which was rapid and continued.

Cornudet sat motionless, thinking.

At the end of three hours on the way, Loiseau put up the cards and said: "I am hungry."

His wife drew out a package, whence she brought a piece of cold veal. She cut it evenly in thin pieces and they both began to eat.

"Suppose we do the same," said the Countess.

They consented to it and she undid the provisions prepared for the two couples. It was in one of those dishes whose lid is decorated with a china hare, to signify that a *pâté* of hare is inside, a succulent dish of pork, where white rivers of lard cross the brown flesh of the game, mixed with some other viands hashed fine. A beautiful square of Gruyère cheese, wrapped in a piece of newspaper, preserved the imprint "divers things" upon the unctuous plate.

The two good sisters unrolled a big sausage which smelled of garlic; and Cornudet plunged his two hands into the vast pockets of his overcoat, at the same time, and drew out four hard eggs and a piece of bread. He removed the shells and threw them in the straw under his feet; then he began to eat the eggs, letting fall on his vast beard some bits of clear yellow, which looked like stars caught there.

Ball-of-Fat, in the haste and distraction of her rising, had not thought of anything; and she looked at them exasperated, suffocating with rage, at all of them eating so placidly. A tumultuous anger swept over her at first, and she opened her mouth to cry out at them, to hurl at them a flood of injury which mounted to her lips; but she could not speak, her exasperation strangled her.

No one looked at her or thought of her. She felt herself drowned in the scorn of these honest scoundrels, who had first sacrificed her and then rejected her, like some improper or useless article. She thought of her great basket full of good things which they had greedily devoured, of her two chickens shining with jelly, of her *pâtés,* her pears, and the four bottles of Bordeaux; and her fury suddenly falling, as a cord drawn too tightly breaks, she felt ready to weep. She made terrible efforts to prevent it, making ugly faces, swallowing her sobs as children do, but the tears came and glistened in the corners of her eyes, and then two great drops, detaching themselves from the rest, rolled slowly down her cheeks. Others followed rapidly, running down like little streams of water that filter through rock, and, falling regularly, rebounded upon her breast. She sits erect, her eyes fixed, her face rigid and pale, hoping that no one will notice her.

But the Countess perceives her and tells her husband by a sign. He shrugs his shoulders, as much as to say:

"What would you have me do? It is not my fault."

Mrs. Loiseau indulged in a mute laugh of triumph and murmured:

"She weeps for shame."

The two good sisters began to pray again, after having wrapped in a paper the remainder of their sausage.

Then Cornudet, who was digesting his eggs, extended his legs to the seat opposite, crossed them, folded his arms, smiled like a man who is watching a good farce, and began to whistle the "Marseillaise."

All faces grew dark. The popular song assuredly did not please his neighbors. They became nervous and agitated, having an appearance of wishing to howl, like dogs, when they hear a barbarous organ. He perceived this but did not stop. Sometimes he would hum the words:

> "Sacred love of country
> Help, sustain th' avenging arm;
> Liberty, sweet Liberty
> Ever fight, with no alarm."

They traveled fast, the snow being harder. But as far as Dieppe, during the long, sad hours of the journey, across the jolts in the road, through the falling night, in the profound darkness of the carriage, he continued his vengeful, monotonous whistling with a ferocious obstinacy, constraining his neighbors to follow the song from one end to the other, and to recall the words that belonged to each measure.

And Ball-of-Fat wept continually; and sometimes a sob, which she was not able to restrain, echoed between the two rows of people in the shadows.

The Best of the World's Best Books
COMPLETE LIST OF TITLES IN
THE MODERN LIBRARY

For convenience in ordering use number at right of title

MISCELLANEOUS

MODERN LIBRARY GIANTS

A series of full-sized library editions of books that formerly were available only in cumbersome and expensive sets.
THE MODERN LIBRARY GIANTS REPRESENT A
SELECTION OF THE WORLD'S GREATEST BOOKS

These volumes contain from 600 to 1,400 pages each

Interior by Melanie Kahane, A. I. D.

No modern library is complete
without THE AMERICAN
COLLEGE DICTIONARY

1472 pages • 7″ x 10″ • large, clear type, Buckram binding, thumb-indexed $6.00
Buckram binding, without index, $5.00 • Special red Fabrikoid binding, in hand-
some gift box, $7.50 • De luxe red leather binding, gold edges, gift box, $15.00